Dr. A  4a

Study the past, if you would divine the future.
—Confucius

Nehru's 97 Major Blunders

Revised & Enlarged Edition, Sep-2018

Rajnikant Puranik

Pustak Mahal
www.pustakmahal.com

Publishers
PUSTAK MAHAL®

Administrative office and sale centre
J-3/16, Daryaganj, New Delhi-110002
☎ 011-23276539, 23272783, 23272784, 23260518
E-mail: info@pustakmahal.com • *Website:* www.pustakmahal.com

Branches
Bengaluru: ☎ 080-22234025, 40912845
E-mail: pustakmahalblr@gmail.com
Mumbai: ☎ 022-22010941, 22053387
E-mail: unicornbooksmumbai@gmail.com

NEHRU'S 97 MAJOR BLUNDERS by *Rajnikant Puranik*

Copyright © 2018 Rajnikant Puranik
www.rkpbooks.com
Categories: Non-fiction, History
ISBN: 978-81-223-1608-7
Reprint Edition: March 2019
Abridged Version of "Revised, Enlarged & Unabridged Second Digital Edition, June 2018"

First PustakMahal Hardback Edition: November, 2016
First Digital Edition: July 2016. Copyright © 2016 Rajnikant Puranik

---

Word "Blunders" is used in this book as a general term to also include failures, neglect, wrong policies, bad decisions, despicable and disgraceful acts, usurping undeserved posts, etc.

All rights reserved. No part of this publication may be reproduced, distributed or transmitted in any form or by any means, whether electronic/digital or print or mechanical/physical, or stored in an information storage or retrieval system, without the prior written permission of the copyright owner, that is, the author, except as permitted by law. However, extracts up to a total of 1,000 words may be quoted without seeking any permission, but with due acknowledgement of the source. For permission, please write to rkpuranik@gmail.com.

Printed at: Glorious Printers, Delhi

Other well-researched books by Mr. Puranik

"I see it as clearly as I see my finger: British are leaving not because of any strength on our part but because of historical conditions and for many other reasons."
—Mahatma Gandhi

And, the "historical conditions and other reasons" were not of the Congress/Gandhi's making—they were despite them.

This book presents a comprehensive view of all the main groups and individuals associated with the Indian Freedom Movement right since the late nineteenth century: Political Parties, Revolutionary Groups, INA, Revolutionaries, Gandhians, and Non-Gandhians. Particulars of the prominent Muslim leaders, Britishers, and Governor Generals are also included. 'Relevant International Timelines' includes prominent international timelines relevant from the Indian angle. The mega chapter 'Interesting Indian Timelines' chronologically covers all timelines, events, and developments relevant to the Freedom Movement right since 1600 CE.

The last chapter 'What Really Led to Freedom & Partition' summarises the REAL reasons behind the Freedom, Partition, and Pakistan.

...[then] it seemed to me that Jawaharlal should be the new President [of Congress in 1946—and hence Prime Minister] ...I acted according to my best judgement but the way things have shaped since then has made me to realise that this was perhaps the greatest blunder of my political life... My second mistake was that when I decided not to stand myself, I did not support Sardar Patel.
— **Abul Kalam Azad, 'India Wins Freedom'**

The problem of the [princely] states is so difficult that only you can solve it.
—**Gandhi to Sardar Patel**

Patel possessed the organising ability of Bismarck, the astute statesmanship of Chanakya, and the single-minded devotion to the cause of national unity of Abraham Lincoln.
—**VV Giri, ex-President of India**

Here was a man [Sardar Patel] with a crystal-clear mind who could see to the core of the problem within the shortest possible time...
—**Frank Anthony**

Leaving no vital aspect uncovered, this book comprehensively covers Sardar Patel's stellar leadership role in an engaging and gripping manner, and is interspersed with a large number of interesting episodes.

Available at: **amazon** and **Flipkart** *or* Visit Our Website: **www.pustakmahal.com**

A Note on Citations & Bibliography

Citations are given as super-scripts in the text, such as {Azad/128}.

Citation Syntax & Examples

{Source-Abbreviation/Page-Number}
e.g. {Azad/128} = Azad, Page 128

{Source-Abbreviation/Volume-Number/Page-Number}
e.g. {CWMG/V-58/221} = CWMG, Volume-58, Page 221

{Source-Abbreviation} ... for URLs (articles on the web), and for digital books (including Kindle-Books), that are searchable, where location or page-number may not be given.
e.g. {VPM2}, {URL15}

{Source-Abbreviation/Location-Number}... for Kindle Books
e.g. {VPM2}, {VPM2/L-2901}

{VPM2/438/L-2901} = Page 438 for Printed/Digital Book; and L-2901 for Location 2901 for a Kindle Book. Applicable, where citations from both type of books given.

Example from Bibliography Table at the end of this Book

Azad	B	Maulana Abul Kalam Azad—*India Wins Freedom*. Orient Longman. New Delhi. 2004
CWMG	D, W	*Collected Works of Mahatma Gandhi*. Vol. 1 to 98. http://gandhiserve.org/e/cwmg/cwmg.htm
URL15	U	Article 'Nehru vs Patel: Ideological Rift, Hardly a Trivial One. Rakesh Sinha, Sunday Express. 10-Nov-2013. www.pressreader.com/india/sunday-express8291/20131110/282033324959792
VPM2	K, D	V.P. Menon—*The Transfer of Power in India*. Orient Longman. Chennai. (1957) 1997. books.google.co.in/books?id=FY5gI7SGU20C

The *second column* above gives the *nature of the source*: B=paper Book, D=Digital Book/eBook other than Kindle, K=Kindle eBook, U=URL of Document/Article on Web, W=Website, Y=YouTube.

Preface

Study the past, if you would divine the future.
—Confucius

Those who do not learn from history are doomed to repeat it.
—George Santayana

But for a series of major blunders by Nehru across the spectrum—*it would not be an exaggeration to say that he blundered comprehensively*—India would have been on a rapidly ascending path to becoming a shining, prosperous, first-world country by the end of his term, and would surely have become so by early 1980s—provided, of course, Nehru's dynasty had not followed him to power. Sadly, the Nehru era laid the foundations of India's poverty and misery, condemning it to be forever a developing, third-rate, third-world country. By chronicling those blunders, this book highlights THE FACTS BEHIND THE FACADE.

The '*Revised, Enlarged & Unabridged, June-2018 Edition*' (Second Edition) of the book comprises (a)122 Major Blunders compared to 97 of the first Digital Edition of July 2016; (b)over twice the matter, and number of words; and (c)exhaustive citations and complete bibliography. This is an abridged version of the same.

Blunders is used in this book as a general term to also include failures, neglect, wrong policies, bad decisions, despicable and disgraceful acts, usurping undeserved posts, etc.

It is not the intention of this book to be critical of Nehru, but historical facts, that have often been distorted or glossed over or suppressed must be known widely, lest the mistakes be repeated, and so that India has a brighter future.

— Rajnikant Puranik
www.rkpbooks.com

To the fond memory of my late parents
Shrimati Shakuntala
Shri Laxminarayan Puranik

Thanks to
Devbala Puranik, Manasi and Manini
for encouragement and support

Table of Contents

Nehru's Positives 9
Pre-Independence Blunders 11
Blunder–1: Usurping Congress Presidentship in 1929 11
Blunder–2: Setting Jinnah on Path to Pakistan 12
Blunder–3: Scoring Self-Goal—Ministry Resignations 15
Blunder–4: Leg-up to Jinnah & the Muslim League 18
Blunder–5: Assam's Security Compromised 20
Blunder–6: Nehru's Undemocratic Elevation as the PM 22
Blunder–7: Aborted 'Cabinet Mission Plan' for United India 26
Blunder–8: NWFP Blunder 1946 30
Blunder–9: Making Jews out of Hindu Sindhis 31
Blunder–10: Giving Away 55 Crores to Pakistan 35
Blunder–11: Pre-Independence Dynasty Promotion 37
Blunder–12: What Really Led to India's Independence? 37
Blunder–13: Nehru/Top-Gandhians vs. Others in British Jails 45
Blunder–14: Clueless on the Roots of Partition & Pakistan 48
Blunder–15: Unplanned & Grossly Mismanaged Partition 51
Blunder–16: No Worthwhile Policy Formulations! 55

Integration of the Princely States 58
Blunder–17: Independent India dependent upon the British! 58
Blunder–18: Nehru Refused J&K Accession when Offered! 60
Blunder–19: Allowing Kashmir to be almost Lost 62
Blunder–20: Unconditional J&K Accession Made Conditional 64
Blunder–21: Internationalisation of the Kashmir Issue 67
Blunder–22: Inept Handling of the J&K Issue in the UN 68
Blunder–23: PoK thanks to Nehru 70
Blunder–24: Nehru's Shocking Callousness in J&K 74
Blunder–25: Article-370 thanks to Nehru 75
Blunder–26: Article 35A for J&K 79
Blunder–27: Nehru's Blood Brother Who Deceived 80
Blunder–28: Wanting Maharaja to Lick his Boots 85
Blunder–29: Kashmiri Pandits vs. Kashmiri Pandits 87
Blunder–30: Sidelining the One Who Could have Tackled J&K 89
Blunder–31: Junagadh: Patel vs. Mountbatten–Nehru 93
Blunder–32: Would-have-been Pakistan-II (Hyderabad) 97

External Security **104**
𝐵𝑙𝑢𝑛𝑑𝑒𝑟–33 : Erasure of Tibet as a Nation 104
𝐵𝑙𝑢𝑛𝑑𝑒𝑟–34 : Panchsheel—Selling Tibet; Harming Self 112
𝐵𝑙𝑢𝑛𝑑𝑒𝑟–35 : Not Settling Boundary Dispute with China 114
𝐵𝑙𝑢𝑛𝑑𝑒𝑟–36 : The Himalayan Blunder: India-China War 124
𝐵𝑙𝑢𝑛𝑑𝑒𝑟–37 : Criminal Neglect of Defence & External Security 131
𝐵𝑙𝑢𝑛𝑑𝑒𝑟–38 : Politicisation of the Army 135
𝐵𝑙𝑢𝑛𝑑𝑒𝑟–39 : Anti Armed-Forces 136
𝐵𝑙𝑢𝑛𝑑𝑒𝑟–40 : Lethargic Intelligence Machinery. No Planning 138
𝐵𝑙𝑢𝑛𝑑𝑒𝑟–41 : Suppressing Truth 139
𝐵𝑙𝑢𝑛𝑑𝑒𝑟–42 : Himalayan Blunders, but No Accountability 143
𝐵𝑙𝑢𝑛𝑑𝑒𝑟–43 : Delayed Liberation of Goa 146
𝐵𝑙𝑢𝑛𝑑𝑒𝑟–44 : Nehru's NO to Nuclear Arms 147
𝐵𝑙𝑢𝑛𝑑𝑒𝑟–45 : No Settlement with Pakistan 148
𝐵𝑙𝑢𝑛𝑑𝑒𝑟–46 : Responsible for 1965-War too, in a way 148
𝐵𝑙𝑢𝑛𝑑𝑒𝑟–47 : International Record in Insecure Borders 149

Foreign Policy **150**
𝐵𝑙𝑢𝑛𝑑𝑒𝑟–48 : Nehru–Liaquat Pact 1950 150
𝐵𝑙𝑢𝑛𝑑𝑒𝑟–49 : Letting Go of Gwadar 152
𝐵𝑙𝑢𝑛𝑑𝑒𝑟–50 : Indus Water Treaty—Himalayan Blunder 153
𝐵𝑙𝑢𝑛𝑑𝑒𝑟–51 : No Initiative on Sri Lankan Tamil Problem 155
𝐵𝑙𝑢𝑛𝑑𝑒𝑟–52 : Erroneous Nehru-Era Map 156
𝐵𝑙𝑢𝑛𝑑𝑒𝑟–53 : Advocating China's UNSC Membership, Sacrificing
               Ours! 157
𝐵𝑙𝑢𝑛𝑑𝑒𝑟–54 : Rebuffing Israel, the Friend-in-Need 162
𝐵𝑙𝑢𝑛𝑑𝑒𝑟–55 : Neglecting Southeast Asia 164
𝐵𝑙𝑢𝑛𝑑𝑒𝑟–56 : India vs. the US & the West 165
𝐵𝑙𝑢𝑛𝑑𝑒𝑟–57 : 'Non-Aligned' with National Interests 167
𝐵𝑙𝑢𝑛𝑑𝑒𝑟–58 : Foreign to Foreign Policy 168

Internal Security **170**
𝐵𝑙𝑢𝑛𝑑𝑒𝑟–59 : Compounding Difficulties in Assam 170
𝐵𝑙𝑢𝑛𝑑𝑒𝑟–60 : Neglect of the Northeast 172
𝐵𝑙𝑢𝑛𝑑𝑒𝑟–61 : Ignoring Illegal Proselytization 173
𝐵𝑙𝑢𝑛𝑑𝑒𝑟–62 : Ungoverned Areas 176
𝐵𝑙𝑢𝑛𝑑𝑒𝑟–63 : Insecurity of the Vulnerable Sections 177

Economy **180**
𝐵𝑙𝑢𝑛𝑑𝑒𝑟–64 : Throttled Industrialisation 180
𝐵𝑙𝑢𝑛𝑑𝑒𝑟–65 : Neglect of Agriculture 183

Blunder–66 : Builder of 'Modern' India.. 184
Blunder–67 : Grinding Poverty & Terrible Living Conditions.......... 185
Blunder–68 : Pathetic India vs. Other Countries................................ 188
Blunder–69 : Nehruvian (and NOT 'Hindu') Rate of Growth.......... 190
Blunder–70 : Nehru's Socialism: The 'God' that Failed..................... 193

Misgovernance **199**
Blunder–71 : Debilitating Babudom & Criminal-Justice System..... 199
Blunder–72 : That Strange Indian Animal: VIP & VVIP................... 204
Blunder–73 : Corruption in the "Good" Old Days............................. 206
Blunder–74 : Nepotism in the "Good" Old Days............................... 211
Blunder–75 : Nehru & Casteism.. 212
Blunder–76 : Messy Reorganisation of States..................................... 213
Blunder–77 : Poor Leadership & Administration.............................. 216
Blunder–78 : Squandering Once-in-a-lifetime Opportunity............ 220

Educational & Cultural Mismanagement..**223**
Blunder–79 : Neglect of Education.. 223
Blunder–80 : Messing Up the Language Issue.................................... 224
Blunder–81 : Promoting Urdu & Persian-Arabic Script.................... 229
Blunder–82 : Neglect of Sanskrit... 230
Blunder–83 : Being Creative with History... 231
Blunder–84 : Distortion of History by Nehru..................................... 237
Blunder–85 : Rise of the Parasitic Leftist-'Liberal' Class................... 242
Blunder–86 : Mental & Cultural Slavery.. 244
Blunder–87 : Distorted, Self-Serving Secularism................................ 248
Blunder–88 : Nehru & Uniform Civil Code (UCC)............................ 251
Blunder–89 : 'Sickularism' vs. Somnath Temple................................. 253
Blunder–90 : Would-have-been Communal Reservation.................. 255
Blunder–91 : Not Seeking Reparations from the British................... 257

Dynacracy & Dictatorial Tendencies..**260**
Blunder–92 : Nehru's Dictatorial Tendencies...................................... 260
Blunder–93 : Nehru—Power Trumps Principles................................ 263
Blunder–94 : Restricting Freedom of Expression............................... 264
Blunder–95 : Nehru & Democracy.. 265
Blunder–96 : Promoting Dynasty & Dynacracy.................................. 266
Blunder–97 : Not Limiting the Term of the PM.................................. 271

Evaluating Nehru..**273**
Bibliography..**281**

NEHRU'S POSITIVES

Shashi Tharoor titled his book 'Nehru: the Invention of India'. Yes, Nehru was honest, upright, knowledgeable, secular, cultured, hard-working, and a man of integrity. He was a capable leader, who gave his all to the nation. One also has to appreciate Nehru's physical fitness, despite his busy and stressful life—it was thanks to yoga and his healthy life style. His was reportedly a singularly unmedicated body till about two years before his death.

He wrote books, and they were good, though not great. They were rather average.

He was courageous—unlike the current nobodies moving under loads of security. Once during the 1947 riots, when he saw a person being attacked in Chandni Chowk, he stopped his car and personally charged-in to save him.

He was a popular leader. He valued the virtues of parliamentary democracy, secularism and liberalism. He was one of the founders of the Non-Aligned Movement.

As an unfailing nationalist, he implemented policies which stressed commonality among Indians while still appreciating regional diversities. He was instrumental in setting up of the Planning Commission, National Laboratories, IITs, IIMs, and a vast public sector.

Nehru was personally an honest person. If you read MO Mathai's book 'Reminiscences of the Nehru Age'{Mac}, you would come across many examples of his uprightness. MO Mathai was his PA. Like when Mathai suggested to him that he could deduct expenses for typing and other such incidentals from his income from sale of his books when filing income-tax returns to get deduction that was legally permissible, Nehru answered in the negative saying that when he had not incurred those expenses how could he seek deduction, even if legally allowed.

There is another good example from Kuldip Nayar's 'Beyond the Lines':{KN}

"This incident might prick the conscience of today's leaders. Bhim Sen Sachar, then chief minister of Punjab, approached Nehru with an embarrassing request. Vijayalakshmi Pandit had stayed at the Shimla Circuit House, then part of Punjab, and had not paid the bill of Rs 2500. Sachar was told by his governor, C.

Trivedi, to put the expense under some miscellaneous state government account. However, Sachar was a stickler for propriety. Nehru said that he could not clear the bill at one go but would pay the Punjab government in instalments. Nehru sent the amount in five instalments, each time drawing a cheque on his personal account."{KN}

Unfortunately, Nehru allowed others to be corrupt—reminds one of Manmohan Singh!

This book does not elaborate on Nehru's positives, as there are a host of books that sing his praises—readers may please refer to them. A mammoth official, semi-official and unofficial army of sycophantic netas and babus, sarkari historians, Leftist-Marxist academics, and obliging, self-serving media persons have been at the job of eulogising Nehru since independence, and therefore, there is a deluge of material highlighting Nehru's 'greatness'. Why add a few more drops in that ocean?

The purpose of this book is to summarise and highlight as many vital and critical aspects of Nehru—that are often swept under the carpet—as possible within the constraints of a short book. For historical background and details on 'Erasure of Tibet as a nation', 'India-China War', 'Integration of the Princely States', and other topics, and Nehru's role in them, please read the book "Foundations of Misery: The Nehruvian Era 1947-64" available on Amazon both in the digital and in paperback edition. Please also check www.rkpbooks.com.

PRE-INDEPENDENCE BLUNDERS

Not many blunders are listed under Nehru's 'Pre-independence Blunders' below, compared to his 'Post-independence Blunders' later, because in the former period Nehru was not fully in-charge. There was Mahatma Gandhi on top, and there were many other leaders of stature, to keep him in check. Despite that, whenever Nehru held an official position bestowing him with some discretion, and an opportunity presented itself,...

Blunder–1:
Usurping Congress Presidentship in 1929

Jawaharlal Nehru was given an unfair leg up on Sardar Patel in 1929 by Gandhi, and made President of the Congress, despite the following facts that overwhelmingly made Sardar the deserving candidate.

Patel had led the Bardoli Satyagraha of 1928 whose resounding success had made him a national hero, and bestowed on him the title *Sardar*. The Bardoli Satyagraha was the first successful practical implementation of the Gandhian non-violent technique involving the rural masses on the ground. Nehru lacked such credentials.

Besides, Sardar Patel was much senior to Jawaharlal, and a larger number of Pradesh Congress Committees (PCCs: legal body to elect President) had recommended him over Jawaharlal. Yet, Gandhi, most unjustly and undemocratically, asked Patel to withdraw! Gandhi thereby tried to establish an unjust pecking order where Jawaharlal came before Patel. Netaji Subhas Bose had subsequently written: *"The general feeling in Congress circles was that the honour should go to Sardar Vallabhbhai Patel."*{RG5/322} Acharya Kripalani had remarked that Gandhi's reasons for preferring Jawaharlal "were personal rather than political...the two were emotionally attached to each other, deny it though they may".{RG/183}

Motilal had a major role to play in his son Jawaharlal's undeserved elevation. Motilal was the Congress President in 1928. He desired that his position be inherited by his son. Subsequent to Patel's Bardoli win, Motilal wrote to Gandhi on 11 July 1928: "I am quite clear that the hero of the hour is Vallabhbhai, and the least we can do is to offer him the crown [make him President of the

Congress]. Failing him, I think that under all the circumstances Jawahar would be the best choice."{RG2/L-2984}

Motilal actively canvassed for Jawaharlal with Gandhi. Nepotism and "fight" for freedom went together: Nehrus from Motilal downwards ensured their family was well taken care of; and that it came first, ahead of the nation! In the long run, the nation paid heavily for Motilal's brazen nepotism, exemplarily emulated by his dynasty. The presidentship during 1929-30 was particularly significant: the one who became president was likely to be Gandhi's successor; and he was also to declare the goal of the Congress as "purn swaraj" or complete independence.

Jawaharlal was also favoured by Gandhi with an unprecedented second consecutive term in 1930, then another two terms in 1936 and 1937, topped by the critical term in 1946! Such privilege was not accorded to any other leader—even Sardar Patel was made President only once for one year!

The Old Man's weakness for the westernized Nehru over the home-spun fellow Gujarati [Patel] was yet another aspect of "Swadeshi" Gandhi's self-contradictory personality. How Jawaharlal managed to become the "spiritual son" of Gandhi is a mystery.

Wrote MN Roy in "The Men I Met":

"It can reasonably be doubted if Nehru could have become the hero of Indian Nationalism except as the spiritual son of Gandhi...To purchase popularity, Nehru had to suppress his own personality..."{Roy/11}

Blunder–2:
Setting Jinnah on Path to Pakistan

Before the 1936-37 provincial elections, the Congress did not expect to get enough seats to form a government on its own in UP. That was because of the other parties in the fray who had strong backing of landlords and influential sections. So as to be able to form a government, it had planned for a suitable coalition with the Muslim League. So that the Muslim League got enough seats for a coalition to be successful, Rafi Ahmad Kidwai of the Congress (who had been private secretary of Motilal Nehru, and after Motilal's death, a principal aide of Jawaharlal Nehru) had persuaded, jointly with Nehru, several influential Muslims, like Khaliq-uz-Zaman (third in the AIML hierarchy after Jinnah and Liaqat Ali Khan) and Nawab

Mohammad Ismail Khan, who had the potential to win, *to fight the elections on behalf of the Muslim League*—as Muslims fighting on behalf of the Muslim League had better chances of winning. They fought and won. But, after the elections, when the Congress found it could form the government on its own, without the help of the Muslim League, it began to put unreasonable conditions.{DD/181-83}

To Jinnah's proposal of inclusion of two Muslim League Ministers in the UP cabinet, Nehru, who was the Congress President then, and was also looking after the UP affairs, put forth an amazing, arrogant condition: the League legislators must merge with the Congress! Specifically, the terms sought to be imposed, inter alia, by Nehru–Azad were:

> "The Muslim League group in the UP Legislature shall cease to function as a separate group. The existing members of the Muslim League party in the United Provinces Assembly shall become part of the Congress Party... The Muslim League Parliamentary Board in the United Provinces will be dissolved, and no candidates will thereafter be set up by the said Board at any by-election..."{Shak/187}

The above humiliating condition that was the death warrant for the League was naturally rejected by Jinnah.{Gill/179-80}

In Bombay, with the Congress Chief minister designate BG Kher willing to induct one Muslim League minister in the cabinet in view of lack of absolute majority of the Congress, and the fact that the Muslim League had done well in Bombay in the Muslim pockets, Jinnah sent a letter in the connection to Gandhi. Gandhi gave a curiously mystical and elliptically negative reply to Jinnah on 22 May 1937:

> "Mr. Kher has given me your message. I wish I could do something, but I am utterly helpless. My faith in [Hindu-Muslim] unity is as bright as ever; only I see no daylight out of the impenetrable darkness and, in such distress, I cry out to God for light..."{CWMG/Vol-71/277}

Jinnah then wanted to meet Gandhi; but Gandhi advised him to rather meet Abul Kalam Azad, by whom he said he was guided in such matters. Rebuffed and humiliated Jinnah then decided to show Congress-Nehru-Gandhi their place. The incident led other Muslim leaders also to believe that a majority Congress government would always tend to ride rough-shod over the Muslim interests. It is claimed that, thanks to this imbroglio, the badly hurt pride of the

Muslims led them to move away from the Congress and quickly gravitate towards the Muslim League, and ultimately to separation.

The incident actually proved a blessing-in-disguise for Jinnah and the Muslim League for they realised their politics needed to be mass-based to counter the Congress. Membership fee for the AIML was dramatically dropped to just two-annas. There was a huge move to increase membership among the Muslim masses, and it paid rich dividends: the membership dramatically rose from a few thousand to well over half a million!

Jinnah told his followers that he had done enough of begging the Congress in the past; he would see to it now that the Congress begged of him.{RZ/70-71}

The humiliated Muslim League aspirants Khaliq-uz-Zaman and Nawab Mohammad Ismail Khan, whose ambitions were thwarted by the Congress and Nehru, thereafter became the pillars of Muslim reaction and played a critical role in swinging the Muslim opinion in favour of partition and Pakistan.

The British were only too glad at the development. The Secretary of State Birkenhead wrote to the Viceroy: "I have placed my highest and most permanent hopes in the eternity of the communal situation."{Muld/42}

It was unwise of the Congress and Nehru not to show a little generosity towards the League. *Reportedly, Sardar Patel and GB Pant were willing for a coalition with the Muslim League as per the pre-election understanding, but Nehru, in his "wisdom" and hubris, decided to act arrogant, and led the way for the ultimate parting of ways with Jinnah and the Muslim League, and for Partition and Pakistan—Nehru was the Congress President in 1936 and 1937.* Jinnah's bitter reaction on 26 July 1937 to Nehru's unjust act was:

"What can I say to the busybody President [Nehru] of the Congress? He [Nehru] seems to carry the responsibility of the whole world on his shoulders and must poke his nose into everything except minding his own business."{DD/181-82}

The fissure caused by Nehru's impetuosity was never healed.

There is an opinion that had the Congress been accommodating towards the AIML post-1937 elections, AIML may not have hurtled forward towards Partition and Pakistan. Besides, it would have prevented counterfactual speculations. Wrote Maulana Azad:

"...I have nevertheless to say with regret that this ['Blunder-7'] was not the first time that he [Nehru] did immense harm to the national cause. He had committed an almost equal blunder in 1937 when the first elections were held under the Government of India Act [of 1935]{Azad/170}...

"Jawaharlal's action gave the Muslim League in the UP a new lease of life. All students of Indian politics know that it was from the UP that the League was reorganised. Mr Jinnah took full advantage of the situation and started an offensive which ultimately led to Pakistan{Azad/171}...

"The [Nehru's] mistake of 1937 was bad enough. The mistake of 1946 [of Nehru: 'Blunder-7'] proved even more costly."{Azad/172}

Wrote MC Chagla: "To my mind, one of the most potent causes which ultimately led to the creation of Pakistan was what happened in Uttar Pradesh [United Provinces in 1937]. *If Jawaharlal Nehru had agreed to a coalition ministry and not insisted on the representative of the Muslim League signing the Congress pledge, perhaps Pakistan would never have come about.* I remember Jawaharlal telling me that Khaliquz Zaman [to whom Nehru had denied a birth in the UP cabinet in 1937] was one of his greatest and dearest friends, and yet he led the agitation for Pakistan... Uttar Pradesh was the cultural home of the Muslims. Although they were in a minority in the State, if Uttar Pradesh had not gone over to the cause of separation, Pakistan would never have become a reality."{MCC/81-2}

Blunder–3:
Scoring Self-Goal—Ministry Resignations

Good Show by the Congress in 1936-37 Provincial Elections

In the 1936-37 provincial elections in 11 provinces, the Congress won an absolute majority in 5 (UP, Bihar, Madras, CP (Central Provinces) and Orissa), and emerged as the largest party in 4 (Bombay, Bengal, Assam and NWFP). The Congress ministries were formed in a total of 8 provinces. They were headed (called Premiers) by Govind Ballabh Pant in UP, Shrikrishna Sinha in Bihar, NB Khare in CP, BG Kher in Bombay, Rajaji in Madras. Bishwanath Das in Orissa, Gopinath Bardoloi in Assam, and Dr Khan Sahib in NWFP.

On the other hand, the Muslim League's show was poor. It secured less than 5% of the Muslim votes. It won a mere 6%

(108/1585) of total seats. Its share (108/(372+108=480)) in the Muslim seats was also low: 22.5%. It failed to form a government on its own in any province. This rankled with Jinnah and the AIML, and also with the British, who didn't want the Congress to get powerful.

Good Performance of Congress Ministries during 1937-39

The hard-won (thanks mainly to the efforts of Sardar Patel) Congress ministries in the provinces since 1937, under the strict vigilance of Patel, had begun to perform better than expected. To guide and coordinate the activities of the provincial governments, a central control board known as the Parliamentary Sub-Committee was formed, with Sardar Patel, Maulana Abul Kalam Azad and Rajendra Prasad as members. A number of measures in the interest of the general public had been taken. Many Congress ministers set an example in plain living. They reduced their own salaries. They made themselves easily accessible to the common people. In a very short time, a very large number of ameliorative legislations were pushed through in an attempt to fulfil many of the promises made in the Congress election manifesto.

Emergency powers acquired by the provincial governments through the Public Safety Acts and the like were repealed. Bans on illegal political organizations such as the Hindustan Seva Dal and Youth Leagues and on political books and journals were lifted. All restrictions on the press were removed. Securities taken from newspapers and presses were refunded and pending prosecutions were withdrawn. The blacklisting of newspapers for purposes of government advertising was given up. Confiscated arms were returned and forfeited arms licenses were restored. In the Congress provinces, police powers were curbed and the reporting of public speeches and the shadowing of political workers by CID agents stopped. Another big achievement of the Congress Governments was their firm handling of the communal riots. Rajaji's premiership of Madras during 1937-39 was brilliant.

Britain Declared War (WW-II) on Behalf of India

The German–Soviet Non-aggression Pact, also called the Molotov–Ribbentrop Pact, or the Nazi–Soviet Pact, was signed between Nazi Germany and the Soviet Union in Moscow on 23 August 1939, in the presence of Stalin. Soon after, on 1 September 1939, Germany invaded Poland (Soviet Union did so on 17 September 1939). In response, Britain declared war against

Germany two days later—on 3 September 1939. *On the same day, the Viceroy of India, Linlithgow, also announced that India, along with Britain, had joined the war (WW-II).*

In Protest, Nehru & Socialists Force Congress Ministries to Resign

The Congress had expected to be consulted by the British before declaring war on behalf of India. The AICC had declared in May 1939 that the Congress would oppose any attempt to impose a war on India without the consent of its people. Yet, the British authorities just didn't bother. The Congress felt rebuffed and enraged. It also demonstrated that the British considered the Gandhian 'threat' as no threat. They knew that the Gandhian non-violence was an insurance against any real problem for the Raj.

In protest against the British-India declaring war without consulting the Congress, the CWC meeting at Wardha on 22-23 October 1939 decided not to co-operate with the British in the war (WW-II). The move was spear-headed by Nehru and the socialists, who also advocated that the Congress Provincial Governments resign by the month-end in protest. Patel and Gandhi were not in favour of non-cooperation with the British in the war, and of the ministries resigning; but Nehru & Co—the socialists—insisted upon it. The resignations were effectively a victory of the Congress Left.

Resignation of Congress Ministries: A Big Nehruvian Blunder

Under pressure from Nehru&Co, the Congress Ministries resigned in November 1939. *It was politics of futile gesture—a big blunder; a political suicide.* Wrote Balraj Krishna:

"Yet, he [Patel] seemed to be in agreement with Gandhi insofar as the continuance of the Congress Ministries was concerned. This was typical of him as the party boss and as an administrator, who saw obvious political gains in holding on to power. Linlithgow's thinking tallied with Patel's. He had written to the King that 'Jinnah had become alarmed by the defection of a growing number of Muslims from the Muslim League to the Congress', because the Ministers could help their friends' and 'inconvenience their opponents'. Such defections, however probable, could not have taken place because of the Congress giving up power in the provinces. The Editor of The Hindu, K. Srinavasan,... 'blamed Nehru for "the dreadful blunder" of withdrawing the provincial Ministers from office.'"{BK/199-200}

"The withdrawal was a triumph for the Congress Left—a triumph which had serious political repercussions. It threw the Congress into wilderness and gave Jinnah absolute freedom to play a game that strengthened his position with the British and helped him, in the end, get Pakistan. The inappropriateness of the resignations lay in their being most inopportune and untimely, especially when Linlithgow had formed a favourable opinion of the Congress leaders and the Congress as a party. He considered the latter to be 'the only one worthy of the name, and certainly the only one possessing an active and widespread organisation in the constituencies.' It was an achievement due to Patel's effective Chairmanship of the Congress Parliamentary Board. In Patel, Linlithgow had found 'a sense of humour, a shrewd and active brain and a strong personality', and Patel clearly saw the point about avoiding speculative hypothesis as a basis of argument."{BK/199-200}

The ill-advised action of Nehru&Co was like giving up all the gains of the 1937-elections; and passing them on to the then defeated AIML. While for the Congress it was self-emasculation that greatly weakened it and drastically slashed its bargaining position, throwing it into wilderness, for the British and for Jinnah the Congress Ministries' resignations were "good riddance".

Blunder–4:
Leg-up to Jinnah & the Muslim League

Resignation of the Congress ministries in 1939 ('Blunder-3' above) was welcomed both by Jinnah and the British authorities. Jinnah couldn't help calling it the *'Himalayan Blunder'* of the Congress, and was determined to take full advantage of it. Jinnah and the Muslim League went to the extent of calling upon all Muslims to celebrate 22 December 1939 as the *"Deliverance Day"*—deliverance from the "misrule" of the Congress. Thanks to Nehru's blunder, the stars of the Muslim League began to rise. 1939-onwards Muslim League was on the ascendency, even as the clout of the Congress eclipsed.

The worst effect of the resignations was on NWFP. This overwhelmingly Muslim province (95%) was ruled in conjunction with the Congress by the Khan brothers. It was a show-piece for the

Congress, and a negation of all that Jinnah and the Muslim League stood for—majority Muslim province under the Congress. Resignation by the ruling Congress-Khan brothers was god-sent for Jinnah and the British. Both quickly manipulated to install a Muslim League government, and make popular the divisive agenda. In the Pakistan that the British had planned inclusion of NWFP was a must, and that was only possible if the Congress and the Khan-brothers were dislodged. Linlithgow did all he could to install a Muslim League government in NWFP, including meeting Jinnah personally{Sar/48}, and instructing the then Punjab Governor Sir George Cunningham to render all necessary assistance to Jinnah{Sar/49}. Viceroy Linlithgow had been playing a dangerous and irresponsible divisive game in India's North-West, particularly in Punjab and NWFP that ultimately led to the Partition carnage.

It is worth noting that Nehru and the Congress were unnecessarily too obsessed with the Centre and the Central legislature, where Jinnah was able to play a wrecker. Had the Congress continued in its ministries, and had it played its cards well in the provinces in the Muslim-majority areas, they could have derailed Jinnah. The Unionist Party headed by Sikandar Hyat Khan that ruled Punjab was a Muslim-Hindu-Sikh coalition. The Krishak Proja Party headed by Fazlul Huq, a nationalist Muslim, dominated Bengal. Ghulam Hussain Hidayatullah had formed a Hindu-Muslim coalition in Sind, independent of the Muslim League. If the Congress had intelligently coordinated its efforts with these parties, it could have sidelined Jinnah. But, what to speak of doing that ground work and strengthening its ties with the non-Muslim-League Muslim parties, the Congress itself chose to get irrelevant.

Congress opposition to the British declaration of World War-II on behalf of India, its non-cooperation with the British in that regard, and the unconditional, whole-hearted support extended to the British by Jinnah and the Muslim League ensured the rise of the Muslim League and the gradual eclipse of the Congress, so much so that thereafter it were the British, Jinnah and the Muslim League who dictated the terms of independence, Partition and Pakistan. Wrote VP Menon in 'The Transfer of Power in India':

> "Had it [Congress] not resigned from the position of vantage in the Provinces the course of Indian history might have been different... By resigning, it showed a lamentable lack of foresight and political wisdom. There was little chance of its being put out of office; the British Government would surely have hesitated to

incur the odium of dismissing ministries which had the overwhelming support of the people. Nor could it have resisted an unanimous demand for a change at the Centre, a demand which would have been all the more irresistible after the entry of Japan into the war. In any case, it is clear that, *but for the resignation of the Congress, Jinnah and the Muslim League would never have attained the position they did...*"{VPM2/152/L-2901}

Blunder–5:
Assam's Security Compromised

With the annexation of Assam in 1826, the British brought in the peasantry from the over-populated East-Bengal for tea plantation and other purposes. The Muslim League, in order to dominate the predominantly non-Muslim Assam and the Northeast, and make it yet another Muslim-majority region, strategized back in 1906 in its conference at Dacca to somehow increase the Muslim population in Assam, and exhorted the East-Bengal Muslims to migrate and settle in Assam. The fact of large-scale migration was also noted in the Census report of 1931. Congress leaders Bordoloi, Medhi and others raised this serious issue of migration, but did not get due support from the Congress leadership at the Centre.

In the 1930s and later, when the Muslims of East Bengal (now Bangladesh) began migrating to Brahmaputra valley in Assam for livelihood, pooh-poohing the grave warnings from sane quarters, pseudo-secular, naive Nehru made an irresponsible statement: "Nature abhors vacuum, meaning where there is open space how can one prevent people from settling there?" Savarkar responded with his masterly prediction: "Nature also abhors poisonous gas. The migration of such large numbers of Muslims in Assam threatened not just the local culture but would also prove to be a national security problem for India on its north-east frontier."

In 1938, when a Muslim League-headed coalition fell in Assam, Netaji Subhas Bose favoured a bid by the Congress to form a government. Several Congress leaders were opposed to the idea, particularly Maulana Azad. Sardar Patel backed Subhas Bose fully; and finally a Congress ministry led by Gopinath Bordoloi took office. With Bordoloi in office it was hoped that the Muslim migrations would be stemmed, and the game of the Muslim League would be defeated.

However, thanks to the unwise move of Nehru and his left supporters, the Congress ministries in the provinces resigned in 1939 ('Blunder-3' above). This forced Gopinath Bordoloi to also resign in Assam, although Netaji Subhas Bose and Patel wanted Bordoloi government to continue. This was God-sent, rather Allah-sent, for the Muslim League. Pro-British Sir Syed Mohammad Saadulla of the Muslim League, from whom Bordoloi had wrested power, again took over. With the Congress in limbo on account of the unwise surrender of power in the provinces (thanks to Nehru&Co), followed by the imprisonment of its leadership in 1942 Quit India, Saadulla ruled uninterrupted for the next seven years shoring up the Muslim base in Assam.

Saadulla brought in a Land Settlement Policy in 1941 that allowed immigrants (Muslims) from East Bengal to pour into Assam, and hold as much as 30 bighas for each homestead. He boasted to Liaquat Ali Khan that through his policies he had managed to quadruple the Muslim population in the lower four districts of the Assam Valley. In short, the demographic position became much worse in Assam thanks to the wrong decision of Nehru.

~~~

The initial British Plan of 1946 for the Indian Independence clubbed Assam and Bengal together in Group-C. Such an inclusion would have had the consequence of Assamese being in a minority, to be overruled into ultimately being absorbed in East-Pakistan. Sensing this ominous possibility, Bordoloi opposed being clubbed into Group-C, contrary to what Nehru had agreed to. With Nehru remaining unamenable, Bordoloi started mass agitation. He fought the Muslim League's effort to include Assam and other parts of the Northeast Region (NER) in East Pakistan. The Congress Party at the national level, led by Nehru, would have acquiesced to the Muslim League had it not been for a revolt by Bordoloi, backed by the Assam unit of the Congress Party and supported by Mahatma Gandhi and the Assamese public. When we talk of the Northeast we must first pay our tributes to Gopinath Bordoloi but for whom Assam and the Northeast may not have been part of India.

Blunder–6:
Nehru's Undemocratic Elevation as the PM

Based on the ground-level practical experience since 1917, it could be said with certainty in 1946 that Nehru was no match for Sardar Patel for the critical post of the prime minister. Of course, Nehru as PM in practice confirmed beyond a shred of doubt that it should have been Sardar, and not him, who should have been the first PM of India—as this book amply brings out.

Legal Procedure for the Election of the Congress President

Whoever became the president of the Congress in 1946 would have also become the first prime minister of India, hence the presidential election was critical. As per the laid down procedure in practice for many decades, only the Pradesh Congress Committees (PCCs) were the authorised bodies to elect a president. There were 15 such PCCs They were supposed to send their nomination to the Congress Working Committee (CWC). The person who received maximum nominations was elected as President. There being 15 PCCs, at least 8 PCCs had to nominate a specific individual for him or her to gain the majority to become president. In 1946, the last date of nominations for the post of the president was 29 April 1946.

Result of the Election : Sardar Won Unopposed

The Congress Working Committee (CWC) met on 29 April 1946 to consider the nominations sent by the PCCs. 12 of the 15 (80%) PCCs nominated Sardar Patel[RG/370]; and 3 PCCs out of the 15 (20%) did not nominate anyone.[ITV] It therefore turned out to be a non-contest. Sardar Patel was the only choice, and an undisputed choice, with not a single opposition.

What was noteworthy was that on 20 April 1946, that is, nine days before the last date of nominations of 29 April 1946, Gandhi had indicated his preference for Nehru. Yet, not a single PCC nominated Nehru!

Hijacking of the Election by Nehru-Gandhi

Looking to the unexpected (unexpected by Gandhi) development, Gandhi prodded Kripalani to convince a few CWC members to propose Nehru's name for the party president. Gandhians like Kripalani slavishly went by what their guru, the Mahatma, directed. Kripalani promptly and unquestioningly complied: He got a few to propose Nehru's name. Finding this queer development, Sardar Patel enquired with Gandhi, and sought his advice. Gandhi counselled him to withdraw his name. Patel complied promptly, and didn't raise any question. That cleared the way for Nehru. The "democratic" Nehru didn't feel embarrassed at his and Gandhi's blatant hijacking of the election, and shamelessly accepted his own nomination.

Said Kripalani later: "Sardar did not like my intervention."{RG/371} Years later Acharya Kripalani had told Durga Das:
"All the P.C.C.s sent in the name of Patel by a majority and one or two proposed the names of Rajen Babu in addition, but none that of Jawaharlal. I knew Gandhi wanted Jawaharlal to be President for a year, and I made a proposal myself [at Gandhi's prodding] saying 'some Delhi fellows want Jawaharlal's name'. I circulated it to the members of the Working Committee to get their endorsement. I played this mischief. I am to blame. Patel never forgave me for that. *He [Sardar Patel] was a man of will and decision. You saw his face. It grew year by year in power and determination...*"{DD/229}

Nehru's Obduracy

Finding none had recommended Nehru, Gandhi, reportedly, did tell Nehru: *"No PCC has put forward your name...only* [a few members of] *the Working Committee has."*{RG/371} Nehru, however, responded with complete silence to this pregnant remark.{RG/371} Despite his grand pretentions of Gandhi as his father figure, and he being his son, chela and follower, Nehru remained silently defiant and let it be known to Gandhi he would not play second fiddle to anyone. It appears that all the "sacrifice" for the nation by Motilal and his son was geared to ultimately grab power for the Nehru dynasty! It has even been claimed that Nehru tried blackmail: he threatened to split the Congress on the issue.

Gandhi's Rationale'

Somebody asked Gandhi why he favoured Nehru. Reportedly, Gandhi's reason was he wanted both Nehru and Patel together to lead the nation, but while Nehru would not work under Sardar Patel, he knew that in the national interest he could persuade Sardar Patel to work under Nehru, as Sardar would not defy him.{ITV} *What Gandhi said amounts to this*: that Sardar Patel, even though senior and more experienced, and backed by majority, was patriotic enough to work under Nehru in the national interest, if so prodded by Gandhi; Nehru, junior, less experienced, and not backed by a single PCC, wanted only to become PM, and was not patriotic enough to work under Patel, in the national interest, even if persuaded by Gandhi! Durga Das recounted the following:

> "I asked Gandhi... He [Gandhi] readily agreed that Patel would have proved a better negotiator and organiser as Congress President, but he felt Nehru should head the Government. When I asked him how he reconciled this with his assessment of Patel's qualities as a leader, he laughed and said: 'Jawaharlal is the only Englishman in my camp... [then, why talk of swadeshi and swaraj!] Jawaharlal will not take second place. He is better known abroad than Sardar and will make India play a role in international affairs [Why not make him Foreign Minister then? Although, Nehru made a mess of the foreign policy—pl. see 'Blunder-48–58']. Sardar will look after the country's affairs. They will be like two oxen yoked to the government cart. One will need the other and both will pull together.'"{DD/230}

Nehru–Gandhi Act : Why Grossly Improper?

Gandhi's actions must be judged in the background of his being a "Mahatma", and an "Apostle of Truth and Non-Violence". As Gandhi had himself stressed, "non-violence" didn't have a narrow interpretation as just lack of violence, but a broad interpretation where things like anger, illegal and unjust acts also came within the broad definition of violence. What Gandhi and Nehru manoeuvred was not only illegal, immoral and unethical, but also against the interest of the nation. Here are the reasons for the same:

(1) *Illegality-1*: PCCs alone were authorised to elect the president. There was nothing in the Congress constitution to permit that rule to be overturned. How could Gandhi overrule what 15 PCCs had recommended? On what legal basis? Gandhi's action was illegal.

(2) *Illegality-2*: Gandhi had resigned from the primary membership of the Congress back in 1934 to devote himself to "constructive work" (Were political work and fighting for freedom "destructive"?). Thereafter, he had never rejoined the Congress. How could a non-member of the Congress like Gandhi dictate who should be the president of the Congress, or even participate in CWC meetings? Yet, another illegality.

(3) *Unreasonable-1:* Did Gandhi put on record his reasons for

overruling the recommendations of the PCCs? No.

(4) *Unreasonable-2*: Did Gandhi put on record why Patel was not suitable as the president, and hence the first PM, and why Nehru was a better choice? No.

(5) *Unreasonable-3*: Was there a proper, detailed, and threadbare discussion in the CWC on why Patel was not suited for the post, and therefore why the recommendations of the PCCs should be ignored? And, why, instead, Nehru should be chosen? No.

(6) *Unreasonable-4*: If CWC was not convinced of the recommendations of the PCCs, why didn't it refer the matter back to the PCCs, and ask them to re-submit their recommendations, with detailed reasoning? The decision could have been postponed.

(7) *Against National Interest-1*: How could responsibility of such critical nature be assigned to a person without doubly ensuring that person's relative suitability through fair and democratic discussions among all CWC members, and, of course, finally through voting.

(8) *Against National Interest-2*: National interests demanded that the choice of person was dictated not by personal biases, and diktats, but by suitability, and mutual consensus, and the reasons should have been put on record.

(9) *Dictatorial & Undemocratic-1*: How could an individual like Gandhi dictate who should or should not be the president, and hence the first PM? And, if that was fine for the Congress, then why the sham of elections, and votes of the PCCs?

(10) *Dictatorial & Undemocratic-2*: What kind of freedom "fighters" we had in the Gandhian Congress that they didn't even assert their freedom within the CWC, or show their guts against the slavery of Gandhi, and voice their opinions? Was an individual Gandhi correct, and were the 15 PCCs wrong?

(11) *Unethical-1*: Leave apart the legal and other aspects, was it ethical and moral and truthful for Gandhi to do what he did? If indeed he thought he was correct, and all others were wrong, the least that was expected from him was to explain his logic and reasoning. Or, was he above all that? Do what you want—no questions asked!

(12) *Unethical-2*: How could a person being nominated for president, and therefore as the first Indian PM, be so devoid of integrity, fair-play and ethics as to blatantly be a party to the illegality of throwing the recommendations of the PCCs into a

dustbin, and allowing oneself to be nominated?

(13) *Unembarrassed*: Did it not embarrass Nehru that he was usurping a position undemocratically through blatantly unfair means? Did it behove a future PM?

(14) *Blot & Blunder*: Overall, it was a blot on the working of the CWC, and on the CWC members, and particularly Gandhi and Nehru, that they could so brazenly commit such a blunder, which ultimately cost the nation heavy.

For full details, please refer to the unabridged digital version of this book or the author's book 'Sardar Patel: The Iron Man Who Should have been India's First PM' available on Amazon.

Blunder–7:
Aborted 'Cabinet Mission Plan' for United India

Prime Minister Clement Attlee told the House of Commons on 15 March 1946: "If India elects for independence she has a right to do so." The Raj had, at last, decided to pack up. A British Cabinet Mission comprising three cabinet ministers—Lord Pethick-Lawrence, the Secretary of State for India, Sir Stafford Cripps, President of the Board of Trade, and AV Alexander, the First Lord of the Admiralty—arrived in India on 23 March 1946 at the initiative of Attlee to discuss and plan for the Indian independence, and the transfer of power to Indian leadership. Their discussions with the INC (Indian National Congress) and the AIML (All-India Muslim League) did not yield a common ground acceptable to both.

So as to make headway, the Cabinet Mission unilaterally proposed a plan (*"16 May Cabinet Mission Plan"*) announced by PM Attlee in the House of Commons on 16 May 1946, which, *among other things, stated that independence would be granted to a UNITED dominion of India, which would be a loose confederation of provinces, and the Muslim League's demand for Pakistan was turned down.*

Thanks to Gandhi, Nehru had become the President of the Congress at the end of April 1946, and hence the would be first PM. Nehru did a blunder at the very start of his Presidency. After the AICC ratification of the CWC's acceptance of the 'May 16 Cabinet Mission Plan' on 25 June 1946, Nehru remarked at the AICC on 7 July 1946: "*...We are not bound by a single thing except that we have decided to go into the Constituent Assembly... When India is free, India* *will do just what she likes...*"{Mak/83}

At a press conference in Mumbai three days later on 10 July 1946, he declared that the Congress would be *"completely unfettered by agreements and free to meet all situations as they arise"*{Azad/164}, and that *"the central government was likely to be much stronger than what the Cabinet Mission envisaged."* Nehru also emphasised that the Congress regarded itself free to change or modify the Cabinet Mission Plan as it thought best.{Azad/165}

How could Nehru talk of unilaterally changing what was mutually agreed upon by the Congress, the Muslim League, and the British? What then was the sanctity of the agreement? Nehru then made controversial remarks on the grouping proposed in the May 16 Plan.

Consequences of Nehru's Blunder :
(a)Jinnah's Renewed Call for Pakistan
(b)Calcutta Carnage, followed by Noakhali & Other Riots.

As it was, Jinnah was under severe pressure from his colleagues and supporters for having accepted the 'May 16 Plan', and thus giving up on an independent Islamic State of Pakistan. Nehru's statement gave Jinnah an excuse to repudiate his earlier acceptance of the Plan, and demand a separate state of Pakistan. Patel wrote to DP Mishra:

"Though President [Nehru] has been elected for the fourth time, he often acts with childlike innocence, which puts us all in great difficulties quite unexpectedly. You have good reason to be angry but we must not allow our anger to get the better of ourselves... He has done many things recently which have caused us great embarrassment. His action in Kashmir, his interference in Sikh election to the Constituent Assembly, his Press conference immediately after the AICC are all acts of emotional insanity and it puts tremendous strain on us to set matters right..."{Mak/86}

Maulana Azad called Nehru's act *"one of those unfortunate events which change the course of history."*{Azad/164} Maulana Azad wrote:

"...The Working Committee [CWC] accordingly met on 8 August [1946] and reviewed the whole situation. I pointed out that if we wanted to save the situation, we must make it clear that the statement of the Congress President [Nehru] at the Bombay Press Conference [on 10 July 1946: pl. see above] was his personal opinion... Jawaharlal argued that he had no objection...

but felt that it would be embarrassing to the organisation and also to him personally..."{Azad/166}

The Congress tried its best to back-track on Nehru's statement, and issued statements reassuring its commitment on 'May 16 Plan'. But, the deed was done. Jinnah had got the excuse and the opportunity he wanted. Wrote Maulana Azad, who had always favoured Nehru over Patel, in his autobiography:

> "...Taking all facts into consideration, it seemed to me that Jawaharlal should be the new President [of Congress in 1946—and hence PM]. Accordingly, on 26 April 1946, I issues a statement proposing his name for Presidentship... [Then] I acted according to my best judgement but the way things have shaped since then has made me to realise that this was perhaps the greatest blunder of my political life... My second mistake was that when I decided not to stand myself, I did not support Sardar Patel. We differed on many issues but I am convinced that if he had succeeded me as Congress President he would have seen that the Cabinet Mission Plan was successfully implemented. He would have never committed the mistake of Jawaharlal which gave Mr. Jinnah an opportunity of sabotaging the Plan. I can never forgive myself when I think that if I had not committed these mistakes, perhaps the history of the last ten years would have been different."{Azad/162}

Jinnah and the AIML exploited Nehru's faux pas to the hilt. Jinnah contended with the British that Nehru's remarks amounted to "a complete repudiation" of 'May 16 Plan', and therefore he expected the British government to invite him, rather than the Congress, to form a government. In the absence of any action in that respect from the British government, the Muslim League Council met at Bombay during 27–30 July 1946. Jinnah took the extreme step: he got the Muslim League to revoke its acceptance of the 'May 16 Plan', and gave a sinister call for the launch of "direct action to achieve Pakistan". Asking the qaum to observe 16 August 1946 as Direct Action Day, Jinnah said on 30 July 1946: "*Today we bid goodbye to constitutional methods. Throughout, the British and the Congress held a pistol in their hand, the one of authority and arms and the other of mass struggle and non-cooperation. Today we have also forged a pistol and are in a position to use it... We will have either a divided India, or a destroyed India.*"{BK/250}

The date 16 August 1946 was cleverly chosen. It was a Friday in

the month of Ramzan, on which the Muslims were likely to gather in large numbers in mosques. Handbills exhorted:
> "Let Muslims brave the rains and all difficulties and make the Direct Action Day meeting a historic mass mobilization of the Millat."
>
> "Muslims must remember that it was in Ramazan that the Quran was revealed. It was in Ramazan that the permission for jihad was granted by Allah."{PF/253}

This is from a pamphlet written by SM Usman, the then Mayor of Calcutta:
> "...By the grace of God, we are crores in India but through bad luck we have become slaves of Hindus and the British. We are starting a Jehad in your name in this very month of Ramzan... Give your helping hand in all our actions—make us victorious over the Kaffirs—enable us to establish the kingdom of Islam in India... by the grace of god may we build up in India the greatest Islamic kingdom in the world..."{Mak/110}

HS Suhrawardy, the then Premier of Bengal, also held the portfolio of Law & Order. He transferred Hindu police officers from all key posts prior to 16 August, and ensured that while 22 of the 24 police stations had Muslims as in-charge, the remaining 2 had Anglo-Indians. Further, to mobilise large Muslim crowds, he declared 16 August as a public holiday. Goondas and bad characters were mobilised by the AIML from within the city and outside to create trouble. While Muslim leaders gave provocative speeches on 16 August, Suhrawardy crossed all norms for a Premier and told the gathered mammoth crowd that he had seen to it that the police and military would not interfere... Suhrawardy even usurped the charge of the Police Control Room on 16 August. He made sure that any Muslim arrested for rioting was released immediately! However, after the initial heavy set back and casualties, once the Hindus and Sikhs began to hit back causing counter damage, something the AIML had not reckoned, Suhrawardy promptly called in the army.{Mak/111-15}

The cumulative result of all the above was the *Calcutta Carnage*, the *Great Calcutta Killings*, the worst communal riot instigated by the Muslim League, that left 5,000 to 10,000 dead, 15,000 injured, and about one lakh homeless! Like Dyer, the butcher of Jallianwala Bagh Massacre of 1919, Suhrawardy came to be known as 'the butcher of Bengal' and 'the butcher of Calcutta'.{Swa1}

Wrote Maulana Azad:
"Sixteen August 1946 was a black day not only for Calcutta but for the whole of India.... This was one of the greatest tragedies of Indian history and I have to say with the deepest of regret that a large part of the responsibility for this development rests with Jawaharlal. His unfortunate statement that the Congress would be free to modify the Cabinet Mission Plan reopened the whole question of political and communal settlement..."{Azad/170}

Nehru's indiscretion put paid to the scheme of united India, precipitated Jinnah's call for Pakistan, and resulted in the ghastly *Direct Action* described above.

Blunder–8:
NWFP Blunder 1946

Congress had won the elections in NWFP, and Dr Khan Sahib (Khan Abdul Jabbar Khan), brother of Khan Abdul Ghaffar Khan, was heading the ministry.

NWFP was another province the Muslim League was targeting along with Bengal, Assam, Punjab, and Sind. Although the provincial government of NWFP was in the hands of the Congress, the British Governor Olaf Caroe, and the local British civil servants, were rabidly anti-Congress, and pro-Muslim League. Why? They must have been instructed by the HMG to back the Muslim League and ensure NWFP became part of Pakistan. Incidentally, Sir Olaf Caroe was the person who authored "Wells of Power: The Oilfields of South Western Asia, a Regional and Global Study", and persuasively wrote an article on Pakistan's potential role in the Middle East, and hence Pakistan's strategic importance for the British. The British were favouring Jinnah in their own interest. Like elsewhere, the Muslim League, backed by the British, had been looking for and exploiting all opportunities to discredit local Muslim leaders not aligned to the Muslim League, defame them as pro-Hindu and anti-Muslim, and rouse the local Muslim population against the Hindus.

Negligently, the Congress was doing little to counter the Muslim League propaganda and violence. Instead, it gave ready excuses to the AIML to indulge in its nefarious game when Nehru visited NWFP as the head of the Interim Government, despite advise to the contrary by the NWFP Chief Minister, Sardar Patel, and others.

Nehru had the delusion he was very popular—even among Muslims! The results were predictable. The situation went worse for the local Congress Provincial Government, and the Muslim League gained an upper hand, through communal rumour-mongering, and false, skilful propaganda, backed by the British Governor, and the British officers. The height (or, rather, the low) of the British Governor Olaf Caroe's partisan role was reached when he tried to buy over NWFP Chief Minister Dr Khan Sahib by assuring him that he would help him and his cabinet colleagues continue as ministers in Pakistan if they severed their connection with the "Hindu Congress"! Jinnah gleefully looked upon Nehru's visit as godsent, and managed to paint Nehru and the Congress as unpopular among the Muslims of NWFP.

Blunder–9:
Making Jews out of Hindu Sindhis

Brutal Islamisation of the Hindu Citadel

Sindh is the home of the oldest civilization in the world—the Indus or Sindhu Valley Civilization, highlighted by the excavations at Mohenjo-daro—dating back to over 7000 BCE. The 3,180 km long Indus or Sindhu River that originates near Lake Mansarovar in the Tibetan Plateau runs through Ladakh, Gilgit-Baltistan, Western Punjab in Pakistan, and merges into the Arabian Sea near the port city of Karachi in Sindh. Sindhu means water in Sanskrit. Name India is derived from Indus. Sindhu river has a number of tributaries. The Indus delta is mentioned in the Rig-Veda as Sapta Sindhu (Hapta Hindu in the Iranian Zend Avesta), meaning 'seven rivers'.

Why was Sindh not Partitioned?

Sindh came under the British in 1843, and was included as a part of the Bombay Presidency. At the time of partition Sindh was a British India province. It was bordered by Baluchistan and West Punjab (to the north), and by the Princely States of Bahawalpur (northeast), Las Bela (west), Kalat (west), and Khairpur (east: Sindh province surrounded it from three sides). To its east was Rajasthan, and Gujarat was to its south.

As per the last census of 1931 before independence, Sindh's population was about 4.1 million, of which 73% were Muslims, 26% were Hindus, and the remaining 1% were Christians, Sikhs, etc. Hindus were concentrated in urban areas, while Muslims dominated the countryside. Hindus were in absolute majority in four of Sindh's five largest cities (for example, Hyderabad was 70% Hindu), the exception being Karachi which was about 48% Muslim, 46% Hindu, and the remaining 6% non-Muslims belonged to other religions—there also Muslims were not in absolute majority. Four sub-districts to the southeast—Umarkot, Nagar Parkar, Mithi, and Chachro—adjoining India had Hindu majority of 57%. Several nearby sub-districts too had about 40–45% Hindu population.

Looking to the above position, Sindh could have been partitioned to give space to the Hindu Sindhis. Southeast Sindh, plus certain adjoining areas to compensate for Hindu Sindhis leaving other parts of Sindh, could have been Hindu or Indian Sindh. Looking to sub-regional Hindu-Muslim ratio of Sindh, the Congress could have tried to have part of Sindh carved out for the Hindus. Considering that the Muslim League had secured only 46% of the votes in Sindh, and the nationalist Muslims had polled three votes for every four polled by the League, the Congress could have insisted for a plebiscite in regions with Hindu dominance. However, the Congress seemed to have abandoned Sindh as 'a far off place', like Chamberlain had abandoned Czechoslovakia to Hitler in 1938 on the pretext that it was 'a far off country about which we know little'.

Khairpur was a Princely State adjoining India on the east, and surrounded on the other three sides by Sindh. Its Mir had offered to Nehru its merger with India. But, the offer was declined by Nehru, and India sent their accession papers back to them! Had the offer been accepted, Khairpur plus the adjoining Hindu-majority area could have been Hindu or Indian Sindh.

Notwithstanding the above, nothing was done for the Hindu Sindhis. They were deprived of their homeland of thousands of years. They became the new Jews, although their history and homeland was several thousand years older than those of the Jews and Israel. Why that injustice? Why Gandhi, Nehru, and other Indian leaders did little for them?

One argument is that the Thar Desert formed a natural boundary between India and Pakistan, and Sindh fell beyond the Thar Desert. That's a reasonable argument if India–Pakistan partition was done taking the natural boundaries into account. But, that was not the case. Where was the natural boundary between the East Punjab that became part of India, and the West Punjab that went to Pakistan—

Pre-Independence Blunders

allowing drug pedlars and terrorists to cross into India from Pakistan. Or, that between the East Bengal (Pakistan, now Bangladesh) and West Bengal (India), that has allowed Bangladeshi refugees to inundate India. Or, that between J&K and Pakistan and PoK, that allows terrorists from Pakistan to filter through. If Punjab, Bengal, and J&K could do without a natural border, why not Sindh? Why shouldn't there have been a Hindu or Indian Sindh?

Another argument is that this kind of partition could not have been done in all regions. Otherwise, why not earmarked areas say in UP for Muslims? There are several reasons for this. There was NO Muslim-majority district then in UP. Partition was restricted to border areas, and not anywhere within India or within Pakistan. Sindh fell in the border area. Initially, the concept of Pakistan was restricted ONLY to northwest India—it did not even include East Bengal.

When the Muslim League proposed Sindh as one of the components of their future Pakistan in the 1930s and later, or when the Groupings (Group-A, B, C) were proposed, Indian leaders and Hindu Sindhis should have objected to the inclusion of whole of Sindh as a Muslim-majority area in Pakistan. They didn't.

However, the real reason nothing was done to retain a part of the homeland for them, like it was done for the Punjabis and Bengalis, seems to be that unlike the Sikhs or the Hindu Bengalis, the Hindu Sindhis did not fight for it. Hindus of Sindh were generally not aggressive or bellicose like the minority non-Muslims in Punjab. The world at large is too cruel and indifferent to the plight of any given section of people unless they themselves fight and sacrifice for their rights. Jews suffered for centuries till they asserted themselves with the creation of Israel. Tibetans, with their non-violent Buddhism, have been deprived of their nation. Yezidis and Kurds, who have been at the receiving end for centuries, are now fighting back. On account of their cultured past of thousands of years, and their engagement in businesses, the Hindu Sindhis had been too peaceful to resist, agitate and fight.

Yet, something was expected from the India leadership of Gandhi & Co, in whom the Sindhis had reposed their faith. All one can say is that perhaps the nature of our freedom movement, and the quality and competence of our national leaders left a lot to be desired. Sadly, Gandhi–Nehru & Co suffered from an inherently defective worldview, thinking and vision, and were too poor as strategists, tacticians and implementers on the ground to be able to outsmart the British or the Muslim League, or stand up to their designs—not just with regard to Sindh, but in all other matters too! Sardar Patel had that genius, but Gandhi–Nehru combine often overlooked him, or did not allow him a free hand.

Making Jews of Hindu Sindhis

At the time of independence there were about 1.4 million (accounting for the increase in population since the 1931 census) Hindu Sindhis, most of whom, to save themselves from the violence, decided to leave, especially after the influx of the Muslim refugees (Mohajirs) who started looting their (Hindu Sindhis) properties and evicting them from their homes. By June 1948, about a million Hindu Sindhis had left Pakistan for India. Migrations continued thereafter, and tapered off in 1951.

Although Hindu Sindhis were deprived of their homeland, cultural identity, businesses, land, shops, properties, residential quarters—making beggars out of prosperous families—no one batted an eyelid, not the UN, or a Human Rights Organisation, or the US, or the UK, or the Pakistanis with whom they had stayed for centuries, or even the Indians! They became like the Jews of the past (before Israel was created in 1948), or the Tibetans of the 1950s, or the Kashmiri Pandits of 1990s, or the Kurds and the Yezidis of the current times.

India was a poor country, and thanks to Nehruvian economic policies, it remained a poor country. There was little that Nehruvian India offered to the hapless Hindu Sindhi refugees, who had lost everything. They were condemned to their miserable fate, and dumped in outer areas of several cities and towns, without any worthwhile help or facilities. Yet, one has to salute the spirit and hard work of the Hindu Sindhi community which without any governmental help gradually stood on its own feet, and became prosperous.

If the Indian leaders, that is, Gandhi & Co, had followed the Ambedkar-suggested model (detailed elsewhere in this book) of partition, and peaceful population and property exchange, not only would the Hindu Sindhi community have been adequately compensated for the loss of their assets in Pakistan, they would not have suffered violence and deprivation.

Blunder–10:
Giving Away 55 Crores to Pakistan

India and Pakistan had agreed in November 1947 that Rupees 55 crores remained to be transferred to Pakistan, as its share of the assets of undivided India. However, at the insistence of Patel, India informed Pakistan, within two hours of the agreement, that the actual implementation of the agreement would hinge on a settlement on Kashmir. Said Patel: *"In the division of assets we treated Pakistan generously. But we cannot tolerate even a pie being spent for making bullets to be shot at us. The settlement of assets is like a consent decree. The decree will be executed when all the outstanding points are satisfactorily settled."*{RG/461}

Pakistan had been pressing India for rupees 55 crores (over USD 500 million in today's terms). In the Cabinet meeting in January 1948 Patel stated that the money if given would surely be used by Pakistan to arm itself for use in Kashmir, hence the payment should be delayed. Dr Shyama Prasad Mukherjee, NV Gadgil and Dr BR Ambedkar backed Patel. Nehru too expressed his total agreement. The Cabinet therefore decided to withhold the money. Patel told in a Press Conference on 12 January 1948 that the issue of 55 crores could not be dissociated from the other related issues.{RG/462}

Gandhi conveyed to Patel the next day (13 January 1948) that withholding 55 crores from Pakistan was what Mountbatten had opined to him as *"a dishonourable act... unstatesman-like and unwise"*{RG/462}, and what he [Gandhi] thought was immoral. Patel was furious and asked of Mountbatten: *"How can you as a constitutional Governor-General do this behind my back? Do you know the facts?..."*{RG/462}

Gandhi was apparently innocent of the fact that Mountbatten and the British were bent upon favouring Pakistan—even on Kashmir, despite Pakistan's aggression. How could a top leader be so blind to the realities? Unfortunately, Nehru, rather than supporting Patel, and sticking to what he had himself agreed to, and had got passed in the Cabinet, went back on his commitment, and commented to Gandhi: *"Yes, it was passed but we don't have a case. It is legal quibbling."*{RG/463}

Gandhi and Nehru, rather than being prudent about what was in the best interest of the nation, went by what the British colonial representative Mountbatten, having his own axe to grind, had to say, and the Cabinet decision was reversed to let Pakistan have the money, and trouble India further in J&K! Going by the net results, effectively, it appears that for Gandhi maintaining "Brand Mahatma", and its associated "morality" was more important—the question is why didn't Gandhi and Mountbatten consider the immorality of Pakistan in attacking Kashmir which had already acceded to India? If Pakistan had agreed to desist from its illegal action in Kashmir, it would have got the money anyway. Further, Gandhi wanted to look good in the eyes of the Muslims in Pakistan and India. Ignore national interest for the sake of appeasement, and your own image! And for Nehru, kowtowing to Mountbatten and Gandhi was a priority, rather than standing up for the Cabinet decision, of which he was a part. People like Sardar Patel were out of place in such a scenario. Gandhi went on a fast to force the issue in his favour (it was one of the several issues that led him to fast). Patel yielded, Gandhi won, and India lost. Wrote Rajmohan Gandhi:

> "Wounded by Mountbatten's backbiting and Jawaharlal's disloyalty and bitter at Gandhi's stand on the 55 crores, Patel felt too that the timing of Gandhi's fast 'was hopelessly wrong'."{RG/464}

All those leaders, including Mountbatten and Nehru, who encouraged or prompted Gandhi into that unreasonable position were indirectly guilty of his untimely death. Patel had said something similar to General Roy Bucher:

> "At our meeting in Dehra Dun, the Sardar [Patel] told me that those who persuaded the Mahatma to suggest that monies (Rs. 55 crore) held in India should be despatched to Pakistan were responsible for the tragedy, and that after the monies were sent off, the Mahatma was moved up to be the first to be assassinated on the books of a very well-known Hindu revolutionary society. I distinctly remember the Sardar saying: 'You know quite well that for Gandhi to express a wish was almost an order.'" It was on Gandhi's insistence that [his] security had been withdrawn."{BK2/xxi-xxii}

Pre-Independence Blunders

Blunder–11:
Pre-Independence Dynasty Promotion

Jawaharlal Nehru's dynastic tendencies, inherited from his father Motilal, were apparent in the 1930s itself, much before he became the prime minister.

After the 1937 elections when the ministry was being formed in UP, Govind Ballabh Pant (who became the Chief Minister) and Rafi Ahmed Kidwai proposed to Nehru inclusion of Mrs Vijaylakshmi Pandit [Nehru's sister] in the ministry, which Nehru readily agreed. Why did they do so? Not because they considered Vijaylakshmi competent! But, by doing so, they hoped to receive Nehru's favour, and hoped to save themselves from unnecessary interference and outbursts of Nehru!{DD}

On Vijaylakshmi Pandit, there is an episode of the time Nehru was head of the Interim Government in 1946, as written by Stanley Wolpert in his book, 'Nehru: A Tryst with Destiny':

"Liaquat Ali Khan and Nehru almost came to blows in the interim government's cabinet, when Nehru named his sister Nan [Vijaylakshmi Pandit] as India's first ambassador to Moscow. Liaquat was livid at such autocratic blatant nepotism, but his protests fell on deaf ears. Nehru yelled louder and threatened to resign immediately if Dickie [Mountbatten] supported Liaquat in the matter."{Wolp2/398}

Blunder–12:
What Really Led to India's Independence?

Often, when one points out the blunders of Nehru, the same are sought to be white-washed by highlighting that "after all, Nehru (along with other Gandhians) won for us our freedom"! So, was it Gandhi-Nehru-Congress that made the British 'Quit India'? The prevalent myth says, "Yes". But, was it really so? NO.

'Quit India' Movement of 1942 fizzled out in about two months. After Quit India, Gandhi did not launch any movement. Is one to infer that the call to Quit India given in 1942 was acted upon by the British after a lapse of five years in 1947? That there was some kind of an ultra-delayed tubelight response? Quit India call heard after a delay of five years!

Recorded the noted historian Dr RC Majumdar: "*Far from claiming any credit for achievements of 1942 [Quit India], both Gandhi and the Congress offered apology and explanation for the 'madness' which seized the people participating in it.*"—quoted by the author Anuj Dhar in his tweet of 1 July 2018. Anuj Dhar also tweeted: "*The claim that Quit India led to freedom is a state sanctioned hoax.*"{AD1}

Britain hinted at independence in 1946, and announced it formally in 1947, even though there was hardly any pressure from the Congress on Britain to do so. Many of the Rulers of the Princely States in fact wondered and questioned the Raj as to why they wanted to leave (they didn't want them to—it was a question of their power and perks, which were safe under the British) when there was no movement against them, and no demand or pressure on them to leave.

The British initially announced the timeline as June 1948 to leave India. Later, they themselves preponed it to August 1947. If the British didn't wish to leave, and it was the Congress which was making them leave, why would the British voluntarily announce preponement of their departure? The long and short of it is that Gandhi and Gandhism and the Gandhian Congress were NOT really the reasons the British left. Gandhi himself admitted as much.

What They Said

What Gandhi had himself said:

"*I see it as clearly as I see my finger: British are leaving not because of any strength on our part but because of historical conditions and for many other reasons.*"{Gill/24}

The "historical conditions and other reasons" were not of Gandhi's making, or that of the Congress—they were despite them. In the context of the choice of the national flag in 1947 Gandhi had said: "*…But what is wrong with having the Union Jack in a corner of our flag? If harm has been done to us by the British it has not been done by their flag and we must also take note of the virtues of the British. They are voluntarily withdrawing from India, leaving power in our hands…*"{CWMG/Vol-96/86-87}

S.S. Gill:

"It seems presumptuous to pick holes in Gandhi's campaigns and strategies, and appear to belittle a man of epic dimensions, especially when the nationalist mythologies render it sacrilegious to re-evaluate his achievements. Great men of action, who perform

Pre-Independence Blunders

great deeds, do commit great mistakes. And there is no harm in pointing these out. In one sense it is a Gandhian duty, as he equated truth with God."{Gill/75}

"It is generally believed that Gandhi's greatest achievement was the liberation of India from colonial rule. But historical evidence does not support this view."{Gill/24}

Dr BR Ambedkar:
"...*The Quit India Campaign turned out to be a complete failure*... It was a mad venture and took the most diabolical form. It was a scorch-earth campaign in which the victims of looting, arson and murder were Indians and the perpetrators were Congressmen... Beaten, he [Gandhi] started a fast for twenty-one days in March 1943 while he was in gaol with the object of getting out of it. He failed. Thereafter he fell ill. As he was reported to be sinking the British Government released him for fear that he might die on their hand and bring them ignominy... On coming out of gaol, he [Gandhi] found that he and the Congress had not only missed the bus but had also lost the road. To retrieve the position and win for the Congress the respect of the British Government as a premier party in the country which it had lost by reason of the failure of the campaign that followed up the Quit India Resolution, and the violence which accompanied it, he started negotiating with the Viceroy... Thwarted in that attempt, Mr. Gandhi turned to Mr. Jinnah..."{Amb3}

Nirad Chaudhuri:
"...After being proved to be dangerous ideologues by that [world] war, the pacifists have now fallen back on Gandhi as their last prop, and are arguing that by liberating India from the foreign rule by his non-violent methods he has proved that non-violent methods and ideas are sound. Unfortunately, the British abandonment of India before Gandhi's death has given a spurious and specious plausibility to what is in reality only a coincidence without causal relationship... And finally, he [Gandhi] had no practical achievement, as I shall show when I deal with his death. What is attributed to him politically is pure myth..."{NC/41}

Freedom: the Real Reasons

Till the early 1940s the British were well-ensconced in power, and looked forward to comfortably sailing through for several more decades—notwithstanding the Gandhian agitations of over two decades since 1918. If they played politics between the Congress and the Muslim League it was only to prolong their rule, and not to give independence or create Pakistan. They never perceived the Gandhian non-violent methods as threats to their rule. Then what changed that they left? Those major factors are detailed below.

1) WW-II and its Consequence
UK's Precarious Economy, and WW-II Exhaustion.

1.1) The UK was in a precarious economic condition as a consequence of the Second World War. It was hugely debt-ridden, and the maintenance of its colonies had become a tremendous drag on the UK exchequer. The Britain had colonised India to loot, and not to invest in it or to maintain it. The money flow had to be from India to Britain to justify continuance of the colony; and not the other way round, which had begun to happen.

> "The Empire was no longer turning a profit, or even paying its way... The result was what the historian Correlli Barnett has called 'one of the most outstanding examples of strategic over-extension in history'."{PF/197}

The famous UK economist John Maynard Keynes, who also happened to be an economic advisor to the UK, presented the war cabinet in 1945 with a financial analysis that showed that running the British Empire had cost 1,000 million pounds for each of the past two years, rising post-war to 1,400 million pounds per year; and that without the US financial assistance, the UK would go bankrupt!{Tim}

The British exchequer was forced to freeze debt repayment. Britain owed the largest amount to India in war debt: 1250 million pounds!{Chee/3} {Wire1}

1.2) By the end of the WW-II territorial colonisation had ceased to be a viable enterprise, and decolonisation began. In fact, around the time India got its independence, many other colonies (like Sri Lanka, Burma–Myanmar, etc.) also got their independence, although there was not much of an independence movement in those colonies that would have forced the colonisers to leave. During 1947 Britain also pushed plans through the UN that would enable it to leave Palestine; and finally Israel was created on 14 May 1948.

1.3) Militarily, administratively, financially, and above all, mentally the British were too exhausted after the Second World War to continue with their colonies.

2) Netaji Bose, INA and Army Mutinies

2.1) The military onslaught of Netaji Subhas Chandra Bose and his INA hugely shook the British, and the Indian army.

2.2) The Viceroy was shocked to learn of thousands of soldiers of the British-Indian army switching over to INA (to support the enemy nation Japan) after the fall of Singapore in 1942. It meant the Indian soldiers in the British-Indian army could no longer be relied upon. What was more—there was a huge support for Netaji Bose and the INA among the common public in India.

Wrote Maulana Azad in his autobiography: "After the surrender of Japan, the British reoccupied Burma and many officers of the Indian National Army (INA) were taken prisoner. They did not repent their action in having joined the Indian National Army and some of them were now facing trial for treason. All these developments convinced the British that they could no longer rely on the armed forces..."{Azad/142}

2.3) The INA Red Fort trials of 1945-46 mobilised public opinion against the British on an unprecedented scale, so much so that the Congress leaders like Nehru (who had till then, and later too, opposed Netaji and INA) had to demonstratively pretend their support to the INA under-trials to get votes in the 1946 general elections.

2.4) The Indian Naval Mutiny of 1946 and the Jabalpur Army Mutiny of 1946, both provoked partially by the INA trials, convinced the British that they could no longer trust the Indian Army to suppress Indians, and continue to rule over them.

2.5) In the context of the Indian colony, Sir Stafford Cripps stated in the British Parliament on 5 March 1947 that Britain had only two alternatives: either to (1)transfer power to Indians, or (2)considerably reinforce British troops in India to retain hold. The latter (option-2), he judged as impossible!{Gill/24}

2.6) Comments Narendra Singh Sarila: "In South-east Asia, Bose blossomed, and,...played an important role in demoralizing the British military establishment in India. Indeed, it is a toss-up whether Gandhiji's or Bose's influence during the period 1945-46— even after Bose's death—played a more important role in destabilizing British rule in India."{Sar/125}

2.7) Wrote MKK Nayar: "The reason why Britain unilaterally granted freedom even before Congress had intensified its agitation was on account of Netaji's greatness. Army jawans who had never dared to utter a word against the British had united as one to declare that INA's soldiers were patriots. Men of the Navy fearlessly pointed guns at British ships and establishments and opened fire. It was the same soldiers who had for a hundred years obeyed orders like slaves, even to massacre unhesitatingly at the notorious Jallianwala Bagh. They had now united to express their opinion and Naval men had shown their readiness to raise the flag of revolt. Attlee and others probably realized that Indian soldiers may no longer be available to hunt Indians. This may have prompted them to leave with dignity and self-respect."{MKN}

2.8) Stated Dr BR Ambedkar: "...The national army [INA] that was raised by Subhas Chandra Bose. The British had been ruling the country in the firm belief that whatever may happen in the country or whatever the politicians do, they will never be able to change the loyalty of soldiers. That was one prop on which they were carrying on the administration. And that was completely dashed to pieces [by Bose and INA]. They found that soldiers could be seduced to form a party - a battalion to blow off the British. I think the British had come to the conclusion that if they were to rule India, the only basis on which they would rule was the maintenance of the British Army."{Amb}

2.9) The British historian Michael Edwardes wrote: "It slowly dawned upon the government of India that the backbone of the British rule, the Indian Army, might now no longer be trustworthy. The ghost of Subhas Bose, like Hamlet's father, walked the battlements of the Red Fort (where the INA soldiers were being tried), and his suddenly amplified figure overawed the conference that was to lead to Independence."{ME/93}

2.10) Chief Justice PB Chakrabarty of Calcutta High Court, who had also served as the acting Governor of West Bengal in India after independence, wrote in his letter addressed to the publisher of Dr RC Majumdar's book 'A History of Bengal'{IT1}:

"You have fulfilled a noble task by persuading Dr. Majumdar to write this history of Bengal and publishing it ...In the preface of the book Dr Majumdar has written that he could not accept the thesis that Indian independence was brought about solely, or predominantly by the non-violent civil disobedience movement of Gandhi. When I was the acting Governor, Lord Atlee, who had given us independence by withdrawing the British rule from India, spent two days in the Governor's palace at Calcutta during his tour of India. At that time I had a prolonged discussion with him regarding the real factors that had led the British to quit India. My direct question to him was that since Gandhi's 'Quit India' movement had tapered off quite some time ago and in 1947 no such new compelling situation had arisen that would necessitate a hasty British departure, why did they have to leave?

"In his reply Atlee cited several reasons, the principal among them being the erosion of loyalty to the British Crown among the Indian army and navy personnel as a result of the military activities of Netaji [Subhas Bose]. Toward the end of our discussion I asked Atlee what was the extent of Gandhi's influence upon the British decision to quit India. Hearing this question, Atlee's lips became twisted in a sarcastic smile as he slowly chewed out the word, **'m-i-n-i-m-a-l!'**"{Gla/159} {Stat1}

The Chief Justice also wrote: "Apart from revisionist historians, it was none other than Lord Clement Atlee himself, the British Prime Minster responsible for conceding independence to India, who gave a shattering blow to the myth sought to be perpetuated by court historians, that Gandhi and his movement had led the country to freedom."

3) Pressure from the US

The Cripps Mission of March-April 1942, the first one in the direction of freedom for India, was under the pressure from the US. The US felt that the best way to secure India from Japan was to grant it freedom, and obtain its support in the war. US President Roosevelt had constantly pressurised Britain on India, and had specially deputed Colonel Louis Johnson to India as his personal representative to lobby for the Indian freedom.{Sar/104} The US wanted Britain to settle the Indian issue so that India could provide whole-hearted support in WW-II. Shimla Conference was called on 25 June 1945 by Viceroy Wavell for Indian self-government again under pressure from Americans to get full Indian support to dislodge Japan from its occupied territories of Burma, Singapore and Indonesia.

The Japanese surrender following the dropping of atom-bombs dramatically enhanced the US military clout. The US thereafter insisted that the Atlantic Charter be also made applicable to the European colonies in Asia (it was, after all, a question of grabbing markets for the US capitalists), and they all be freed.

Thanks to the war, Britain had almost gone bankrupt, and was dependent on massive American aid. It could not therefore ignore or withstand the US pressure. Clement Attlee himself acknowledged in his autobiography that it was difficult for Britain to keep sticking on to the Indian colony given the constant American pressure against the British Empire.

Wrote Maulana Azad: "I have already referred to the pressure which President Roosevelt was putting on the British Government for a settlement of the Indian question. After Pearl Harbour, American public opinion became more and more insistent and demanded that India's voluntary cooperation in the war effort must be secured [by giving it freedom]."{Azad/47}

The fact of American help and pressure in getting independence for India is not adequately acknowledged by India.

Apart from the US, the Chinese Generalissimo Chiang Kai-shek, part of the Allies in WW-II, had also throughout pressed the British Government to recognise India's independence to enable it to render all help it was capable of.{Azad/41}

The Chicago Tribune in its valedictory tribute to Churchill had mentioned that "we [the US] have no interest in maintaining [or allowing the UK to maintain] her oppressive empire."{PC/366}

4) Gandhi & the Congress?

Gandhi and the Congress were among the minor reasons and non-decisive factors the British left.

5) The British Sought Freedom from India!?

It may sound ironic but by 1946–47 it was actually Britain which sought freedom from India!

As Patrick French puts it: "The role given to him [Mountbatten] by Attlee's government was to be the lubricant of imperial withdrawal; nothing more. His task was to give Britain—a harassed, war-torn, penniless little island—*freedom from its Indian Empire*, which had turned from a valuable asset into a frightening burden."{PF/289}

For full and further details, please refer to the unabridged digital version of this book available on Amazon.

Blunder–13:
Nehru/Top-Gandhians vs. Others in British Jails

In sharp contrast to the British prisoners, and the top Gandhians, who were treated very well in jails, the condition of Indian political prisoners, including revolutionaries, in jails was terrible: their uniforms were not washed for several days; rats and cockroaches roamed their kitchen area; reading and writing materials were not provided to them. Being political prisoners, they expected to be treated like one, rather than as common criminals. They demanded equality with the jailed Europeans in food standards, clothing, toiletries, and other hygienic necessities, as well as access to books and a daily newspapers. They also protested against their subjection to forced manual labour. To force the issue, Bhagat Singh and colleagues, including Jatin Das, began hunger strike. Jatin was martyred on 13 September 1929 in Lahore jail after a 63-day hunger strike.

Talking of suffering and sacrifices, many were tortured and whipped in British jails—but, never the top Gandhian Congress leaders. Nehru himself describes in his book of severe whipping of other imprisoned freedom-fighters in jails. For most Gandhiites, especially the top ones, the jails were, relatively speaking, comfortable. While ruthlessly persecuting the other freedom fighters, the British kid gloved Gandhi & Co, and incarcerated them under comfortable conditions. When arrested in 1930, the British took due care to provide all provisions for the health and comfort of Gandhi. That their (top Gandhians, including Azad and Nehru) life in Ahmednagar jail during 1942-45 was not all that terrible can be inferred from the following episodes. Wrote Rajmohan Gandhi:

> "On the day of their arrival [in jail], Kripalani recalls Azad showing 'towering rage': he threw out the Jailor who had brought ready-to-drink tea for them in an aluminium kettle along with loaves of bread on an aluminium plate and glasses for the tea. The Congress President 'ordered' the jailor to bring tea in a pot, milk in a jug and sugar in a bowl, plus cups, saucers and spoons. The jailor, an Indian, complied. According to Pattabhi, he was 'bravely performing his duties with visible regard for his new guests and with unshakeable loyalty to his old masters'."{RG2}

Describes Maulana Abul Kalam Azad in his autobiography:
> "Dinner was served to us soon after on iron platters. We did not

like them and I told the jailer that we were accustomed to eat from China plates. The jailer apologised and said that he could not supply us with a dinner set then but it would be obtained the next day. A convict from Poona had been brought to serve us as our cook. He could not prepare food according to our taste. He was soon changed and a better cook appointed."{Azad/91}

The routine of the leaders in Ahmednagar jail, that included Azad, Nehru, Patel, etc., used to be generally: breakfast at 7am, lunch at 1pm, bridge from 1pm to 3pm, rest from 3pm to 5pm followed by tea (alternately, writing or reading work between lunch and tea), games from 6pm to 7pm, dinner from 7pm to 8.30pm followed by coffee, then retire.

Gandhi was "imprisoned" between 1942 and 1944 in the grand Aga Khan Palace in Pune.

This is not to say that jail was fun place. It must have been a very dull and tedious and an oppressive place, where you are cut off from the world. And to be in jail for such long periods must have got on to their nerves. However, at least, they were relatively better placed compared to non-Gandhiite freedom-fighters, and lower-level Gandhiites, who were ill-fed, and ill-treated.

Nehru had access to newspapers, magazines and books in Naini and other jails. He also had ample supply of reading and writing materials. He wrote *Glimpses of World History* in Naini jail between 1930 and 1933; *An Autobiography* during 1934-35 in Bareilly and Dehra Dun jails; *Discovery of India* between 1942 and 1945 in Ahmednagar Jail.

Jails were almost a holiday vacation for the top Gandhians. Wrote Asaf Ali: Nehru almost had a bungalow to himself in his so-called jail with curtains of his choicest colour—blue. He could do gardening at leisure and write his books. When his wife was sick, his sentence was suspended even without he asking for it!{URL70}

It is said that Sir Harcourt Butler, the then Governor of UP, had even sent quality food and a champagne bottle to Motilal Nehru in his prison{Sar/323}, out of consideration for their association. As per MJ Akbar's book: "...but this, Motilal [Nehru] told me [Arthur Moore, a former editor of 'The Statesman'], is what happened. His [Motilal's] first morning in prison an ADC from Government House [Sir Harcourt Butler was the governor] arrived at lunchtime with a half-bottle of champagne wrapped in a napkin, and every single day of his imprisonment this was repeated."{Akb/123-4}

Writes Nehru in his autobiography:
"Personally, I have been very fortunate, and almost invariably, I have received courtesy from my own countrymen and English. Even my gaolers and the policemen, who have arrested me or escorted me as a prisoner from place to place, have been kind to me, and much of the bitterness of conflict and the sting of gaol life has been toned down because of this human touch...Even for Englishmen I was an individual and not merely one of the mass, and, I imagine, the fact that I had received my education in England, and especially my having been to an English public school, brought me nearer to them. Because of this, they could not help considering me as more or less civilized after their own pattern..."

Sadly, the top Gandhian leaders like Gandhi, Nehru did nothing to ensure revolutionaries and other freedom fighters got just treatment equivalent to them as freedom fighters. No non-cooperation, no andolan, no civil disobedience, no fast to support them or get them justice. In sharp contrast, Lokmanya Tilak had done all he could to support other freedom fighters, including revolutionaries. This when the revolutionaries had whole-heartedly supported Gandhi's Non-Cooperation Movement of 1920-22.

Savarkar and other prisoners in *Kaalapani* (a precursor to Gulag Archipelago and Guantanamo Bay prisons of our times) were subjected to brutally inhuman treatment. Prisoners were manacled; gruel to eat was riddled with worms; inmates, formed in groups, were chained like bullocks and hauled to oil mills, grinding mustard seed for endless hours. Prisoners were flogged.(URL70)

Had even 5% of the above treatment been meted out to the likes of Nehru and other top Gandhians, they would have given up the fight for freedom. However, the sacrifices of Savarkar and others were not recognised. What is most noteworthy is that while many who suffered in the fight for freedom remained faceless and unacknowledged, Nehrus enjoyed all the fruits of their sacrifice—and many, many times more. It was the most profitable investment they made, with returns thousands of times more, and through the decades, for the whole dynasty and descendants!

Blunder–14:
Clueless on the Roots of Partition & Pakistan

Though vociferously most anti-fascist and anti-Nazi, Nehru and his socialist colleagues had advocated rabidly anti-British stand when the British-India declared war (WW-II) on Germany. Why? There were no prior consultations with the Congress. Please see 'Blunder-3'. It is worth noting that being more a socialist and a communist sympathiser than an "internationalist", Nehru changed his tune soon after Russia joined the war on the side of Britain, and against Nazis. This lack of support by the Congress to the British war efforts in WW-II made the British anti-Hindus and anti-Congress, and made them favourably disposed towards the Muslims and the AIML. Wrote VP Menon in 'The Transfer of Power in India':

> "Moreover, the Congress opposition to the war effort [WW-II] and the [Muslim] League's de facto support for it convinced the British that the Hindus generally were their enemies and the Muslims their friends, and this consideration must have added force to the silent but effective official support for the policy of partition."{VPM2/438/L-8234}

Based on their negative experiences with the Congress in WW-II, and positive experiences with the Muslim League, and driven by the several major strategic considerations, Britain developed a vested interest in the creation of Pakistan: (1)The UK and the West wanted to secure 'Oil and the Middle East', and for that they felt a Muslim Pakistan as a border state would be critical. (2)The leadership of the proposed Muslim Pakistan was willing to be their accomplice in the cold war. (3)The proposed Muslim Pakistan was willing to provide military bases to the UK and the West. (4)Nehru, with his leftist, pro-Russia and pro-Socialist-Communist leanings was not likely to be an ally of the UK and the West in the cold war. Sadly, Gandhi and the remaining Congress leadership had not clarified their stand in the matter. Unfortunately, what the "internationalist & foreign-affairs expert" Nehru articulated passed off as India's foreign policy.

DN Panigrahi states in his book 'Jammu and Kashmir, The Cold War and the West':

> "Clement Attlee [UK PM, 1945-51], in his official as well as private correspondence, categorically stated that Kashmir was an issue so germane to 'the Muslim world' that *they must support Pakistan keeping in view British interest in the Middle*

East. ...the western powers, including Britain, considered Pakistan 'as a key factor in international politics by virtue of being Muslim' and because of its proximity with the Middle East. ...Sir Olaf Caroe...an ICS officer...wrote an article on Pakistan's potential role for Middle East defence...in 1949...his influential book, 'Wells of Power: The Oilfields of South Western Asia, a Regional and Global Study'. He argued that Middle Eastern oil held the key to progress and to international relations in the world in the future..."{Pani/3}

"The main thrust of the Caroe's argument was that the competition for oil would determine the future relationships of the powers and that 'the danger of attack of Soviet Russia was less likely in Europe than in the Middle East'. Second, he argued that *Pakistan, apart from having a strategic position in the region, was a Muslim country, and hence had a better chance of serving British interests in the Middle East than India...*"{Pani/24-5}

Since the First World War India's primary usefulness to Britain was less as a market for commercial exploitation and more in the field of war and defence, and in maintaining and securing its Empire. Through India as the base, and its Indian army, Britain controlled other countries in Asia. It could ill-afford to altogether give up its two-century old Empire, without having a firm foothold at least in part of India. That's when it cooked up the idea of Pakistan.

The West wanted to check the expansionist ambitions of communist Russia and China towards the Middle-East and the Indian Ocean. How to do that? The regions adjoining Russia and China had to be under their influence: that is, north-western India bordering Russia and J&K. Pakistan was willing to be an ally of the West in their cold war with the communists, hence critical to their strategy, along with J&K; while India, with its little likelihood of cooperating with the West in military matters, and forming an alliance with them, given India's anti-West dogma, Nehruvian pro-Russia bend, and protestations of non-violence, was dispensable. *The British military establishment too had become a strong proponent of Pakistan on account of its promise of cooperation in military matters.* Pakistan was actually midwifed by the UK and the US as a bulwark against Russia; and that's why they always came to its rescue lest it should fail.

Narendra Singh Sarila quotes in his book 'The Shadow of the Great Game: The Untold Story of India's Partition' a report of the

British chiefs of staff: *"The area of Pakistan [West Pakistan or the northwest of India] is strategically the most important in the continent of India and the majority of our strategic requirements would be met...by an agreement with Pakistan alone..."*{Sar/28}{DG/17}

Once the British realised India would deny them military cooperation after independence, they settled in favour of Pakistan, which was willing to cooperate with them, be their lackey, and help them in securing the Middle East and the Indian Ocean area. Yet another reason the British army and bureaucracy was favourable towards Pakistan was that they were being offered positions and employment in Pakistan.

"Field Marshal Lord Montgomery argued that it would be a tremendous asset if 'Pakistan, particularly the North-West', remained within the Commonwealth. The bases, airfields and ports in 'North West India' would be invaluable..."{DG/16-17}

The UK would have had no difficulty if they were sure that India—undivided India—after Independence, would serve as their ally. Had they felt reassured on those issues critical to their national and foreign policy interests, there would have been no Partition or the J&K imbroglio. What did India gain out of Nehru's socialism and pro-Soviet tilt? Nothing. India's economy went to dogs, and no one took India seriously in foreign affairs. It was Nehru's fads of socialism and pro-Soviet bend that led to Britain and Western nations, including USA, going against India, and resulting in the tragedy of partition, and the problem of Kashmir.

Had it been a wise Indian leadership that was adequately enlightened on the international affairs, and the vested interests of Britain and the West, and their Oil and Cold-war strategy, they would have been careful and tactful enough to have reassured Britain, the US, and the West on their cooperation (but, in practice, actually done what was in the best national interest of India, after independence). *And, in any case, being pro market-economy, and pro-West, compared to being socialistic and pro-Russia (as Nehru was), was far more beneficial for India.* But, when, despite being political leaders, you spend precious years in jail and outside hand-spinning yarn, experimenting with nutrition and indigenous medicines, and with truth, fasting, and non-violence, rather that deliberating on the crucial post-independence issues of economy, poverty and prosperity, internal and external security, and foreign policy, what can be expected?

Wrote Narendra Singh Sarila fittingly:
"But the Indian leaders remained plagued by the Indians' age-old weakness such as arrogance, inconsistency, often poor political judgement and disinterest in foreign affairs and questions of defence."{Sar/405}

"Protected by British power for so long and then focused on a non-violent struggle, the Indian leaders were ill prepared, as independence dawned, to confront the power play in our predatory world. Their historic disinterest in other countries' aims and motives made things none the easier. They had failed to see through the real British motivation [*despite Nehru's claim as an internationalist and a foreign-affairs expert*] for their support to the Pakistan scheme and take remedial measures..."{Sar/406}

"By the end of 1946, they [Indian leaders] had been manoeuvred into such a corner that if Sardar Patel had not stepped forward 'to have a limb amputated', as he put it, and satisfy Britain, there was a danger of India's fragmentation, as Britain searched for military bases in the bigger princely states by supporting their attempts to declare independence."{Sar/406}

Blunder–15:
Unplanned & Grossly Mismanaged Partition

Partition caused sudden displacement of about 14 million Hindus, Sikhs and Muslims, loss of their properties; and murder and slaughter of an estimated one to three million: there are no definite figures—an exercise for a proper count was never carried out! Wrote Patrick French:
"The number of people killed during the creation of independent India and Pakistan has never been established. It was in the interest of the governments of Attlee, Jinnah and Nehru to play down the scale of the massacres, since they all bore a measure of responsibility for what had happened. ...As Marn Singh, an eye specialist [a victim of Punjab partition]... remembered: 'Personally I believe it was the fault of politicians, who were keen for power, especially that Mr Jinnah, who hoped to gain a nation without even damaging the crease of his trousers, like some lord

of England.'"{PF/348, 351}

Trains carrying refugees from either side were looted, and passengers were slaughtered. There was mass dishonouring, brutality and rapes. JA Scott, the then British DIG of Police in Rawalpindi had stated: *"I could never believe that such barbarous acts as were committed on innocent people in rural areas of Rawalpindi district could be possible in Punjab."*{Bali/18}

Winston Churchill had accused Mountbatten of killing two million Indians!{AA/12} Mountbatten's critic Andrew Roberts had commented: "Mountbatten deserved to be court-martialled on his return to London."{Tunz/252}

Once the partition was agreed upon in principle by all the concerned and contending parties, it should have been carried out in a well thought-out, planned and professional manner. *That responsibility lay principally with the British, and particularly with the Viceroy Mountbatten, and with the heads of the two governments—Nehru and Jinnah.* Of course, the responsibility also lay with the Congress, the Muslim League, and the other political parties and organisations, and their leaders. Sadly, everyone failed the people.

For such a hugely major operation like partition of a country, and creation of a new country, no blue print was prepared, no planning was done either to ensure security and safety of people and their property, or to provide for their rehabilitation. It was just hurriedly and haphazardly put through, exposing millions to grave risk.

The bitter, unfortunate truth was that having decided to quit India, the Raj didn't really care. They had already decided to withdraw British troops from active service and repatriate them before the transfer of power. The British were too much in a hurry to get out. If they could be here for about two centuries to exploit and oppress, why not a few months more to secure Indians, as a compensation? But, Mountbatten and the British were least bothered about the Indians. They maintained only limited British troops to secure the left-over British. Having decided to leave, the Raj didn't wish to risk British lives. If Hindus and Muslims indulged in killing, looting and raping each other, so be it! Would demonstrate all the more how things would degenerate without them! British colonialism was a hugely cruel, greedy, selfish project. Why the British who had managed law and order covering millions for many,

many decades in India failed at this critical juncture? Accusing the Raj of dereliction of duty, Sardar bitterly complained to Mountbatten: *"The British had little difficulty when it was a question of putting down Indian freedom movements."*

The point, however, is why the Indian and the Pakistani leaders, whose people were to be so frightfully affected, failed to read the writing on the wall? That terrible things were bound to happen should have been very well known to them after what happened on the 'Direct Action Day' in Calcutta in August 1946, in Noakhali in East Bengal, and in Bihar, and in scores of other places down the decades, including the most horrible Moplah Rebellion of 1920s in Malabar, Kerala, where Muslims butchered Hindus! Weren't they aware that what actually happened was bound to happen if they didn't take sufficient care? What precaution and care did they take?

Expectedly, our clueless, non-violent Gandhian leaders had done absolutely nothing to keep people safe. They could have heeded Dr BR Ambedkar's wise and elaborate plan in his book "Pakistan or the Partition of India"{Amb3} given several years back on peaceful transfer of population. But, with "Mahatma" and "scientifically-minded, rational" Nehru as leaders, who would listen to the genuinely wise persons like Dr Ambedkar. If things had been planned well and foreseen, there could have been an agreement between the Congress and the Muslim League for a well-designed protocol for smooth and orderly transfer of population (as Ambedkar had suggested), as per the wishes of the concerned families and groups. Further, if the time was deemed too short to make adequate preparation for smooth transfer of power to the two domains, partition and independence could have been delayed by a month or so. Where was the tearing hurry?

Why those responsible—the leaders on either side—have not been singled out and made accountable? Why the blame has been put on general public on either side, and their inhumanity? How could Mountbatten, the main person responsible, escape the blame, and lord it out? Why was compensation not demanded from the British, the actual party responsible? If what is described below was possible, why thousands were allowed to be brutalised and slaughtered? It is from *"Empires of the Indus"* by Alice Albinia:

> "In 1947, Hameeda Akhtar Husain Raipuri was a young mother...
> She came to Karachi at Partition with her family from Aligarh...
> As the wife of a civil servant in the Education Ministry,

Hameeda's introduction to Karachi was comparatively orderly. The train that brought her from Delhi was one of the first to be attacked; but it was full of government employees, and thus was well defended by the army. 'A gentleman was waiting at the station at Karachi with the keys to our flat in Napier Barracks,' she says, 'another was holding out a ration card.' So the family settled into their new country, full of hope..."{AA/15}

That is, had all trains been well-guarded, like in the above case, thousands of deaths, loot and rapes could have been easily avoided. Similarly, had proper planning been done, and had a bigger and stronger military, para-military, police or armed volunteer force deployed well in advance, with political leaders, social workers and volunteers to assist them, most of the other tragedies could also have been avoided.

Instead of doing the above, Mountbatten and his British staff had done the opposite—they had ensured that all the British troops were withdrawn before the partition. This is what Sir Evan Meredith Jenkins, the last governor of the Punjab, had advised Mountbatten (who too was of similar opinion): *"I think it will be wise to avoid postponing the relief [withdrawal] of British troops for too long. It would be awkward if trouble on a large scale started while the relief was in progress. My own advice would therefore be to make the change before the end of July [1947]."*{Wolp3/165}

Further, why shouldn't Mountbatten, Nehru, and the Congress have planned for augmenting the strength of the police and army by induction of Indians. Well-trained returning INA soldiers were readily available. But, the British and the Congress (especially Nehru) bias against anything remotely related to Netaji Subhas and his INA came in the way!

Rather than ensuring sufficiency of troops to control possible trouble, Nehru had grandly and irresponsibly declared: *"I would rather have every village in India go up in flames than keep a single British soldier in India a moment longer than necessary."* But, if Nehru was happy having the highest post of the Governor General (till June 1948), and the highest posts in the Army with the British after independence, why not the soldiers to save poor citizens?

Blunder–16:
No Worthwhile Policy Formulations!

Nehru, Gandhi and other Congress leaders had all the time in the world prior to independence to formulate all relevant national policies for the post-independence period. But, did they do so? NO.

From 1915 onwards, when Gandhi returned from South Africa, the top Gandhian leaders had 32 long years till independence in 1947 to study, discuss, argue, and thrash out all issues vital to independent India. When in the British jails together for many years, they had long, uninterrupted and undisturbed times to work out all details under the sun for free India.

Yet, among the greatest weaknesses of the Freedom Movement was the failure of the Congress to formulate an enlightened constitution suited to India much prior to 1947. Not just the verbose one full of legalese, but also a short lucid one readable and understandable by non-experts, like the American constitution. After independence, it should have been taught in schools as a compulsory subject.

Of course, a much greater weakness of the Freedom Movement was the failure of the Congress to formulate well thought-out policies on economy, finance, taxation, agriculture, industries, education, science and technology, culture, language, administration, law and justice, internal security, external security, foreign policies, and so on, well in advance of the freedom in 1947. They should also have studied how the Western nations, especially the US, had managed to drastically reduce poverty, and became prosperous, and how India could emulate them after gaining freedom. Even if there could not be agreement on various issues, differing options with their pros and cons, along with practical examples from various countries, should have been documented as a guide for future. Expert teams should have been formed with such an end in mind. Finance for the study-teams should have been arranged. There was enough talent to deploy. There were enough financiers to back them. There was no dearth of time. The freedom movement stretched on for several decades! The Congress had all the time in the world to formulate India's future constitution and policies at least six times over.

Most of the leaders who were jailed over long periods had the additional advantage of undisturbed time at their disposal to read, study, think, discuss and thrash out details on various aspects related to the future constitution and policies.

Twelve top Congress leaders—Vallabhbhai Patel, Nehru, Maulana Azad, Kriplani, GB Pant, Pattabhi Sitaramayya, Narendra Dev, Asaf Ali, Shankarrao Deo, PC Ghosh, Syed Mahmud, and Hare Krushna Mahtab—were in Ahmednagar Fort jail for about three years from 1942 to 1945. But that overlong period of three years generated no short or detailed plans or policies or expert-studies on anything of relevance to the immediate or mid-term or long-term future of India, or even on the burning problem of the day: way forward towards freedom!

Gandhi, Nehru, Patel, and other top Congress leaders spent a number of years in the British jails where (unlike the revolutionaries and others who were whipped or tortured, and were deprived of the basic facilities) free from any compulsory labour or torture or hardship, they had the facilities of reading and writing and discussions. Yet, they hardly produced a work which could be considered of worthwhile practical use and implementation after independence.

In jail, Gandhi indulged in his fads of naturopathy, nutrition, fasting, enema, and medicinal quackery; and in flood of words through innumerable letters and articles that didn't really contribute much to what really mattered. When not in jail, Gandhi enjoyed playing dictator in his ashrams making life difficult for the inmates, and engaging people in all kind of time-pass activities like spinning yarn and so on.

Collected works and other writings of Gandhian leaders contain no serious discussions on any of the crucial topics listed earlier, and the most critical of all—the economic policies. It was as if they had no interest in ascertaining how to make India prosperous after independence. It was as if Adam Smith, Milton Friedman, Friedrich Hayek, and host of other notable economists did not exist for them. It was as if the study of economics and how to manage a modern state was irrelevant for them.

As became obvious during Nehru's post-independence era, despite "Glimpses of World History" India miserably failed in foreign affairs, defence and external security, and despite "Discovery of India" India failed to discover its forte, and became a basket case. Other leaders didn't help much either in defining well before independence what India's future policies should be. That gave

Nehru a free ride; and he royally blundered unchecked. Of course, Patel was able to limit Nehru's blunders as long as he was alive.

Wrote Rustamji: "Another shortcoming that could be mentioned is that in those years we did not think that the freedom would come so soon [Given Gandhian methods, independence was always a distant dream—and when it finally came, it was NOT thanks to Gandhi-Nehru-Congress: pl. check 'Blunder-12']. So, we never prepared, studied or made arrangements for running governments in the proper way."{Rust/216}

> Commented Nirad Chaudhuri very appropriately:
> "...*In the Indian nationalist movement there was not only a total absence of positive and constructive ideas, but even of thinking. These shortcomings were to have their disastrous consequence in 1947... The intellectual poverty of the nationalist movement gradually became intellectual bankruptcy, but nobody perceived that because the hatred of the British rule left no room for rational ideas... Over the whole period with which I am dealing [1921-52] none of them [Gandhi, Nehru...] put forth a single idea about what was to follow British rule... What was even more astonishing, none of these leaders were qualified to put forward any positive idea because none of them had any worthwhile knowledge of Indian history, life, and culture...*"{NC/31-2}

INTEGRATION OF THE PRINCELY STATE

Blunder–17:
Independent India dependent upon the British!

Nehru Plumped for the British—Mountbatten

God only knows why India chose to appoint Mountbatten, a British, as the Governor General (GG) of India after independence! Jinnah didn't do that blunder—he himself became the GG of Pakistan. Mountbatten as GG managed what the Raj desired—to the detriment of India. It was thanks to Nehru that Mountbatten became the GG. Why did the freedom-fighters choose a foreigner, a British, for the top post? Weren't competent Indians available? If Jinnah as GG could manage Pakistan, couldn't an Indian as GG manage India?

Nehru had adopted Mountbatten as his guru and guide. Reflects much on Nehru's judgement of people. Where Nehru was not readily amenable, Mountbatten reportedly used his wife Edwina to get Nehru around. Maulana Azad, a pro-Nehru person, expressed bewilderment in his autobiography as to how a person like Jawaharlal was won over by Lord Mountbatten; mentions Nehru's weakness of being impulsive and amenable to personal influences, and wonders if the Lady Mountbatten factor was responsible for certain decisions.{Azad/198}

Mountbatten was a representative of Britain, and it was natural for him, rather, expected of him, to safeguard and promote the interests of Britain; and keeping the British Government informed of the goings on, including confidential matters. India and Pakistan also had British army chiefs. In case the Indian leaders felt that having a British GG, and a British C-in-C, did help in some way, they should have accounted for the fact that it could also be counter-productive in certain cases—and it did prove to be so. Their basic allegiance being to Britain, between them, these British were able to manipulate matters—many contrary to the interests of India.

Mountbatten & Partition Mayhem

Much is made of Mountbatten, but he had been a failure in most of his past assignments. He belonged to navy, and in the Admiralty he was long known as the *"Master of Disaster"*.{Tunz/156}

Mountbatten was widely held responsible for his gross mismanagement resulting in the horrifying scale of the partition mayhem. Please check 'Blunder-15'. *Winston Churchill had accused Mountbatten of killing two million Indians!*{AA/12} Mountbatten's critic Andrew Roberts had commented: *"Mountbatten deserved to be court-martialled on his return to London."*{Tunz/252}

After the partition and its tragedy, there had been three assassination attempts on Jinnah by the aggrieved victims. Jinnah was so rattled he had remarked that the person most responsible for the disaster of partition was Dickie Mountbatten.{Tunz/301}

Wrote Maulana Azad:
"I also asked Lord Mountbatten to take into consideration the likely consequences of the partition of the country. Even without partition there were riots in Calcutta, Noakhali, Bihar, Bombay and Punjab... If the country was divided in such an atmosphere there would be rivers of blood flowing in different parts of the country and the British would be responsible for such carnage... Without a moment's hesitation Lord Mountbatten replied, 'At least on this question I shall give you complete assurance. I shall see to it that there is no bloodshed or riot. I am a soldier, not a civilian. Once partition is accepted in principle, I shall issue orders to see that there are no communal disturbances... If there should be slightest agitation, I shall adopt measures to nip the trouble in the bud... I shall order the Army and the Air Force to act and use tanks and aeroplanes to suppress anybody who wants to create trouble.'"{Azad/207}

Wrote Durga Das: "I concluded my report by stating that Mountbatten had hurried through with partition without making sure that the Boundary Force would be able to maintain peace."{DD/264}

Mountbatten Machinations in J&K, Junagadh & Hyderabad

Britain wanted Kashmir, a strategic territory, to be under their influence. That was possible if it was either independent or with Pakistan, which was pro-West. Towards this aim, Mountbatten ensured that as GG he did not remain just a titular head. He manipulated to get himself appointed as '*Head of the Defence Committee of India*' ensuring that the C-in-C of the Indian and the Pakistani Army and the Supreme Commander, Auchinleck, reported to him. In that capacity, Mountbatten secretively co-ordinated with the transitional British Commander-in-Chief of the Pakistan Army; had private strategy sessions with the transitional British C-in-C of the Indian Army, without the knowledge of the Indian leaders; and manipulated to the extent feasible, decisions and actions in the direction the British Government wanted.

Sarila points out in 'The Shadow of the Great Game':
"Another factor that distinctly influenced the situation was Nehru's offer to Mountbatten to chair the Defence Committee of the Indian Cabinet. It was this committee and not the Indian Cabinet as a whole that made decisions on Kashmir war policy. This power gave the governor-general enormous power to influence the course of fighting."{Sar/357}

Nehru was mainly responsible for having Mountbatten appointed as the GG of independent India; and was perhaps the only factor in making him the Head of the Defence Committee.

Wrote Durga Das in 'India from Curzon to Nehru & After':
"...Patel added that Nehru was unduly amenable to Mountbatten's influence. Nehru had 'always leaned on someone'. He was under Bapu's protective wing and 'now he leans on Mountbatten'."{DD/240}

The role of Mountbatten in the integration of the three states that created problems—Junagadh, Hyderabad and J&K—was dubious. Where the British interests were not affected—in respect of the other Princely States—he did try to help India. But, where the British interests clashed with the Indian interests, he helped the British interests. It was Mountbatten who made Nehru refer the J&K issue to the UN, thus internationalising a domestic issue. Mountbatten attempted to also refer the Junagadh and the Hyderabad cases to the UN. Fortunately, they were firmly rejected by Sardar Patel. British did all that was possible to prevent Indian army action in Hyderabad.

Blunder–18:
Nehru Refused J&K Accession when Offered!

By June-July 1947 Maharaja Hari Singh of J&K had begun to take steps towards final accession with India, including replacement of his pro-Pak PM Ram Chandra Kak with Mehr Chand Mahajan, a lawyer, and a Congress nominee on the Boundary Commission, who later became the Chief Justice of India. Looking to all this, Nehru should have created a conducive atmosphere, and taken Hari Singh into confidence, so that Maharaja's decision to accede to India could be expedited, and all the subsequent troubles on account of his late accession would have been avoided. Instead, *Nehru acted adversarial with the Maharaja.*

"There have been suggestions that the Maharaja had decided in August 1947, or certainly by mid-September, that he had no option but to join India, and that he was just waiting for the best moment and the most advantageous terms," wrote Andrew Whitehead in 'A Mission in Kashmir'.{AW/101}

When in August–September 1947, Maharaja Hari Singh indeed offered Kashmir's accession to India; most unbelievably, it was refused by Nehru, who first wanted Sheikh Abdullah to be freed and installed as the prime minister of the State—something not acceptable to the Maharaja. *Was it not queer? The nation being favoured with accession laying down conditions, rather than the state agreeing to merge!* Nehru's ways, driven by his hubris, were indeed bizarre and alarming!! (In sharp contrast you had Jinnah offering a signed blank sheet along with his own fountain pen to Maharajas of Jodhpur, Jaisalmer, and Bikaner to put down their conditions for accession to Pakistan, saying: *"You can fill in all your conditions."*{BK/337}) Had the accession been accepted, the Indian army could have been deployed in Kashmir well in advance of the invasion by the Pakistani-raiders, preventing both the creation of the PoK, and the terrible tragedy of loot, killings and rapes.

States Sarila in 'The Shadow of the Great Game':
"Mountbatten added: 'He [Sardar Patel] has also attacked Nehru for the first time saying *"I regret our leader has followed the lofty ideas into the skies and has no contact left with earth or reality"'*...This outburst probably reflected Patel's frustration with Nehru at the time, for refusing to accept the Maharaja of Kashmir's accession to India unless and until a government under Sheikh Abdullah was installed."{Sar/370}

It was undemocratic and irresponsible of Nehru, and an illegal act, not to have obtained the concurrence of the cabinet before taking such a major decision of not accepting J&K accession. It is quite likely that Mountbatten had dissuaded him from accepting accession, as the British wanted J&K to accede to Pakistan.

Blunder–19:
Allowing Kashmir to be almost Lost

The Pakistani raiders were almost on the outskirts of Srinagar by 22 October 1947, and the Maharaja desperately sought help. Looking to the precarious situation, Sardar Patel proposed sending the Indian Army to J&K. However, Mountbatten insisted that unless the *Instrument of Accession* was signed by J&K in favour of India (the offer earlier refused by Nehru ['Blunder-18'], most likely at the instance of Mountbatten himself!), India should not send army to Kashmir, and Nehru concurred.

On Friday, 24 October 1947, the Pakistani raiders attacked the Mohore Power House causing black out in Srinagar. Defence Committee of India, headed by Mountbatten, met the next morning on Saturday, 25 October 1947, and rather than ordering action to save Srinagar, directed VP Menon, Sam Manekshaw and a few senior military officers to fly to Srinagar the same day to check the position first hand. This was actually a deliberate ploy of Mountbatten to pass time and not allow counter-action by India, and let Pakistan gain an upper hand by force, as the British desired—because Mountbatten would have known through the British C-in-C of Pakistan what Pakistan was up to. (C-in-C of both India and Pakistan were British!)

VP Menon and company flew to Srinagar and found the state of affairs to be worse than what was reported. They advised Maharaja Hari Singh to hurry to the safety of Jammu. Hari Singh drove the same night to Jammu, 200 kilometres away. MC Mahajan, the premier of J&K, VP Menon, Sam Manekshaw, and colleagues returned to Delhi from Srinagar early next morning on Sunday, 26 October 1947, and reported the desperate situation to the Defence Committee. They advised that it would not be possible to save Srinagar and its people unless the troops were immediately airlifted. Even the Srinagar air-strip was in danger of being imminently occupied by the raiders, in which case even that only possibility of air-lifting troops would close.

Notwithstanding the desperate situation, and knowing that unless help was sent immediately, both the Muslims and the Pandits of Srinagar would be butchered by the Pakistani raiders, and the Valley of Kashmir would be lost to Pakistan, Mountbatten still insisted that the Instrument of Accession be first signed in favour of India. Nehru simply went along with his guru Mountbatten. *It didn't*

External Security

seem illegal to Mountbatten and Nehru that the raiders backed by the Pakistani army should invade J&K, which had not signed any Instrument of Accession in Pakistan's favour; but it seemed illegal to them to send Indian army help to save people getting looted, raped and butchered!

As desired, VP Menon flew to Jammu the same day—Sunday, 26 October 1947—to have the Instrument of Accession signed by Hari Singh, which he did. The Instrument of Accession signed by Hari Singh on Sunday, 26 October 1947, and brought back by VP Menon, was accepted by Mountbatten on Monday, 27 October 1947. With the signing of the *Instrument* and its acceptance, J&K legally became a part of India, and it became incumbent upon India to defend its territory, and throw out the raiders.

In the Defence Committee meeting held on Monday, 27 October 1947 Sam Manekshaw apprised the members of the Military situation. He said the raiders were hardly seven to nine kilometres from Srinagar; and unless the troops were flown in immediately, Srinagar would be lost, because going by road would take days, and once the raiders got to the airport and Srinagar, it would not be possible to fly-in the troops. He further informed that everything was ready at the airport, and the troops could be immediately airlifted, once the orders were issued.

However, Mountbatten—serving the pro-Pakistani British interests—tried to stall sending the Indian army, saying it was too late, raiders being already at the door of Srinagar. But, who made it late in the first place—Mountbatten himself! *As usual, Nehru prevaricated.*

Notably, even when the need for action became urgent, *"Mountbatten threw his weight against any precipitate action, emphasising the need for further information,"* writes C Dasgupta in his book, *'War and Diplomacy in Kashmir 1947-48'*{DG/45}. Even after further information was available through VP Menon and Sam Manekshaw, who had been specially flown to Srinagar for the purpose on 25 October 1947, and who advised urgent airlift of troops, *Mountbatten showed reluctance.* Writes Dasgupta *"...the service chiefs [all British], supported by Mountbatten, sought to dissuade the ministers from an airlift on the grounds that it involved great risks and dangers."*{DG/47}

Sardar Patel finally intervened. Recounted Sam Manekshaw, who later became the first Field Marshal in the Indian army, in his interview with Prem Shankar Jha{Jha1}:

"At the morning meeting he [VP Menon/Patel] handed over the (*Accession*) thing. Mountbatten turned around and said, 'come on Manekji (He called me Manekji instead of Manekshaw), what is the military situation?' I gave him the military situation, and told him that unless we flew in troops immediately, we would have lost Srinagar, because going by road would take days, and once the tribesmen got to the airport and Srinagar, we couldn't fly troops in. Everything was ready at the airport. *As usual Nehru talked about the United Nations, Russia, Africa, God almighty, everybody, until Sardar Patel lost his temper. He said, 'Jawaharlal, do you want Kashmir, or do you want to give it away.' He (Nehru) said, 'Of course, I want Kashmir.' Then he (Patel) said 'Please give your orders.'* And before he could say anything Sardar Patel turned to me and said, 'You have got your orders.' I walked out, and we started flying in troops..."{Jha1/135}

It has also been reported that the J&K premier, Mehar Chand Mahajan, even threatened to proceed to Karachi and offer Kashmir to Jinnah, if India could not secure safety of the people of J&K. Despite tremendous practical difficulties, lack of preparation, and the short notice, the Indian Army rose to the occasion and chased the raiders out of the valley. It is worth factoring-in the fact that had the Indian army not reached Srinagar in time, there would have been a large scale massacre and mayhem by the Pakistani raiders in Srinagar and surrounding areas, which in turn would have had repercussions all over India. But, Mountbatten and the British didn't seem to value Indian lives. British were serving pro-Pakistani British interests. But, Nehru? Had Sardar Patel not acted, and had it been left to Nehru and Mountbatten, the whole of Kashmir would have been lost to Pakistan.

Blunder–20:
Unconditional J&K Accession Made Conditional

Was the 'Instrument of Accession' signed by Maharaja Hari Singh for J&K different from the other Princely States, and did it incorporate some special provisions? NO. The Instrument of Accession was standard and common for all Princely States. There was no provision in it for any ruler to add or subtract conditions. It was required to be signed unchanged.

Enclosing his signed 'Instrument of Accession' in the standard format (like for all the other princely states), Maharaja Hari Singh wrote to the Governor-General of India Mountbatten on 26 October 1947:

> "With the conditions obtaining at present in my state and the great emergency of the situation as it exists, I have no option but to ask for help from the Indian Dominion. Naturally they cannot send the help asked for by me without my State acceding to the Dominion of India. I have accordingly decided to do so and I attach the Instrument of Accession for acceptance by your Government."{Jag/86}

With regard to J&K, it is worth re-emphasising that (a)the Instrument of Accession signed was no different from those signed by the other Princely States; (b)it was signed by Hari Singh unconditionally; and (c)it was accepted by the Governor General, Lord Mountbatten, unconditionally. That is, the whole process was no different from the one that applied to the other 547 Princely States that acceded to India (please note that the other 14 of the 562 had acceded to Pakistan).

Through a separate letter, however, Mountbatten advised Maharaja Hari Singh that the accession was subject to reference to the people of J&K:

> "In the special circumstances mentioned by Your Highness, my Government [so, Mountbatten regarded independent India's government as his government!] have decided to accept the accession of Kashmir State to the Dominion of India. Consistent with their policy that, in the case of any State where the issue of accession has been the subject of dispute, the question of accession should be decided in accordance with the wishes of the people of the State, it is my Government's wish that, as soon as law and order have been restored in Kashmir and her soil cleared of the invader, the question of the State's accession should be settled by a reference to the people..."{AW/114}{Jag/86}

Notably, the Maharaja had put no conditions on accession. In fact, even Sheikh Abdullah, who had favoured accession to India, never insisted on this condition—rather, he wanted it to be unconditional, lest any uncertainty should remain.

Who gave Mountbatten the authority to write such a letter? Who was he to make the accession conditional? Was he still the Viceroy of the British India serving the British interests, or was he the

Governor General of independent India? Why did Nehru not object? Why had the Indian Cabinet and leaders, particularly Nehru, not made it clear to him that he could not act on his own on critical matters—that he had to take the permission of the cabinet? One can understand conditions being stipulated by the party offering you the favour of accession. But, for the party being favoured with accession to stipulate conditions—that's absurd.

Had it been a Governor General who was an Indian like say Dr Ambedkar or Dr Rajendra Prasad or Rajagopalachari or Mahatma Gandhi (Wonder why he didn't wish to take on any official responsibility after independence, and leave the top post to a British!) himself, and not a British like Mountbatten, would he have tried to make the accession conditional? And, had he done so, would the Indian public have ever forgiven him? Or, was it that Nehru acquiesced to writing of such a letter by Mountbatten? (—yet another blunder?) Even if the deed was done without Nehru's knowledge (unlikely), Nehru should have objected to it and should have got it annulled or withdrawn.

Stipulation of 'Reference to People': Illegal

The Indian Independence Act 1947 enacted by the British Parliament also incorporated the Memorandum on States' Treaties and Paramountcy of 12 May 1946 as per which the princely states were to regain full sovereignty with the creation of the two dominions of India and Pakistan from the British India on 15 August 1947, with the ruler of the Princely State being the ONLY authority to offer accession to India or Pakistan, or to remain independent, regardless of the religious composition of the people of that state, *there being NO provision for 'reference to the people' or plebiscite.*

Therefore, with the signing of the *Instrument of Accession* unconditionally by the Maharaja of J&K on 26 October 1947 in favour of India, J&K's accession to India was full, final, irrevocable and totally legal as per the International Law. Legally, that separate letter of Mountbatten (please see above) made absolutely NO difference. In fact, Mountbatten's action of writing the above letter was unconstitutional and illegal. Even Nehru had NO legal authority to approve of such a letter. What is more, there was NO cabinet sanction for it!

India should have stuck to this incontestable legal position of the irrevocable accession of J&K to India, like for the other 547 states, on the strength of the signing of the *Instrument of Accession*. This is *what Sardar Patel strongly advocated.* Even US considered ours as an ironclad legal position in 1948. Writes C Dasgupta in his book, *'War and Diplomacy in Kashmir 1947-48'*: "The fundamental difference between the American and British positions lay in the fact that the United States was prepared in 1947-48 to recognise India's sovereign rights in Kashmir."{DG/121} However, Nehru failed to leverage on that.

The funny thing is that the *"reference to the people"* or plebiscite was requested neither by Maharaja Hari Singh, nor by Sheikh Abdullah, nor by the people of J&K, nor even by Jinnah(!!) at that time! It was only thanks to Mountbatten and Nehru!{Hing/200}

Blunder–21 :
Internationalisation of the Kashmir Issue

Nehru unnecessarily internationalised what was purely an internal issue by taking the J&K issue to the UN, again under the influence of the British Mountbatten. Wrote V Shankar in 'My Reminiscences of Sardar Patel, Volume 1':

"Lord Mountbatten persuaded Pandit Nehru to make a broadcast in which he was to announce that the accession would be subject to a plebiscite under the UN auspices. This was scheduled at 8.30pm on 28 October [1947]. Sardar used to insist on seeing the texts of important broadcasts including those of the prime minister. Pandit Nehru had a very busy day and could not send the text before 8.15pm. Sardar read it and noticed the embarrassing commitment. He tried to contact Pandit Nehru but the latter had left for the Broadcasting House. Sardar then commissioned me to go to the Broadcasting House and ask Pandit Nehru to delete the offending phrase 'under UN auspices'..."{Shan1}

However, by the time Shankar reached the place, the Mountbatten-inspired deed was done by Nehru. It was imprudent on the part of Nehru to have made this commitment of "plebiscite under UN auspices" at the instance of a British, Lord Mountbatten, having his own axe to grind, without taking the cabinet and the patriotic Indians who mattered—Sardar Patel and others—into confidence! Wrote the veteran Congressman DP Mishra:

"...Soon after, I heard Nehru's voice on All India Radio at Nagpur, committing the Government of India to the holding of plebiscite in Kashmir. As from my talk with Patel, I had received the impression that the signature of the Maharaja had finally settled the Kashmir issue. I was surprised by Nehru's announcement. When I visited Delhi next, I pointedly asked Patel whether the decision to hold a plebiscite in Kashmir was taken at a meeting of the Cabinet. He sighed and shook his head. It was evident that Nehru had acted on Mountbatten's advice, and had ignored his colleagues."

Reference to the UN was something Sardar Patel, Dr Ambedkar and others were against, however, Nehru again went ahead with it publicly in his radio broadcast on 2 November 1947. Despite sane advice, Nehru scored a self-goal for India by formally referring the J&K matter to the UN on 1 January 1948. With the issue internationalised, India suffered greatly, both domestically and internationally. It became like the sword of Damocles. The UK, the US and their allies, led by the UK, began playing politics of favouring Pakistan over India, ignoring the fact of Pakistani aggression in J&K.

That the member-nations of the UNSC acted in their own selfish national interests and engaged in power-game was apparently not known to the foreign-affairs expert Nehru. *As usual, Nehru himself realised his blunder after the act.* Nehru regretted the Kashmir issue "has been raised to an international level... by reference to the Security Council of the UN and most of the great powers are intensely interested in what happens in Kashmir... [Kashmir issue] has given us a great deal of trouble... the attitude of the great powers has been astonishing. Some of them have shown active partisanship for Pakistan... We feel we have not been given a square deal."{BK2/159}

Blunder–22:
Inept Handling of the J&K Issue in the UN

India and Pakistan presented their cases at the UN in January 1948. The Indian case was presented by Gopalaswami Aiyangar, Minister for Kashmir Affairs, specifically appointed by Nehru in his cabinet. Aiyangar was the leader of the Indian team that also included Sheikh Abdullah. Quipped Chaudhry Sir Muhammad Zafrullah Khan (1893-1985), the Pakistani representative in the UN, when he came to know about Gopalaswami Aiyangar as India's representative: *"You are offering me Kashmir on a platter."*{BK/387}

It is worth noting that Zafrullah Khan had an illustrious career. Educated at London's King's College, he had been a member of the All-India Muslim League, and had served as its president between 1931 and 1932. He was the Minister of Railway of British India in 1935. He sat on the British Viceroy's Executive Council as its Muslim member between 1935 and 1941. He represented India at the League of Nations in Geneva in 1939. He was the Agent-General of British India to China in 1942. He became judge at the Federal Court of India. He was the foreign minister of Pakistan (1947-54), the president for the UN General Assembly (1962), and the judge (1954-61, 1964-73), vice-president (1958-61) and the president (1970-73) of the International Court of Justice.

(Incidentally, Zafrullah Khan was an Ahmadiyya, like Abdus Salam (1926–1996), a Pakistani theoretical physicist, who shared the 1979 Nobel Prize in Physics. Abdus Salam left Pakistan in 1974 in protest against the passage of the parliamentary bill declaring the Ahmadiyya Community as NOT-Islamic. Jinnah and Aga Khan, both Shias, were the prime movers of Pakistan. Shias too are at the receiving end in Pakistan.)

Expectedly, while Zafrullah Khan's presentation was brilliant, and received all-round praise, that of Aiyangar's was an unmitigated disaster!

Earlier, instead of Aiyangar, the name of Sir Girija Shankar Bajpai, the then Secretary-General (senior-most position) in the Ministry of External Affairs and certainly a much more capable person, was suggested; but, on account of opposition he was dropped, as he was known to have been too close to the British during the pre-independence period.{Akb3/129} But then, why was he made the Secretary-General at all!

Sardar Patel was opposed to Gopalaswami Aiyangar leading the Indian team in the UN. He considered him to be not competent enough. Patel had instead suggested the name of CP Ramaswami Iyer, who had been the Diwan of Travancore. CP, as he was called, was a very competent intellectual, statesman and a diplomat, with many foreign contacts in the UK and the US. He would have presented India's case effectively. But, Nehru ignored **Patel's advice,** and stuck to Gopalaswami Aiyangar. Here is a tell-tale **description of** what happened in the UN, as told by Shakunthala Jagannathan, **CP's** granddaughter:

> "I was a student living in New York, when the question of Kashmir came up in the U.N. Accompanied by several Indian and American friends, I attended the Security council session, oozing

with confidence on India's stand. First came Sir Zafrullah Khan's impassioned and brilliant speech on behalf of Pakistan which was powerful enough to shake up our confidence. When he sat down, we Indians breathed a sigh of relief. The Indian delegation was then asked to present their case. The delegate concerned put up his hand, stood up, and said, "I protest!"... We had expected that our case, so much stronger, would shake up the U.N.! Instead our presentation on that day resulted in a debacle, right before our eyes..."{SJ/45-46}

Yet another wrong choice of Nehru was to include Sheikh Abdullah in the Indian delegation. Wrote Howard Schaffer: "The Indians had made Abdullah a member of their UN delegation, no doubt in the expectation that he would be an effective spokesman for India's cause. They could not have calculated that he would undercut their position by calling for Kashmir's independence in a private conversation with Austin. Apparently caught by surprise, the ambassador gave Abdullah no encouragement..."{Sch} Incidentally, Warren R. Austin was the US permanent representative—their ambassador—to the UN.

Nehru's initial blunder was to take an internal, domestic matter of India to the UN, and make it international. However, having referred the matter to the UN, it was expected of the international-affairs-expert Nehru to put his best foot forward, and win the case for India. Unfortunately for India, Nehru obliged Pakistan with a follow-up blunder: appointing an incompetent to present India's case!

Blunder–23:
PoK thanks to Nehru

It was thanks to Nehru's wrong decision that 'Pakistan Occupied Kashmir' (PoK) came into existence, when the Indian army was on the verge of getting the whole of J&K vacated.

Indian Army's Grand Achievements

Let's look at the two concrete cases from among the many feats of daring and bravery by the Indian army which helped throw the enemy out.

Pakistani raiders' determined bid to occupy Ladakh was frustrated by the superior Indian strategy of airlifting troops to Leh.

External Security

Air Commodore Mehar Chand flew his plane amazingly to 23,000 feet above sea-level—without oxygen—on an unchartered course to land his plane, with troops, at Leh at the height of about 12000 feet!

Another daring feat was that of Major-General Thimayya. He took his tanks to a height of about 12000 feet on the snow-capped Zojila Pass—something unique in history, as nobody had taken tanks to such heights and in such hazardous conditions before—and routed the enemy, destroying all their bunkers.

Incidentally, it was this brave and competent Thimayya who was humiliated by Krishna Menon, when he was Defence Minister in Nehru's cabinet, forcing Thimayya to resign! Later, after Thimayya withdrew his resignation at the instance of Nehru, even Nehru behaved with him in a way that amounted to his double humiliation!!

Thanks to the Indian Army, the raiders were forced to retreat, and were on the run. This war, started by Pakistan in October 1947, lasted 15 months, and ended on 1 January 1949.

How Nehru Allowed Creation of PoK

The capture of Muzzafarabad, now the capital of PoK, was imminent. The Army, however, was ordered to suspend all offensive operations with effect from *1 January 1949*, even though the enemy did not cease fighting. The Indian Army was very disappointed by the decision, but orders were orders. Thanks to ordering of ceasefire with immediate effect by Nehru, *PoK—Pakistan Occupied Kashmir—* came into existence; else the whole of Kashmir would have been with India. And, now it is this PoK which is used by Pakistan to send terrorists into J&K.

> Shakespeare had rightly articulated:
> *There is a tide in the affairs of men,*
> *Which, taken at the flood, leads on to fortune;*
> *Omitted, all the voyage of their life*
> *Is bound in shallows and in miseries;*
> *And we must take the current when it serves,*
> *Or lose our ventures.*

As per a report, the ceasefire decision was remote-controlled by Mountbatten, who was by then back in England—such influence Mountbatten still exercised over Nehru.

> Commented General SPP Thorat:
> "Our forces might have succeeded in evicting the invaders, if the Prime Minister had not held them in check, and later ordered the

ceasefire... Obviously great pressure must have been brought to bear on him by the [former Governor-General]... Panditji was a great personal and family friend of Lord Mountbatten."{BK2/160}

The military commanders directly involved in the operations of clearing J&K from the raiders and the Pak-army were General Officer C-in-C, Western Command, KM Cariappa, and the Operational Commander Major-General Thimayya.

As per the biography of late Field Marshal KM Cariappa, they both requested Nehru in December 1948 for a little more time to clear J&K of Pakistani raiders completely, but Nehru did not heed them. Thimayya had told Nehru that the Army needed two weeks more to regain lost territory but Nehru was adamant. It is said that Thimayya found Nehru's attitude inexplicable, and left Teen Murti Bhavan, the official residence of the PM, in disgust. When Cariappa asked Nehru about the decision a few years later, Nehru conceded that the ceasefire order ought to have been delayed!

Britain had marked out two areas that had to absolutely go to Pakistan—despite J&K accession to India. One was the northern area along the Chinese, Russian and Afghanistan borders comprising Gilgit, Hunza, Nagar, Swat and Chitral. This area commanded as much strategic importance to Britain and the West as NWFP in Pakistan. Mountbatten had ensured NWFP went to Pakistan, even though its leader, Khan Abdul Ghaffar Khan, was opposed to the partition of India.

The other area was the western strip adjoining Pakistani Punjab to secure Pakistan from India, comprising Muzzafarabad, Mirpur, Bhimbar, Kotli and adjoining areas. Muzzafarabad is now the capital of PoK. What the British had planned, they managed to achieve—thanks to the way Nehru acted, or failed to act. How the British managed to fool India even after independence! Reflects also on the then Indian leadership.

After J&K acceded to India on 26 October 1947, Major William Brown of the Gilgit Scouts, although a British contract officer of the Maharaja of J&K, had the Governor Ghansara Singh imprisoned on 31 October 1947, as per a pre-meditated plan, and hoisted the Pakistani flag there on 2 November 1947, and declared its accession to Pakistan!

This was totally an illegal action on the part of the British meant to deliberately deny India access to Central Asia. Mountbatten would surely have known of the goings on, but did nothing, or rather, allowed the illegality to quietly happen. Major Khurshid Anwar was one of the Pakistani army officers who had organised and lead the Pakistani Pathan tribal invasion of J&K. His deputy, Major Aslam Khan, took charge of Gilgit from Brown. In 1948, Brown was honoured with the "Most Exalted Order of the British Empire".

Wrote NV Gadgil, the then Cabinet Minister for Works and Mines in the Nehru's Cabinet, in his autobiography 'Government from Inside':

"In truth, Nehru did not show much enthusiasm for Kashmir's accession at the time... Both the Maharaja and [Meherchand] Mahajan [Premier of Kashmir] pressed for the acceptance of Kashmir's accession, but Nehru would not move. [Nehru then was being guided by Sheikh Abdullah]... If our army had not received instructions to stop fighting before that date [1 January 1949], it would have cleared the raiders from whole of Kashmir...

"The restrain imposed upon our army was motivated by the hope that Pakistan would be satisfied with a bit of Kashmir occupied by it. Of course, some of us opposed this view... Sheikh Abdullah was an ordinary person elevated to an extraordinary position by the Government of India...

"I am afraid that Nehru is responsible for the prolongation of the problem through his willingness to compromise at every stage... Had Vallabhbhai [Patel] been the man to handle the Kashmir question, he would have settled it long ago. At least, he would never have settled with a partial control of Jammu & Kashmir. He would have occupied the whole of the State and would never have allowed it to be elevated to international importance." {Mak/445-6} {DFI} {HJS}

MO Mathai, the then private secretary to Nehru, wrote: "Nehru... ordered a ceasefire in Kashmir at a time when our forces were in a sound position and poised to roll back the enemy. *Nehru's decision, which was impulsive, was a grievous error much resented by the armed forces.* Nehru's was an imitative and an absorptive mind... Essentially, Gandhi's was an original mind, while Nehru's was a second-rate one. He was all heart and less mind. This is reflected in his books also."{Mac/170}

Wrote BM Kaul in 'Confrontation with Pakistan': "We were politically unwise in accepting the ceasefire in view of our successes at the time in Uri, Tithwal, and Kargil."{YGB/17}

As per the article "Nehru's Pacifism and the Failed Recapture of Kashmir" by Sandeep Bamzai in ORF:
"To keep abreast with the developments in Kashmir, Nehru had dispatched his private secretary and 'eyes and ears' Dwarka Nath Kachru to the frontline...

"Some of Kachru's correspondence is extremely damaging, the prism far too revealing of how the Indian Army first pushed back the raiders and then vanquished the Pakistan Army regulars, even having them on the run... Previously unpublished correspondence [Nehru-Kachru] reveal that Nehru's pacifism—guided by the principles of fair play [?!] and the fact that India had referred the Kashmir matter to the United Nations erroneously on Lord Mountbatten's insistence—meant that the Indian Army was refused permission to go all the way and reclaim what eventually became PoK and the Northern Areas..."{URL51}

Nehru can be squarely blamed for the creation of the J&K problem, and the creation of the PoK. However, those problems did not arise on account of just one or two unfortunate decisions of Nehru. There was enough scope to correct or reverse those initial one, two, or three wrong decisions. But he persisted with his wrong position. And, made a further series of blunders.

Blunder–24:
Nehru's Shocking Callousness in J&K

Here is an account by of a Hindu survivor who was a witness to the Mirpur tragedy reproduced from Swarajya Mag{Swa2}:
"On November 23 [1947], Prem Nath Dogra and Professor Balraj Madhok met Brigadier Paranjape, the Brigade Commander of the Indian Army in Jammu, and requested him to send reinforcements to Mirpur [a strategic place where more than one hundred thousand Hindus and Sikhs were held up during first Pakistani aggression over Kashmir]. Paranjape shared their agony but expressed his helplessness because—as per instructions from the army generals—consultation with Sheikh Abdullah was mandatory in order to deploy Indian troops anywhere in Jammu and Kashmir. Paranjape also informed the delegation that Pandit Nehru would come to Srinagar on

November 24 [1947] and they should meet him. On November 24, Pandit Dogra and Professor Madhok met Nehru and once again told him about the critical situation in Mirpur. They requested him to order immediate Indian troops reinforcement to the beleaguered Mirpur City. Professor Madhok was amazed at Pandit Nehru's response—Pandit Nehru flew into a rage and yelled that they should talk to Sheikh Abdullah. Prof Madhok again told Pandit Nehru that Sheikh Abdullah was indifferent to the plight of the Jammu province and only Pandit Nehru could save the people of Mirpur. *However, Pandit Nehru ignored all their entreaties and did not send any reinforcements to Mirpur."*{Swa2}

Mirpur later fell to Pakistani artillery, and became part of PoK. The Hindus and Sikhs encountered a genocide, and worst orgies of rape and barbarity.

Blunder–25:
Article-370 thanks to Nehru

How Nehru-Abdullah Ensured Article-370

Article-370 on J&K is thanks to Nehru, who brought it about at the instance of Sheikh Abdullah, despite opposition by many, including Dr BR Ambedkar and Sardar Patel.

Gopalaswami Aiyangar, appointed by Nehru, moved Article 306A—which later became Article 370 in the Indian Constitution—in the Constituent Assembly on 17 October 1949 guaranteeing special status to J&K. This was at the instance of Sheikh Abdullah, and with the concurrence of Nehru. Although many in the Constituent Assembly were not in favour of it, they consented, keeping in view Nehru's wish, who was then the main person steering the J&K policy. Those not in favour included Ambedkar, Maulana Hasrat Mohani, Sardar Patel, and many others. India, which was a Dominion, became a Republic on 26 January 1950, and Article 370 came into force for J&K. Why was special provision made for J&K? Why Article 370? Let's examine.

J&K had nominated four representatives to the Indian Constituent Assembly in June 1949—the nominations were made by Yuvraj Karan Singh on the advice of the Council of Ministers of the

State's Interim Government led by Sheikh Abdullah. The J&K representatives in the Indian Constituent Assembly chose to act differently from the other Princely States—at the behest of Sheikh Abdullah. While the other Princely States were agreeable to a common Constitution, J&K representatives stated they were not inclined to accept the future Constitution of India, and they would rather have their own separate State Constitution. This, they insisted, was allowed as per clause 7 of the Instrument of Accession. It is another matter that the representatives of the other States could also have taken the same position as J&K, for they too had signed the *Instrument of Accession*, which had the same content and format as that signed for J&K by the Maharaja. The J&K representatives also stated that till their new State Constitution was framed, they would be governed by the old Constitution Act of 1939.

It was to accommodate this that a special provision had to be made for J&K in the Constitution of India. That provision is Article 370. Of course, Article 370, labelled *"Temporary provisions with respect to the State of Jammu and Kashmir"* was conceived as a temporary arrangement, with hopes of a full integration in time to come. J&K State Constitution came into effect on 26 January 1957, comprising 158 Sections, of which Section 3 says, *"The State of Jammu and Kashmir is and shall be an integral part of the Union of India."*

But why were such special provisions allowed. They could have been blocked by the Constituent Assembly? Interestingly, poor Hari Singh was already out of the picture. Special provisions or no special provisions—he stood neither to gain nor to lose. It was Abdullah, who after getting rid of the Maharaja, was trying to secure and upgrade his status.

Nehru had brought in Gopalaswami Ayyangar as a Minister without Portfolio to look after the J&K affairs. Before his visit to Europe, Nehru had finalised the draft provisions relating to J&K with Sheikh Abdullah, which later became Article 370. He had entrusted to Gopalaswami Ayyangar the task of piloting these provisions through the Constituent Assembly. Ayyangar did the needful. His presentation provoked angry protests from all sides. Most were opposed to any discriminatory treatment for J&K. The proposal of Article 370 was torn to pieces by the Constituent Assembly. Ayyangar was the lone defender, and Maulana Azad was not able to effectively support him. In the debate, Maulana Hasrat Mohani of UP stated that while he was not opposed to all the concessions that were being granted to his friend Sheikh Abdullah, why make such discrimination; if all those concessions were to be granted to the Kashmir, why not to the Baroda ruler too.

Dr Ambedkar was firmly opposed to it. Nehru had sent Abdullah to Dr Ambedkar to explain to him the position and to draft an appropriate Article for the Constitution. Ambedkar had remarked:
"Mr Abdullah, you want that India should defend Kashmir, India should develop Kashmir and Kashmiris should have equal rights as the citizens of India, but you don't want India and any citizen of India to have any rights in Kashmir. I am the Law minister of India. I cannot betray the interest of my country."{SNS/106}

Nehru, who was then abroad, rang up Patel and requested him to get the Article 370 through, and it was for that reason alone that Patel relented, as Sardar did not wish to embarrass Nehru in his absence. But Sardar commented, "*Jawaharlal royega* [Nehru will rue this]."{RG/517}

Strangely, Nehru made a statement on Kashmir in 1952, when Sardar Patel was no more, "Sardar Patel was all the time dealing with these matters." Wrote V Shankar:
"When I was working as his [Gopalaswami Ayyangar] joint secretary the self-same Article [370] came in for criticism in the Lok Sabha. In defence, Pandit Nehru took the stand that the Article was dealt with by Sardar in his absence and he was not responsible for it. I met Gopalaswami the same day evening as he was walking on the lawn of his residence. I questioned the bonafides of Pandit Nehru's stand. Gopalaswami's reaction was one of anger and he said, 'It is an ill return to the Sardar for the magnanimity he had shown in accepting Panditji's point of view against his better judgment.' He added, 'I have told Jawaharlal this already.'"{Shan2/63}

Adverse Consequences of Article-370

There are many adverse consequences of Article 370. Some of them are:

(1)Regionalism, parochialism and secessionism. (2)Denial of fundamental right to an Indian citizen to settle in J&K permanently. (3)Denial of fundamental right to an Indian citizen to purchase property in J&K. (4)Deprivation of right to vote to an Indian citizen, as he or she cannot become a citizen of J&K. (5)Denial of jobs—an Indian citizen, who is not also a citizen of J&K, cannot get a job in

J&K. (6) A woman, who is a permanent citizen of the State, loses her property, including ancestral property, if she gets married to a man who is not a citizen of the State. Also, she can't get a job in the State, nor can she get admission in colleges getting financial aid from the State or the Union Government. (7) Hindu immigrants who were ousted from their ancestral homes in West Pakistan at the time of partition and settled in J&K have not yet been given citizenship. This includes their children and grand-children.

Of course, the biggest negative is that it has come in the way of full integration of the State, which has gravely harmed both the people of J&K and India. Article 370 helps protect the corrupt J&K politicians from the more stringent central provisions, and keeps them out of reach of CAG. To the general public, it does not benefit. It is actually counter-productive. If J&K were like any other state in India, there would have been much more private investment in it, leading to prosperity.

Jagmohan, who had also been Governor of J&K, writes in his book, '*My Frozen Turbulence in Kashmir*':

"Article 370 is nothing but a feeding ground for the parasites at the heart of paradise. It skins the poor. It deceives them with its mirage. It lines the pockets of the 'power elites'. It fans the ego of the new 'sultans'. In essence, it creates a land without justice...It suffocates the very idea of India and fogs the vision of a great social and cultural crucible from Kashmir to Kanyakumari...

"Over the years, Article 370 has become an instrument of exploitation at the hands of the ruling political elites and other vested interests in bureaucracy, business, the judiciary and bar...It breeds separatist forces which in turn sustain and strengthen Article 370. Apart from politicians, the richer classes have found it convenient to amass wealth and not allow healthy financial legislation to come to the State. The provisions of the Wealth Tax and other beneficial laws of the Union have not been allowed to operate in the State under the cover of Article 370..."{Jag/230}

Even if Article 370 had to be introduced for whatever reason, it could have been made applicable only to the Valley, and Jammu and Ladakh could have been kept out through certain special provisions, or by spinning them off as separate mini-states or union territories. That would at least have ensured Jammu and Ladakh developed unhindered by the needless restrictions that were the by-products of Article 370. Why make Jammu and Ladakh suffer for the politics of the Valley? There are enough statistics to show that the people of Jammu and Ladakh have been short-changed and benefits have been largely cornered for the Valley.

The Article 370 is labelled "Temporary provisions with respect to the State of Jammu and Kashmir", and is included in Chapter 21 of the Constitution dealing with "Temporary, Transitional & Special" provisions. High time this temporary provision was done away with.

Blunder–26:
Article 35A for J&K

Following the '1952 Delhi Agreement' between Nehru and the then J&K Premier Sheikh Abdullah, Article 35A was added to the Indian Constitution in a hush-hush manner (without routing it through the Parliament as required under Article 368) through a Presidential Order of 1954 (in exercise of the powers conferred by Article 370) on the advice of the Union Government headed by Nehru empowering the J&K state to define 'Permanent Residents' (PR) of the state, and accord them rights and privileges denied to other citizens of India.

Under the above provisions 'Permanent Resident Certificates' (PRC) are issued to the Permanent Residents of J&K. Among the debilitating and discriminating provisions for the Indian citizens who don't hold PRCs are that they can't own immovable property in J&K, they can't get jobs in the J&K govt, they can't get admission in a college run by the J&K govt, nor avail of any scholarships. Also, if a woman who holds a PRC marries a man who doesn't hold a PRC then her children and husband can't exercise any right in the state, are not entitled to PRC, and can't inherit her immovable property in J&K.

This Article 35A, along with the Article 370, has been at the root of non-complete integration of J&K with India, and hinders development of the region, as outsiders are handicapped in investing in the region.

The Article has since been challenged in the Supreme Court on several strong grounds, some of which are as follows. (a) It is illegal because it was added to the Constitution without following the proper, laid-down (under Article 368) procedure of the Parliamentary route. (b) It violates Article 14: Equality before the

Law. (c)It violated women's right to marry as per their choice.

It is ironical that Article 35A is supposed to be an extension of Article 35 which deals with the 'Fundamental Rights' when 35A actually violates the fundamental rights of an overwhelming majority. Curiously, 35A is not listed after Article 35 in the Constitution, but is included in the Appendix.

A telling example of the consequences of the iniquitous Article 35A is the plight of about 200 Valmiki families brought to J&K as 'Safai Karamcharis' in the 1950s on the promise of grant of PRC. However, even after many decades PRCs have not been granted to them, and to their children. Many, who have since acquired required educational qualifications, can't apply for government jobs in the absence of PRC. They can vote for the Lok Sabha elections but not for J&K legislature, or for the local bodies. Their colony has not been regularised. Another painful example is that of about two lakh Hindu-Sikh refugees who migrated to J&K from West Pakistan in 1947 after Partition—none have received PRC, and they can neither acquire immovable property in J&K, nor avail of educational and other facilities! They are Indian nationals, but not citizens of the J&K state. Their cry for justice has gone unheard for decades.

The worst thing about the Article was that although passed on 14 May 1954, it was made applicable retrospectively from 14 May 1944, well before independence! Hindus from Pakistan entered Jammu in 1947 after partition, and were thus handicapped, thanks to this Article—demonstrates how insensitive Nehru was to their plight. Had they been Muslims Nehru's stand would have been different and accommodating—like it was in case of the Muslims from East Bengal.

It is high time this iniquitous Article 35A is dumped along with the Article 370 from which it flows. In this context one thing can definitely be said of Nehru. While he failed to solve any of the many problems of India in his overlong innings of 17 years, he did manage to manufacture fresh ones, like those through these Articles 370 and 35A—purely his creations.

Blunder–27:
Nehru's Blood Brother Who Deceived

A critical player in the J&K saga was Sheikh Mohammed Abdullah, born in 1905 in Soura, a village on the outskirts of Srinagar. He became famous as Sher-e-Kashmir: the Lion of Kashmir. Sheikh Abdullah's father was Sheikh Mohammed Ibrahim, a middle class manufacturer and trader of shawls. Sheikh Abdullah's grandfather was a Hindu Kashmiri Pandit by the name of Ragho Ram Koul, who was converted to Islam in 1890 and was named Sheikh Mohammed Abdullah, the name his grandson took. Sheikh Abdullah married Akbar Jahan in 1933. She was daughter of Michael Harry Nedou and his Kashmiri wife. Michael owned a hotel at the tourist resort of Gulmarg—his father was a European proprietor of a chain of hotels in India including Nedous Hotel in Srinagar.

Sheikh Abdullah did MSc in Chemistry from Aligarh Muslim University in 1930. It was at the University that he became politically active. He formed the Muslim Conference, Kashmir's first political party, in 1932, and later renamed it to National Conference in 1938. The Muslim Conference founded by Sheikh Abdullah was reportedly communal: some say that he later changed its name to National Conference only for tactical reasons. Sheikh Abdullah was a protagonist of Kashmiri nationalism linked to Islam; and his role model was Dr Mohammad Iqbal, a scion of another Kashmiri Pundit convert to Islam—like himself—who propounded the ideology of Pakistan way back in 1930.

Although Gandhi had thought it prudent to keep himself aloof from the affairs of the Princely States, Nehru had set up "The All-India States' Peoples' Conference" for the States in 1939. Nehru had associated himself with Sheikh Abdullah in that capacity. He was supportive of his agitations. Sheikh Abdullah and his colleagues were arrested on several occasions by the Maharaja for their political agitations. Sheikh Abdullah launched the *Quit Kashmir* agitation against the Maharajah in May 1946 leading to his arrest. The agitation, felt most Congress leaders, was opportunist and malevolent, and driven by selfish consideration of self-promotion—after all, Maharaja was not an outsider like the British. Sheikh Abdullah indulged in such acts knowing he would receive tacit support of Nehru. Although Sheikh Abdullah had tried to project his fight against the Maharaja as a fight against the feudal order, and a fight for the people of J&K—something the gullible, socialist Nehru believed—in reality his purpose was communal, to get Muslim support, and grab power.

Alarmed at the acts of Sheikh Abdullah, and Nehru's support to him, the Kashmiri Pandits had telegrammed Sardar Patel on 4 June 1947:

"The statements of Pandit Jawaharlal Nehru concerning Kashmir affairs being entirely unverified and tendentious are universally condemned and resented by Hindus of Kashmir. By encouraging Sheikh Abdullah's Fascist and Communal Programme he is doing great disservice to the people of Kashmir. His [Abdullah] unwarranted and wrong statements about facts and demolishing mosques inflame Muslims against Hindus..."{Mak/406-7} {BK/374}

Sheikh Abdullah had endeared himself to Nehru—who had called him *my blood-brother*—and others by projecting an anti-feudal, democratic, leftist, pro-India, pro-Congress, and above all, a secular image: perhaps to get Hari Singh out of the way, and then to sit in his place; for his later actions belied that image, and disappointed and shocked Nehru. S. Gopal, Nehru's biographer, had written that Nehru regarded Abdullah as 'an old friend and colleague and blood-brother'. Nehru held Abdullah beyond suspicion, and trusted him fully. *For Nehru, Abdullah was Kashmir, and Kashmir was Abdullah!*{BK/372} To have reposed such blind faith in Sheikh Abdullah and in his capability to deliver, grossly overestimating his popularity and remaining innocently unsuspicious of his intentions, even to the extent of being unfair, unjust and insulting to the Maharaja, reflected negatively on the expected leadership qualities from Nehru.

Sheikh Abdullah was made 'Head of the Emergency Administration' in J&K on 30 October 1947 by Maharaja Hari Singh at the instance of Nehru and Mahatma Gandhi. He took oath as Prime Minister of Kashmir on 17 March 1948. He was accused of rigging elections to the Constituent Assembly in 1951. He was dismissed as Prime Minister on 8 August 1953, and was arrested and later jailed for eleven years upon being accused of conspiracy against the State in what came to be known as the 'Kashmir Conspiracy Case'. Bakshi Ghulam Mohammed was appointed in his place—it was he who had arrested Sheikh Abdullah. Wrote MO Mathai:

"When Feroze Gandhi [Indira Gandhi's husband] heard of the arrest of Sheikh Abdullah in 1953 he came to my study beaming. He said that Bakshi did a foolish thing in arresting Sheikh Abdullah, and added that Bakshi should have had Sheikh Abdullah taken to the top of a lonely hill on the Azad Kashmir border, pushed down and shot, and published the news that Abdullah had fled to Pakistan." {Mac2/L-5660}

Sheikh Abdullah was released on 8 April 1964. Nehru passed away on 27 May 1964. Sheikh Abdullah was later interned from

1965 to 1968. He was exiled from Kashmir in 1971 for 18 months. Consequent to the Indira-Sheikh accord of 1974, he became the Chief Minister of J&K and remained in that position till his death in 1982.

Sardar Patel's Correct Assessment of Sheikh Abdullah

BN Mullik, who was the then Deputy Director of the IB—the Intelligence Bureau—with charge of Kashmir, and later head of the IB, wrote in his book, *'My Years with Nehru: Kashmir'*[BNM2] that his report of Kashmir of 1949 stating, inter alia, intense local anti-Pak feelings and no weakening in Sheikh Abdulla's ideological commitment to India so pleased Nehru that he had copies of the report circulated to all embassies and ministries. However, the realist and wise Sardar Patel, with a gift for making right judgements, was not amused. Here are extracts from the book:

"...Sardar Vallabhbhai Patel was unhappy. This report of mine apparently went against the views which he had held about Kashmir in general and Sheikh Abdullah in particular. *He suspected that the Sheikh was not genuine and was misleading Pandit Nehru and was not happy that the report should have been given such wide circulation...* A few days after I had sent the report, the Home Secretary informed me that the Sardar did not agree with my assessment and had taken exception to the fact that I had submitted this report without first consulting him...

"I got a summons to see the Sardar the next day. He was not well and was seated on his bed. He looked at me quietly for some time. Then he asked me whether I had written the report, a copy of which was in his hands. I replied in the affirmative. He asked me why I had sent a copy of this to Jawaharlal without consulting him. I replied that I had submitted the report to the Director. Sardar Patel then enquired whether I knew that Jawaharlal had sent copies of this report to all our embassies abroad and what was my reaction to this. I said that I had heard about the circulation only the previous day from the Home Secretary and I was naturally happy to hear that the Prime Minister thought so well of my report that he had thought fit to circulate it to our Ambassadors abroad. *The Sardar then said that he did not agree with my assessment of the situation in Kashmir in general and of Sheikh Abdullah in particular...*

"The Sardar then gave me his own views about Sheikh Abdullah. *He apprehended that Sheikh Abdullah would ultimately let down*

India and Jawaharlal Nehru and would come out in his real colours; his antipathy to the Maharaja was not really an antipathy to a ruler as such, but to the Dogras in general and with the Dogras he identified the rest of the majority community in India. In his slow voice, he firmly told me that my assessment of Sheikh Abdullah was wrong, though my assessment of public opinion in Kashmir valley about accession was probably correct. After having pointed out what he considered to be my error in judgment, he was, however, good enough to say that *he agreed with my views that I should submit only independent assessments to the Government and not tailor them to suit the known or anticipated views of particular leaders. He said that I would soon discover my error but*, at the same time, he complimented me on the way the report had been written and the pains I had taken over it. *This was the greatness of the Sardar.* Whilst disagreeing with my views, he recognised my right to express them...

"That day I came back to my office wondering whether I had really made a mistake in my assessment of Kashmir and whether what the Sardar had said was not right after all. Events, as they turned out subsequently, proved that the Sardar was right and I was not. Within three years we found ourselves fighting against Sheikh Abdullah. Sardar Patel was dead by then. Yet, I feel that possibly events might have turned out differently and the subsequent pain, turmoil, and embarrassments could have been avoided if the special difficulties of Kashmir had been understood by all concerned and they had guided their talks and modified their actions on the basis of this understanding. *Probably, things would not have come to this pass at all if the Sardar was still living, because Sheikh Abdullah had a very wholesome respect and fear for him.*"{BNM2/16-17}

Nehru Realises his Blunder

Nehru ultimately realised his blunder after he discovered what Sheikh Abdullah really was. Wrote Balraj Krishna: "*Nehru himself came round to Patel's view later in 1962, when he told Mullik of Abdullah's 'communal activities throughout the period he had acted as the National Conference leader. It was the Pakistani aggression which had mellowed him a little for a short time, because the tribals had committed gruesome atrocities on the Muslim population in the Valley. But, as soon as he became Prime Minister, he came out in his* true colours once again and started his anti-Hindu activities... his entire outlook and behaviour was based on the fact that the Kashmir Valley had a Muslim majority.'"{BK/395}

Blunder–28: Wanting Maharaja to Lick his Boots

Most unwisely, while Nehru had treated Maharaja Hari Singh ignominiously, he gave all his support to Sheikh Abdullah, little appreciating that Maharaja's signature on the Instrument of Accession was necessary for J&K to be part of India.

When Abdullah launched the 'abusive and mischievous'{BK/375} *Quit Kashmir* agitation against the Maharajah in May 1946 leading to his arrest ('Blunder-27'), Nehru decided to go to the Valley in June 1946 to free Abdullah. Though prohibited to enter the State, Nehru decided to defy the ban. He proclaimed that he wanted to take on the autocratic and the feudal rule that prevailed in Kashmir. Autocratic and feudal rule prevailed in the other 547 Princely States too that ultimately merged with India: Did Nehru go to any of those 547 states to similarly protest—especially the recalcitrant Nizam-ruled state of Hyderabad, where Hindus had been brutally at the receiving end of the Razakars? Nehru did not seem to realise that the support of the princes and their collaboration would be indispensable in the coming months for persuading them to accede to India. To take on the Maharaja at that stage, and that too as Congress president, did not appear to be politically wise. Sardar Patel and others tried to dissuade him, yet he went. Sardar Patel wrote to DP Mishra:

"Though President [Nehru] has been elected for the fourth time, he often acts with childlike innocence, which puts us all in great difficulties quite unexpectedly. You have good reason to be angry but we must not allow our anger to get the better of ourselves... He has done many things recently which have caused us great embarrassment. His action in Kashmir, his interference in Sikh election to the Constituent Assembly, his Press conference immediately after the AICC are all acts of emotional insanity and it puts tremendous strain on us to set matters right..."{Mak/86}

Even Gandhi, when he went for his only visit to Kashmir in 1947, pointedly rejected the hospitality of the Maharaja, and remained the guest of the National Conference of Abdullah. Rebuffed thus by

Gandhi, having been consistently rubbed the wrong way, experiencing the hostility of Nehru towards him over the last many months, and watching the commitment being shown to his arch enemy, Abdullah, why Hari Singh, anybody in his place—Nehru himself, were he in Maharaja's shoes—would have hesitated to accede to India. Hari Singh realised he would have no future with Nehru and Gandhi at the helm. Pakistan he surely did not wish to join. But he did not relish the insistence from Nehru (when Maharaja offered accession in September 1947) to first hand over power to Sheikh Abdullah—as if he were some foreign power who should hand over power to a native. So, the Maharaja started considering his option for independence, which was legally permissible.

If Nehru had dealt with Hari Singh wisely looking to the political options, like Sardar Patel had done in respect of all the other 547 Princely States, had Nehru not allowed his personal bias to dominate, had Nehru accommodated Maharaja suitably, had Nehru convinced him that his interests would be suitably protected if he joined India, Hari Singh may not have dithered and would have signed the Instrument of Accession well before 15 August 1947; and J&K would never have been an issue at all!

Apart from, "*I thought he [Nehru] wanted to make the Maharaja lick his boots...*"{MND/47}; Mountbatten had made another observation: "I am glad to say that Nehru has not been put in charge of the new [Princely] States Department, which would have wrecked everything. Patel, who is essentially a realist and very sensible, is going to take it over...Even better news is that VP Menon is to be the Secretary."{BK2/91}

States V Shankar in his book, 'My Reminiscences of Sardar Patel':{Shan}

"...Pandit Nehru regarded it as axiomatic that only Sheikh Abdullah could deliver the goods and was prepared to make any concessions to him to seek his support... Sardar did not trust Sheikh nor did he share Pandit Nehru's assessment of his influence in the State. He felt that our case in Jammu and Kashmir had to be met on the basis of the Maharaja executing the Instrument of Accession, the thought of antagonising the one on whose signature on that document alone we could justify our legal case in Jammu and Kashmir was distressing to him.

"...Sardar also felt it would be in the long-term interests of India to utilise the Maharaja's undoubted influence among the various sections of the people to force a permanent bond between the State and India...He [Sardar] was doubtful if the weakening of the administrative authority by the Maharaja to the extent demanded by the Sheikh was in the interests of the State and India. He felt that the last thing that should occur at that critical period was for the Maharaja and the Sheikh to work at cross-purposes with each other or for the already disillusioned people of the State to harbour doubts about the future of the Government or the Maharaja.

"...Sardar Patel also came into conflict with Pt Nehru and Gopalaswami Ayyangar owing to the personal rift between the Maharaja and Sheikh Abdullah. It can scarcely be denied that the latter wanted the Maharaja's head on a charger and taking advantage of the wrong assessment by Pandit Nehru and Gopalaswami Ayyangar ... he literally wanted to dictate his own terms..."

Blunder–29:
Kashmiri Pandits vs. Kashmiri Pandits

The tormentors of the Kashmiri Pandits (*KP*s) have been Kashmiri Pandits themselves, or Kashmiri-Pandit-Converts. Most notably, *people like Pandit Nehru who created the Kashmir problem in the first place; and then, rather than solving it, made it more complicated.*

Wrote B Krishna in his book 'Sardar Vallabhbhai Patel':
"Nehru's bias in favour of Abdullah was evident from what he said in August 1945 at the annual session of the National Conference at Sopore in the Valley, '*If non-Muslims want to live in Kashmir, they should join the National Conference or bid goodbye to the country...If Pandits do not join it, no safeguards and weightages will protect them.*'"{BK/374}

Nehru threatening his own people! And, not for any wrong committed by them. But to undemocratically force them to back a person [Sheikh Abdullah] who turned out to be a bigot, and an anti-national. Half a million Kashmiri Pandits would, some forty-five years later, pay for Nehru's sins, and be ethnically cleansed out of Kashmir—their home for thousands of years.

Incidentally, Sheikh Abdullah himself was a Kashmiri Pandit

convert. The second-generation-convert Sir Allama Muhammad Iqbal, one of the main promoters of the idea of Pakistan, had a major influence on Jinnah in gradually turning him from a liberal, advocating Hindu-Muslim unity, into a bigot. As per the article "Iqbal's Hindu Relations" by Khushwant Singh in 'The Telegraph' of 30 June 2007{KS2}, Iqbal's (1877–1938) father was one Rattan Lal Sapru, a Kashmiri Pandit. He was the revenue collector of the Afghan governor of Kashmir. He was caught embezzling money. The governor offered him a choice: he should either convert to Islam or be hanged. Rattan Lal chose to stay alive. He was named Nur Mohammad after conversion. The Saprus disowned Rattan Lal and severed all connections with him.

Those who drove out the Kashmiri Pandits from the valley also happen to be Kashmiri-Pandit-Converts. Fundamentalist Islam is supremacist, intolerant, cruel, and inhuman like the ISIS.

That KPs have been their own worst enemies is highlighted by the following interesting historical episode: Rinchin was a Buddhist from Ladakh. Hinduism (Shaivism) was then the dominant religion in Kashmir. Islam was on the fringe, and was at the time being propagated by Saiyyid Bilal Shah, popular as Bulbul Shah. After Sahadev fled and Dulacha left, Sahadev's Army Chief, Ramchandra, occupied the throne of Kashmir. But Rinchin, who had a key post in Sahadev's administration, plotted and eliminated Ramchandra, and sat in his place in 1320 CE. To pacify the public provoked by the misdeed, Rinchin married Kotarani, daughter of Ramchandra. At Kotarani's behest, discarding Buddhism, Rinchin adopted Shaivism to become acceptable to the public. But the Kashmiri Pandits refused to accept him in their fold, saying that his conversion was not feasible—a legend says they couldn't decide which caste to put him in. As a reaction to the rebuff, and at the instance of Shah Mir, Rinchin then approached Bulbul Shah, who converted him to Islam, and gave him the name Sultan Malik Sadruddin. Rinchin later built a mosque called the Bodro Masjid, venerated both by the Ladakh Buddhists and the Kashmiri Muslims. With the king converted to Islam, many others followed. And thus Islam spread in the Kashmir Valley.

This is how Pandits scored a self-goal. So, in a way, the Kashmiri Pandits have themselves to blame for inadvertently giving a push to the Islamisation of the Valley, though it was the later state-backed campaign—through preaching, patronage, incentives, torture and forced conversions—that reduced the Pandits from an overwhelming majority to a minority.

Blunder–30:
Sidelining the One Who Could have Tackled J&K

The matter of Princely States was under the States Ministry, which was under the charge of Sardar Patel. Patel had ably dealt with the complexity of over 500 Princely States. As such J&K should also have been left to Patel. However, Nehru, as Prime Minister, had decided to handle J&K himself. Without the concurrence of Sardar, and without even the courtesy of informing him, Nehru appointed N Gopalaswami Ayyangar, a former Dewan of J&K and a constitutional expert, as a Cabinet Minister without portfolio, to assist him (Nehru) in handling Kashmir. It was this Gopalaswami who had very badly messed up India's case in the UN later ('Blunder-22'). Sardar became aware of Gopalaswami's role indirectly when he [Gopalaswami] issued a note in connection with J&K, without consulting Sardar. Wrote Patel to Gopalaswami on 22 December 1947: "This question should have been referred to and dealt with by the Ministry of States... I would suggest that the relative papers may now be transferred to the States Ministry and in future the Kashmir administration may be asked to deal with that Ministry direct."

Gopalaswami let the position be known to Sardar (that what he was doing was at the behest of PM Nehru), and expressed his willingness to dissociate himself from the J&K matter if DyPM Patel so desired. Realising the position, Patel wrote back to Gopalaswami the next day on 23 December 1947: "I would rather withdraw my letter and let you deal with matters as you deem best than give you cause for annoyance." Meanwhile, Nehru, when he became aware of Patel's above letter of 22 December 1947, chose to write a rather harsh and bossy letter to Patel on 23 December 1947{Arpi5}:

"Gopalaswami Ayyangar has been especially asked to help in Kashmir matters. Both for this reason and because of his intimate knowledge and experience of Kashmir he had to be given full latitude. I really do not see where the States Ministry comes into the picture, except that it should be kept informed of steps taken. All this was done at my instance and I do not propose to abdicate my functions in regard to matters for which I consider myself responsible. May I say that the manner of approach to Gopalaswami was hardly in keeping with the courtesy due to a colleague?"{RG/447/L-7686}

Response to such an intemperate letter was on expected lines.

Patel wrote to Nehru on 23 December 1947 {Arpi5}:
"Your letter of today has been received just now at 7 p.m. and I am writing immediately to tell you this. It has caused me considerable pain. Before I received your letter I had already written to Gopalaswami a letter of which a copy is enclosed herewith. If I had known (that) he had sent you copies of our correspondence I would have sent to you a copy of my letter to him straightaway. In any case, your letter makes it clear to me that I must not or at least cannot continue as a Member of Government and hence I am hereby tendering my resignation. I am grateful to you for the courtesy and kindness shown to me during the period of office which was a period of considerable strain."{RG/447}

Apparently, the letter was not sent at Gandhi's instance, upon Mountbatten's advice that without Patel the Government could not be run.{BK2/162}

Disenchanted and frustrated with Nehru's hubris, and his improper and thoughtless ways, Patel expressed to Gandhi his wish to dissociate himself from the government in December 1947 and again in January 1948. Wrote Balraj Krishna:

"In taking away Kashmir from the States Ministry and placing it under the charge of Ayyangar who was Minister without Portfolio, Nehru was acting under Abdullah's influence. To all intents and purposes, he was discarding Patel for Abdullah, ignoring how Patel had stood by his side both as a loyal friend and as a pillar of strength through the tempestuous, nerve-wracking, fateful months preceding and following the transfer of power."{BK/388}

Nehru wrote a long note to Gandhi on 6 January 1948 seeking his arbitration for his differences with Patel. Gandhi referred the letter to Patel. Patel responded to Gandhi:

"I have tried my best to appreciate what he [Nehru] says on the subject [Hindu-Muslim relations], but howsoever much I have tried to understand it on the twin basis of democracy and Cabinet responsibility, I have found myself unable to agree with his conception of the Prime Minister's duties and functions. That conception, if accepted, would raise the Prime Minister to the position of a virtual dictator, for he claims 'full freedom to act when and how he chooses'. This in my opinion is wholly opposed to democratic and Cabinet system of government. The Prime Minister's position, according to my conception, is certainly pre-eminent; he is first among equals. However, he has no overriding powers over his colleagues; if he had any, a Cabinet and Cabinet responsibility would be superfluous..."{LMS/177}

Wrote Durga Das: "Two days earlier [before Gandhi's assassination on 30 January 1948] I had met Azad and learnt from him that tension between Nehru and Patel had mounted to a point where the Prime Minister had angrily thumped the table at a Cabinet meeting and said: *'Patel, you do what you like. I will not have it.'* ...Nehru's outburst was basically sparked by the feeling, fed by his courtiers and hangers-on, *that Patel was taking the country to the Right*... [Now, what was wrong in taking the country to the right! Nehru took the country to dogs with his leftism and poverty-perpetuating socialism!] ...When I called on Patel the following day, he told me that *Nehru* had *'lost his head'* and he, for his part, had made up his mind *not to stand 'the nonsense any more'*. He said he was going to see Gandhi and tell him he was quitting. I said Bapu would never agree to let him go... Patel quietly replied: 'The old man has gone senile. He wants Mountbatten to bring Jawahar and me together.'...."{DD/277}

Before Gandhi could resolve Patel-Nehru differences, he was assassinated on 30 January 1948. That forced Nehru and Patel together. For the sake of the nation, and to honour the request of the departed soul (Gandhi), Patel sacrificed himself. Patriotically speaking, Patel should not have given way to sentimentality upon Gandhi's death, and for the sake of the good of the nation, he should have fought out Nehru to its logical end: that is, he should have marshalled all his forces, unseated Nehru, saved India from the depths to which Nehru had ultimately condemned it to, and taken India towards the heights like only he could have.

Notably, even the Deputy Prime Minister of J&K between 1947-53, Bakhshi Ghulam Muhammad of the National Conference, had become so disturbed and alarmed at the way the J&K issue was being messed up that he met Sardar Patel and requested:

"Why do you [Sardar Patel] not take over the problem and finish it like Hyderabad? Patel replied cryptically: You go to your friend [Nehru] and tell him to keep his hands off Kashmir problem for two months and I will undertake to solve it."{Mak/440-41}

Writes Rajmohan Gandhi in his book 'Patel–A Life':

"Patel was as strongly against the reference to the UN and preferred 'timely action' on the ground, but Kashmir was Jawaharlal's baby by now and Vallabhbhai did not insist on his prescriptions when, at the end of December, Nehru announced that he had decided to go to the UN. Jawaharlal obtained Mahatma's reluctant consent... Patel's misgivings were amply fulfilled after India invited the UN's assistance..."{RG/448}

Jayaprakash Narayan, who had been pro-Nehru and anti-Patel had this to admit later:

"Kashmir issue, being left to Nehru, proved to be unfortunate for the nation. Because of Panditji's mishandling, the issue did no longer remain an internal affair, as it should be, but is smouldering as an international issue in the United Nations and its Security Council, making it possible for Pakistan to rake it up every now and then. Many a veteran leader in the country maintains that had the matter been handled by the Sardar, he would have found a satisfactory solution, and thus prevented it becoming a perennial headache for us and a cause of bitterness and animosity between India and Pakistan."{BK/396-7}

Sardar Patel had reportedly remarked to HV Kamath that had Nehru and Gopalaswami Aiyangar not made Kashmir their close preserve, separating it from his portfolio of Home and States, he would have tackled the problem as purposefully as he had already done for Hyderabad. Sardar Patel had told Air Marshal Thomas Elmhirst: *"If all the decisions rested on me, I think that I would be in favour of extending this little affair in Kashmir to a full-scale war with Pakistan... Let us get it over once and for all, and settle down as a united continent."*{BK2/157}

Communist MN Roy, no friend of Patel, was also of the opinion that had Kashmir affair remained with Patel, he would have solved it soon after partition. He wrote in "Men I Met" on Patel:

"...Could Sardar Patel have had his way on the Kashmir issue, India would not be today spending fifty percent of her revenue on military budget... the Sardar had no choice but to play the game, but one could be sure that he loathes the stupidity clothes in the glamour of popular heroes [hint on Nehru]..."{Roy/17}

Blunder–31:
Junagadh: Patel vs. Mountbatten-Nehru

Junagadh was a Princely State whose area was about 3,337 square miles, and it was ruled by Nawab Sir Mahabatkhan Rasulkhanji (or Nawab Mahatab Khan III) at the time of independence in 1947. There are many stories of the eccentricity of the Nawab and of his love for dogs, including his expenditure of £21,000 on the wedding of two of his dogs{Tunz/216}. In the chapter 'A Junagadh Bitch that was a Princess' in 'Maharaja'{JD}, Diwan Jarmani Dass states that on the occasion of the marriage of his favourite bitch Roshanara, the Nawab had invited Rajas, Maharajas, Viceroy and other distinguished guests, had declared state holiday for three days, and had entertained over 50,000 guests. The book describes the crazy reception of the bridegroom—a dog:

> "The bridegroom's party was received by the Nawab of Junagadh at the railway station, accompanied by 250 male dogs in gorgeous clothes and jewellery who came in procession from the palace to the station on elephants with silver and gold howdahs. The Ministers and officials of the State and the members of the Royal family of Junagadh were also present at the station to receive Bobby, the bridegroom."{JD/198}

Junagadh is to the south-west of Kathiawar. Its neighbours were all Indian States, and to its south and south-west is the Arabian Sea. Junagadh had no geographical contiguity with Pakistan. Its distance by sea, from Port Veraval to Karachi, is about 300 miles. Out of its population of about 6.7 lacs, 82% were Hindu.

The people of the state desired merger with India. However, the Nawab signed the *Instrument of Accession* in favour of Pakistan on 15 August 1947. He was aided by his diwan, Sir Shahnawaz Bhutto—father of the late Prime Minister of Pakistan, Zulfikar Ali Bhutto—who was close to Jinnah. The accession was kept a closely guarded secret by Pakistan. Jinnah had reckoned that if sufficient time passed before the matter became known, India would accept the accession as a fait accompli. It was only on 13 September 1947—about a month after the accession—that India was informed that Pakistan had accepted Junagadh's accession and had also signed the *Standstill Agreement*.

The British too knew of the accession earlier, but had kept quiet. Mountbatten promptly recognised Junagadh as Pakistani territory, and advised so to the King in his report. He even stated in his report: "My chief concern as Governor-General was to prevent the Government of India from committing itself on the Junagadh issue to an act of war against what was now Pakistan territory."{BK2/119}

Mountbatten revealed: "Pakistan is in no position even to declare war, since I happen to know that their military commanders [British, at the top level, at that time] have put it to them in writing that a declaration of war with India can only end in the inevitable and ultimate defeat of Pakistan."{BK2/120}

Mountbatten was least concerned that Junagadh, a Hindu-majority state (which was not even a border-state), had acceded to Pakistan. In sharp contrast, he was much concerned that J&K had acceded to India, and played all his dirty games to ensure that the accession became disputed by fooling the gullible Nehru. After Junagadh had acceded to Pakistan Mountbatten wanted to make sure India did not use its armed forces to occupy Junagadh. He played his tricks on Nehru and Gandhi to ensure the same. Expectedly, Nehru, the PM, remained silent! Jinnah had correctly assessed that an ever indecisive and vacillating Nehru would only indulge in his usual *"international situation and international reaction"* high-talk, but would, again as usual, soft-pedal the whole matter in order to avoid taking any decision or action. As for Lord Mountbatten, the cunning Jinnah knew Mountbatten would not allow India to take any precipitate action. All that Jinnah wanted was that there should be no physical action from India's side. Gandhi, being a pacifist, and more concerned about his "Mahatma" label and its associated brand of "non-violence", never considered appropriate action to gain back Junagadh. Given Nehru-Gandhi inaction, only Sardar Patel could have been the rescuer.

"He [Sardar Patel] rejected Nehru's soft-pedalling in the suggestion that 'it would be desirable for us to send a message to the British Government about the Junagadh affair' with a polite comment: 'I am not quite sure whether we need say anything to the British Government at this stage.' Patel was not willing to let India revert to the pre-Independence years and allow the British to play their earlier partisan role which was pro-Muslim and pro-Jinnah."{BK/359}

Sardar Patel vehemently objected to the "forcible dragging of over 80 percent of Hindu population of Junagadh into Pakistan by

External Security

accession in defiance of all democratic principles". Jinnah and Mountbatten had failed to factor-in the fact that if there were pacifists on India's side unassertive on India's interests like Gandhi and Nehru whom they could manage, fool-around and outmanoeuvre; there was also a wise, don't-meddle-with-us Iron-Man on India's side.

All of Mountbatten's diversionary tactics failed to work on Sardar Patel. Mountbatten tried his options one after the other, as each failed. He counselled Patel on one premise after another: Adverse world opinion! Needless war! War when so many urgent tasks demanded attention! Why not refer the matter to the UNO? If at all necessary, use only the Central Reserve Police, not the Indian Army!

Sardar Patel rejected all of Mountbatten's options and suggestions, and went in for military operations to settle the issue once and for all. That required guts—something that Nehru and Gandhi lacked. Patel did not let the matter linger, like in cases of Kashmir or Hyderabad. Patel tactfully kept Mountbatten in the dark, and moved troops before Mountbatten came to know. Kathiawar Defence Force, a newly created command of Indian troops, was first deployed in the territory adjoining Junagadh, and then occupied Babariawad and Mangrol, which Junagadh had claimed as its territory.

Sardar planned and executed the Junagadh operation so well that the Nawab of Junagadh fled to Pakistan on *26 October 1947* leaving the state to Shahnawaz Bhutto, who, facing collapse of the administration, invited India on 7 November 1947 to intervene, and left for Pakistan on 8 November 1947. The Indian army moved in on *9 November 1947*, and Sardar Patel arrived to a grand reception on the Diwali day of 13 November 1947.

The Nawab fled with his dogs, emptying the treasury of cash and valuables. Leonard Mosley recounts in 'The Last Days of the British Raj': "*The Nawab had already fled to Pakistan in his private plane. He crammed aboard as many of his dogs as he could, plus his four wives. One of them discovered, at the last moment, that she had left her child behind in the palace and asked the Nawab to wait while she fetched her. The moment she left the airfield, the Nawab loaded in two more dogs and took off without his wife...*"{Mos/210-1}

Wrote V Shankar: "...But he [Sardar Patel] had to contend with two important factors, one of them being Lord Mountbatten...Sardar had to be particularly patient because very often Lord Mountbatten succeeded in enlisting Pandit Nehru's sympathies for his point of view...He was convinced that, in this matter of national importance, police action could not be ruled out in the case of Hyderabad and that the threat of its accession to Pakistan must be removed at all costs. As regards Junagadh he was not prepared for any compromise and finally succeeded in evolving and executing his own plans despite Lord Mountbatten's counsels against precipitating matters or his suggestion of a plebiscite [under UN auspices] ...He [Sardar] remarked with a twinkle in his eye, *'Don't you see we have two U.N. experts—one the Prime Minister [Nehru] and the other Lord Mountbatten—and I have to steer my way between them. However, I have my own idea of plebiscite. You wait and see...'"*{Shan1}

Writes C Dasgupta in his book, 'War and Diplomacy in Kashmir 1947-48':

"At the end of September [1947], the Indian government decided that a show of force was unavoidable. Sardar Patel pointed out that by sending its armed personnel into Babariawad, Junagadh had committed an act of war against India. The princely state which had acceded to India had a right to expect that India would protect them against aggression. A weak posture would undermine India's standing with the Princely States and would have repercussions in Hyderabad, where the Nizam was holding out against accession. In an effort to head him off from this course of action, *Mountbatten suggested lodging a complaint to the United Nations against Junagadh's act of aggression... Patel observed that possession was nine-tenths of the law and he would in no circumstances lower India's position by going to any court as a plaintiff.* The Governor-General asked him whether he was prepared to take the risk of an armed clash in Kathiawar leading to war with Pakistan. The Deputy Prime Minister [Sardar Patel] was unmoved. He said he was ready to take the risk..."{DG/27}

Sardar was really a Sardar—he lived up to his title! Without Sardar, one does not know what other Kashmir-like states or additional Pakistans would have been created—especially, if Mountbatten and Nehru had a free run. If Sardar Patel had not taken the action that he did in Junagadh, and allowed the status quo—its accession to Pakistan on 15 August 1947—to continue, India would have faced difficult situation in Hyderabad. Indeed Kasim Rizvi, the leader of Hyderabad's Razakar, had questioned: "Why is the Sardar

External Security [97]

thundering about Hyderabad when he cannot control even little Junagadh?"{BK/358}

A plebiscite was held in Junagadh by India. At the instance of Sardar Patel, it was conducted not by the UN, but by an Indian ICS officer, CB Nagarkar, on 20 February 1948, in which 99%—all but 91 persons—voted to join India. Sardar was not gullible like Nehru to allow himself to be made a fool of by letting Mountbatten have his way, refer the matter to the UN—which Mountbatten had suggested for Junagadh too—and allow domestic matters to be internationalised, and be exploited by Pakistan and the UK.

Blunder–32:
Would-have-been Pakistan-II (Hyderabad)

At the time of Independence, Hyderabad was a premier State, with an area of about 2,14,000 square kilometres, population of 16 million, and an annual revenue of 26 crores. It had its own coinage, paper currency and stamps. 85% of its population of 1.6 crores was Hindu. However, the Police, the Army, and the Civil Services were almost completely the preserve of the Muslims. Even in its Legislative Assembly set up in 1946 the Muslims were in majority, despite forming a mere 15% of the population.

Soon after the announcement of the *3-June-1947 Plan* or the *Mountbatten Plan* of the partition of India, Nizam declared on 12 June 1947 that he would neither join India nor Pakistan, but would remain independent. He wanted to secure the Dominion Status, like the one proposed for partitioned India and Pakistan, although the same was not allowed for any Princely State.

Razakars and Nizam

A fanatical Muslim organisation, Ittehad-ul-Muslimeen, headed by one Kasim Razvi had been fomenting trouble. They came to be known as the Razakars. At the instance of Kasim Razvi, Nizam appointed Mir Laik Ali as Prime Minister and president of his Executive Council. Laik Ali was a Hyderabadi businessman, who had also been a representative of Pakistan at the UN till September 1947. With this the Hyderabad Government came virtually under Razvi. Razvi later met Sardar and Menon in Delhi to tell that Hyderabad would never surrender its independence, and that Hindus were happy under Nizam; but *if India insisted on a plebiscite, it is the sword* which would decide the final result. Razvi further told Sardar Patel, "We shall fight and die to the last men," to which Patel responded, "How can I stop you from committing suicide?"{RG/476}

In his speeches in March 1948 and later, Kasim Razvi exhorted the Muslims "to march forward with Koran in one hand and a sword in the other to hound out the enemy." He declared that "the 45 million Muslims in India would be our fifth columnists in any showdown"{BK2/138}. Razvi challenged that "if the Indian Union attempted to enter Hyderabad, it would find nothing but the bones and ashes of 15 million Hindus residing in the State."{BK/408}. He boasted on 12 April 1948 that "the day is not far off when the waves of bay of Bengal would be washing the feet of our Sovereign"{BK/409}; and that he would "hoist the Asaf Jahi flag on the Red Fort in India". Razakars continued their criminal anti-Hindu activities.{BK/409}

At the suggestion of his British and Muslim advisers, the Nizam had planned out several ways to strengthen his position: acquiring port facilities at Goa from Portugal; getting approval for a rail-corridor from Hyderabad to Goa; taking mine-leases in mineral-rich Bastar; readying more air-fields; acquiring weapons; recruiting more Muslims in the army; recruiting British soldiers; getting Muslims from other states to move into Hyderabad state; converting Dalits to Islam; unleashing militia comprising local Muslims, Pathans and Arabs to intimidate non-Muslims; scaring away Hindus out of Hyderabad state; and so on.

Mir Laik Ali had bluffed and boasted: "If the Union Government takes any action against Hyderabad, a hundred thousand men are ready to join our army. We also have a hundred bombers in Saudi Arabia ready to bomb Bombay."{URL16}

Nizam-British-Mountbatten-Nehru vs. Sardar Patel

Like their pro-Pakistan attitude, many in the Press in Britain and many prominent British leaders were pro-Hyderabad and anti-India. Hyderabad had been their *most faithful ally*, and they wanted it to be independent and pro-Britain. They did not care if it was a cancer right in the heart of India and had predominant Hindu population of over 85%. Their stand and support, and that of Pakistan, emboldened the Razakars and the Nizam.

While Mountbatten and the British had nothing to say on the grossly unethical, illegal and even barbarous acts of Pakistani raiders in J&K, and of Razakars in Hyderabad; he was liberal in his moral lectures to India, and wanted India "*to adopt ethical and*

External Security

correct behaviour towards Hyderabad, and to act in such a way as could be defended before the bar of world opinion."{BK2/129}

V Shankar writes in 'My Reminiscences of Sardar Patel'{Shan}: "Hyderabad occupied a special position in the British scheme of things and therefore touched a special chord in Lord Mountbatten...The *'faithful ally'* concept still ruled the attitude of every British of importance... all the other rulers were watching whether the Indian Government would concede to it a position different from the other states...

"Lastly, *on Hyderabad, Pandit Nehru and some others in Delhi were prepared to take a special line;* in this Mrs Sarojini Naidu and Miss Padmaja Naidu, both of whom occupied a special position in Pandit Nehru's esteem, were not without influence. There were also forces which were not slow or hesitant to point out the special position of the Muslims in the state... *Apart from Lord Mountbatten's understandable* sympathy *for the Muslim position in Hyderabad, shared by Pandit Nehru,* in anything that concerned Pakistan even indirectly, he was for compromise and conciliation to the maximum extent possible..."{Shan}

Nehru never showed similar indulgence towards the Maharaja of Kashmir. Indeed, he was unreasonably hostile to the Maharaja of Kashmir, unnecessarily friendly and brotherly towards Sheikh Abdullah; but indulgent towards the Nizam under whose regime the innocent Hindus were being terrorised by the Razakars and Muslim militias. Mountbatten, also Chairman of the Defence Committee, had recorded:

"Pandit Nehru said openly at the meeting, and subsequently assured me privately, that he would not allow any orders to be given for operations to start unless there really was an event, such as a wholesale massacre of Hindus within the State, which would patently justify, in the eyes of the world, action by the Government of India."{RG/480-81}

By October 1947 Sardar Patel had got sick of negotiations with the Nizam's representatives, and wanted to break off the negotiations. However, Mountbatten pleaded for more time. Why? The British didn't wish to displease their faithful ally. Patel was not the only person deciding. There were Gandhi, Nehru, Mountbatten and others. Despite Sardar's objections, a Standstill (status quo) Agreement was signed between India and Hyderabad in November

1947 for a year. In the subsequent months, Hyderabad loaned rupees twenty crores to Pakistan, placed orders for arms elsewhere, and stepped up its nefarious, anti-Hindu activities through Razakars. Multiple delegations had discussed numerous proposals with Hyderabad, all to no avail. Mountbatten too tried, but failed. Finally, his tenure over, Mountbatten left India on *21 June 1948*. But, before leaving, he tried once more to get very favourable terms for the Nizam by getting Sardar Patel to sign a document as a farewell gift to him. Sardar signed knowing the stubborn Nizam would reject those terms. And, Nizam did reject the document! The moment that happened Sardar declared that thenceforth Hyderabad would be treated on par with other states, and not as a special state.

Operation Polo, thanks to Sardar Patel & Despite Nehru

Distressed about Nehru's reluctance to act, Patel had written to NV Gadgil on 21 June 1948:

"I am rather worried about Hyderabad. This is the time when we should take firm and definite action. There should be no vacillation; and the more public the action is the greater effect it will have on the morale of our people, both here and in Hyderabad, and will convince our opponents that we mean business. There should be no lack of definiteness or strength about our actions. If, even now, we relax, we shall not only be doing a disservice to the country, but would be digging our own grave."{BK2/141}

One JV Joshi, in his letter of resignation from the Nizam's Executive Council, wrote that law and order had completely broken down in many districts and that the Nizam's Police—comprising almost exclusively of Muslims—was colluding with the Razakars in loot, arson and murder of Hindus, and molestation and rape of their females. He stated having himself witnessed such scenes and even scenes where Brahmins were killed and their eyes gouged out. It was estimated that besides the Hyderabad State forces of over 40,000, there were about 2,00,000 Razakars with small arms, and a number of Pathans lately imported. It became morally difficult for India to remain a mute witness to the mayhem, that turned worse by August 1948.

Resistance by Nehru & the British to Any Action

On the use of force by India to settle the Hyderabad issue, V Shankar writes{Shan}:

"The entire staff for the purpose had been alerted and the timing depended on how long it would take for Sardar to overcome the resistance to this course by C Rajagopalachari, who succeeded Lord Mountbatten as Governor General, and by Pandit Nehru, who found in C Rajagopalachari an intellectual support for his non-violent policy towards Hyderabad.." Shankar quotes Sardar's response to a query, "Many have asked me the question what is going to happen to Hyderabad. They forget that when I spoke at Junagadh, I said openly that if Hyderabad did not behave properly, it would have to go the way Junagadh did. The words still stand and I stand by these words."

"...The situation in Hyderabad was progressing towards a climax. Under Sardar's constant pressure, and *despite the opposition of Pandit Nehru and Rajaji*, the decision was taken to march into Hyderabad and thereby to put an end both to the suspended animation in which the State stood and the atrocities on the local population which had become a matter of daily occurrence."{Shan}

Wrote MKK Nayar: "Indian Army's C-in-C was an Englishman named Bucher and the Southern Command was headed by Lieutenant General Rajendra Singhji. Patel knew that Nehru would not agree to military intervention, but anyway sent an instruction through V P Menon to Rajendra Singhji to be ready to act if the need arose. Major General Chaudhry commanded the First Armored Division which was stationed in the South and Rajendra Singhji decided to keep it ready for war."{MKN}

In the Cabinet meeting on 8 September 1948, while the States Ministry under Sardar Patel pressed for occupation of Hyderabad to put an end to the chaos there; *Nehru strongly opposed the move* and was highly critical of the attitude of the States Ministry [under Sardar Patel].

MKK Nayar also wrote: "Patel believed that the army should be sent to put an end to the Nizam's highhandedness. At about that time, the Nizam sent an emissary to Pakistan and transferred a large sum of money from his Government's account in London to Pakistan. At a cabinet meeting, Patel described these happenings and advised that the army may be sent to end the terror-regime in Hyderabad. Nehru who was usually calm, peaceful and good mannered, lost his self-control and said, *'You are a total communalist and I shall not accept your advice.'* Patel remained unfazed and left the room with his papers. He stopped attending cabinet meetings and even speaking with Nehru after that."{MKN}

Wrote Kuldip Nayar: "...*Reports circulating at the time said that even then Nehru was not in favour of marching troops into Hyderabad lest the matter be taken up by the UN... It is true that Patel chafed at the 'do-nothing attitude of the Indian government'...*"{KN}

Sardar Patel's daughter's 'The Diary of Maniben Patel: 1936-50' states: "About Hyderabad, Bapu [her father, Sardar Patel] said if his counselling had been accepted—the problem would have been long solved...Bapu replied [to Rajaji], '...Our viewpoint is different. I don't want the future generation to curse me that these people when they got an opportunity did not do it and kept this ulcer [Hyderabad princely state] in the heart of India...It is States Ministry's [which was under Sardar Patel] function [to make Hyderabad state accede to India]. How long are you and Panditji going to bypass the States Ministry and carry on...Bapu told Rajaji that Jawaharlal continued his aberration for an hour and a half in the Cabinet—that we should decide our attitude about Hyderabad. The question will be raised in the UN...Bapu said, 'I am very clear in my mind—if we have to fight—Nizam is finished. We cannot keep this ulcer in the heart of the union. His dynasty is finished.' He (Jawaharlal) was very angry/hot on this point."{Mani/210}

Nehru was so opposed to the use of force against Hyderabad that after Patel got the same approved by the cabinet Nehru called his cabinet colleague Dr Shyama Prasad Mukherjee and remonstrated with him for supporting Patel on the issue, and warned him [being a Bengali] that India's action would lead to retaliation by Pakistan, which was likely to invade West Bengal, and bomb Calcutta. Unexpected by Nehru, Mukherjee nonchalantly responded that the people of Bengal and Calcutta had enough patriotism to suffer and sacrifice for the national cause, and would be overjoyed when they learn that General JN Chaudhuri, a Bengali, had conquered Hyderabad!

Sardar's Decisive Action & Attempt to Abort it

Sardar Patel finally prevailed. A decision was finally taken on 9 September 1948 to carry out *Operation Polo* against Hyderabad by sending troops under the command of Major-General JN Chaudhuri.

Very tactfully, Sardar Patel waited for Mountbatten to first go from India for ever, which he did on 21 June 1948—lest he should interfere in the matter. Patel's most formidable obstacle lay in Mountbatten and Nehru, who had been converted by Mountbatten

External Security

to his point of view—not to let Indian Army move into Hyderabad. Had Gandhi been alive, perhaps Nehru-Gandhi combine would not have allowed the action that Sardar took—Gandhi being a pacifist. Wrote V Shankar:{Shan}

> "Sardar [Patel] was aware of the influence which Lord Mountbatten exercised over both Pandit Nehru and Gandhiji; often that influence was decisive... Sardar had made up his mind that Hyderabad must fit into his policy regarding the Indian states... I know how deeply anguished he used to feel at his helplessness in settling the problem with his accustomed swiftness... the decision about the Police Action in Hyderabad in which case Sardar [Patel] described the dissent of Rajaji and Pandit Nehru as *'the wailing of two widows as to how their departed husband [meaning Gandhiji] would have reacted to the decision involving such a departure from non-violence.'*"

Sardar Patel had fixed the zero hour for the Army to move into Hyderabad twice, and *twice he had to postpone it under intense political pressure from Nehru and Rajaji* [C.R.]. When the zero hour was fixed the third time by Patel, again it was sought to be cancelled in response to the appeal of the Nizam to Rajaji. Nehru and Rajaji instead directed VP Menon and HM Patel to draft suitable reply to Nizam on his appeal. Nehru and Rajaji didn't realise that the Nizam was all along buying time to strengthen himself, and not to reach any amicable settlement. By then Sardar had had enough of Hamlet Nehru.

While the reply to Nizam was being readied, Sardar Patel, summarily announced that the Army had already moved in, and nothing could be done to halt it. This he did after taking the Defence Minister, Baldev Singh, into confidence!{DD/285}

The operations commenced on 13 September 1948, and after about four days of operations lasting 108 hours{VPM1/256}, the Hyderabad Army surrendered, with Major-General El Edroos, commander of the Hyderabad Army, asking his troops to yield; and Major-General JN Chaudhuri entered Hyderabad city on 18 September 1948, taking charge as Military Governor. His administration continued till December 1949. Kasim Razvi was arrested on 19 September 1948.

For further details, please refer to the unabridged digital version of this book or the author's book 'Sardar Patel: The Iron Man Who Should have been India's First PM' available on Amazon.

EXTERNAL SECURITY

Blunder–33:
Erasure of Tibet as a Nation

This is our only foreign debt, and some day we must pay the Mantzu and the Tibetans for the provisions we were obliged to take from them.
— Mao Zedong, when he had passed through the border regions of Tibet during the Long March

In the 8th century, Tibetan King Trisong Dentsen had defeated China, which was forced to pay an annual tribute to Tibet. To put an end to mutual fighting, China and Tibet signed a treaty in 783 CE where boundaries were confirmed, and each country promised to respect the territorial sovereignty of the other. This fact is engraved on the stone monument at the entrance of the Jokhang temple, which still stands today. The engraving is both in Chinese and in Tibetan.

I [Sardar Patel] have been eating my heart out because I have not been able to make him [Nehru] see the dangers ahead. China wants to establish its hegemony over South-East Asia. We cannot shut our eyes to this because imperialism is appearing in a new garb...He is being misled by his courtiers. I have grave apprehensions about the future.
—Durga Das, reporting his talks with Sardar Patel{DD/305}

Allowing Tibet to be Erased as a Nation

Nehru allowed Tibet, our peaceful neighbour and a buffer between us and China, to be erased as a nation, without even recording a protest in the UN, thereby making our northern borders insecure, and putting a question mark on the future of the water resources that originate in Tibet.

The Tibetan Government protested to the UN against the Chinese aggression. But, as Tibet was not a member of the UN, it was simply recorded by the UN Secretariat as an appeal from an NGO. Their appeal, in a way, was pigeonholed. In view of this handicap, Tibetans requested the Government of India to raise the Tibet issue in the UN. But, India was not willing to do so, lest China should feel antagonised! What to speak of helping our neighbour who had appealed to us for help, we shamelessly advised the victim to seek peaceful settlement with the aggressor China. Even worse, when through others, the Tibet's appeal came up on 23 November 1950 for discussions in the UN General Assembly, we opposed the discussions on a very flimsy ground—that India had received a note from China that the matter would be resolved peacefully!

Even though China had invaded Tibet, KM Panikkar, the Indian Ambassador in Beijing, went so far as to pretend that there was lack of confirmation of the presence of Chinese troops in Tibet and that to protest the Chinese invasion of Tibet would show China in bad light—as an aggressor—which would have a negative effect on India's efforts of ensuring entry of China in the UN! Such was the crazy Nehru-Panikkar line! Tibet and our own national security interests were sought to be sacrificed to help China enter the UN!!

With no one to sponsor the Tibetan appeal, possibility of some joint action was discussed by the Commonwealth delegation to the UN. *In the meeting, the Indian representative advised that India did not wish to raise the Tibetan issue in the UNSC, nor did India favour its inclusion in the UN General Assembly agenda*!

See the irony: Nehru referred to the UN what India should never have referred—the J&K issue, it being India's internal matter. But, Nehru refused to refer a matter to the UN that India should certainly have referred—Tibet, despite its criticality both to India's external security, and to the survival of a peaceful neighbour. When Nehru should not have acted, he did act; and when he should have acted, he didn't! Both, his action and his inaction, led to disastrous consequences for India. *Nehru's strategy was India's and Tibet's tragedy.*

Independent India's Indifferent Approach

India was in desperate need of a Sardar Patel to drive its strategic thinking. Nehru, by stating on 1 November 1950 in an interview to the Unites Press that "*India has neither the resources nor the inclination to send armed assistance to Tibet*"{Arpi/374} and that "*We can't save Tibet*" seemed to wash his hands off the whole affair so critical to India's security, and seemed to suggest that other than armed intervention, which India didn't wish to undertake, there was nothing India could do—when there was much the India could have very well done, other than its own armed intervention!

Independent India Indifferent to its own Security!

While the independent India was an indifferent India—

indifferent to its own security—British-India had done all it could to keep India's northern borders secure by ensuring Tibet remained free from foreign powers. According to Claude Arpi:
"A few months before India's Independence, not only was Tibet a de facto independent State and the British wanted it to remain so, but they were ready to carry out a military action to protect Tibet's status. For this, a detailed military intervention plan was prepared by the General Staff of the British Army...The purpose of the Memo [a Top Secret Memo of 1946] was to find a solution in case of 'domination of Tibet by a potentially hostile major power [which] would constitute a direct threat to the security of India.'...Neither Russia nor China must be allowed to violate Tibetan autonomy...since it would then be possible for them to build roads and airfields to their own advantage, which would vitally affect India's strategic position."{Arpi/371}

That's foresight, strategic thinking and meticulous planning!

Talking of strategic thinking, what to speak of viceroys and generals, even a British explorer, Francis Younghusband, who led the British Mission to Lhasa in 1904, had this to say in his book 'India and Tibet', first published in 1910:
"...apart from questions of trade, we want to feel sure that there is no inimical influence growing up in Tibet which might cause disturbance on our frontier [northern India]. That is the sum total of our wants. The trade is not of much value in itself, but, such as it is, is worth having. We have no interest in annexing Tibet...but we certainly do want quiet there... Before the Lhasa Mission, Russian influence...was the disturbing factor; now it is the Chinese influence, exerted beyond its legitimate limits and with imprudent harshness [reference to Zhao Erfeng's invasion of 1909]. Either of these causes results in a feeling of uneasiness, restlessness, and nervousness along our north-eastern frontier, and necessitates our assembling troops and making diplomatic protests..."{FY/420}

Wrote Brig. Dalvi: "In October 1950 I was a student at the Defence services Staff College in Wellington, South India. Soon after the news of the Chinese entry in into Tibet reached us, the Commandant, General WDA (Joe) Lentaigne, strode into the main lecture hall, interrupted the lecturer and proceeded to denounce our leaders for their short-sightedness and inaction, in the face of Chinese action...*he said that India's back door had been opened...He predicted that India would have to pay dearly for failure to act...His last prophetic remark was that some of the students present in the hall would be fighting the Chinese before retirement."*{JPD/15}

Olaf Caroe, Secretary to the Government of India in the External Affairs Department in 1945, and one of the foremost British strategic thinkers had written:

"From the point of view of India's internal economy and administration the maintenance of this buffer [Tibet] between the frontiers of India and China is of great advantage. Recent wartime conditions have shown that China is a difficult neighbour... The more substantial the buffer that can be maintained between India and China, the better for future relations..."{Arpi/349}

Britain had been unambiguous in its approach: It didn't want a new neighbour to its north—neither China, nor the Soviet Union.

It can be said that from the Tibetan angle it was their misfortune India gained independence from the British in 1947. Had that independence been delayed, and had the British been still ruling India at the time of the Chinese aggression of Tibet in 1950, Britain would certainly not have just watched helpless—it would have ensured the Chinese were resisted and thrown out of Tibet. Alternately, it can be said that it was Tibet's misfortune that Nehru was then at the helm in India. Had it been Sardar Patel, or some other Patel-like leader, China would not have got the walk-over.

Significantly, while the British and China were well aware of the strategic importance of Tibet, India under Nehru remained irresponsibly ignorant. For Nehru, it was the convenient, laid-back, no-need-for-action 'Hindi-Chini-Bhai-Bhai' at all costs—even at the cost of the nation.

In sharp contrast to Nehru, there were notable prescient observers in addition to Sardar Patel, like KD Sethna of a Mumbai weekly 'Mother India', who wrote back in November 1950: *"Let us not blink the fact that Tibet is useful to China principally as a gate of entry to India. Sooner or later attempts will be made to threaten us..."*{Arpi/348}

Could China have been prevented?

China could have been prevented from taking over Tibet by bringing about international pressure. China was in a vulnerable position in 1950: it was fully committed in Korea and was by no means secure in its hold over the mainland. There would have been wide international support for the cause of Tibet, if India, the nation which had inherited from British-India the treaty with Tibet, and which was directly affected, had taken the initiative. The world opinion was strongly against the Chinese aggression, and all the countries were looking to India, the most affected country, to take the lead. Even if India did not wish to itself meddle militarily, it could at least have helped the military efforts by others, or tried to thwart China diplomatically. The Economist wrote:

"Having maintained complete independence of China since 1912, Tibet has a strong claim to be regarded as an independent state. But it is for India to take a lead in this matter. If India decides to support independence of Tibet as a buffer state between itself and China, Britain and USA will do well to extend formal diplomatic recognition to it."{URL61}{URL62}

Writes Prasenjit Basu in 'Asia Reborn': "The Americans were keen to support Tibet's claim to sovereignty but needed support from India (or possibly Nepal) to solidify the claim. But the proto-communist Nehru (who believed, in his simple heart, that communism was the wave of the future, and the forces of history would inevitably lead to the triumph of communism) contemptuously brushed off the American offer of support. Nehru told his cabinet that it was not possible for India to help Tibet fend off the well-armed PLA (but he did not address the question of whether American support could have augmented the military potential of a combined effort)."{PB}

Wrote Dr NS Rajaram:{URL43}

"...It is nothing short of tragedy that the two greatest influences on Nehru at this crucial juncture in history were Krishna Menon and K.M. Panikkar, both communists... The truth is that India was in a strong position to defend its interests in Tibet, but gave up the opportunity for the sake of pleasing China. It is not widely known in India that in 1950, China could have been prevented from taking over Tibet... Patel on the other hand recognized that in 1950, China was in a vulnerable position, fully committed in Korea and by no means secure in its hold over the mainland. For months General MacArthur had been urging President Truman to 'unleash Chiang Kai Shek' lying in wait in Formosa (Taiwan) with full American support. China had not yet acquired the atom bomb, which was more than ten years in the future. India had little to lose and everything to gain by a determined show of force when China was struggling to consolidate its hold... In addition, India had international support, with world opinion strongly against Chinese aggression in Tibet. The world in fact was looking to India to take the lead... Nehru ignored Patel's letter as well as international opinion and gave up this golden opportunity to turn Tibet into a friendly buffer state. With such a principled stand, India would also have acquired the status of a great power while Pakistan would have disappeared from the radar screen of world attention. *Much has been made of Nehru's blunder in Kashmir, but it pales in comparison with his folly in Tibet. As a result of this monumental failure of vision—and nerve—India soon came to be treated as a third rate power, acquiring 'parity' with Pakistan...*"{URL43}

Even if India did not have the military strength to confront and prevent China, there were so many other steps that India could have taken: express disapproval; provide moral support to Tibet; lodge protest in the UN; mobilise world opinion against Chinese action; grant recognition to Tibet as an independent nation; persuade other nations to also do so; demand plebiscite in Tibet to ascertain the opinion of the public—China had agreed for a plebiscite in Mongolia, that led to its independence; work towards ensuring complete independence for Tibet through peaceful means. Even if the final favourable outcome took decades it didn't matter—at least there would have been hope. Had India taken the initiative many nations would have supported India. In fact, many did pass resolution in favour of Tibet in the UN later, which India, the affected country, did not support!

One could argue that doing so would have made China an enemy of India? Well, did China care for our friendship when it attacked our friend and neighbour Tibet? Are friendships only one-sided? Foreign policy cannot be based on cowardice! Or, in being too nice to the other party in the hope that they would reciprocate. The US felt disappointed India had resigned itself to leave Tibet to its fate, and do nothing! The then US ambassador to India, Loy Henderson, described the Indian attitude as '*philosophic acquiescence*'.

Several prominent Indian leaders and citizens decided to form a committee and observe the *Tibet Day* in August 1953 to protest Chinese invasion of Tibet. Nehru wrote to Balwantray Mehta of AICC on 24 August 1953:

"...Obviously, *no Congressman should join such committee or participate in the observance of 'Tibet Day'*. This is an unfriendly act to China and is against the policy we have pursued during these years. There is absolutely no reason for observing such a day now... I think we should inform members of the Party that they should keep aloof from this. If you remind me, I shall mention this at the Party meeting tomorrow..."{JNSW/Vol-23/483}

Nehru's Strange & Baffling Rationalization

Reportedly, Nehru tried to rationalise India's inaction on various pretexts, the most bizarre among them being that Tibetan society was backward and feudal, and that reforms were bound to upset the ruling elite, and so on. Wrote Walter Crocker: "It was being said in Delhi in 1952-53 that *Nehru, in private and semi-private, justified the Chinese invasion of Tibet...*"{Croc/73} Says Arun Shourie in "Are we deceiving ourselves again?":

"Panditji has now come down firmly against the order in Tibet: it isn't just that we cannot support Tibet. His position now is that *we must not support Tibet*. The reason is his progressive view of history! The Tibet order is feudal. And how can we be supporting feudalism?..."{AS/79}

"Panditji reiterates the other reasons for neither acting nor regretting the fact of not acting: 'We must remember that Tibet has been cut off from the world for a long time and, socially speaking, is very backward and feudal. Changes are bound to come there to the disadvantage of the small ruling class and the big monasteries... I can very well understand these feudal chiefs being annoyed with the new order. We can hardly stand up as defenders of feudalism.'"{AS/100}

Crazy, perplexing and inexplicable! What does Nehru's logic lead to? It is all right for a country that is backward and feudal to be taken over by another country if that would help it progress! By that logic, the USA could have colonised most of Asia and Africa that was backward and feudal—including India, which also fell in that category—and Nehru would have been fine with that! And, how was the brutal communism of China superior to Buddhist feudalism!!

Why the Untenable Approach?

Why did Nehru operate in such a way?

One. Sacrifice the meek, and satisfy the bully. Wrote Arun Shourie:

"...response of the [Indian] Government has been to be at its craven best in the belief, presumably, that, *if only we are humble enough to the python, it will not swallow us...*"{AS/26} Said Winston Churchill: *"An appeaser is one who feeds a crocodile, hoping it will eat him last."* It was like substituting a very peaceful and harmless neighbour for a dangerous bully. Watching the way India capitulated, Chinese perhaps developed contempt for India and its leaders. Mao respected only the strong, and not the weak who bent over backwards to please him. India's pusillanimity must have emboldened China.

Two. It suited Nehru temperamentally. Nehru was a pacifist, and did not have a stomach to face up to difficult situations.

What was the result? Those who abandon their friends and neighbours, especially weaker ones, in their difficulties, should know that their own time would also come. And it came. As India realised in 1962. What was once a most secure border became the most insecure border, thanks to Nehru.

President Dr Rajendra Prasad had famously remarked, *"I hope I am not seeing ghosts and phantoms, but I see the murder of Tibet recoiling on India."*{RP2}

He had also written: "In the matter of Tibet, we acted unchivalrously, but even against our interest in not maintaining the position of a buffer state, for it had thus exposed the frontier of 2,500 miles to the Chinese... I have very strong feeling about it. I feel that the *blood of Tibet is on us...* but the Prime Minister does not like the name of Tibet to be mentioned even now and regards any mention of its liberation as 'manifest nonsense'."{KMM/Vol-1/289}

Nehru Admits his Blunder

During his last days in 1964, Nehru was reported to have said: *"I have been betrayed by a friend. I am sorry for Tibet."* Betrayal? One does not understand! In international politics, if you are naive and incompetent to take care of your own interests, you would keep getting betrayed.

For complete details on Tibet, please refer to the author's other books "Foundations of Misery: The Nehruvian Era" or "Kashmir, Tibet, India-China War & Nehru" available on Amazon.

Blunder–34:
Panchsheel—Selling Tibet; Harming Self

"This great doctrine [Panchsheel] was born in sin, because it was enunciated to put the seal of our approval upon the destruction of an ancient nation which was associated with us spiritually and culturally... It was a nation which wanted to live its own life and it sought to have been allowed to live its own life..."
—Acharya Kriplani[Arpi2]

Despite what China did to Tibet, India signed the 'Panchsheel Agreement' with China on 29 April 1954. The agreement itself was titled "Agreement on Trade and Intercourse between the Tibet region of China and India" thus acknowledging Tibet as a part of China. India gained nothing through the Agreement, and all benefits accrued to China. Chinese leaders must have been laughing at the naivete of the Indian leadership.

India did not even insist on prior settlement of borders. Reportedly, Girija Shankar Bajpai of the External Affairs Ministry had advised on settlement of the borders prior to the signing of Panchsheel, but his suggestion was ignored by all the three concerned: KM Panikkar, Krishna Menon, and Nehru. Our ambassador to China, KM Panikkar, was later derisively referred to as "ambassador of China".

Dalai Lama wrote poignantly in his autobiography, "Yet I was conscious that outside Tibet the world had turned its back on us. Worse, India, our nearest neighbour and spiritual mentor, had tacitly accepted Peking's claim to Tibet. In April 1954, Nehru had signed a new Sino-Indian treaty which included a memorandum known as *Panchsheel*...According to this treaty, Tibet was part of China."[DL/113]

Acharya Kriplani had said on the floor of the Parliament in 1954: "Recently we have entered into a treaty with China [Panchsheel]. I feel that China, after it had gone Communist, committed an act of aggression against Tibet. The plea is that China had an ancient right of suzerainty. This right was out of date, old and antiquated. It was never exercised in fact. It had lapsed by the flux of time. Even if it had not lapsed, it is not right in these days of democracy by which our Communist friends swear, by which the Chinese swear, to talk of this ancient suzerainty and exercise it in new form in a country which had and has nothing to do with China... England went to war with Germany not because Germany had invaded England, but because it had invaded Poland and Belgium..."{AS/137}

Dr Ambedkar disagreed with the Tibet policy of India and felt that "there is no room for Panchsheel in politics". He said that "if Mr Mao had any faith in the Panchsheel, he certainly would treat the Buddhists in his own country in a very different way."

Dr Ambedkar also commented:

"The Prime Minister has practically helped the Chinese to bring their border down to the Indian border. Looking at all these things it seems to me that it would be an act of levity not to believe that India, if it is not exposed to aggression right now, is exposed to aggression..."{DK/455-6}

Wrote Walter Crocker in 'Nehru: A Contemporary's Estimate': "India, step by step, renounced the hard-won special position in Tibet which Britain had bequeathed to her, and she accepted Chinese suzerainty in principle and Chinese sovereignty in fact. Nehru dismissed the notion of Tibet as a buffer state—'A buffer between whom?'—and described India's previous special position there as an outmoded relic of imperialism. India's renunciation was sealed in a series of Sino-Indian agreements, the most important being the Agreement on Trade and... signed in 1954 [Panchsheel]..."{Croc/74-75}

India did this despite its own stand to the contrary earlier. The flag of Tibet was put up on 15 August 1947 in the Parliament, acknowledging Tibet as a separate nation. Right up to 1949, Nehru, in his official communications, used words like the Tibet Government, our two countries, and so on, leaving no doubt that India recognised Tibet as a separate, independent nation.

Panchsheel is actually a most eloquent example of the naivety of the Indian diplomacy and a shining example of what an international agreement should not be! Yet, upon criticism of the Panchsheel in parliament, Nehru had brazenly stated that in the realm of foreign affairs he could never take so much credit as for the India-China settlement over Tibet! An amazing assertion indeed!!

Blunder–35 :
Not Settling Boundary Dispute with China

Nehru failed to negotiate with China on a peaceful settlement of borders, so vital to India's security. Doing so was not difficult considering that China at that time was not strong, had numerous external and internal problems to contend with, and was therefore willing for a "give and take", particularly 'Aksai Chin—McMahon Line swap': recognition of McMahon Line by China in return for India's recognition of China's claim on Aksai Chin, with minor adjustments.

Status of India-China Border at Independence

India had borders with Tibet, but not with China. However, after the forcible annexation of Tibet by China in 1950 and its mute acceptance by India, what were Indo-Tibetan borders became Indo-China borders. As part of the *Great Game* that Britain played of check-mating Russia which was expanding south into Asia, Britain made adjustments to the northern boundaries of India—some with the consent of the other party and some without—to keep northern India safe from Russia and China. Britain was adept at cartographic aggression, unilateral cartographic changes and cartographic flip-flops, adjusting the boundaries to suit its strategic requirements, that varied with times. *That left free India a bad legacy of unclear and disputed borders.*

Two Major Disputed Border-Regions

(1) Aksai Chin

Aksai Chin ('The Desert of White Stones') is to the north of Ladakh. It is located at a height of between 17,000 to 19,000 feet. Its eastern border touches Tibet, and the northern border touches Xinjiang province of China. Aksai Chin was in physical possession of China, and they had built a highway there in the 1950s joining Tibet with Xinjiang [Sinkiang], there being no other land-route to connect the two. Aksai Chin was uninhabited, barren and of no strategic or economic importance for India; and considering India had no legally sound claim on it (please see the history below), there was little point, and indeed unwise, for Nehru to act adamant on it, especially when China was prepared for a quid pro quo on the McMahon Line in the northeast. General Thimayya had himself stated in 1959 that Aksai Chin was of no strategic significance for India.

Border History related to Aksai Chin

A *'Boundary Commission'* set up by Britain in *1847* tasked to determine the eastern border of J&K had considered the traditional natural eastern boundary of Ladakh formed by the *Karakorum ranges* as adequate, pointing out also the possible disputed position of Demchok. *Aksai Chin fell beyond the Karakorum ranges into Tibet, that became part of China in 1950.*

In *1892* China erected a boundary marker at the Karakoram Pass with an inscription that the Chinese territory began there, and laid claim to the *Karakoram Pass, Shahidulla* and the tract between the *Kuen Lun ranges* and the *Karakoram ranges*, that included *Aksai Chin*. Britain didn't mind. All they wanted was that the area should be out of reach of the Russians—in those days Britain was worried about Russia, and not China, which it considered a weak, harmless nation. In the connection, the British Foreign Department had noted:

"...We had always hoped that they [Chinese] would assert effectively their rights to Shahidulla and the tract between Kuen Lun and Karakoram range [which included Aksai Chin]... We see no occasion to remonstrate with China on account of erection of the boundary pillar... We favour the idea of getting 'no mans' land filled up by the Chinese, subject to future delimitation of boundaries."{DW/54-55}

In *1899 Macartney-MacDonald Ladakh-Tibet line* was proposed by Britain to the Chinese Government, *which had left Aksai Chin to Tibet. The Karakoram Mountains formed a natural boundary for this border.* This Line was presented to the Chinese by the British Minister in Peking, Sir Claude MacDonald. The Chinese did not respond to the note, and the British took that as Chinese acquiescence. *This Line is approximately the same as the current Line of Actual Control in Ladakh. Britain never attempted to make a physical presence in Aksai Chin or exert authority there in any form. Post-independence Indian government also took no steps to actually extend their control beyond the Karakoram range into the Aksai Chin plains.*

That the British Government continued to hold to the above proposal (which included Aksai Chin as part of Tibet) was confirmed in the map accompanying the Shimla Convention (please see details further down) of 1914.{Max/35}

Significantly, the maps of the *Survey of India* were showing the northern borders as *'Boundary Undefined'* till 1954 like the British had been showing. In his book, AG Noorani mentions that a map annexed to the Mountbatten's Report on his Viceroyalty labelled these boundaries as 'Boundary Undefined'.(Noor/210) Map annexed to a White Paper on Indian States released in July 1948 by the Ministry of States under Sardar Patel also did not show these borders as clearly defined(Noor/221). However, the maps were unilaterally altered after July 1954 at the instance of Nehru, and began to show a clear, demarcated border—that included Aksai Chin—as *unilaterally decided by India.*

(2) McMahon Line

The McMahon Line was finalised in the Shimla Convention of 1914. The Shimla Convention arranged by the British, to which Tibet and China were invited and were represented by Lonchen Shastra and Ivan Chen respectively, conducted eight formal sessions between 6 October1913 and 3 July 1914. Sir Henry McMahon, the then foreign secretary of British-India, was the chief negotiator and the British Plenipotentiary at the Convention, assisted by Charles Bell. Lonchen Shastra and Ivan Chen had to get orders and clarifications from Lhasa and Nanjing respectively, that took a long time on account of the distances and conventional communication network; and that was the reason the Convention stretched for so long a period—about 10 months.

China initially objected to the presence of Tibet in the Convention saying it had no independent status and was part of China, but then went along fearing Britain may proceed unilaterally with Tibet, like Russia did with Mongolia, ignoring China.

The Convention proposed granting China control over *Inner Tibet* while recognizing the autonomy of *Outer Tibet* under the Dalai Lama's rule. Outer Tibet comprised Western and Central Tibet including Lhasa, Chamdo and Shigatse, and areas skirting the British-India frontier; while Inner Tibet included Amdo and part of Kham. Both China and Britain were to respect the territorial integrity of Tibet, and abstain from interference in the administration of Outer Tibet. Further Outer Tibet could not be converted into a province of China.

The border between northeast India and Tibet was also discussed and finalised between Tibet and British-India during the Convention—it came to be known as the *McMahon Line*. China was not invited to the discussions on the McMahon Line because it was a boundary settlement between Tibet and India, and not between

China and India. It was not a secret negotiation, and China knew about it—and raised no objections.

Ivan Chen initialled the draft Convention on 27 April 2014. However, two days later, on 29 April 2014, China repudiated Chen's action and refused to proceed with full signature. It is worth noting that China refrained from full signature not because it had problems with Inner–Outward Tibet per se, but because Tibet and China could not agree to the dividing line between the two. Britain and Tibet signed the Convention on July 3, 1914.(Arpi/126) Even as late as 1947, China, under the Nationalists, had conveyed to the then Indian government they didn't recognise the McMahon Line.

The text of the draft Convention or that of the final Convention did not specifically and explicitly talk about the Indo-Tibetan border or the *McMahon Line* at all, the Line was shown only in the annexed map. Article IX of the Convention simply and briefly stated: "For the purpose of the present Convention the borders of Tibet, and the boundary between Outer and Inner Tibet, shall be shown in red and blue respectively on the map attached hereto."

The *McMahon Line* was a thick red-line drawn on a double-page map, hence it is inaccurate and susceptible to alternate interpretations and disputes. As proper follow-up protocols that should have used cartographic techniques to identify the location of the agreed line on the ground through a joint survey were not taken up, the line remained inexact, leaving scope for controversial claims. The Indian maps showed it as a dashed/broken-line till 1954 to indicate it was roughly defined but not yet demarcated, that is, marked on the ground consequent to a ground survey. However, after July 1954, the Indian maps began showing it as a solid line indicating it was well-demarcated—at the instance of Nehru!

Through the McMahon Line, McMahon had effectively advanced the borders of British-India further north and added 50,000 odd square miles of territory that was till then administered by Tibet, including Tawang, that had the famous Tibetan-Buddhist monastery. Tawang was on the trade-route and British desired control over it. Though reluctant, Tibet agreed to the give-away as a bargain for its rights on the Outer Tibet.

Later, the Tibetans claimed they had most reluctantly agreed for Tawang and other areas (which till then were theirs), as part of British-India—that is, their depiction to the south of the McMahon Line—as a quid pro quo for Britain keeping its part of the bargain:

getting China to agree to Outer/Inner Tibet and sign the Convention. Since China had refused to sign the Convention, not only the Tibetans had a right to both the Outer and Inner Tibet, they also had claims on Tawang and such other areas relinquished by them then. Soon after Indian independence, Tibet had asked India for return of the territories on its boundary acquired by the British!

With India having agreed to Tibet being a part of China, and not an independent nation, a doubt was implicitly cast upon the validity of the treaties which were agreed to by Tibet, but not by China. India effectively did a self-goal through its Tibet policy—Dalai Lama rightly pointed out that to deny the sovereign status of Tibet when the McMahon Line was agreed to in 1914 was to deny the validity of the McMahon Line itself.

What should have been done post-Independence

India should not have allowed Tibet, which was a buffer with China, to disappear as an independent nation. That blunder having been done, the following sensible steps should have been taken:

Step-1: Both India and China should have taken stock of the fact of unsettled borders, and let the public in both the countries know of the same, lest there be any wrong impression, false propaganda, and unwarranted politics.

Step-2: A team comprising experts from both the countries should have done ground survey and should have tried to define the boundaries.

Step-3: Those areas that the expert-team failed to resolve could have been left for further discussions at a higher level, where they could have been resolved in a spirit of give and take.

But, were the above sensible steps taken? Unfortunately, no! Contrary to expectations, one is shocked to learn that while China was agreeable for these sensible steps, India was not! Nehru had other ideas—odd, brazen and unreasonable!! Please see below.

India Unilaterally Changed Maps in July-1954

In his memo of 1 July 1954 to the Secretary General of the Ministry of External Affairs and the Foreign Secretary, Nehru's directives were [*comments in italics within square brackets are author's remarks*]:{JNSW/Vol-26/481-2}

"6. In future, we should give up references, except in some historical context, to the McMahon Line or any other frontier line by date or otherwise. We should simply refer to our frontier. Indeed, the use of the name McMahon is unfortunate and takes us back to the British days of expansion. [*But, then, Nehru was not talking of a new, proper, just line/boundary mutually negotiated between independent India and China after junking the colonial McMahon Line of the imperialist/expansionist Britain. He was all for sticking to the colonially laid down lines like McMahon Line—only he didn't want the legacy of the British names, which lent a negative, expansionist flavour.*]

7. All our old maps dealing with this frontier should be carefully examined and, where necessary, withdrawn. New maps should be printed showing our Northern and North Eastern frontier without any reference to any 'line'. These new maps should also not state there is any undemarcated territory. The new maps should be sent to our Embassies abroad and should be introduced to the public generally and be used in our schools, colleges, etc.

"8. Both as flowing from our policy and as consequence of our Agreement with China [*which agreement?*], this frontier should be considered a firm and definite one which is not open to discussion with anybody. There may be very minor points of discussions. Even these should not be raised by us. It is necessary that the system of check-posts should be spread along the entire frontier. More especially, we should have check-posts in such places as might be considered disputed areas.

"9. ...Check-posts are necessary not only to control traffic, prevent unauthorised infiltration but as a symbol of India's frontier. As Demchok is considered by the Chinese as a disputed territory, we should locate a check-post there. So also at Tsang Chokla..."{JNSW/Vol-26/481-2}

This decision of Nehru was fraught with risks because the new maps of 1954 publicly committed India to a cartographic position that was known to have been of ambiguous provenance.

Nehru aligned himself with the maximalist position of the British on the northern borders, whether or not agreed to by China or Tibet in the past, declared them as well-demarcated Indian borders, even where the British had themselves shown the border as undefined. Nehru also formulated a policy where no talks or discussions or negotiations were to be encouraged on boundary issues. Even in new maps, we made blunders. Kuldip Nayar states in 'Beyond the Lines':

> "...To India's dismay our maps showed some of our territory as part of China. The home ministry wrote to the states asking them to burn the maps or at least smudge the border with China on the Assam side because they did not exactly delineate the Indian border. The Chinese exploited our confusion and used our maps to question our claim."[KN]

Even if one assumes, for the sake of argument, that the new Indian maps were drawn with due care after ascertaining the historical facts and the traditional boundaries, and India had sufficient justification for what it claimed as its boundary; the critical question is: Were the borders agreed to by the other party? Did India possess agreements, documents and maps to prove its claims? If not, should India not have discussed with China and tried to convince them of India's position? India could have taken the maximalist position to start with in the negotiations. But, negotiations India should have done. A unilaterally-drawn map is a mere cartographic claim, it is not a title to land. It settles nothing, it can have no legal or international acceptance, unless concurred with by the other party. Simply said, it takes two to settle a boundary.

China's Stand & Willingness for a Negotiated Settlement

As brought out above, historically, China had not agreed to any border with India and signed any boundary agreement, except for the borders with Sikkim.

The stand of the Peoples Republic of China from 1949 onwards was that they wanted to remove the blot of the British imperialist humiliation China had suffered with regard to the borders and on other matters, and rather than accepting the unjust and illegal British-drawn borders, they desired discussions, negotiations and a joint ground survey to settle the borders in a just and mutually acceptable manner in the spirit of give and take, and not with a view to grab area they were not entitled to. They also wanted to dispense with the British-given names, and give the boundaries new Indian–Chinese names.

Chinese communists, having just ascended the power in 1949, desired a settled border, especially because they already had several severe headaches—internal troubles, Korea, Taiwan, Tibet and a belligerent US—and didn't want to add to them.

China Settles Borders Peacefully with Other Countries

That the above was so was proved by the agreement China finalised with Myanmar (Burma) in 1960—the new Burma-China border is roughly along the McMahon Line, with certain adjustments accepted by both the sides. China also settled its boundaries amicably through negotiations with Nepal and Pakistan, and signed boundary agreements. India remained the only exception.

Nehru's Unreasonable Stand & Unwillingness to Negotiate

China did try on several occasions to settle India-China borders through negotiations and took initiatives in that direction, but what should have happened—peaceful, negotiated settlement through talks—did not happen, for Nehru had his own ideas, like unilaterally changing the maps (as detailed above), claiming the borders are already settled, and refusing to negotiate.

In July 1952, China proposed settlement through peaceful negotiations of India's inherited rights and assets in Tibet, and the related issues, that obviously included the borders. However, Nehru & Co decided in their wisdom not to raise border issues. Why? It might open the Pandora's box and open up the whole border for negotiations. What was the way out? Claim borders were already settled, and therefore there was nothing to negotiate.

The Indian Ambassador to China KM Panikkar had advised: *"[If] China raises the issue [of the McMahon Line], we can plainly refuse to reopen the question and take our stand that the Prime minister took [in his public statement], that the territory on this side of the McMahon Line is ours, and that there is nothing to discuss about it."*{Max/77}

It was this self-deluding approach that led Nehru&Co not to discuss and settle the boundary issue when they signed the only-give-give-and-no-take Panchsheel Agreement with China in 1954.

However, Sir Girija Shankar Bajpai who had been the Secretary-General in the Ministry of External Affairs did not agree with the above stand, and pointed out that China had asked for settlement of pending problems, and that the Chinese *"never having accepted the McMahon Line as the frontier between Tibet and us, can hardly regard this frontier as settled. Naturally, they have no intention of raising it until it suits their convenience."*{Max/77}

Nehru had advised the Secretary General of the Ministry of External Affairs on 3 December 1953: *"I agree about the attitude we should take up in regard to the frontier, we should not raise this* question [of boundaries]. If the Chinese raise it, we should express our surprise and point out that this [boundaries] is a settled issue..."{JNSW/Vol-24/598}

As per Neville Maxwell's "India's China War":
"India reiterated that her boundaries with China could not be a matter of negotiation, claiming that they stood defined 'without the necessity of further or formal delimitation'. China replied that 'this attitude...of refusing to negotiate and trying to impose a unilaterally claimed alignment on China is in actuality refusal to settle the boundary question'; and she warned that while India maintained that position and kept up her 'unreasonable tangling', China would 'absolutely not retreat an inch' from her own stand. That China was equably and equitably settling her boundaries with her neighbours tended to throw an adverse light on India's position. Peking prodded at that sore point: *'Since the Burmese and Nepalese Governments can settle their boundary questions with China in a friendly way through negotiations and since the Government of Pakistan has also agreed...to negotiate a boundary settlement, why is it that the Indian Government cannot negotiate and settle its boundary question...'"*{Max/214}

India avoided raising the border issue with China following Nehru's decision—even when Panchsheel was signed in 1954, and later when Zhou Enlai had overlong five rounds of discussions with Nehru between 25 and 27 June 1954{JNSW/Vol-26/365-406}. For over a decade since the independence, Nehru talked with Zhou Enlai on everything under the Sun except the boundary issues. Records quoted in various books on the subject show that Chinese Premier Zhou Enlai did raise the boundary matter with Nehru several times, but India soft-peddled or avoided the issue. China was also not insistent. No objections or protests from the Chinese were taken to mean their acquiescence to our position. So, as a "strategy", India maintained silence, kept mum on the issue.

This is from 'Beyond the Lines' by Kuldip Nayar:
"...I was only the home ministry's information officer and had no official locus standi, but it was obvious that the Polish ambassador was on a mission. He invited me for a chat at his chancery and expected me to convey what he had said to [Gobind Ballabh] Pant [Nehru's Home Minister]. At the beginning of the conversation he said that the proposal he would make had the support of all Communist countries, and specifically

External Security

mentioning the Soviet Union. His proposal was that India should accept a package political deal, getting recognition for the McMahon Line in exchange for handing over control of some areas in Ladakh [Aksai Chin] to China. He said that the areas demanded had never been charted, and nobody could say to whom they belonged. What was being claimed to be India's was what had been forcibly occupied by the UK. No power could honour 'the imperialist line', nor should India insist upon it. Whatever the odds, China would never part with the control of the road it had built. That was lifeline between Sinkiang and other parts of China, he argued. I conveyed the proposal to Pant who gave me no reaction, his or that of the government."{KN}

In response to a very long letter of Nehru of 26 September 1959, wrote Chou En-Lai on 7 November 1959:{URL21}

"...As the Sino-Indian boundary has never been delimited and it is very long and very far or comparatively far from the political centres of the two countries, I am afraid that, if no fully appropriate solution is worked out by the two Governments, border clashes which both sides do not want to see may again occur in the future. And once such a dash takes place, even though a minor one, it will be made use of by people who are hostile to the friendship of our two countries to attain their ulterior objectives..."{URL21}

After several incidents and exchanges of letters between the two countries to diffuse the situation, China wrote in December 1959 repeating its stand on the border but suggesting maintenance of the status quo pending formal delimitation of the border and withdrawal of the armed forces of the two sides by 20km or so on either side, and stoppage of patrolling by the armed forces.

Nehru strangely continued to maintain the borders were settled and there was nothing to negotiate.

Zhou Enlai, Marshal Chen Yi, Foreign Minister, and a big official Chinese delegation visited New Delhi in 1960 to settle the border dispute. The Chinese position was the same as what Zhou had earlier conveyed in writing to India on several occasions. However, *China was reportedly willing to accept the McMahon Line as the boundary in the east—with possibly some adjustments and a new name—like they had done with Myanmar (Burma) provided, in return, India dropped its claims over Aksai Chin. Once this broad framework was agreed to, the officials from the two countries could do a survey and determine the exact alignments of the borders.* Unfortunately, adhering to his stated position, Nehru declined.

Finding the deadlock, Zhou then suggested steps similar to his letter of December 1959 to diffuse the situation till an amicable settlement was reached. Nothing came of these.

Chou had come with high hopes after having settled the borders with Burma, but left disappointed—he articulated Chinese position in a press-conference at Delhi before leaving and expressed his disappointment. Reportedly, Zhou found Nehru's adamant stand on Aksai Chin inexplicable and unexpected for several reasons: (a)India had never occupied or ruled or set its foot in Aksai Chin; (b)in the opinion of China, India had no valid and legal ground to lay claim on it; (c)it was barren and nothing grew there; and (d)it was of no strategic or economic importance for India.

Nehru had admitted his mistake, yet...

This is what Nehru had himself admitted in the Parliament in 1959: *"Seven or eight years ago I saw no reason to discuss the frontier with the Chinese Government because, foolishly if you like, I thought there was nothing to discuss."*{AS/154}

What is the position now? India would be happy to do what China had repeatedly proposed in the 1950s and early 1960s, but what Nehru had declined. But, now being a super power, China is playing difficult. In personal life, as also in the life of a nation, what you don't do when it can and should be done, you fail to achieve later. Time and tide wait for none. Who is paying for the missed opportunities?

For further details on this and the next blunder, please refer to the unabridged digital version of this book available on Amazon.

For complete details on this and the next several blunders, please refer to the author's other books "Foundations of Misery: The Nehruvian Era" or "Kashmir, Tibet, India-China War & Nehru" available on Amazon.

Blunder–36:
The Himalayan Blunder: India-China War

India and China had a record going back thousands of years for never having fought a war between them. Nehru, through his unwise and ill-considered policies, broke that record, though unwillingly. Nehru's 'forward policy' and his failure in settling the borders resulted in India-China war and its consequent human and financial loss, besides loss of face for India and Indians before the international community. Here, we are talking of what India could control, not what China had in mind.

Summarising Himalayan Blunders

It was not just one Himalayan blunder, but like the Himalayan range, a range of blunders by Nehru over a fifteen-year period since independence across domains—External Security, Defence, Foreign Policy, and so on—that led to the disaster that shamed India and the Indians before the world. The same are summarised below, followed by coverage of some of them in detail further down.

Blunder-1. Allowing Tibet to be annexed by China, and recognising China's claim over Tibet. This allowed Tibet-India borders to become China-India borders, bringing with them all the associated problems ('Blunder-33' above).

Blunder-2. Not settling the border-issue with China, and being inflexible about it ('Blunder-35' above).

Blunder-3. Signing *Panchsheel* agreement with China in 1954 without first settling the borders.

Blunder-4. Changing of Indian maps unilaterally after July 1954 without mutual discussions with the other party—China.

Blunder-5. Nehru's refusal to consider the proposal of the Chinese delegation in 1960 of East-West give-and-take swap on the McMahon Line and Aksai Chin.

Blunder-6. Ill-conceived, non-forward-looking forward policy of establishing indefensible border posts in disputed areas, provoking China, or giving China the excuse to attack.

Blunder-7. Absurd assumption on the part of Nehru and his close group that China would not attack even if India established certain posts in the disputed areas.

Blunder-8. Leaving the forward posts grossly under-manned and under-armed, with inadequate logistics in place.

Blunder-9. Politicisation of the army high command. Favouritism. Putting in place sycophants and submissive officers at top positions who would kowtow to political bosses. Eventually, some of these chosen submissive officers contributed to the humiliation of India.

Blunder-10. Gross neglect of defence and external security.

Blunder-11. Appointment by Nehru of insufferably arrogant and incompetent protégé Krishna Menon as Defence Minister.

Blunder-12. Nehru's indiscretion of publicly declaring on 12 October 1962, barely 8 days before the war started, that he had instructed the Army to "*evict the Chinese*"! Does one give operational orders publicly? Wars are meant to be waged silently and anonymously. Mature nations and mature leaders are not expected to indulge in empty bluffs! There was no worth-while plan to either evict the Chinese, or to resist them if they attacked!!

Blunder-13. After mere 4 days of fighting, during which the damage had not been too much, China offered a ceasefire on 24 October 1962 suggesting withdrawal by 20km by both the sides from the line of actual control, followed by talks and negotiated settlement on the border-dispute. Nehru didn't agree! India's major humiliation in the war happened later after 14 November 1962—that could have been avoided, had India taken up the Chinese offer.

Blunder-14. On 21 November 1962 China declared unilateral ceasefire and offered the same terms it offered on 24 October 1962 and again suggested talks, discussions, joint ground survey and negotiated settlement. India agreed for ceasefire, but did not take up the offer for talks. It was worth resolving the dispute.

Blunder-15. Nehru should have done whatever it took to amicably settle the border-dispute with China, and should not have left it open for the generations to follow, like he did for Kashmir, because with the passage of time, as China became stronger and stronger, settlement became difficult.

Blunder-16. Nehru should have set up a fully-empowered Commission for a comprehensive enquiry into all aspects of the debacle with a mandate to recommend action against the negligent and the guilty, and suggestions for the steps to be taken going forward. The findings should have been made public. That was the minimum expected of a democratic country. However, nothing of the sort was done.

Blunder-17. Nehru should have resigned in the aftermath of the rout. Not just offered to resign—the offer he didn't make anyway—he should have actually resigned or should have been made to resign. Democratic norms demanded it. It would have been a good lesson for the future politics of India—you can't do a series of major blunders, yet continue in power. Not just as a lesson, but also on account of its beneficial effects. Had he resigned another competent person—and there were many—who would not have carried

Nehru's baggage, would have looked at the issue afresh and reached a permanent settlement on the borders with China.

III-Conceived Forward Policy

With Nehru-Krishna Menon deciding to unilaterally fix India's border with China, India went ahead with its plan of physical presence on the frontiers. It began building forward check-posts under its *hare-brained Forward Policy*—which was actually a "bluff" masquerading as a military strategy. Their locations were as per the border unilaterally determined by India, and not as per any mutual discussions or agreement with China. There was, therefore, a possibility of China's objection, and even Chinese action to demolish the posts. The fact was that the boundaries were not settled, so what was say within Indian boundary for India, may have been within Chinese boundary for China. If you had not settled the boundaries, controversies were bound to arise (please see 'Blunder-35'). But, rather than negotiating a boundary with China and reaching a peaceful settlement, Nehru-Menon & Co, in their wisdom—their Forward Policy—convinced themselves that it is they who would determine the boundary, and in token thereof, establish their posts, like markers. That China could object, and then attack and demolish those posts, and even move forward into India did not seem to them a possibility. Why? Because, reasoned Nehru: any such "reckless" action by China would lead to world war, and China would not precipitate such a thing! That what they were themselves doing was also "reckless" did not apparently strike the wise men.

The decision on the 'Forward Policy' was reportedly taken at the PMO on 2 November 1961 in a meeting attended by Nehru, Krishna Menon, General PN Thapar (COAS), Lieutenant General BM Kaul (CoGS), BN Mullik (Director–IB), Brig. DK Palit, and the then Foreign Secretary.{KNR/205-6}

Wrote Kuldip Nayar in 'Beyond the Lines':
"...Nehru ordered that police check-posts be established to register India's presence in the Ladakh area. As many as 64 posts were built, but they were not tenable. Home Secretary Jha told me that it was the 'bright idea' of B.N. Malik, the director of intelligence, to set up police posts 'wherever we could', even behind the Chinese lines, in order to 'sustain our claim' on the territory. This was Nehru's 'Forward policy', but then Jha said, 'Malik does not realise that these isolated posts with no support from the rear would fall like ninepins if there was a push from

the Chinese side. We have unnecessarily exposed the policemen [Assam Rifles were posted] to death.' He went on to say: 'Frankly, this is the job of the army, but as it has refused to man the posts until full logistical support is provided, New Delhi has pushed the police.'"{KN}

Arun Shourie quotes Nehru in 'Are we deceiving ourselves again?': "*It is completely impracticable for the Chinese Government to think of anything in the nature of invasion of India.* Therefore I rule it out... It is necessary that the system of check-posts should be spread along this entire frontier. *More especially, we should have check-posts in such places as might be considered disputed areas...* As Demchok is considered by the Chinese as a disputed territory, we should locate a check-post there. So also at Tsang Chokla..."{Noor/223-4}, {AS/103}

China seemed to have viewed India's Forward Policy as a deliberate attempt to usurp Chinese territory, and provoke war. As things stood, China was suspicious of India's intentions. Wrote Rustamji: "*His [Nehru's] mistake was that he did not accept or realise how our 'forward policy' was being received in China.*"{Rust/215} Several analysts, including Neville Maxwell{Max}, are of the opinion that *Nehru's ill-conceived Forward Policy that was rolled-out December 1961 onwards was at the root of the 1962 India-China War.*

"Mao commented on Nehru's Forward Policy with one of his epigrams: 'A person sleeping in a comfortable bed is not easily aroused by someone else's snoring.'...[commented Mao:] 'Since Nehru sticks his head out and insists on us fighting him, for us not to fight with him would not be friendly enough. Courtesy emphasises reciprocity.'"
—Henry Kissinger, 'On China'{HK/L-3012}

No Preparation—Yet, Orders to Throw Out the Chinese!"

In response to a reporter's query, Nehru grandly declared at the airport on 12 October 1962 on his way to Ceylon[Sri Lanka] that he had already "*ordered the armed forces to clear the Chinese from the NEFA*".{URL23}{MB2/137} Confirming this, on October 14, Indian Defence Minister V.K. Krishna Menon told a meeting of Congress workers at Bangalore that the Government had come to a final decision to 'drive out the Chinese'. He declared that the Indian Army was determined to fight the Chinese to the last man.{URL23}

In its jingoism, the press lapped up the comment. Wrote the Statesman: "Mr Nehru...has told the country...that the armed forces have been ordered to throw the Chinese aggressors out of NEFA and that until Indian territory in that area is cleared of them there can be no talks with China." Even foreign newspapers reported it, some headlining the news to the effect that Nehru had declared war on China. The 'New York Herald Tribune' headed its editorial 'Nehru declared war on China'. The Chinese People's Daily also reported it, advising Nehru to *"pull back from the brink of the precipice, and don't use the lives of Indian troops as stakes in your gamble."*{Max/345}

The question is: Does one give operational orders publicly? It amounted to declaring war, and giving Chinese the excuse to retaliate. Wars are meant to be waged silently and anonymously. Mature nations and mature leaders are not expected to indulge in empty bluffs—there was no worth-while plan to either evict the Chinese, or to resist them if they attacked!! With the AHQ dumbfounded at Nehru's surprise "throw out" orders, General Thapar rushed to the Defence Minister Krishna Menon and pointed out the orders were contrary to what was mutually agreed: not to attack or engage the Chinese! Responded Menon, unconcerned: "This is a political statement. It means action can be taken in ten days or a hundred days or a thousand days."{DD/363}

Commented Mao: "Since Nehru sticks his head out and insists on us fighting him, for us not to fight with him would not be proper. Courtesy emphasises reciprocity."

Responded Zhou Enlai: "We don't want a war with India. We have always strove in the direction of avoiding war. We wanted India to be like Nepal, Burma or Mongolia, i.e. solve border problems with them in a friendly fashion. But Nehru has closed all roads. This leaves us only with war. As I see it, to fight a bit would have advantages. It would cause some people to understand things more clearly."

Mao agreed: "Right! If someone does not attack me, I won't attack him. If someone attacks me, I will certainly attack him."{Arpi/479} Mao directed: "First, the PLA had to secure a victory and knock Nehru to the negotiating table; and second, Chinese forces had to be restrained and principled."{Arpi/481}

The Debacle

Alarmed by the Indian massing of troops in Dhola and the Indian attempts at Yumtsola on 10 October 1962 thanks to General BN Kaul, or, taking that as an excuse, Chinese overran Dhola on 20 October 1962 heralding the 1962-war. BM Kaul has to be blamed for it. Having seen the situation first-hand, General Kaul, as a responsible professional, should have put his foot down on India's *forward policy* misadventure to save the Indian army from the sure debacle it was staring at.

This is from the book, 'Himalayan Blunder', by Brigadier JP Dalvi, an eyewitness, and an actual participant in the war:

"At 5 on the morning of 20th October 1962 massed Chinese artillery opened up a heavy concentration on the weak Indian garrison, in a narrow sector of the Namka Chu Valley... Massive infantry assaults followed, and within three hours the unequal contest was over. The route to the plains of Assam lay wide open. The Chinese exploited their initial successes and advanced 160 miles into Indian territory... reaching the Brahmaputra Valley by 20th November. They swept aside the so-called impregnable defences of Sela Pass; Bomdilla was literally overrun; the monastery town of Towang fell without a fight. India's panicky reaction included the scrambling of ill-equipped, ill-trained for mountain warfare and unacclimatised military formations... The Chinese were amazed at this..."{JPD/1}

President Dr Radhakrishnan was so aghast that when someone told him of a rumour that BM Kaul had been taken prisoner by the Chinese, he commented, "*It is, unfortunately, untrue.*"{Max/410} Wrote S Gopal, Nehru's official biographer: "*Things went so wrong that had they not happened it would have been difficult to believe them.*"

Nehru Admits his Blunder

This is what Nehru himself admitted:

"We were getting out of touch with reality in the modern world and we were living in an artificial atmosphere of our creation...".{Zak/149}

"We feel India has been ill-repaid for her diplomatic friendliness toward Peking... Difficult to say the Chinese have deliberately deceived us... We may have deceived ourselves..."{AS/38}

For further details, please refer to the unabridged digital version of this book available on Amazon.

Blunder–37:
Criminal Neglect of Defence & External Security

The art of war is of vital importance to the State. It is a matter of life and death, a road either to safety or to ruin. Hence it is a subject of inquiry which can on no account be neglected.
—Sun Tzu, 'Art of War'

Again and again, military men have seen themselves hurled into war by the ambition, passions and blunders of civilian governments, almost wholly uninformed as to the limits of their military potential and almost recklessly indifferent to the military requirements of the war they let loose.
—Alfred Vagts, 'The History of Militarism'{Max/289}

For a country that had been under the foreign domination for about a millennium, first under the Muslim invaders, and then under the British, it was natural to expect that its own Indian rulers would give top priority to its external security after independence in 1947.

But, did that happen? No. Nehru and the Congress, brought up on the lethal dose of non-violence, pacifism and Gandhism, substituted wishful thinking for realpolitik, and negligently put India's external security requirements on the back-burner. (Please also check 'Blunder-16'.)

Nehru seemed to be clueless, even irresponsible, in not realising what it took for the country of the size of India, with its many inherited problems, to be able to defend itself adequately and deter others from any designs over it. On one hand, Nehru failed to settle border-issue with China, and on the other, he did precious little to militarily secure the borders we claimed ours. Nehru and his Defence Minister Krishna Menon ignored the persistent demands for military upgradation.

Wrote SK Verma in "1962: The War That Wasn't":
"With Bose's exit and Sardar Patel's death in 1950, there was no one who could provide the necessary inspiration for the reconstruction of an army (that had so far served British interests) into an integrated military instrument that could identify potential threats and tackle them militarily. Nehru, *unlike Bose and Patel*, veered away from building military power."{SKV/L-646}

Jaswant Singh wrote that "*independent India simply abandoned the centrality of strategic culture as the first ingredient of vigorous and bold national policies.*"{JS2}

The seeds of India's disgraceful debacle in 1962 India-China War were sown soon after Independence by none other than Nehru himself, as would be shockingly obvious from the following incident. Shortly after independence, the first Army Chief of independent India Lt General Sir Robert Lockhart (first army chiefs of India and Pakistan were British then!), as per the standard procedure, took a strategic defence plan for India to Nehru, seeking a Government directive in the matter. Unbelievably, Lockhart returned shell-shocked at Nehru's response:

"The PM took one look at my paper and blew his top. 'Rubbish! Total rubbish! We don't need a defence plan. Our policy is ahimsa [non-violence]. We foresee no military threats. Scrap the army! The police are good enough to meet our security needs', shouted Nehru."{URL32}

Nehru actually went ahead and reduced the army strength by about 50,000 troops after independence despite the looming threat in Kashmir, and the Chinese entry into Tibet.{URL33}

Noted MO Mathai in the context of Khrushchev-Bulganin visit to India: "Several times Khrushchev emphasised the need for a first-class aircraft industry for a large country like India and volunteered to send some of Soviet Union's best experts in the field. Somehow it did not register with Nehru and no follow-up action was taken. It was only after the Chinese invasion that we woke up to the grim realities and secured Soviet collaboration in the production of modern military aircraft."{Mac2/4541}

Wrote RNP Singh in 'Nehru: A Troubled Legacy':
"Nehru took the matter of defence so lightly that in an answer to a question on Indian defence against a potential aggressor, he asserted that the nation had the spirit *to defend itself by lathis (sticks) and stones if need be*; 'Therefore, I am not afraid of anybody invading India from any quarter.' While delivering a speech in Parliament, Nehru once advised in an idealistic manner, '*If you better your morale and determine not to surrender, nothing can conquer you.*' Nehru... told a press conference: '*I think the proper way to consider defence is to begin to forget the military aspect.*'"{RNPS/120}

Given such a mind-set, only God could have saved India in times of disaster. Unfortunately, God too abandoned India in the 1962 War. Perhaps God was cheesed off by the "rational", "scientific-minded", atheist-agnostic Nehru! Despite the "Glimpses of World History" and the "Discovery of India", Nehru failed to discover that India suffered slavery for well over a millennium on account of its weakness to defend itself. No wonder, he neglected modernisation of the army, strengthening of defence, and pacts with powerful nations to deter enemies and ensure India's security.

General Thapar had submitted a note to the government in 1960 pointing out that the equipment that the Indian army had and their poor condition was no match to that of China and even Pakistan. Prior to the operations against China to get certain territories vacated, Thapar had impressed upon Nehru that the Indian army was unprepared and ill-equipped for the task it was being asked to undertake. He even got Nehru to cross-check these stark realities from some of his senior staff. Yet, Nehru persisted, saying China would not retaliate! General Thapar told Kuldip Nayar on 29 July 1970, as stated by Nayar in his book 'Beyond the Lines': "Looking back, I think I should have submitted my resignation at that time. I might have saved my country from the humiliation of defeat."{KN}

Nehru's government indifferent approach to defence rested on the presumption that 'China would not attack' India. Wrote Durga Das:

"If [*Krishna*] Menon was guilty of hugging the illusion [that 'China would not attack'], so was Nehru, perhaps to a greater degree. He openly ticked off General Thimmaya, Chief of Army Staff, at a Governor's Conference months earlier for even suggesting the possibility of an attack by China. Many others in the cabinet were not innocent. Either through ignorance or fear of going contrary to the Prime Minister [*that was Nehruvian democracy, FoE, and quality of Cabinet System of Government for you!*], they endorsed his complacent attitude."{DD/361}

General Thapar, the Chief of Army Staff, had requested for urgent additional funding to make good the gross deficiencies in armaments in July 1962, that happened to be about three months before the actual war. When the request was referred to Nehru, he shot it down saying China would not resort to force.{DD/362}

The army had made it sufficiently clear to Nehru and Menon that being out-gunned, out-tanked, and out-manned by the Chinese, they wouldn't be able to hold against them. Yet, the wise politicians persisted with their hare-brained 'Forward Policy' ('Blunder-36').

Earlier, the India's army chief KS Thimayya had repeatedly raised the issue of army's gross weaknesses in defending itself from China. Frustrated at his failure to get the needful done despite his entreaties to Krishna Menon and Nehru, this is what he told his fellow army-men in his farewell speech upon retirement in 1961: "*I hope I am not leaving you as cannon fodder for the Chinese. God bless you all!*"

Thimayya had earlier remarked:

"I cannot, even as a soldier, envisage India taking on China in an open conflict on its own. China's present strength in man-power, equipment and aircraft exceeds our resources a hundredfold with the full support of the USSR and we could never hope to match China in the foreseeable future. It must be left to the politicians and diplomats to ensure our security."{Arpi/473-4}

Commented Brig. Dalvi:{JPD/2}

"There was no overall political objective; no National Policy; no grand strategy and total unreadiness for military operations in the awesome Himalayan mountains, against a first-class land power... We did not study the pattern of weapons and communications equipments that we may require. Army Schools of Instruction were oriented towards open warfare. There was little emphasis on mountain warfare despite the Army's deployment in Kashmir from 1947... The Army was forgotten; its equipment allowed to become obsolete, certainly obsolescent; and its training academic and outdated. We merely tried to maintain what we had inherited in 1947...The political assumptions of our defence policies were invalid and dangerous..."

"In October 1962 Indians were shocked beyond words to discover that we had no modern rifle, although we were supposed to be ready to 'manufacture' an aircraft; and had the know-how to make an atom-bomb... Assam Rifles posts [under the forward policy] were deployed non-tactically and they were ill-armed and even worse equipped that the Regular Army. At best, they could only function as border check-posts and yet their task was 'to fight to the last man and the last round'...There were no inter-communication facilities between Assam Rifles' posts and the nearest Army sub-unit...The standard explanation was that there was a general shortage of wireless sets in the country. The Assam Rifles was a separate private army of the External Affairs Ministry. And who would dare bell the cat about the extraordinary command system?"

Reportedly, at a meeting of the Defence Council in September 1962 [a month before the Chinese attack], while the Army Commander in Ladakh had stated, "*If China attacks massively, we shall be annihilated,*" the head of the Eastern Command had said, "*If China decides to come down in a big way, we are in no position to hold it anywhere in NEFA.*"

Although, despite severe handicaps, Indian soldiers did their very best, the fact remains that it was a pathetically ill-prepared, ill-fed, ill-clothed, ill-supplied, and ill-armed Indian Army—exposed to the elements, cold and hungry—that was forced into the misadventure, and it had to pay a very heavy price. For a relatively minor operation against the Portuguese in Goa in 1961, "one battalion was short of 400 pair of footwear and went into the battle in PT shoes,' as narrated by General BM Kaul.

Nehru's Wild Claim!

Despite the above facts, Nehru stated (bluffed?) in the Parliament:
"I can tell this House that at no time since our independence, and of course before it, were our defence forces in better condition, in finer fettle...than they are today. I am not boasting about them or comparing them with any other country's, but I am quite confident that our defence forces are well capable of looking after our country."{Max/132}

Blunder–38:
Politicisation of the Army

Politicisation of the army high command was one of the reasons India performed miserably in the India-China War. Instead of heeding sound military advice, Nehru and Menon had put in place submissive officers at the top in the military, who would carry out their orders. Krishna Menon ill-treated people. He was offensive to the top-brass of the military. He antagonised many through his acerbic comments, sarcasm and supercilious behaviour. He had publicly humiliated top brass of the army. Eventually, some of their chosen submissive officers contributed to the humiliation of India.

General Verma had dared to write to the higher authorities the facts of poor operational readiness. He was asked to withdraw his letter. He refused and wanted the letter to be put on record. That honest, forthright and very capable officer was victimised—ultimately he resigned. Wrote Inder Malhotra:

> "To cap it all, it was Menon's penchant to play favourites that was responsible for the disaster of Lt.-General B.M. Kaul, with hardly any experience of combat, being appointed the commander in the battlefield and retaining that position even when he was lying ill in Delhi."{IM1}

It was the same Nehru protégé General BM Kaul who, to please Nehru, took forward the 'forward-policy', was responsible for the 'Dhola' disaster, and landed India in a soup. BM Kaul had replaced General Umrao Singh, an able, upright professional, who had been removed for not falling in line with what the political leadership (Nehru and Menon) wanted—he had objected to the reckless putting up of forward posts. Having undertaken to do what Umrao Singh had hang-ups about, Kaul could not very well turn around and express difficulties. Someone who would play the politicians' game was urgently needed and Kaul had willingly stepped into that role.

Wrote GS Bhargava in his book 'The Battle of NEFA':

> "...a new class of Army Officer who could collude with politicians to land the country in straights in which it found itself in September-October 1962. Since qualities of heart and head ceased to be a passport to promotion for military officers...the more ambitious among them started currying favour with the politicians."{GSB}

Blunder–39:
Anti Armed-Forces

It may sound odd, but Nehru&Co were so obsessed about continuing in power, and so unnecessarily and irrationally concerned of the possibility of the army coup, that they went to insane level of check-mating that possibility—even to the extent of harming the Indian defences, Indian external security, and the morale of the Army.

The top bureaucracy, noticing Nehru's suspicion for and bias against the army, cleverly manoeuvred a note declaring the Armed

Forces Headquarters as the "attached" office of the Defence Ministry. That ensured ascendency for the top babu of the Defence Ministry—the Defence Secretary—over the army chief. The post of Commander-in-Chief, the main advisor on military matters, was abolished. That role was given to the President of India—the President became formally the Supreme Commander of the Armed Forces! The real motive was to remove the possibility of the Army Commander-in-Chief ever challenging the civilian authority. When you had adopted the complete British political system, bureaucratic system and the army system lock, stock, and barrel, and when there had been no occasion in the pre-independence period either in India or Britain when the Commander-in-Chief had booted out the civilian authority, why that uncalled for concern? The British-Indian army under the British, during the pre-independence days, though under the political control of the Governor General, enjoyed a large degree of autonomy, and was not subservient to the bureaucracy. That changed post-independence.

Rather than recognising the tremendous contribution of the Indian Armed Forces in the First and the Second World War, and giving them pride of place, the political class and the bureaucratic class conspired to downgrade the position of the Military top brass, by instituting various changes in the pecking order, reporting channels, and the constitution of the committees.

The place next in stateliness and grandeur to the Viceroy palace was the residence of the British Commander-in-Chief, then called Flagstaff House. That house should have been allocated to Field Marshal KM Cariappa. But, Nehru, leaving his spacious York Road residence, promptly allocated it to himself—such were the Gandhian values of simplicity imbibed by him. Flagstaff House was later renamed as *Teen Murti Bhavan*.

Changes were done where the bureaucrats began to be ranked higher than the senior military officers. With respect to the top IAS babus, the three Service Chiefs have been downgraded. They interact with the Defence Secretary who is the interface between the Armed Forces and the Union Cabinet. Matters related to Defence Production and Defence Purchases also came principally under the bureaucrats in the Defence Ministry (though army men were represented in committees). Whichever domain, department, sector the babus, the IAS stepped in that area went to dogs. Babus, who knew next to nothing on the defence matters, started dictating terms and making money. Politicisation and favouritism became the order of the day, and professionalism went for a toss. Instead of exercising 'political control' over the military, what is exercised in practice is 'bureaucratic control'. Defence Secretary is the boss and the Service Chiefs have a subservient role, with the military isolated from real decision-making! Such was the Nehruvian hubris that side-lining the military-seniors, even purely military matters tended to be decided by Nehru, Krishna Menon, other politicians, and bureaucrats—like the hare-brained "Forward Policy" ('Blunder-36): even the post-facto inputs of the Indian army on its military and strategic implications were ignored by Nehru-Menon.

Worst was keeping the military weak, lest they ever challenge the civilian authority. Military remained grossly under-funded. It continued with the obsolete Second World War equipments. During the Nehruvian times the Defence Ministry had very low importance. Senior ministers shunned it, as it was considered not an important enough portfolio for a senior politician!

Blunder–40:
Lethargic Intelligence Machinery. No Planning

Despite the fact of unsettled borders, skirmishes as far back as 1959, and the real possibility of war, there was grossly inadequate defence preparation and no contingency plan in place. Even assuming there had actually been no war, common sense dictated that allowing for its possibility, alternate plans, accounting for all contingencies, should have been in place. That also required intelligence inputs on the Chinese preparedness, their strategy and their weaknesses and strengths. While it seems China had sufficient knowledge on India on all aspects relevant to winning war against it through its network of agents; India's intelligence was woefully poor. Here are glaring examples.

China declared unilateral ceasefire on 21 November 1962. However, even such an important announcement of China became known to the government belatedly. Wrote Kuldip Nayar:

> "...A cavalcade of cars moved to the prime minister's residence. Nehru had just woken up and was totally unaware of the Chinese offer. This was typical of our intelligence agencies and of the functioning of the government. Though the statement on the ceasefire had reached newspaper offices just before midnight, the government was unaware of it. Even the official spokesman

whom the pressman awoke for a reaction expressed ignorance. What a way to fight a war, I thought."{KN}

BG Verghese wrote in "The War We Lost":
"Around midnight, a transistor with one of our colleagues crackled to life as Peking Radio announced a unilateral ceasefire and pull back to the pre-October 'line of actual control'...Next morning, all the world carried the news, but AIR still had brave jawans gamely fighting the enemy as none had had the gumption to awaken Nehru and take his orders as the news was too big to handle otherwise! Indeed, during the preceding days, everyone from general to jawan to officials and the media was tuned into Radio Peking to find out what was going on in our own country."{URL19}

The above are only illustrative examples. When on critical matters you had no intelligence or prior information, what to speak of other matters. The life of our brave jawans came cheap. Just dump them in the war without any proper protective gear or arms, and without any intelligence on the enemy positions and preparation! With the strategic thinking and strategic planning itself being absent, where was the question of intelligence to assist those processes.

Blunder–41:
Suppressing Truth

People feel shocked when they learn of the background and the details of the India-China War because under the cover of "national security interests" things have been hidden away from the public, despite such a long lapse of time. Wrote Brigadier JP Dalvi:
"The people of India want to know the truth but have been denied it on the dubious ground of national security. The result has been an unhealthy amalgam of innuendo, mythology, conjecture, outright calumny and sustained efforts to confuse and conceal the truth. Even the truncated NEFA Enquiry [Henderson-Brooks Report] has been withheld except for a few paraphrased extracts read out to the Lok Sabha on 2nd September 1963. For some undisclosed reason, I was not asked to give evidence [despite being on the frontline during the war] before this body nor (to the best of my knowledge) were my

repatriated Commanding Officers [Dalvi and others were taken prisoner by the Chinese and released in 1963]."{JPD/xv}

Like a dictator Nehru kept the whole thing under wraps. Wrote Neville Maxwell: "...This was true of the handling of the boundary question [with China] which was kept away not only from the Cabinet and its Foreign Affairs and Defence Committees, but also from Parliament until armed clashes made it impossible to suppress."{Max}

No democratic country remains so secretive. Both the UK and the USA, as also other democratic countries, make all official documents available after a lapse of certain years, as per their law, so that historians, academics, researchers, experts, leaders and others can study them. This helps writing of correct history, drawing proper conclusions, and learning lessons for the future. But, in India, the leaders and the bureaucrats are ever afraid of their incompetence and dishonesty being exposed. They are bothered about their present and their survival, the future of the country is not their business. You ignore history and its lessons at your own peril and hence, to draw useful lessons for future from the debacle, it is necessary to raise uncomfortable questions:

"What was the nature of the border dispute? Why the issue was not resolved through talks? Why didn't India settle it in 1954 itself at the time of signing the Panchsheel? Was Indian position justified? Did Chinese arguments have substance? Why did India change its maps in 1954—on what grounds? Were there solid grounds for India to be so adamant on its stand? Why was the Chinese offer of a swap-deal on McMahon Line and Aksai Chin not accepted? Why was the forward policy adopted? Why the Indian defence preparedness was so poor? Had there been politicisation of the army? Why was the Indian performance in the war so pathetic? What should be India's stand going forward? How to resolve the dispute? How to strengthen India's defence?..."

Accountability should have been established and those responsible should have got their just deserts. The findings of the enquiry should have been made public, along with a road-map for the future. That's democracy!

The India-China war of 1962 was indeed independent India's most traumatic and worst-ever external security failure. Any democratic country, worth its salt, would have instituted a detailed enquiry into all aspects of the debacle. But, what happened in practice? Nothing! The government was brazen enough not to set up a comprehensive enquiry. Why let their own mistakes be found? Why punish themselves? Why be made to resign? Why vacate your positions? People don't deserve to know! It was an autocratic democracy. Don't disclose—cite "national interest". *Although, it was not national interest, but pure self-interest, that drove the decision.* Sweep under carpet whatever is unpalatable. Just put all the blame on the Chinese and on a few scapegoats.

The above would be obvious from the following. During the lull in the war—24 October to 13 November 1962—this is what Nehru said in the Rajya Sabha on 9 November 1962: *"People have been shocked, all of us have been shocked, by the events that occurred from October 20 onwards, especially of the first few days, and the reverses we suffered. So I hope there will be an inquiry so as to find out what mistakes or errors were committed and who were responsible for them."* During the lull period India was making its preparations and those in power in Delhi were sure India would give a befitting reply to the Chinese. However, the subsequent war of 14-20 November 1962 proved even more disastrous. *Sensing its consequence upon him, Nehru conveniently forgot about the enquiry.*

Although no enquiry was set up by the Indian Cabinet or the Government, the new Chief of Army Staff, General Chaudhuri, did set up an Operations Review Committee headed by Lieutenant-General TB Henderson-Brooks, aka HB, of the Indian army—an Australian-born, second-generation English expatriate who had opted to be an Indian, rather than a British, citizen in the 1930s—with Brigadier Premendra Singh Bhagat, Victoria Cross, then commandant of the Indian Military Academy, as a member.

However, the terms of reference of the Committee were never published; it had no power to examine witnesses or call for documents; and it had no proper legal authority. The purpose was to ensure it didn't morph into a comprehensive fact-finding mission that could embarrass the government. Reportedly, its terms of reference were very restrictive confined perhaps to only the 4 Corps' operations. However, going by the fact that the report, referred to as the Henderson-Brooks Report or Henderson-Brooks/Bhagat Report or HB/B Report (submitted in April 1963) of even such a handicapped Committee has been kept classified and top secret even till today signifies that the Committee went beyond its limited terms of reference, did some very good work and managed to nail the root causes, which the powers that be wanted to remain hidden. Perhaps, had the HB report been made public, Nehru would have had to resign.

Wrote Kuldip Nayar in 'Beyond the Lines'{KN}:
"...in September 1970, [General] Thapar [who headed the army at the time of the war] approached Indira Gandhi...to allow him to see the [HB] report... She did not however concede the request...When I was a Rajya Sabha member from 1996, I wanted the report to be made public. The government refused to do so 'in public interest'. My hunch was that the report had so severely criticized Nehru that the government, even headed by the BJP, did not want to face the public anger that would have been generated... I used the RTI facilities in 2008 when I wanted access to the Henderson Brooks inquiry report...[but didn't succeed]..."{KN}

As per the Hindustan Times report titled 'Incorrect maps given to China led to 1962 war' of 22 October 2012:
"...India presented contradictory maps on the McMahon Line to China in the fifties and in 1960-61, which ultimately led to the war with China in 1962. This revelation was made by Wajahat Habibullah, former chief information commissioner (CIC), perhaps the only civilian besides defence secretaries to have officially accessed the top secret Henderson Brookes-Bhagat report. *'We had given maps with serious contradictions on the layout of the McMahon Line to China. This led the Chinese to believe that one of the pickets being controlled by our forces in the Northeast was theirs—according to one of the maps given to them by us,'* said Habibullah, declining to name the picket along the Arunachal Pradesh border with China...Accordingly, on October 20, 1962, the Chinese army crossed over to occupy the border picket, leading to open hostilities...Habibullah got the go-ahead to access to the report after journalist Kuldip Nayar's appeal under the RTI Act in 2005 [or, was it 2008?] to get a copy of the report."{URL63}

Wrote Claude Arpi:
"Unfortunately, historians and researchers have never been allowed access to original materials to write about Nehru's leadership during the troubled years after Independence. It is tragic that the famous 'Nehru Papers' are jealously locked away

in the Nehru Memorial Library. They are, in fact, the property of his family! I find it even more regrettable that during its six years in power, the NDA government, often accused of trying to rewrite history, did not take any action to rectify this anomaly. Possibly they were not interested in recent history! ...As a result, today history lovers and serious researchers have only the 31 volumes published so far of the Selected Works of Jawaharlal Nehru (covering the period 1946 to 1955) to fall back on. This could be considered a partial declassification of the Nehru Papers, except for the fact that the editing has always been undertaken by Nehruvian historians, making at times the selection tainted. The other problem is that these volumes cover only the writings (or sayings) of Nehru; notes or letters of other officials or dignitaries which triggered Nehru's answers are only briefly and unsatisfactorily resumed in footnotes."{Arpi2}

Blunder–42:
Himalayan Blunders, but No Accountability

Such was the economy practised in sharing information with the public, the media, and even the parliament, and such was the economy with truth in Nehru's democratic India that the blame for debacle in the India-China War came not on Nehru, the principal person responsible, but on Menon. Such was the ignorance of the opposition that Kriplani and others asked Nehru to take over the defence portfolio from Menon! The poor fellows had no idea that the disaster both in the foreign policy and in the defence was actually thanks to Nehru. Menon was only a protégé of Nehru, did his bidding, and became Defence Minister only in 1957.

Krishna Menon was reluctantly made the scapegoat. COAS Thapar resigned. BM Kaul resigned. But, not Nehru. Wrote Brigadier JP Dalvi in his book 'Himalayan Blunder':

"When the inevitable disaster came Nehru did not even have grace or courage to admit his errors or seek a fresh mandate from the people. He did not even go through the motion of resigning; he merely presented his trusted colleagues and military appointees as sacrificial offerings..."{JPD/249}

"Instead of gracefully accepting responsibility for erroneous policies, the guilty men sought alibis and scapegoats. In any developed democracy the Government would have been replaced, instead of being allowed to continue in office and sit in judgement on their subordinates..."{JPD/161}

"We must also learn that a democracy has no room for proven failures. This is not a matter of sentiment. Mr Chamberlain was removed after Hitler invaded France in May 1940 with Cromwell's classic plea, 'For God's sake, go'. Mr Anthony Eden was forced out of office after the disastrous Suez adventure of 1956..."{JPD/161}

Not only that, Nehru was not even willing to remove the Defence Minister Krishna Menon. Nehru told Yashwant Rao Chavan who had come to Delhi to attend a meeting of the Chief Ministers: *"You see, they want Menon's blood. If I agree, tomorrow they will ask for my blood."*{DD/364}

Finding it difficult to resist pressure, Nehru played his old game of a threat of his own resignation. Nehru had threatened to resign on several earlier occasions to have his way safe in the knowledge that people would back off. But, not this time. When he found that the trick won't work and he himself would have to go, he quickly backed off and asked Menon to resign. Meanwhile Indira Gandhi had approached Vice-President Zakir Hussain to persuade her father to drop Menon, as that was the only way to appease the enraged public and the media. Nehru actually remonstrated with those who criticised him, and later even took revenge against some!

Here is Israel and Golda Meir's example, in sharp contrast to that of India and Nehru's:

After its decisive victory against the joint Egypt-Syria-Jordan-Iraq army in 1967 in the Six-Day War, following its victories in 1948 at the time of its birth, and later, Israel was a little laid back and unprepared, thinking Arabs wouldn't dare attack again. Also because Israel had nuclear weapons by then to deter the Arabs. The attack of 1973 therefore came as a surprise to it. In 1973, Yom Kipper, the holiest day of the year for the Jews, fell on 6 October. It is on that day when Israel and the Jews the world over were busy observing Yom Kipper that the Egyptian and the Syrian armies launched a surprise attack against Israel in the Sinai Peninsula and the Golan Heights respectively. Still, after the initial setbacks and panic, it rose to the challenge, and repelled the combined attack, emerging triumphant. The war came to be known as the Yom Kipper War.

Golda Meir was the president then. Even though Israel's ultimate victory was spectacular and decisive, they immediately instituted an enquiry to fix responsibility for the initial setbacks and the panic reaction, and the lapses that led to the attack coming as a surprise. The preliminary report took just a few months and was released on April 2, 1974—it actually named names of those responsible. Several top-ranking staff were asked to resign. Golda Meir was not named, but taking overall responsibility, she resigned on April 10, 1974—after mere eight days of release of the report, which was only a preliminary report! This, even though Israel, under Golda Meir, had actually won the war decisively and turned the tables on the Arab countries that had attacked them!

Contrast the above with Nehru and India. Even though India lost pathetically in the 1962 India-China War, Nehru government instituted no enquiry; and Nehru did not even make a gesture of an offer to resign. What was the alibi offered to the gullible public? The nation was told that the borders were well-settled, and that the unprovoked attack from China was what the innocent India got for doing all the good to China. Even Rajaji, otherwise in opposition to Nehru by then, blamed it on the treachery of the Chinese. Perhaps, at that time Rajaji did not know all the facts. You do a Himalayan blunder, but you receive sympathy—Nehru, the poor chap, was stabbed in the back by the Chinese! How publicised misinformation can turn the scales.

Everyone remembers a popular song of those times penned by poet Pradeep and sung by Lata Mangeshkar. It went like this: "*Aai mere watan ke logo, jara aankh me bhar lo paani, jo shaheed hue hai unki, jara yaad karo kurbani...*" The song is invariably played on August 15 every year. Lata told in an interview when she had sung that song in Nehru's presence, Nehru had wept! So sensitive was he!! Again, additional praise. But, who was responsible for his own tears and tears in the eyes of crores of Indians, in the first place? Had sensible policies been followed, this huge tragedy that befell the nation, and the consequent tears, could have been avoided.

Blunder–43:
Delayed Liberation of Goa

Goa, Daman and Diu, and Dadra and Nagar Haveli—collectively known as the Estado da Índia—continued to remain occupied by Portugal after independence. They covered an area of about 4,000 sq km, and a population of about 6.4 lakh comprising about 61% Hindus, 37% Christians, and 2% Muslims. India finally carried out air, sea and land strikes under the armed-action code-named 'Operation Vijay", and liberated all the Portuguese-occupied Indian territories in December 1961, after a two-day operation. Dadra and Nagar Haveli were liberated earlier in 1954.

Why should it have taken 14 long years after the Indian independence to throw out the Portuguese in 1961? Couldn't Nehru get a small territory vacated?

During a long discussion on Goa in the Foreign Affairs Committee in 1950, *Sardar Patel* kept to himself listening to the various tame alternatives, then suddenly said at the end, "*Shall we go in? It is two hours' work!*" Patel was very keen to fulfil the assurance given to the Goa Congress in his letter of 14 May 1946 promising freedom from foreign domination. *He was all for using force to settle the matter quickly. But, Nehru was much too soft to take any effective steps.* Patel felt exasperated.{BK/521}

Wrote Durga Das: "Gandhi advised the people [Indians] of the French and Portuguese possessions in India not to revolt against their overlords on 15th August but to trust Nehru to do for his kith and kin what he was doing to assist the Indonesians to become free. Indirectly, *Gandhi was voicing the fact that he differed from Patel's view on Goa and Pondicherry and other foreign enclaves* and agreed with Nehru's that the question of their liberation could wait for some time."{DD/250}

If Sardar Patel's advice had been heeded, Goa would have been part of the Indian Union by 1948 itself. However, with pacifists like Nehru and Gandhi desired action could always wait, and self-deluding talks substituted for decision and action. Left to Gandhi and Nehru, and had Patel not been on the scene, while Hyderabad and Junagadh would have been another Kashmir or Pakistan; there would have been dozens of independent Princely States sucking up to Britain or Pakistan, and becoming permanent headaches!

Blunder–44:
Nehru's NO to Nuclear Arms

The then US president John F Kennedy was an admirer of Indian democracy, and when he learnt that China was on its way to detonate a nuclear device, he wanted that it ought to be a democratic country like India, and not communist China, which should have nuclear capability. The Kennedy administration was ready to help India out with nuclear deterrence. But, Nehru rejected the offer.

Currently, India has been canvassing support from various countries to become a member of Nuclear Suppliers Group (NSG)—in vain, so far. Had Nehru gone along with Kennedy's advice, India would have detonated a nuclear device well before China. *Had that happened, not only would India have been a member of the NSG long, long ago, but China would not have dared to attack India, nor would Pakistan have taken liberties to attack India in 1965.*

Former foreign secretary Rasgotra disclosed:

"...Kennedy's hand-written letter was accompanied by a technical note from the chairman of the U.S. Atomic Energy Commission, setting out the assistance his organisation would provide to Indian atomic scientists to detonate an American device from atop a tower in Rajasthan desert, the release said... In the letter, Kennedy had said he and the American establishment were aware of Nehru's strong views against nuclear tests and nuclear weapons, but emphasised the political and security threat China's test would spell for Nehru's government and India's security, it said, adding the American leader's letter emphasised that 'nothing is more important than national security.'"{URL49}

Gandhian 'Ahimsa' had not only totally vitiated free India's approach to retaining its own freedom by strengthening its defence and external security; but also gave excuse to pacifists like Nehru to not fulfil their basic responsibility as prime minister of protecting India, under the garb of the hypocrisy of high moral principles, and being flag-bearers of world-peace. Nehru failed to grasp the deterrence value of nuclear weapons. What is surprising is what were his cabinet colleagues and other leaders of the ruling and the opposition parties doing? Were they mere mute and spineless witnesses to whatever the dictator Nehru chose to do?

Blunder–45:
No Settlement with Pakistan

Nehru failed to reach an accommodation with Pakistan during his life time, making our western and north western borders sensitive, costing us heavy to secure them. The crux of the Indo-Pak dispute was Kashmir; and Pakistan was unwilling for settlement and for no-war pact till the Kashmir issue was resolved. Kashmir would have been a non-issue had Nehru allowed Sardar Patel to handle it; or had Gandhi not made Nehru the first PM. It was Nehru's responsibility to resolve the issues he had created. Nehru unfortunately expired leaving both the issues—Kashmir and Indo-Pak settlement—unsolved.

The India-Pakistan Indus Water Treaty (IWT) of 1960 on sharing of waters from the six Indus-system rivers was an unprecedented (by any nation) generous "give away" (like the India-China Panchsheel agreement later of 1954) by Nehru to Pakistan at the cost of J&K and Punjab (details in 'Blunder–50'), with no reciprocal "take". It didn't occur to Nehru to make it conditional upon Pakistan settling on J&K and other matters to ensure secure western and north western borders.

Intended to palliate India's alarm at Pakistan's entry into SEATO in 1958, General Ayub Khan proposed security alliance/pact with India to Nehru. Nehru summarily and scornfully rejected the proposal remarking security alliance "against whom?"

Blunder–46:
Responsible for 1965-War too, in a way

India's lack of pacts with powerful countries to back it up in case of external attacks (Nehruvian policy (fad) of "Non-Alignment" resulted in it being non-aligned with its own national security interests—'Blunder-57'), its poor showing in 1962-War, the fact of its continued dependence on outdated armaments of World War-II vintage, the exposure of its gross deficiency in modern military hardware, and little efforts even post 1962-war to strengthen itself, prompted Pakistan to take advantage of the situation and attempt to grab Kashmir militarily in 1965.

India and Nehru did not wake up even as Pakistan equipped itself with first-class, modern military hardware from the USA, following its pact with the anti-communist Western Bloc. Shastri was relatively a new entrant as PM, and he had hardly had time to come to grips with things crying for attention, let alone tackle the huge Nehru legacy of untackled problems. The blame for the fact that Pakistan dared to attack India on account of its known unpreparedness, therefore, rests squarely with Nehru. Further, as per the US advice, had India gone nuclear ('Blunder-44'), or had Nehru reached an honourable settlement with Pakistan ('Blunder-45'), Pakistan would not have dared to attack India.

Blunder–47:
International Record in Insecure Borders

Nehru's policies resulted in thousands of kilometres of all land boundaries of India, whether in the north or east or west or northeast or northwest, becoming sensitive and insecure, requiring massive investments to protect them. What is noteworthy is that there were enough opportunities to peacefully settle the boundaries with China in the 1950s and early 1960s, yet most irresponsibly Nehru failed to encash on them ('Blunder-35'). Nehru also failed to settle India's disputes with Pakistan ('Blunder-45').

Thanks to Gandhi's choice for the first PM of India, India is the only country of its size in the world with such a long unsettled border with a giant neighbour, and disputes with another.

Rather than solving a plethora of severe problems crying for attention, the Nehruvian era added new problems, and not just added them, made them more difficult and almost insolvable, the most severe being securing the long borders.

Thanks to the Himalayas, the north from time immemorial has been the most secure natural boundary. Nehruvian policies managed to make them insecure!

Northeast has been made insecure thanks to gross misgovernance, corruption, and insurgency, and to Nehru turning a blind eye to adversely changing demography—thanks to proselytization, and to Muslim migrations from East Pakistan/Bangladesh.

FOREIGN POLICY

Blunder–48:
Nehru-Liaquat Pact 1950

With indescribable atrocities against Hindus in East Bengal going unabated, the GoI made an appeal to Pakistan to call a halt on the same. But, there was little response, till tit-for-tat brought Pakistan to the negotiating table.

It is worth noting in this connection that Gandhian non-violent principles yielded nothing, as this episode illustrates. In Rajlakshmi Debi's Bangla novel Kamal-lata, quoted by Tathagata Roy in his book 'My People, Uprooted: A Saga of the Hindus of Eastern Bengal'[TR] (Chapter 6), there is a conversation described between a Hindu from Mymensingh town and a Muslim from a Calcutta suburb sometime just after partition. In the process of haggling the Muslim says *"Excuse me, but your position and ours are not the same. So long as Mahatma Gandhi is alive we have no fears. But you won't be able to live here [East Bengal] much longer."*

There was a marked difference between Punjab and Bengal in respect of the partition. In Punjab, the carnage was on both sides, East Punjab and West Punjab, although more in the Muslim-dominated West Punjab. In Bengal, the mayhem was mostly in the Muslim-dominated East Bengal. In Punjab, the migration was both ways. In a way, there was a population transfer between West Punjab and East Punjab. In Bengal, the predominant migration was that of Hindus from East Pakistan to West Bengal. There was a reverse migration of Muslims too, but comparatively far less.

However, the continued violence against the Hindus in East Bengal had begun provoking retaliation in West Bengal. For example, the anti-Muslim riots in Howrah turned serious from 26 March 1950 onwards, leading to the beginning of migration of Muslims from West Bengal to East Bengal by March 1950. That is, the population transfer that had happened in Punjab in 1947-48 began to happen in Bengal belatedly by March 1950. It is this which alarmed Pakistan and the Muslim League leaders, who had hitherto been inciting the mobs in East Bengal, and were happy at Hindus being at the receiving end.

It was only when the anti-Muslim riots in Howrah, in retaliation of the on-going carnage in East Bengal, took a serious turn from 26 March 1950 onwards that the Pakistan PM Liaquat Ali made his first conciliatory gesture in a speech at Karachi on 29 March 1950, and expressed his intention to travel to New Delhi on 2 April 1950 to work out a solution with Nehru.

Liaquat Ali hurried to New Delhi on 2 April 1950, and signed the Nehru–Liaquat Pact, also called the Delhi Pact, on 8 April 1950. It provided for safety of refugees when they returned to dispose of their property; return of abducted women and looted property; derecognition of forced conversions; complete and equal right of citizenship and security of life and properties to minorities; and setting up of Minority Commission in each country.

As expected, while India firmly implemented the Pact, not Pakistan. While the anti-Muslim violence in West Bengal was put down with a firm hand, and the migration of Muslims from West Bengal to East Bengal ceased; the violence against the Hindus in East Bengal continued unabated, so also the migration of Hindus from East Bengal to West Bengal. That is, the carnage became only one-sided: that of Hindus in East Bengal. Also, the migration became only one way: Pakistan to India.

Looking to the track-record of the Muslim League leaders, who had themselves been inciting the mobs, Nehru should have known what the result of the pact would be. Sardar Patel was unhappy with the Pact, but being in the cabinet, didn't oppose it. However, Dr Shyama Prasad Mukherjee and KC Niyogee, the two central ministers from West Bengal, immediately resigned from the Union Cabinet in protest against the Pact.

Rather than facilitating transfer of population between West and East Bengal, and removing forever the problem and the poison, Nehru extracted the following "*benefits*" for India from the Nehru-Liaquat pact: (1)Checked depletion of Muslim population from West Bengal and Assam by stopping their migration to Pakistan. (2)Increased the population of Muslims in West Bengal and Assam by allowing their reverse migration—allowing Muslims to return who had migrated. (3)Allowed fresh migration of Muslims from East Bengal. (5)Condemned the Hindus in East Bengal (a)to violence, (b)to second-class status, and (c)to remain at the mercy of Muslims. (6)Forced subsequent migration of Hindus from East Bengal to West Bengal (as the atrocities did not subside in Pakistan).

Blunder–49:
Letting Go of Gwadar

Gwadar is a port-city on the Arabian Sea on the south-western coast of Baluchistan province in Pakistan. It is located opposite Oman across the sea, near the border with Iran, and to the east of the Persian Gulf. Gwadar is a warm-water, deep-sea port, and it has a strategic location between South Asia, Central Asia and West Asia at the mouth of the Persian Gulf, just outside the Straits of Hormuz. The operations of Gwadar's strategic sea port were handed over by Pakistan to China in 2013. Now, thanks to the Chinese money and expertise, Gwadar is all set to emerge as Pakistan's third largest port. Gwadar will be the southern point and the sea terminal of the $46 billion China-Pakistan Economic Corridor (CPEC) that will extend to Kashgar in Xinjiang. The CPEC is part of China's "One Belt, One Road" (OBOR).

Gwadar was not owned by the British at the time of independence. Gwadar was an overseas possession of the Sultanate of Muscat and Oman—it was given as a gift to Oman by the Khan of Kalat in 1783—until Pakistan purchased the territory on 8 September 1958. Pakistan assumed its control on 8 December 1958, and the territory was later integrated into Baluchistan province on 1 July 1970 as Gwadar District.

Oman was on good terms with India, and Sultan of Oman had offered to sell Gwadar to India for mere one million US dollars. However, India under Nehru did not take the offer, and let go of such an excellent strategic location. It was ultimately purchased by Pakistan on 8 September 1958 for three million US dollars.

It had the great potential of a deep water port (which China is now exploiting), but Nehru didn't have the foresight to appreciate its critical benefit. Even if Nehru didn't see much use of the place then as a deep water port, India should have acquired it, so that it could have been used as a bargaining chip with Pakistan, vis-à-vis Kashmir and other matters.

In hindsight, not accepting the priceless gift from the Sultan of Oman was a huge mistake at par with the long list of post-independence strategic blunders by Nehru.

Blunder–50:
Indus Water Treaty—Himalayan Blunder

Nehru's *First* Himalayan Blunder: Tibet's Erasure as a Nation.
Nehru's *Second* Himalayan Blunder: Indus Water Treaty (IWT).
Nehru's *Third* Himalayan Blunder: India-China War.

"No armies with bombs and shellfire could devastate a land so thoroughly as Pakistan could be devastated by the simple expedient of India's permanently shutting off the source of waters that keep the fields and people of Pakistan green."
—David Lilienthal, former Chief, Tennessee Valley Authority, US{Swa6}

"The 'Aqua Bomb' is truly India's most powerful weapon against Pakistan. As the upper riparian state, India can control the flow of the seven rivers that flow into the Indus Basin."{Swa6}

In the India-Pakistan Indus Water Treaty (IWT) of 1960 on sharing of waters from the six Indus-system rivers, Nehru gave away far, far more than what was adequate, miserably failing to envisage India's future needs; and did not even leverage it to have the J&K dispute settled—as the upper riparian state, India could have called the shots, but Nehru, by unwisely agreeing to the World Bank (manipulated by the US and the West) mediation, surrendered all its advantages.{Swa6} India-Pakistan Indus Water Treaty of 1960 has parallel with India-China Panchsheel agreement of 1954. Both had generous "give away" but no reciprocal "take" and both were thanks to Nehru! Wrote Brahma Chellaney:{URL48}

"Jawaharlal Nehru ignored the interests of Jammu and Kashmir and, to a lesser extent, Punjab when he signed the 1960 Indus Waters Treaty, under which India bigheartedly agreed to the exclusive reservation of the largest three of the six Indus-system rivers for downstream Pakistan... In effect, India signed an extraordinary treaty indefinitely setting aside 80.52% of the Indus-system waters for Pakistan—the most generous water-sharing pact thus far in modern world history.

"In fact, the volume of waters earmarked for Pakistan from India under the Indus treaty is more than 90 times greater than what the US is required to release for Mexico under the 1944 US-Mexico Water Treaty, which stipulates a minimum transboundary delivery of 1.85 billion cubic metres of the

Colorado River waters yearly.

"Despite Clinton's advocacy of a Teesta treaty, the fact is that the waters of the once-mighty Colorado River are siphoned by seven American states, leaving only a trickle for Mexico.

"India and Nehru did not envisage—you may call it a lack of foresight on their part—that water resources would come under serious strain due to developmental and population pressures. Today, as the bulk of the Indus system's waters continue to flow to an adversarial Pakistan waging a war by terror, India's own Indus basin, according to the 2030 Water Resources Group, is reeling under a massive 52% deficit between water supply and demand...

"Worse still, the Indus treaty has deprived Jammu and Kashmir of the only resource it has—water. The state's three main rivers—the Chenab, the Jhelum (which boast the largest crossborder discharge of all the six Indus-system rivers) and the main Indus stream—have been reserved for Pakistan's use, thereby promoting alienation and resentment in the Indian state.

"This led the Jammu and Kashmir state legislature to pass a bipartisan resolution in 2002 calling for a review and annulment of the Indus treaty. To help allay popular resentment in the state over the major electricity shortages that is hampering its development, the central government subsequently embarked on hydropower projects like Baglihar and Kishenganga. But Pakistan—as if to perpetuate the alienation in the Indian state—took the Baglihar project to a World Bank-appointed international neutral expert and Kishenganga to the International Court of Arbitration, which last year stayed all further work on the project..."{URL48}

Perplexing thing is that Nehru could settle an international water issue like Indus Water Treaty, for it involved only a generous give-away on the part of India; but he failed to tackle India's own internal river-water disputes like those relating to the sharing of Narmada water, or the Krishna-Kaveri dispute.

Blunder–51:
No Initiative on Sri Lankan Tamil Problem

It is sad that even though the two peoples—the Sinhalese and the Tamils—spring from the same civilisational background, they have been at loggerheads. People from Gujarat and Sindh in India immigrated to Sri Lanka and formed the Sinhala dynasty. Chronicles—Mahavansa and Dipavansa—record the landing of Wijaya in the sixth century BC.

Sadly, the Sri Lankan Tamil problem was allowed to fester and Nehru did little to get the matter resolved in the fifties, when it could have been—and it grew worse.

Both the 'Sri Lankan Citizenship Act of 1948' and the 'Official Language Act of 1956' put the Tamils at a severe disadvantage. Sri Lanka witnessed mayhem of Tamils in 1958, amounting almost to genocide. Tamils everywhere were attacked mercilessly, and their properties were burnt or looted. Sinhala mobs poured kerosene over many Tamils, and burnt them alive. Thousands were injured or killed. Many were internally displaced. It was a case of state-sponsored terror.

Walter Crocker, who was then the Australian ambassador to India, says in his book, 'Nehru: A Contemporary's Estimate', that while India and Nehru spoke against the treatment of Africans in the European colonies, and justifiably so; in contrast, with regard to the ill treatment of Tamils in Ceylon, they did precious little. Writes Crocker: "...and with little done to save Indians in Ceylon from treatment which was worse than the treatment meted out to Africans in European colonies in Africa."

But, that was typical of Nehru. He railed against the discrimination and savagery in distant lands—against blacks in South Africa—but remained conspicuously silent about our own people next door: against the Hindus in East Pakistan (now Bangladesh), or against the Tamils in Sri Lanka. Because, the former required only talking; while the latter required action too!

If India had succeeded in doing the needful in the fifties, much of the trouble that Sri Lanka and the Tamils and the Sinhalese faced subsequently could have been avoided. It is in such cases that the statesmanship of a leader is tested.

Blunder–52:
Erroneous Nehru-Era Map

An error in the Indian maps shows territory as large as Sikkim or Goa in Arunachal Pradesh as belonging to China. The error has yet to be corrected.

Extracts below from an article[URL29] by Madhav Nalapat in 'The Sunday Guardian' of 23 August 2014 are self-explanatory:

"Prime Minister Manmohan Singh rejected an August 2013 request by senior officials in his government to correct a serious error, dating back over 50 years, in India's official maps. In effect, this oversight in official maps mistakenly gave China control of two Arunachal Pradesh "fishtails", a territory as large as Sikkim or Goa, and continuously inhabited by Indian citizens...

"...The two 'fishtail' formations in Arunachal Pradesh were omitted from maps prepared by the Survey of India during the 1960s, although the area has always been under the control of India. No public records exist as to why and how such a significant error was made. In 1962, recognising the fact that this territory was Indian, soldiers from the People's Liberation Army of China, who had occupied the fishtails during November 1962, withdrew after the unilateral ceasefire declared by Beijing that month.

"'Since then and before, the area within the two fishtails has always been occupied by our troops, as well as by the Mishmi tribe, all of whom are citizens of India. Our claim on the territory is incontestable and our maps ought to have been updated to reflect this,' a senior official stated.

"...Asked as to why official maps did not reflect the fact of the 'fishtails' being Indian territory, the reply was that 'as the mistake took place during Nehru's time, it was felt that correcting the maps formally would draw attention to this mistake on the part of the then Prime Minister and thereby tarnish his name'.

"A retired official claimed that 'every government has protected Nehru's reputation by refusing to make public facts dating from the 1940s that they saw as damaging to the image of Nehru'. He and a former colleague saw Prime Minister Manmohan Singh's

Foreign Policy

2013 refusal to formally change the map (a decision taken 'after consultations with the political authority') as part of the effort to protect the reputation of Jawaharlal Nehru by refusing to make public any details of his failures, including the decision to keep secret the Henderson-Brooks Report on the 1962 war, or to draw attention to Nehru's failures even by the necessary step of rectifying them.

"Interestingly, the fact that maps showed the two 'fishtails' as being outside Indian territory was, according to a senior (and now retired) official, 'brought to the attention of then Home Minister P. Chidambaram by the (then) Director-General of the Indo-Tibetan Border Police (ITBP) in 2010, along with reports of Chinese troops entering the area in 2011 and 2012, but the response was to do nothing'..."{URL29}

Blunder–53 : Advocating China's UNSC Membership, Sacrificing Ours!

India has been trying to become a permanent member of the United Nations Security Council (UNSC) for a long time, begging all nations—big and small—including China. But, over five decades ago India was getting the UNSC seat unasked—on a platter! And, Nehru chose to rebuff the offer!! Why? Nehru wanted the position to be given to the People's Republic of China instead! Being generous at India's cost!! But, note the contrast. In 2008, in a conclave of foreign ministers of BRIC countries, when Russia proposed that the BRIC countries support India's Permanent Membership of the UNSC, it was strongly opposed by China!

First, the background. On account of the failure of the League of Nations to prevent World War II, United Nations Organisation (UNO) was formed in 1945 after World War II by the main allies in the War: US, UK, USSR, France and China—ROC (Republic of China) headed by Chiang Kai-shek. These five became the Permanent Members of the UNSC, with veto powers. UNSC also has 10 rotating non-permanent members with a term of two years.

In 1949, Communists took over China and founded People's Republic of China (PRC) under Mao. Chiang Kai-shek and his ROC were driven away to Formosa—now called Taiwan. ROC continued to be a member of the UN till 1971, and not PRC, as US and allies refused to recognise it. They did not wish to have another communist country as a member of the UNSC.

The move by the US to have India in the UNSC in lieu of China started in 1950. In that context, in response to the letter of his sister Vijaya Lakshmi Pandit, who was then the ambassador in the US, Nehru wrote:

> "In your letter you mention that the State Department is trying to unseat China as a Permanent Member of the Security Council and to put India in her place. So far as we are concerned, we are not going to countenance it. That would be bad from every point of view. It would be a clear affront to China and it would mean some kind of a break between us and China. I suppose the state department would not like that, but we have no intention of following that course. We shall go on pressing for China's admission in the UN and the Security Council. I suppose that a crisis will come during the next sessions of the General Assembly of the UN on this issue. The people's government of China is sending a full delegation there. If they fail to get in there will be trouble which might even result in the USSR and some other countries finally quitting the UN. That may please the State Department, but it would mean the end of the UN as we have known it. That would also mean a further drift towards war. India because of many factors, is certainly entitled to a permanent seat in the security council. But we are not going in at the cost of China."{URL37}

Was India under Nehru trying to take a high moral ground? But, why? Why not look to your own country's interest? Besides, was it even ethical, moral, and principled? No. Why support an aggressor of Tibet for the UN and the UNSC? Correct ethical and moral position for India should have dictated trenchant opposition of China for the UN and the UNSC as long as it did not vacate Tibet.

What was bizarre was that even though never requested by China, India had been voluntarily and vigorously advocating Peoples Republic of China (PRC) for the Permanent Membership of the UNSC in lieu of Taiwan! India lobbied with all nations for the UN membership and UNSC permanent seat, not for itself, but for China!

Even though China had invaded Tibet, KM Panikkar, the Indian Ambassador in Beijing, stated that to protest the Chinese invasion of Tibet would be an interference to India's efforts on behalf of China in the UN! That is, complaining against China on behalf of Tibet would show China in bad light—as an aggressor—when it was more important for India to ensure China's entry into the UN, for which India had been trying, and ensure that this effort of India was not thwarted by taking up China's Tibet aggression! What kind of crazy Nehruvian foreign policy was this? *Our own national security interests and the interests of Tibet were sought to be sacrificed to help China enter the UN!!*

Incidentally, there was another irony to India advocating the UN membership of China in the fifties. As per 'Mao: The Unknown Story' by Jung Chang and Jon Halliday[JC], and other books, India thought it was doing a great favour to China by advocating its membership of the UN, and expecting it to feel obliged; however, China resented such overtures, for it abhorred the patronizing attitude of Nehru—more so because China considered itself to be the real leader of Asia, and contemptuously looked at India's pretensions to being a great power merely on rhetoric, with nothing to show for it. Further, China did not really care then—in the fifties—of the UN membership. In fact, it thought that becoming a member would oblige it to abide by the UN charter, when it wanted to actually have a free hand in dealing with Korea and Tibet.

Both the US and the USSR were willing to accommodate India as a Permanent Member of the UNSC (United Nations Security Council) in 1955, in lieu of Taiwan, or in addition to it as a sixth member, after amending the UN charter. *This Nehru refused!* Nehru wanted the seat to be given to PRC (Peoples Republic of China), as Nehru did not want China to be marginalised!

Wrote Nehru in his note of 1 August 1955 on his tour of the Soviet Union and other countries during June-July 1955:

"Informally, suggestions have been made by the United States that China should be taken into the United Nations but not in the Security Council and that India should take her place in the Security Council. We cannot of course accept this as it means falling out with China and it would be very unfair for a great country like China not to be in the Security Council. We have, therefore, made it clear to those who suggested this that we cannot agree to this suggestion. We have even gone a little further and said that India is not anxious to enter the Security Council at this stage, even though as a great country she ought to be there. The first step to be taken is for China to take her rightful place and then the question of India might be considered separately."{JNSW/Vol-29/303}

It was almost as if Nehru, for reasons one cannot fathom, totally ignored India's own strategic interests! It is possible that the US and the USSR were more keen to show PRC its place, than to really promote India. But, so what—if it also served India's interests. India should have been alive to its own self-interest. Why should Nehru have been generous to China at the cost of India! Shashi Tharoor states in his book 'Nehru: The Invention of India':

"Indian diplomats who have seen the files swear that at about the same time Jawaharlal also declined a US offer to take the permanent seat on the United Nations Security Council then held, with scant credibility, by Taiwan, urging that it be offered to Beijing instead... But it was one thing to fulminate against Great Power machinations, another to run a national foreign policy with little regard to the imperatives of power or the need of a country to bargain from a position of strength."{ST/183}

Reads a 'Business Line' article 'UN reforms—a fading mirage?' of 16 September 2009:{URL14}

"Ironically, around 1955, Prime Minister Jawaharlal Nehru was offered the disputed Chinese Permanent Security Council seat by the US to keep out the People's Republic of China, and he also was sounded out by the USSR Prime Minister, Nikolai Bulganin, to allow China to take this seat while giving India a sixth permanent seat in the Security Council. Nehru rejected this offer in deference to China. History may have been different if this offer had been subjected to serious negotiations. Through the decades since, we have been struggling for this seat."{URL14}

S Gopal wrote in his book Jawaharlal Nehru: A Biography (volume two): 'He (Jawaharlal Nehru) rejected the Soviet offer to propose India as the sixth permanent member of the Security Council and insisted that priority be given to China's admission to the United Nations.'{URL50}

When an MP JN Parekh raised a short notice question in the Lok Sabha on whether India had refused a UNSC seat informally offered to her, Nehru's reply was apparently less than honest: "There has been no offer, formal or informal, of this kind. Some vague references have appeared in the press about it which have no foundation in fact. The composition of the Security Council is prescribed by the UN Charter, according to which certain specified nations have permanent seats. No change or addition can be made to this without an amendment of the Charter. There is, therefore, no question of a seat being offered and India declining it. Our declared policy is to support the admission of all nations qualified for UN membership."{URL50}

A Wilson Centre report of 11 March 2015 titled 'Not at the Cost of China: India and the United Nations Security Council, 1950'{URL37} states that both the US and the USSR offered India permanent membership in the UNSC but Nehru refused to accept it, and wanted it to be given to China instead.

Writes Arun Shourie in 'Are we deceiving ourselves again?':
"...The Communists seize power [in China]. Panditji [Nehru] is the first to ensure that India recognizes the new Government. He also urges countries like U.K. to hasten recognition. Although, it is Chiang Kai-shek who has supported India's struggle for independence...Panditji immediately begins championing the cause of the new Government [of China]. He urges the British, the Americans, in fact everyone he can reach, that the Nationalist Government [of Chiang Kai-shek] must be made to vacate its seat in the United Nations, and that seat—which means necessarily the seat both in the General Assembly and the Security Council—must be given over to the Communist Government..."{AS/28-9}

What was even more bizarre was that even after the 1962 India-China war, India supported China in the UN. Declared Nehru's sister Vijaya Lakshmi Pandit, who was leading a delegation to the UN in 1963, that she "doesn't understand that why a world-class organization such as the United Nations has not included a big and powerful country like China."{URL38}

If you analyse India's actions and moves then, we appear to be novices and simpletons! Speaking to students of Lucknow University in November 1951, Ambedkar had said: "The government's foreign policy failed to make India stronger. Why should not India get a permanent seat in the UN Security Council? Why has the prime minister not tried for it?"

Blunder–54:
Rebuffing Israel, the Friend-in-Need

The irony and the absurdity of Nehru's foreign policy is hard not to notice: India under Nehru was amongst the first nations to recognise PRC (People's Republic of China) when Communists took over in 1949; but when it came to Israel, Nehru did not recognise it as a nation till September 1950, even though it was established on 14 May 1948, and most nations of the world had recognised it! While Nehru campaigned for admission of China to the UN and even into the UNSC, sacrificing its own chances ('Blunder-53' above); India not only voted against the UN resolution that had the effect of creating Israel, but also voted against Israel's admission in the UN in 1949! This when China did what it did—annexing Tibet and inflicting 1962 India-China war—while Israel was indeed India's friend-in-need!

On 29 November 1947, the United Nations General Assembly voted on the modified UN Partition Plan of Palestine that effectively included creation of Israel for Jews. Most (33) nations voted in favour: they included the US, the European countries, the Soviet Union and the East-European countries, and the Latin-American countries. 33 countries votes in favour of the UN resolution, and 13 against. There were 10 abstentions and 1 absent. Abstentions included Republic of China and Yugoslavia.

Those against included 10 Muslim nations, namely Afghanistan, Egypt, Iran, Iraq, Lebanon, Pakistan, Saudi Arabia, Syria, Turkey and Yemen, and 3 others, namely Cuba, Greece, and one more country. Guess which? Most regretfully, it was India. This was despite Albert Einstein's personal appeal to Nehru. Here are extracts from the article "When Nehru Shunned Einstein's Request To Support The Jewish Cause":{Swa5}

> "On 11 June 1947, Albert Einstein made an extraordinary intervention in global geo-political affairs by writing to then prime minister-designate of India, Jawaharlal Nehru. He implored India's leader to endorse the 'Zionist effort to recreate a Jewish Homeland in Palestine'. Appealing to Nehru's moral sensibilities, he focused on the ethical question of whether the Jews should be allowed to have a homeland in the 'soil of their fathers'. In his letter, Einstein described the historical wrong done to the Jewish people, who had been 'victimized and hounded' for centuries. He wrote that millions of Jews had died

not only because of the Nazi gas chambers but also because 'there was no spot on the globe where they could find sanctuary'. Zionism was the means to end this anomaly of history, he wrote, and a solution for this persecuted people to settle in a land to which they had 'historic ties'.{Swa5}

A nation which got independence only a few months earlier on 15 August 1947 after having suffered foreign domination, ignominy, insult to its culture and religion and back-breaking exploitation for over 1000 years should have valued independence or creation of another nation, especially those for Jews, who richly-deserved it. Jews had suffered for centuries like the Hindus had suffered, though much longer. We should have had empathy for them. But, Nehru? What can one say of his convoluted thinking, defective world-view and faulty approach! *India could have at least abstained from voting, rather than voting against.*

Nehru could recognise China's sovereignty over Tibet, which had an adverse impact on India, but not build relations with Israel, with which India had much in common, and relations with whom would have been very helpful in various fields. Indira Gandhi, like her father, and Rajiv Gandhi, like her mother, maintained their distance from Israel. What Nehru-Indira Dynasty did was driven by their self-interest of vote-bank politics (Minority Muslim votes) at the cost of the nation. It was left to the wise non-Dynasty Prime Minister Narsimha Rao to establish formal relations with Israel in 1992.

It is worth noting that despite Nehru-Indira Dynasty's unjust treatment of Israel, Israel helped India in whatever manner it could in India's multiple wars with its neighbours. India sought and got arms from Israel both in the 1962 India-China war{Hin1} and in the 1971 Bangladesh war. Israel has been supplying us critical military and security equipments. Its modern and innovative agricultural practices are worth emulating by India. Despite severe lack of natural resources, wars, and enemies on all sides, the new nation of Israel created only in 1948 became a shining first-world nation within a few decades, while India under the Nehru dynasty remained a poor, miserable, third-rate, third-world country.

For details on 'Israel and the Jews' please check the blog-series: http://rajnikantp.blogspot.in/2014/10/israel-jews-i-faqs-truths-fascinating.html

Blunder–55:
Neglecting Southeast Asia

Nehru gave little importance to the relations with Southeast Asian countries, and was patronizing towards them, even though India had much to learn from them looking to their far better economic growth rate. Here is an example of Nehru's snobbishness. Even as India was going around the world with a begging bowl, Nehru didn't flinch from being sarcastic on Southeast Asian countries and their economy, which had actually been doing far better. Wrote Durga Das [*words in italics in square-brackets are author's*]{DD/342}:

> "A talk with the Prime Minister of Thailand was very revealing. He complained that Nehru had characterised the Thai Government as corrupt [*What about the financial scandals in the Nehru government?*] and said the country had a 'Coca-Cola economy'... Thailand, the Prime Minister explained to me, had a long tradition of independence, and if she had taken shelter under the U.S. umbrella it had done so to safeguard her independence. If Nehru was willing to underwrite their security [*it's another matter India could not secure itself!*], the Thais would prefer to be with India since Thai culture was predominantly Indian [*He didn't know that India under Nehru didn't care for its own culture!*]... When I suggested that a visit by the King and the Prime Minister to India would improve matters, he replied that their very experienced Ambassador in New Delhi had warned them against inviting an insult by undertaking such a visit. They treated their ruler as a demi-god, and he would not go to India unless assured of a cordial welcome."{DD/342}.

India had even rebuffed the fast-growing Japan. Krishna Menon, the right-hand man of Nehru, had snubbed offers of the Japanese corporate representatives for collaboration saying it was out of question on account of the vast differences in the policies of the two countries.{DD/346}

Lee Kwan Yew took Singapore's per capita income from $400 in 1959 to $55,000. Yet in the Nehru-Indira era, Indian socialists viewed Lee with contempt as a neo-colonial puppet destined for humiliation and poverty.{URL64}

Blunder–56:
India vs. the US & the West

India would have gained much had it aligned with the West, or had at least been pro-West, or bent a little towards them, especially the US and the UK. Had that been so perhaps there would have been no Kashmir issue, and neither China nor Pakistan would have dared to attack India. Besides, had we adopted the free-market capitalist economy of the West, we would have been in a far, far better shape, and perhaps by 1980 India would have been a first-world nation. Instead, Nehru, although he talked non-alignment, showed his bias towards the Communist bloc. That was because Nehru was basically a Marxist-socialist in outlook. Notably, during the 1962 India-China war, while the communist or the non-aligned nations did not come to India's help, it was the US, of whom the Nehru&Co were very critical, that came to the rescue of India.

With the US, a country vitally important to the India's interests, Nehru's attitude was indifferent, as would be obvious from what follows. Wrote Arthur Schlesinger Jr, Special Assistant to President Kennedy and a distinguished historian, on Nehru's visit to the US in 1961 in his book: "His [Nehru's] strength was failing, and he retained control more by momentum of the past than by mastery of the present... Nehru listened without expression... In conversation he displayed interest and vivacity only with Jacqueline [Kennedy]... The private meetings between the President and the Prime Minister were no better. Nehru was terribly passive, and at limes Kennedy was hard put to keep the conversation going... It was, the President said later, like trying to grab something in your hand, only to have it turn out to be just fog... The following spring, reminiscing about the meeting, Kennedy described it to me as 'a disaster; the worst Head of State visit I have had'... It was certainly a disappointment, and Kennedy's vision of India had been much larger before the visit than it would ever be again. Nehru was obviously on the decline; his country, the President now decided, would be increasingly preoccupied with its own problems and turn more and more into itself. Though Kennedy retained his belief in the necessity of helping India achieve its economic goals, he rather gave up hope, after seeing Nehru, that India would be in the next years a great affirmative force in the world or even in South Asia.{ASJ/524=6}

About Nehru's visit to the US in 1961, wrote Stanley

Wolpert: "The long flight had wearied Nehru, but he perked up as soon as he saw Jackie [Jacqueline Kennedy] and was most excited by the prospect of her imminent visit to India with her lovely sister, both of whom he invited to stay in his house, in the suite that Edwina had always occupied. But Kennedy found Nehru so unresponsive in their talks—which for the most part turned out to be Kennedy monologues—that he later rated his summit with Nehru as 'the worst State visit' he had ever experienced. Nehru's age and reluctance to 'open up' in Washington proved most frustrating to his young host, who also found infuriating Nehru's focus on his wife and his inability to keep his hands from touching her."{Wolp2/480}

This is what Kuldip Nayar wrote on the same visit: "Kennedy organised a breakfast meeting between Nehru and top US economists and foreign policy experts. Nehru was late for the meeting and generally monosyllabic in his responses. The breakfast ended in 20 minutes. Some of them reported this to Kennedy who remarked in the presence of his aides that Nehru had 'lived too long'."{KN}

Apparently, Nehru's actions and behaviour were dictated more by his personal predilections, his arrogance, and his leftist, pro-USSR, pro-communist bend, than by what was in the best interest of an emerging nation like India. Wrote MN Roy: "For her economic development India requires foreign financial aid which can come only from the United States. The latter had repeatedly expressed readiness to extend the help as in the case of Europe. But Nehru's foreign policy has prevented India from receiving the help she requires. From this point of view his visit to the U.S.A. was an all-round failure. It yielded no concrete result, and pleased nobody except himself. He disappointed American statesmen by his refusal to take sides in cold war, and annoyed businessmen by the morbid suspicion of political strings attached to foreign capital. At home, realistic politicians and big business were displeased with Nehru because he failed to bring home the bacon. The all-round failure and disappointment were due to the Actor's [Nehru's] desire to draw applause from the world leftist gallery, and also to increase his popularity with the vocal middle class at home by pandering to their national conceit."{Roy/5-6}

The New York Times described Nehru as *"one of the greatest disappointments of the post-war era"*.{Roy/7}

Blunder–57:
'Non-Aligned' with National Interests

Rather than having strong allies on its side to deter others, India, thanks to Nehru's self-defeating foreign policy of 'Non-Alignment', remained *non-aligned* so that Pakistan (aligned with the West) and China (aligned with the USSR) felt free to attack India, knowing it to be a non-risky business as no country would come to the rescue of a non-aligned India in its hours of distress. Common sense dictated that till you became strong enough to defend yourself, have sensible pacts with some strong nations to take care of your security.

Non-aligned policy fetched no gains for India.{Swa3} If India had aligned itself with the US and the West, not only would India have been much better off economically, neither China nor Pakistan would have dared to attack India, and the Kashmir issue would have been solved in India's favour long ago. By being apparently loosely aligned with the Soviets, India effectively chose to be on the losing side of the Cold War, with all its severe political and economic disadvantages and handicaps.

Pakistan was much smarter. After its creation, its first PM Liaquat Ali Khan accepted an invitation from Moscow—deliberately. The purpose was to alarm the opposite side in the cold war: the US and the UK. Expectedly, the US and the UK made a deal with Pakistan: in return for Pakistan joining the Anglo-American Military bloc, they would support Pakistan on Kashmir and other matters against India.

Wrote Walter Crocker in 'Nehru: A Contemporary's Estimate': "As late as 1956, [John Foster] Dulles [the then US Secretary of State], who distrusted Nehru as much as Nehru distrusted him—as was not concealed when Dulles visited India in 1954—said that 'the conception of neutrality is obsolete, immoral, and short-sighted'. For Dulles, neutrality in all forms, including non-alignment, was a refusal to choose between evil and good; that is to say, between communism and anti-communism."{Croc/94}

All that non-alignment did was it helped project the image of Nehru on the world stage. It helped grant Nehru rhetorical leadership in non-aligned forums, but it did precious little for India. In fact India grievously suffered from that stand. *In short, Nehru's policy of 'Non-Alignment' was not aligned to the Indian national interests.*

Blunder–58:
Foreign to Foreign Policy

The main reason Gandhi had made Nehru India's first PM was his notion that Nehru had good international exposure and expertise in foreign affairs, and would project India well on the international stage. Nehru is credited as the founder of India's foreign policy. Founder he was, but were the foundations solid? Or, were they rickety? Or, were there no foundations at all? Was it all airy ad-hocism, and one-man's-pontifications? Crucially, was it a foreign policy that benefited India? Or, was it merely a device for Nehru for self-posturing and to project himself internationally?

If ours was a good foreign policy, how come all our major neighbours became our enemies? And, a friendly neighbour, Tibet, disappeared as an independent nation? How come all our borders turned insecure during the Nehruvian era, costing us a fortune to defend them? How come no nation came to India's rescue (including Nehru's non-aligned or socialist-communist friends) in its war with China, except the nation Nehru and Krishna Menon always panned—the United States{Red1}; or the nation Nehru refused to recognise—Israel?{Hin1} *You evaluate a policy by its results, not by its verbosity and pompousness.* Wrote Walter Crocker:{Croc/57}

> "He [Nehru] insisted on keeping the portfolio of external affairs for himself. It was a disadvantage to him that he did so, because, as head of the whole government of India, he had to deal with a range of internal problems already too much for one mind. And it was a disadvantage to the Indian foreign office and the Indian diplomatic service. In effect he did damage to both, and at a formative and impressionable stage of their growth..."{Croc/56}

> "...it was not a good service [Foreign Services in Nehru's day]—nothing like good enough for a country of India's importance. There was not enough training or professional competence, not enough esprit de corps, and too much eagerness to please the boss. Nehru was too busy and preoccupied to get to know the necessary detail, or to get to know the officers except for a handful of very senior ones or a few favourites. This encouraged sycophancy, personal ad hoc approaches, and a mixture of amateurishness and subjectivity. Indian embassies were too often sending back to Delhi the kind of reports which they

thought would be congenial to their master. It was scarcely improved by the ambiguous position allowed to Krishna Menon, who in some fields was virtually the second foreign minister for five years or so prior to his fall in 1962..."{Croc/57}

"Nehru rooted India's foreign policy in abstract ideas rather than a strategic conception of national interests. He disdained alliances, pacts, and treaties, seeing them as part of the old rules of realpolitik, and was uninterested in military matters... Nehru tended to put hope above calculation. When he was warned that Communist China would probably seek to annex Tibet, for example, he doubted it, arguing that it would be foolish and impractical adventure. And even after Beijing did annex Tibet in 1951, Nehru would not reassess the nature of Chinese interests along India's northern border..."
—Fareed Zakaria {Zak/148}

This is what *Dr Ambedkar* had to say in his resignation (from the Nehru's cabinet) speech of 27 September 1951:

"The third matter which has given me cause, not merely for dissatisfaction but for actual anxiety and even worry, is the foreign policy of the country. Any one, who has followed the course of our foreign policy and along with it the attitude of other countries towards India, could not fail to realize the sudden change that has taken place in their attitude towards us. *On 15th of August, 1947 when we began our life as an independent country, there was no country which wished us ill. Every country in the world was our friend. Today, after four years, all our friends have deserted us. We have no friends left. We have alienated ourselves.* We are pursuing a lonely furrow with no one even to second our resolutions in the U.N.O..."{Amb5}

Ambedkar criticised Nehru's foreign policy saying: "The key note of our foreign policy is to solve the problems of other countries and not to solve the problems of our own country!"{DK/456}

Nehru himself had this to admit: "We were getting out of touch with reality in the modern world and we were living in an artificial atmosphere of our creation."{Zak149}

INTERNAL SECURITY

Blunder–59:
Compounding Difficulties in Assam

In 'Blunder-5' detailed earlier we saw how Nehru's wrong decision ultimately resulted in adverse demographic changes in Assam, with the influx of Muslims from East Bengal. Taking note of that, any nationalist, concerned about the fate of the indigenous people, their property, their well-being and their culture in Assam, would have ensured that the Muslims migrations from East Bengal were stemmed at least after independence, with the power in our hands. Unfortunately, even after independence, the Government remained ostrich-like, and demographic invasion continued.

What became paramount for the Congress and Nehru after independence were votes—Muslim migrants swelled their vote bank. Why not then turn a blind eye to it, even if the people of Assam and the Northeast suffer! And, all that despite severe opposition of many local Congress leaders like Gopinath Bordoloi and Medhi, who considered such vote-bank politics to be effectively anti-national. Here are extracts from an article titled 'How Bangladeshi Muslims wiped the Assamese out in their own land'[URL40]:

"After partition, the Assamese people expected that there would not be any further trans-migration of Muslims from East Pakistan to their new political territory. Muslim populations in Assam considerably decreased in 1947 partly due to inclusion of Sylhet in Pakistan and also return of sizeable number of earlier immigrants to their original land due to fear of backlash. But the situation changed, when Mainul Haq Chaudhary, the Private Secretary of Jinnah and also a prominent leader of the youth wing of AIML till partition, joined Congress party along with the supporters of Pakistan en-mass. On the eve of partition, he was shaky whether to opt for Pakistan or stay back in India. He was however told by Jinnah, 'wait for ten years, I shall present Assam on a silver plate to you'. Jinnah died in 1948 but the Congress Party fulfilled his promise by inducting Chaudhary in the Cabinet of Congress Government led by Gopi Nath Bordoloi. It is often alleged that Chaudhary stayed back in Assam on the advice of Jinnah and other Pakistani leaders to help the immigrants from

Pakistan for their settlement in Assam...

"Against the evil geo-political design of Pakistan, which scared the Assamese middle class of the threat to their marginalisation in their own land, Government of India never had any organised plan or definite policy. Nehru-Liaquat Pact (April 1950)... rather facilitated the Pakistan Government to accelerate infiltration... It is said that the Congress leadership applauded the increase of Muslim immigrants as a God sent opportunity to consolidate the 'Muslim vote banks' and accordingly ruled Assam without any break for thirty years...

"Moinul Huq Choudhury, who later became a Minister in the Union Cabinet of Indira Gandhi Government and former President of India Fakharuddin Ali Ahmad were widely known for being instrumental in the settlement of illegal Muslim immigrants. Late B.K. Nehru, the Governor of Assam between 1968 and 1973, condemned the infiltration as vote bank politics by the Congress."{URL40}

Congress leaders Bordoloi, Medhi, Bimala Prasad Chaliha and others raised this serious issue of migration, but did not get due support from Nehru and the Congress leadership at the Centre. Wrote Kuldip Nayar in 'Beyond the Lines':

"The state subsequently paid the price...when illegal migration from the then East Pakistan reduced the Assamese-speaking population in Assam to a minority... It was not Chaliha who initiated the issue of illegal migration but his senior in the Congress, Fakhruddin Ali Ahmad, who rose to be India's president. In fact, the entire party was guilty. Its simplistic solution was to win elections in Assam by allowing would-be settlers from across the border into the state thus creating a vote bank...[Gobind Ballabh]Pant [the then Home Minister in Nehru's cabinet] knew that large number of people were coming across the border. After all, his party had connived at the migration since independence..."{KN}

In early sixties, Assam Chief Minister Bimala Prasad Chaliha launched an aggressive campaign to flush out the immigrants. However, Nehru wanted him to go easy on deportations and even stop them!

Blunder–60:
Neglect of the Northeast

The problems of Assam and the Northeast have their roots in the Nehruvian era on account of faulty understanding of the issues, distorted world view, defective grasp of national security interests, and the faulty policies and remedies that flowed from them. Nehru, driven by vote-bank politics, allowed migrations from East-Pakistan—please see previous blunder. Also, no-holds-barred proselytization by the Christian missionaries promoted fissiparous and anti-national tendencies (dealt with in the next blunder).

Nehru's policy of division of Assam into a number of smaller states to satisfy certain ethnic groups has actually been counter-productive. *One*, because there are so many different ethnicities—over 220 ethnic groups. To what extent can one keep dividing? *Two*, it started divisive identity politics. Others too have raised their demand for separation. *Three*, such small states are not economically viable.

Looking to the fact of scores of ethnic groups and languages in the Northeast, Nehru should have understood that sub-dividing the region into multiple states would be an endless process that would give rise to further divisiveness, without doing any good for the people at large, each new state being economically unviable. Egged on by Verrier Elwin, Nehru's advisor on tribal matters and a British missionary and anthropologist, Nehru's broad policy was to treat Nagas and the like as "anthropological specimen". This came in the way of development and integration of the Northeast.

What would have won the hearts of the people and brought them into the mainstream would have been not a State for each group, for that benefits only the elites; but solid, good, empathetic governance, effective criminal-justice system, assurance of security to people, delivery of services, education, health-care, providing connectivity and communications, putting in place adequate infrastructure, and economic development. But, that requires dedicated, committed, competent, empathetic and honest human resources, ensuring which should have been the top-priority task of independent India. But, no. The arrogant, callous, selfish, self-serving, exploitive, rent-seeking, corrupt, anti-people babudom, bureaucracy and the criminal-justice system continued, and rather than being replaced or reformed, became worse and vicious, as amply brought out by Ved

Marwah in his book 'India in Turmoil'{(VM)}.

Further, with socialism as the Nehruvian creed, India had condemned itself to poverty, want and international beggary, and had neither the surplus to invest in development, nor policies to promote private investments and foreign investments. The NE states are unable to take care of either their development or their expenses. All the states have been categorised as Special Category States: they get 90% of the funds as grants from the Centre, and have to only generate the remaining 10%. In other words, all are totally dependent upon the Centre for their expenditure for salaries of government employees, maintenance, and development.

The PCB nexus ("P" for politicians, "C" for contractors, and "B" for businessmen and bureaucrats), and in many regions the PCBI nexus (PCB plus "I" for insurgents) takes care of major portion of the funds. Without ensuring proper end-use of funds, the Central Government keeps announcing special economic packages for the region, most of which go to line the pockets of the PCBI. Continued militancy, and need for development to tackle it, provide a convenient pretext to get more and more funds to loot.

Blunder–61: Ignoring Illegal Proselytization

"It is impossible for me to reconcile myself to the idea of conversion after the style that goes on in India and elsewhere today. It is an error which is perhaps the greatest impediment to the world's progress toward peace. Why should a Christian want to convert a Hindu to Christianity? Why should he not be satisfied if the Hindu is a good or godly man?"—Mahatma Gandhi, Harijan, 30-Jan-1937

"Religion is important for humanity, but it should evolve with humanity. The first priority is to establish and develop the principle of pluralism in all religious traditions. If we, the religious leaders, cultivate a sincere pluralistic attitude, then everything will be more simple. It is good that most religious leaders are at least beginning to recognize other traditions, even though they may not approve of them. The next step is to accept that the idea of propagating religion is outdated. It no longer suits the times." —HH Dalai Lama

Nehru turned a blind eye to illegal and rampant proselytization by the Christian missionaries, feeding on poor, innocent souls like

soul vultures—this adversely affected national interests. Wrote Durga Das in 'India from Curzon to Nehru & After':
"The Constitution-makers swept under the carpet the important matter relating to the scheduled tribes in the Assam hills in the north-east. They adopted a formula virtually placing the region outside the pale of normal Union laws and administrative apparatus. Nehru did this on the advice of Christian missionaries. His colleagues in the top echelons let it pass, treating the matter, in the words of Azad, as 'a Nehru fad'."{DD/274}

It is worth noting that Sir Reginald Coupland (1884–1952), a historian and a professor of the Oxford University who had accompanied the Cripps Mission as an adviser in 1942, had recommended for a statutory guarantee that the work of the Christian missions in the hill tracts of Assam (Assam then included all the NE states) would continue uninterrupted.{DD/207}

Wrote MKK Nair:
"Nehru and Patel did not agree on many issues and Patel used to point out shortcomings in Nehru's approaches to him. Almost everyone knows that the problems of North East India began with Nehru's policy. Patel had vehemently opposed Nehru's plan to administer North Eastern Region under the Foreign Ministry and differentiate it from the rest of India. He explained the repercussions of such a step, but there was no one in the cabinet to oppose Nehru. When implemented, *it became easy for Christian missionaries to tell local people that they were not Indians* and their's was another country because India's Foreign Ministry dealt with it. Nehru created a new cadre, Indian Frontier Administrative Service, to administer the region but selection was like for Indian Foreign Service. However, except for one or two exceptions, everyone chosen was incompetent and did not have the required administrative calibre. *Their clumsy rule and the worse control by the Foreign Ministry were causes for anti-national activities to flourish in Nagaland, Mizoram, Manipur and hill areas of Assam.*"{MKK}

Massive conversions in the Northeast states, particularly Nagaland and Mizoram, have led to secessionist movements. Christian missionaries and a number of foreign-funded NGOs have deliberately propagated and funded the myths of Aryan-Dravidian conflicts and differences (Aryan Invasion Theory [AIT] has long since been discredited). They have been active in anti-Brahmanical and anti-Hindu propaganda. They have taken advantage of the poverty and wants of the dalits and the tribals. Why? All this helps than in conversions. It is they who have fuelled Aryan-Dravidian politics in Tamil Nadu to help them in their proselytization project. It is necessary to realise that conversions (over 99% of them are through enticements and deception, and are illegal) to Christianity or Islam are actually spiritual murders more heinous than physical murders, as they unhinge converts from their roots.

It seems Nehru did not understand the correlation among religion, nation, partition, and divisiveness; despite being a witness to creation of Pakistan. It may be fine to be personally an atheist, or agnostic, or above religion; but it is definitely irresponsible, as a national leader, to ignore the reality of religions, particularly the latter two proselytizing, supremacist, "only true" Abrahamic religions, their effect on people and regions, and their potential for divisiveness. There are 126 Christian-majority, and 49 Muslim-majority countries in the world, but just one Hindu-majority country—that is, India (leaving the tiny country Nepal). Is it not an Indian leader's responsibility to ensure that at least one country remains Hindu-majority, and safe for Hindus, and to which persecuted Hindus elsewhere in the world (like in Pakistan and Bangladesh, and, sadly, even from its own state of Kashmir) could seek refuge. Isn't it the least that Hindus, who have suffered a millennium of slavery and persecution at the hands of Muslims and Christians, must expect from the Indian leaders. People of other religions must, of course, have full freedom as equal citizens; but they can't be allowed to dominate, illegally proselytize, and displace the Hindu majority.

Christian missionaries and their illegal proselytization has created havoc in many parts of India, and it is high time India woke up to them and took effective counter measures. Nehru dynasty never cared about India's religious and cultural foundations and heritage, but non-Dynasty governments need to act differently.

Proselytization in India has been solely for economic reasons, and to a lesser extent on account of societal reasons. Religion or spiritualism, or 'seeking God', or appreciating that the religion one is converting into is "better", has nothing whatsoever to do with it. Hence, all conversions are illegal (barring perhaps 0.01%). There is, of course, no question of the latter two Abrahamic religions, the "religion of compassion", and the "religion of peace", which have caused terrible and indescribable miseries to uncountable millions of locals belonging to other faiths in Africa, Asia, Europe, North America, South America, and Australia through the centuries, being superior or the only true religions. None can come even remotely near the grandness of essential Hinduism. There can, therefore, be no conversion through rational analysis and conviction.

Conversions actually got a fillip thanks to the Nehruvian policies. If you have chosen the socialist path, which benefits only the politicians and the babus, poor can never really come up. Deprived of medical facilities, free education, other necessities, and even food, they become easy targets for conversion. Had India followed free-market policies, India would have been a prosperous first-world nation, with better administration and justice, long ago; leaving little scope for illegal conversions.

Blunder–62: Ungoverned Areas

Large swathes of tribal and other areas remained ignored, neglected and ungoverned during the Nehruvian era and later, leading ultimately to the problems in the Northeast and the huge Naxal-infested red corridor cutting across sections of Chhattisgarh, Jharkhand, Maharashtra, Andhra Pradesh, and Bihar. Further, it was not just tribal areas that were neglected and ungoverned. There were vast swathes of countryside and small towns in UP, Bihar and many other states that were, and remain, hopeless, depressing, lawless, dangerous 'Omkaralands'. What is the root cause? Dirty politics, colonial babudom and misgovernance. In fact, wherever there has been the Indian government outreach into these areas, it has been more to exploit and make money than to serve and provide services. Further, Nehruvian socialism meant economic stagnation, and no surplus to enable deployment of resources or investments in the so-called ungoverned areas, nor policies to encourage private investments for infrastructure in those areas. And, whatever little funds were deployed were siphoned off by the Nehruvian-socialistic babudom.

Blunder–63:
Insecurity of the Vulnerable Sections

Among the very basics expected from any government is safety and security of its citizens, particularly the vulnerable sections like the poor, minorities, dalits, women and children. This is fundamental. Other things come later. People should not feel vulnerable to terrorist, communal, caste, gender or domestic violence. They should be able to breathe freely and live fearlessly—otherwise what is the point of gaining "independence".

Safety is what independent India should have firmly ensured within the first five to ten years of its existence. Not a difficult goal to achieve at all, given the desire and the will. The safety and social justice should have been ensured whatever it took: persuasion, education, publicity, unbiased and empathetic governance and criminal-justice system—even violence where needed.

However, post-independence, there was no change, rather, there was a change for the worse. The heartless anti-weak, anti-poor and corrupt criminal-justice-police system and babudom continued as in the colonial days. There was no reform or replacement. Poor, minorities, dalits, women and children continued to remain highly vulnerable. There were reportedly 243 communal riots between 1947 and 1964 and there was little improvement in the lot of the poor and the Dalits.

This is what Dr Ambedkar had to say in his resignation letter (from the Nehru's cabinet) of 27 September 1951:

"What is the Scheduled Castes [status] today? So far as I see, it is the same as before. The same old tyranny, the same old oppression, the same old discrimination which existed before, exists now, and perhaps in a worst form. I can refer to hundreds of cases where people from the Scheduled Caste round about Delhi and adjoining places have come to me with their tales of woes against the Caste Hindus and against the Police who have refused to register their complaints and render them any help. I have been wondering whether there is any other parallel in the world to the condition of Scheduled Castes in India. I cannot find any. And yet why is no relief granted to the Scheduled Castes? Compare the concern the Government shows over safeguarding the Muslims. The Prime Minister's whole time and attention is devoted for the protection of the Muslims. I yield to none, not even to the Prime Minister, in my desire to give the Muslims of India the utmost protection wherever and whenever they stand in need of it. But what I want to know is, are the Muslims the only people who need protection? Are the Scheduled Castes, Scheduled Tribes... not in need of protection? What concern has he shown for these communities? So far as I know, none and yet these are the communities which need far more care and attention than the Muslims."

It was unfortunate that rather than working and co-ordinating with Dr Ambedkar to get rid of the curse of untouchability in India, and bring succour to the vulnerable sections, Nehru chose to get rid of Dr Ambedkar himself. Nehru even campaigned against him in elections to ensure his defeat! Dr Ambedkar was a multi-dimensional talent, and his services could have been used for many other critical areas too—he was academically and experience-wise most suited to become Finance Minister. It would actually have been great if Sardar Patel had been India's first PM, and after him, Dr Ambedkar.

For a political leader, is it sufficient to be personally non-communal, but do little to ensure communal harmony? If communal riots continue to take place, if the minorities, the dalits and the weaker sections continue to be on the receiving end, what's the use of your being personally non-communal or pro-weaker sections. The real test of secular and socialist leader, and for his empathies with the weak, is what did he achieve on the ground. India and its rulers since independence cut a sorry figure on this aspect.

Most Indians wish the communalism had been firmly curbed within a decade of independence, and secularism and communalism were made non-issues by 1957. If universal education up to class 10 had been made compulsory after independence, if people had been specifically educated on secularism, anti-casteism and women's rights, the post-independence generation would have been different, and even those remaining communal and casteist sections could have been tackled. Had Congress done the actual work on the ground of overhauling our criminal-justice-police system and babudom, launched vigorous educational campaign on the issue, held netas and those in administration and police accountable for disturbances and riots, punished the guilty and made examples of them, and adopted a non-compromising attitude to the issue, the curse of communalism and casteism, and of ill-treatment of poor and dalits would have vanished within a decade of independence. It was not an unachievable target. But, when you yourselves allocate seats and win elections on communal, religious and caste considerations, where is the remedy? Most of the so-called secular-socialistic parties have been great talkers, but, non-doers. They want to keep the secular, communal and casteism pot boiling to win votes, because, in practical terms on the ground, they are incapable of solving any real issues.

In fact, this whole debate on parties, people and groups being secular or communal, casteist or otherwise, pro-dalit or anti-dalit, pro-women or male-chauvinists, traditionalist or modern, conservative or liberal is irrelevant to the issue of safety of vulnerable sections of the society, that is, poor, minorities, dalits, women and children. The real issue is "governance", which includes enforcing "rule of law". Therefore, if a party claims to be secular, the touchstone of its credentials is "governance". If its "governance" is poor it is unfit to be called a "secular" party. Like one measures GDP, per-capita income, literacy, poverty, human development index (HDI), quality of living index and so on, one needs to measure GI, "Governance Index", for each of the states and for the central government. It is this GI which would actually reflect the "Secularism Index" (SI), and the "Anti-Casteism Index" (ACI). SI and ACI can't be measured by your decibel levels and your protestations. It has to be measured by your real actions on the ground reflected in the GI—a tough call.

Take Singapore. Lee Kuan Yew managed to create a unique Singaporean identity within the umbrella of multiculturalism in just the first 15 years of his rule, despite the fact that Singapore never had a dominant culture to which locals and immigrants could assimilate. They have ensured religious and racial harmony through the decades. Singapore has consistently been ranked as the safest country in the world; and among the top five in the Global Competitiveness Report in terms of its reliability of police services.

ECONOMY

Blunder–64:
Throttled Industrialisation

Nehru, through his anti-private-sector policies, throttled industrialisation, and consequently employment generation. Although, in comparison with the deliberate neglect in the British period, the progress in industrialisation during the Nehru period was much better owing to significant public sector investments. Post-independence industrialisation was also helped by the very significant second world war sterling debt repayments by the UK, and aid by other countries like the US, the USSR and Germany. However, when the repayment of the sterling debt by the UK tapered off, and not much further foreign aid was forthcoming, and the public sector into which Nehru had sunk the investment was either in loss or not able to generate adequate surplus, the industrialisation momentum began to taper off, as there were no funds; and given Nehru's socialistic approach, the private sector was anyway shackled!

Further, not learning anything from Japan and others, who had dramatically prospered with their outward-looking, export-led growth, India under Nehru went in for inward-looking, import-substitution model, denying itself a world-class, competitive culture, incentive for production of quality products, share in the world-trade, and the consequent prosperity. Instead, India invested heavily in the inefficient public sector, over-regulated and strangulated private enterprise, shunned foreign capital, and ignored better technology.

Despite Sardar Patel's objections, Nehru pushed through the Industrial Policy Resolution in April 1948 that reserved many areas under the state sector: railways, defence manufacturing, atomic energy, and so on. Further, new enterprises in steel, coal, ship-building, communications, and many others could only be under the state sector. By 1954, Nehru made Parliament accept as the aim of economic development the "socialist pattern of society". Socialism was enshrined in 1955 as the official policy of the Congress at its Avadi session. The 1956 version of the Industrial Policy Resolution made the state even more dominant—it allowed new ventures in textiles, automobiles and defence only to the state, and vested exclusive controls to it over many other sectors. Wrote MKK Nair:

"As a Socialistic pattern of economy had been adopted by the Parliament in December 1954, the new industrial policy embraced the same objective... An important aspect of socialism was establishing Government control over sectors that brought financial wellbeing. With that in view, the importance of public sector was enhanced and industries that would be brought into it were listed. They included explosives, arms, defence equipment, atomic energy, iron & steel, heavy metallic castings, mining machinery, heavy electrical equipment, coal & lignite, petroleum, mining for Iron, Manganese, diamond & minerals for atomic energy, aircraft manufacture, air transportation, railways, ship building, telephone and electricity generation."{MKN}

A series of Five-Year Plans started from 1952 that sank precious investment in the inefficient public sector, and rather than enhancing the growth rate, made it crawl at 3%. Much needed foreign-investment was shunned, thanks to anti-colonial mindset. Many industries were barred for the private sector. When entrepreneurs in the countries in Southeast Asia, like South Korea, were being encouraged to expand and set up industries and their government was offering them cheap credit, here in India we were doing the opposite: GD Birla was refused a license for setting up a steel plant; scores of business proposals of Tatas were rejected; Aditya Birla, looking to the hostile business environment in India, chose to set up industries outside India; ...the list is endless.

Krishna Menon [the right-hand man of Nehru] had reportedly snubbed offers of the Japanese corporate representatives for collaboration saying it was out of question on account of the vast differences in the policies of the two countries!{DD/346}

Given license-permit-quota-raj, reluctance to give licenses to the so-called "monopolies", anti-business policies and extortionist taxes—maximum slab rate being over 80%—industrialisation had to suffer. Industrialisation and industries were sought to be controlled and managed by Nehru's IAS babus who knew next to nothing on how to run an industry. Nehru and the socialists had very simplistic notions on wealth creation: Nehru thought that all it took to have economic prosperity was to invest in industrialisation, especially in heavy industries, and to put babus in charge. Wrote a bureaucrat of those times MKK Nair:

"When factories in other areas began to be set up, experienced managers were not available and ICS officers were appointed to head public sector industries. But their training and experience were not suitable for industrial management. Many of them were too old to grasp the new culture of management. Thus, public sector companies began to be operated like Government departments...

"Both SN Mazumdar, General Manager of Rourkela [Steel Plant] and SN Mehta, General Manager of Bhilai [Steel Plant] were highest level ICS officers. They could work efficiently as Commissioners, Board Members or Chief Secretaries and discharge their duties with great aplomb. But they were frightened to spend two hundred crore Rupees in three years to build a million tonne steel plant. They were past the age to learn new ways of work. What happened in Rourkela and Bhilai got repeated elsewhere too when new public sector projects began to take shape... Industrial management is best left to those who are qualified to do it. If IAS or IPS officers who are neither familiar with nor trained for it are selected for it, it is a sin perpetrated on the public sector..."{MKN}

With the IAS babus in-charge, the expected results followed: Public sector companies began to be run like government departments—lethargic, over-staffed, and corrupt—with no understanding of process or products. Investment in the public sector leviathan was a huge two-thirds of the country's investable funds, but to little avail—the public sector churned out shoddy goods and remained in loss. Of the entire paid-up capital in India, the share of the public sector rose to a massive 70% by 1978, with little benefits accruing to the nation. Our extremely scarce resources were squandered and precious public money was literally burnt by the Nehru and his dynasty in trying to do business.

Gurcharan Das mentions in *India Unbound*{GD} of Kasturbhai Lalbhai establishing Atul chemical plant in collaboration with American Cyanamid in the wilds of Gujarat, building a whole township, and provided jobs to many tribals. When invited to inaugurate it in 1952, Nehru agreed after considerable reluctance. Why? Because, it was in the private sector!{GD/53-54}

Blunder–65:
Neglect of Agriculture

Nehru and his team were seemingly innocent of the basics of economics that without a prosperous agriculture, you can't have agricultural surplus, and without that, you can't feed the growing urban population and sustain industrialisation. Yet, they neglected agriculture. Agriculture was so neglected that by 1957 India's agricultural output fell below that of 1953!

Most countries like Japan and others who rapidly progressed and joined the first-world, first concentrated on agriculture and universal education. Nehru neglected both. Nehru copied the Soviets, without realising that all communist countries faced famines thanks to their stress on heavy industries at the expense of agriculture.

I had quarrelled with him [Nehru] regarding his neglect of the village economy, especially agriculture, and protested to him about his almost total neglect of irrigation which was the key to Indian agriculture... Nehru told me disparagingly, 'You are a villager, you know nothing.' I retorted, 'If you had one-tenth of my regard for the village, the Indian economy would have been different.'...I am not sure if he had any convictions, except for aping the Russian model.
—S. Nijalingappa, 'My Life and Politics: An Autobiography'[Nij]

Nehru went socialistic where he should not have—in industrialisation; and did not go socialistic where he should have—in agriculture and land reforms. The renowned economist Jagdish Bhagwati had suggested that probably Indian needed capitalism in industry and socialism in land. But, Nehru did the reverse—besides wrong notions, the main factor was votes: Why annoy the powerful landlords and landed class? Wrote Kuldip Nayar in 'Beyond the Lines'[KN]: "...I got hold of the report (on land reforms) by Wolf Ladejinsky... His report vehemently criticized the government for having reforms on paper but doing very little on the ground... Surprisingly, it was Nehru who had stopped the report from being made public... Nehru abandoned the proposal to initiate drastic land reforms when he found that the states were opposed to the measure. This sent a wrong message to the country and proved yet again that he hated to join issue when vested interests were involved."[KN]

Blunder–66:
Builder of 'Modern' India

Admirers claim Nehru was the builder of modern India. Is one referring to "modern" India with broken-down, side-lane-like highways, run-down Fiats and Ambassadors, meagre second world-war armaments to take care of its security, perennial food shortages, famines, millions in grinding poverty, both hands holding begging bowls? He did set up a string of research labs, but they did little, and became money sinks. Pathetic communication networks and transport severely affected economic growth, fight against poverty, mobility and national integration.

Many countries, including those in Southeast Asia, which were much behind India at the time India got independence, marched far ahead of India. When you look at their airports, their roads, their metros, their city-buses, their well laid-out cities, their infrastructure, their cleanliness, their everything, you wonder why you have remained a country of crumbling roads, overcrowded locals, overhanging scary ugly mess of mesh of electrical, TV and internet cables blotting the skyline and brutally assaulting even the "chalta hai" sense of terribly intolerable tolerance of the "have given up" generations; a country of absent pavements or encroached pavements or pavements that stink from the use they are not meant for, and where mercifully for the walkers this is not so, they are but patches of broken down pavers, punctuated by uncovered, or partially covered, or precariously or deceptively covered man-holes, awaiting their catch; a nation of stinking slums and impoverished villages, open drains and sewers, rotting garbage, squalor and stink all around, children and men defecating by the road-side—all testimony to criminal absence of the very basics of being modern and civilised...

Most of the Indian towns, cities and metros are dirty, foul smelling and hideous. They look like a defacement of spaces and a blot on the landscape. Cities in the West, Southeast Asia, China and elsewhere get better, cleaner, smarter and spiffier year after year, while ours get worse, more congested, more polluted, more difficult to live in and more squalid.

How's it that we got so left behind? What is it that we did, or did not do, after independence, that everything is so abysmal and pathetic? And all this unmitigated misery despite the overwhelming advantage of India as a nation with first-rate people, plentiful natural resources, grand civilisational heritage, rich culture and languages, unmatched ethical and spiritual traditions, and, above all, relatively better position in all fields—infrastructure, trained manpower, bureaucracy, army—at the time of independence compared to all other nations who have since overtaken us.

Why did we fail to leverage such rich assets of a gifted country? Well, all thanks to Nehruvian policies. Nehruvianism is responsible for keeping India forever a developing, third-world country.

Blunder–67:
Grinding Poverty & Terrible Living Conditions

(Statistics below are till the Nehru Dynasty times of up to UPA-II. Things began to improve since 2014, albeit very gradually.)

Thanks to the Nehruvian economic policies, millions of Indians were condemned to grinding poverty.

We have the largest number of poor—a third of the world's poor! As per the World Bank's estimate, while 69% Indians live on less than US$2 per day, 33% fall below the international poverty line of US$1.25 per day. In terms of GDP per capita, India stands at 129 among 183 countries as per IMF tabulation for 2011. Per capita income in India is little more than half that of Sri Lanka, about a sixth that of Malaysia, and a third that of Jamaica. Things have been improving, but precious decades were lost in poverty-perpetuating Nehruvian economic policies.

Says Darryl D'Monte in an article, *Living off the land*, that appeared in the Hindustan Times: "...Oxford University and the UN Development Programme brought out a *Multidimensional Poverty Index* or MPI which replaced the Human Poverty Index. The researchers analysed data from 104 countries with a combined population of 5.2 billion, constituting 78% of the world's total. It found that about 1.7 billion people in these countries live in multidimensional poverty. If income alone is taken into account, at less than $1.25 a day, a standard measure throughout the world, this amounts to 1.3 billion. The startling fact that emerges from this analysis, which made headlines throughout the world, is that using the MPI, just eight Indian states have more poor people than the 26 poorest African countries combined. These sub-Saharan countries—

like Ethiopia—are considered the worst-off in the world, with pictures of starving children there becoming symptomatic of a deep malaise."

Worldwide rankings for 2012 by the Mercer Quality of Living Survey lists 49 cities. No Indian city makes the grade. Mercer City Infrastructure Ranking, 2012 lists 50 cities. No Indian city appears in the list. Among the prominent cities in the world, the 25 dirtiest include New Delhi and Mumbai having mostly the African cities for company.

Two cities in India, Sukinda and Vapi, rank 3rd and 4th in the world as the most polluted cities! Even our water bodies and rivers, including the most sacred ones, get dirtier by the year. The sacred rivers have been reduced to sewers. The waters of the Ganga are pure and sparkling when it starts from Gangotri, with a BOD, that is, Biochemical Oxygen Demand, of zero, and a DO, Dissolved Oxygen, of over 10. Water with BOD level of less than 2mg per litre can be consumed without treatment; that with BOD level between 2 and 3 mg per litre can be consumed, but only after treatment; and that with BOD level above 3 mg per litre is unfit even for bathing. Ganga-Yamuna water at Sangam in Allahabad has a BOD level of 7.3 mg per litre! It is totally unfit even for bathing!!

To summarise a ToI report, "A pitcherful of poison: India's water woes set to get worse", India ranks third-lowest, a lowly 120, in a list of 122 countries rated on quality of potable water. By 2020, India is likely to become a water-stressed nation. Nearly 50% of Indian villages still do not have any source of protected drinking water. Of the 1.42 million villages in India, 1.95 lacs are affected by chemical contamination of water. 37.7 million are afflicted by waterborne diseases every year. Nearly 66 million people in 20 Indian states are at risk because of excessive fluoride in their water. Nearly 6 million children below 14 suffer from dental, skeletal and non-skeletal fluorosis. In Jhabua district, bone deformities are common among children. Arsenic is the other big killer lurking in ground water, putting at risk nearly 10 million people. The problem is acute in several districts of West Bengal. The deeper aquifers in the entire Gangetic plains contain arsenic. In UP's Ballia district, the problem is so acute that almost every family has been affected—most people are suffering from skin rashes, some have lost their limbs; many are dying a slow death due to arsenic-induced cancer. Bacteriological contamination, which leads to diarrhoea, cholera and hepatitis, is most widespread in India.

The HDI, *Human Development Index*, is a composite statistic of life expectancy, education, and income indices and was published by the UNDP, United Nations Development Programme. In 2016, India ranked 130 on HDI among 187 countries, below even Iraq and Egypt!

The Hunger and Malnutrition (HUNGaMA) report by the Naandi Foundation points out that 42 per cent of under-fives Indian children are severely or moderately underweight and that 59 per cent of them suffer from moderate to severe stunting.

As per another study released on *Mother's Day*, India ranks 76th among 80 "less developed countries" in the world on Mother-care Index, that is 5th worst.

Health-care system—we beat even the poorest countries in Africa in infant mortality rates! The rate is a measure of number of deaths of infants under one year old in a given year per 1,000 live births. Among 221 countries, India ranks 50—rank 1 being the worst—with an infant mortality rate of 46. That is, among 221 countries, 171 countries are better off than India. China's infant mortality rate is 15.62, Singapore's 2.65, while India's is 46.07. Over 400,000 newborns die within the first 24 hours of their birth every year in India, the highest anywhere in the world, a study by an international non-government organisation, "Save the Children", has declared.

Take MMR, the Maternal Mortality Rate, which is the annual number of female deaths per 100,000 live births from any cause related to or aggravated by pregnancy or its management. The MMR includes deaths during pregnancy, childbirth, or within 42 days of termination of pregnancy. India ranks 52—rank 1 being the worst—among 183 countries, with an MMR of 200 deaths per 100,000 live births. MMR is 37 for China and just 3 for Singapore.

Take housing. Government's recent housing survey reveals that 53% of Indian homes are without toilets, 68% are without access to clean tap water, 39% do not have indoor kitchens, and 70% make do with one or two room homes. Figures don't reveal the real horror. Of course, all—men, women and children—suffer; but, the main sufferers are women: having to defecate in the open in the absence of toilets, having to fetch water in the absence of tap-water at home, having to cook without a kitchen!

There are nearly 97 million urban poor living in 50,000 slums in India, 24% of which are located along nallahs and drains and 12%

along railway lines. And, thanks to our lack of planning and neglect, the number of slums and the slum population is on the rise. The worst affected are the children—our future—in these slums.

Singapore and Finland recruit teachers in schools from among the brightest 10% of graduates and offer them salaries on par with engineers. And, in India?

Quality of graduates from engineering and management colleges is so poor many remain unemployable. Our education system—it is a mess.

In literacy, India is 183 among 214 countries—below many African countries. Reports *The Economic Times* of 18 January 2013: "The Annual Status of Education Report (ASER 2012) by NGO Pratham shows that the number of Class V students who could not read a Class II level text or solve a simple arithmetic problem has increased. In 2010, 46.3% of kids in this category failed to make the cut and this shot up to 51.8% in 2011 and 53.2% in 2012...In 2010, 29.1% children in Class V could not solve a two-digit subtraction problem without seeking help. This proportion increased to 39% in 2011 and 46.5% in 2012."

The hitherto Dynasty-driven Nehruvian-socialistic-populist-babudom-dominated dynacratic India rarely disappoints in scoring the top grade—when it comes to the negatives. With the change of guard and exit of the Nehru-Gandhi Dynasty the things have been thankfully improving, and are likely to improve further.

Blunder–68:
Pathetic India vs. Other Countries

India, which was far better placed with respect to many countries in Southeast Asia when Nehru took over the charge of India, was left far, far behind all of them by the end of the Nehru's tenure. Nehru miserably failed to do justice to India's potential.

Let's take a concrete comparative example. After its separation from Malaysia in 1965, Singapore was left as an independent country that was not only poor and backward, and with meagre defensive capabilities, it had NO natural resources—not even water! It had to import water from Malaysia. Lee Kuan Yew, often referred to by his initials as LKY, who became its Prime Minister, lead it through its traumatic separation. Thanks to his enlightened grasp on "what makes a nation strong and prosperous", sound and far-sighted diplomacy and foreign policy, innovative ideas, wise strategy and unmatched competence in governance, he lifted Singapore from a poor, backward, "Third World" nation in 1965 to a "First World" Asian Tiger by 1980—in mere 15 years!

In comparison, what did India achieve during the 17 years of Nehru rule? India had tremendous natural and water resources and the significant colonial legacy of defence, military, trained bureaucracy, industries and infrastructure, particularly railways. However, at the end of Nehru's 17-year rule India remained a poor, third-world country of starving millions begging the world for food and aid.

LKY managed to convert barren Singapore, with no water resources, into a clean, beautiful, green, garden nation. And, what has India done after independence? Converted India into a gigantic garbage bin!

Japan, which had almost the same GDP as India in the early 1950s, grew so fast that by 1980, India's GDP was a mere 17% of Japan's. Japan grew at massive 18% annually during the 15-year period starting 1965 and took its GDP from 91 billion dollars to a mammoth 1.1 trillion dollars by 1980.

Park Chung-Hee of South Korea took his poor, pathetic country— amongst the world's poorest (poorer than India at the time of India's independence)—and placed it on an automatic path to the first-world status: today it is a rich, gleaming, confident country that would leave many advanced first-world western countries behind. South Korea's per capita income is currently 1400% that of India, although at the time of our Independence it was on par!

That Japan achieved what it did, and so also South Korea, Taiwan and Singapore, was because their leaders refused to follow the politically convenient and self-serving populist socialistic path to nowhere. Thanks to the wisdom that dawned upon China, it junked its socialistic past, tremendously improved its governance, and is now a super power both economically and militarily.

Blunder–69:
Nehruvian (and NOT 'Hindu') Rate of Growth

India's poverty is self-inflicted, thanks to the self-destructive policies followed, even though prescriptions for prosperity were available off-the-shelf for many years, and there were any number of real, practical examples to go by. Had Nehru's government focused on its primary responsibilities and desisted getting into business, had it allowed the freedom to public to do business, had it followed free-market economy, India would have shot into double-digit growth rate in the 1950s itself—such were its advantages over other countries—and would long since have been a part of the developed first world, rather than still being a poor, pathetic, struggling, limping, third-rate, third-world country.

While the developing countries of SE-Asia, which had been far behind India in 1947, raced ahead at 9–12% growth rate or more and became highly prosperous, with infra-structure rivalling western countries, India plodded along at what was derisively referred to as the *Hindu rate of growth* of just 3%, and became a basket-case, begging aid and food from all. However, the term "Hindu rate of growth" is highly inappropriate and unfair, besides being derogatory. Let us examine why?

One: The "Nehruvian rate of growth". The low rate of growth was thanks to Nehru-Indira-Rajiv's policies. If rather than the "Hindu rate of growth" it was called the "Nehruvian rate of growth" or "Nehruvian socialistic rate of growth" or "NIDP [Nehru-Indira-Dynasty policies] rate of growth", one would have no quarrel.

Two: The "Colonial rate of growth". The rate of growth during the pre-independence period, the colonial period, was even less! In fact, it had even turned negative during several long periods!! Why was the rate of growth then not called the "Colonial rate of growth" or the "Christian rate of growth" in a pejorative sense? As per the Cambridge University historian Angus Maddison, "India's share of the world income fell from 22.6% in 1700, comparable to Europe's share of 23.3%, to a low of 3.8% in 1952."

Hindu-India had been highly prosperous in the past, thanks to its *massive* "Hindu rate of growth", which is why first the Muslim hordes from the northwest of India, and then the Western countries invaded it. Until the rise of the West, India was possibly the richest country in the world, which is why it presented an irresistible target for the ravaging Muslim hordes, and then the West. Why then was the term "Hindu rate of growth" not used in an adulatory sense?

Three: How do you explain the recent growth rate of over 9%? The same India, after only part junking of the Nehru-Indira-Rajiv socialistic policies, reached a growth rate of over 9%! Junk more of the Nehru-Indira socialistic policies, and the growth rate will rise to double-digits.

Four: Absurdity of religious-cultural connotation. Many Islamic countries prior to the world demand and discovery of oil were very poor. Was their growth rate called the "Islamic rate of growth"? The growth rate during the dark ages of Europe was static or negative, when during the same period India was immensely rich and progressive. Was it ever called the "Christian rate of growth"? Sri Lanka and Myanmar have had long periods of no growth or measly growth. Were they castigated for being under the spell of the "Buddhist rate of growth"? China's growth rate after going communist and till the end of the Mao-period was pathetic. Was it termed the "Atheistic or Communist rate of growth"? Why associate "Hindu" with a rate of economic growth unless there is an ulterior motive of deliberately showing Hinduism in bad light? Of course, many use the term unfeelingly, without being conscious of its implications.

Five: Nehru vs. Hinduism. Nehru was an agnostic, and was more English than Indian, more western than eastern, more "something else" than a Hindu, and therefore it is grossly inappropriate to name a rate of growth, which was thanks to him and his dynasty, as "Hindu".

Six: Why not "Secular" rate of growth? Nehru, Nehru-dynasty and company have raved ad nauseum on "secularism", without ensuring it in practice. Why not credit the growth rate thanks to them as the "Secular rate of growth"?

Seven: Socialism vs. Hinduism. Hindu-India has had long tradition of free international trade and commerce, and of liberal religious and world view. Such an ethos can never accept the Big Brother denouement or the run-up to it. There is an age old Indian proverb: *Raja Vyapari taya Praja Bhikhari.* That is, people become beggars when government enters into business. A belief in self-reliance and an overweening socialistic state on the part of Jawaharlal Nehru and Indira Gandhi actually did India in, rather than something that had anything to do with Hinduism.

Eight: Socialism vs. Mahatma Gandhi and Others. Mahatma Gandhi was no socialist. Nor were the other stalwarts like Sardar Patel, Rajaji and Rajendra Prasad. All the four—Mahatma Gandhi, Sardar Patel, Rajaji and Rajendra Prasad—quite unlike Nehru, could be considered as also representing the Hindu ethos, and perhaps precisely for that reason they were against socialistic claptrap of Nehru.

Nine: A camouflage. In any case, using "Hindu" as in "Hindu rate of growth" in a pejorative sense is not only insulting, it camouflages the real reasons—Nehruvian policies.

But, the question arises as to why did the term "Hindu rate of growth" gain currency? Well, here are the reasons.

One: Raj Krishna. The term was reportedly coined by the economist Raj Krishna to draw attention to the embarrassing rate of growth during the Nehru-Indira period. India being predominantly populated by the Hindus, he called it the "Hindu rate of growth". But, of course, he didn't mean it to be insulting to Hinduism.

Two: Blame Hinduism rather than Socialism. Indian politicians and bureaucrats never wanted to admit that the fault lay with the socialistic apparatus. Why blame self? Especially, why blame something on which you have fattened yourselves? The leftists, socialists and communists got prized slots in the government or government-aided organisations, societies and universities, and dominated the intellectual discourse in India. The whole band didn't mind the blame shifting to the religious-cultural heritage.

Three: The Secularists. For certain class of intellectuals the touchstone of secularism is whether you can be abusive to Hinduism. The term "Hindu" in "Hindu rate of growth" serves that purpose. It serves for them the double purpose: camouflage the ills resulting from socialism, and be also hailed "secular" the cheap way—by casting a slur on Hinduism.

Four: The Colonialists and the India-baiters. Other groups, which received the term with glee, lapped it up, and enthusiastically promoted it to disparage India, were the colonialists or those with the colonial mind-set or the brown sahibs, or the India-baiters. Give power to the Hindus, and what you will get is the "Hindu rate of growth"! Had the Raj continued, things would have been better!!

Blunder–70:
Nehru's Socialism: The 'God' that Failed

The whole political vision of the left, including socialism and communism, has failed by virtually every empirical test, in countries all around the world. But this has only led leftist intellectuals to evade and denigrate empirical evidence... When the world fails to conform to their vision, then it seems obvious to the ideologues that it is the world that is wrong, not that their vision is uninformed or unrealistic.
—Thomas Sowell

All the above economic blunders of Nehru were thanks to his thrusting socialistic policies on poor India. Nehru uncritically accepted socialism. It is strange that while Nehru's books approvingly talk of Marxism and socialism, there is no comparative analysis by him of much more proven competing economic thoughts. It was as if Adam Smith, Alfred Marshall, JS Mill, John Maynard Keynes and others did not exist for Nehru. Nor did he care to read Milton Friedman (1912–2006) or Friedrich Hayek (1899–1992).

Marxism and socialism were something Nehru was sold out on since the 1920s, wrote approvingly about in his books, advocated vigorously all through, and, unfortunately for India, implemented it post-independence in his own Nehruvian way. This is what Nehru said in his presidential address at the Lucknow session of the Congress in 1936:

"I am convinced that the only key to the solution of the world's problems and of India's problems lies in socialism, and when I use this word I do so not in a vague humanitarian way but in the scientific, economic sense. Socialism is, however, something even more than an economic doctrine; it is a philosophy of life and as such also it appeals to me. I see no way of ending the poverty, the vast unemployment, the degradation and the subjection of the Indian people except through socialism. That involves vast and revolutionary changes in our political and social structure, the ending of vested interests in land and industry, as well as the feudal and autocratic Indian States system. That means the ending of private property, except in a restricted sense, and the replacement of the present profit system by a higher ideal of co-operative service. It means ultimately a change in our instincts and habits and desires. In short, it means a new civilisation, radically different from the present capitalist order. Some glimpse we can have of this new civilisation in the territories of the U.S.S.R. Much has happened there which has pained me greatly and with which I disagree, but I look upon that great and fascinating unfolding of a new order and a new civilization as the most promising feature of our dismal age. If the future is full of hope it is largely because of Soviet Russia and what it has done, and I am convinced that, if some world catastrophe does not intervene, this new civilisation will spread to other lands and put an end to the wars and conflicts which capitalism feeds... Socialism is thus for me not merely an economic doctrine which I favour; it is a vital creed which I hold with all my head and heart..."{URL28}

Nehru stuck to his position on socialism and communism despite the increasing evidence of their global failure, and the immense misery and totalitarianism they brought about. And, despite irrationally and unscientifically ignoring the facts and evidence, he flaunted himself as of a rational and scientific temperament.

Marxists call their socialism *scientific* socialism, as if the self-assigned, self-adulatory adjective *scientific* is sufficient to testify to it being *scientific*—correct; however preposterous it might be from a genuine scientific angle, where the litmus test is the real practical proof. Mere dialectics of self-serving arguments and logic does not result in truth! Marxism and socialism as a science or as an alternate economic thought for a nation to build on has miserably failed—it has globally been proven wrong both in theory and in practice.

Those who do not genuinely understand science or scientific-methods are taken-in by mere allusion to something as *scientific*. Many became Marxists because being so implied being *scientific*-spirited, rational, progressive, pro-poor intellectual, aligned to the forces of history! *Rather than being aligned to the forces of history or being on the right side of it, to the dismay of the Marxists, the unfolding history proved them to be on the wrong side; and their "science"— "scientific" socialism—turned out to be an alchemy!*

Further, Marx didn't elaborate on the nature of society and organisation that would replace capitalism, and how it would be managed, except talking vaguely about the *"dictatorship of the proletariat"—without allowing for the possibility of the Frankenstein it would unleash, and the surreal "1984" it would beget.*

The capitalist economic thought, the capitalist societies and the associated democratic system themselves evolved and adapted since the time of Marx in such a way that they not only brought unprecedented prosperity to the concerned nations, they also significantly uplifted the status of the masses—falsifying, in the process, many of the foundations and assumptions of Marx.

In science, society, economics and indeed all disciplines knowledge evolves, concepts change, new theories replace old ones in the light of new experiments, experiences and knowledge gained. To be scientific is to keep an open mind on things, to be willing to change, to be ready to jettison the old in the light of new evidence, and to go by actual practical results. For anything to be scientifically correct, it has to be proved truly and convincingly in practice, without a shadow of doubt. Till the same is done, it remains merely a conjecture, a hypothesis, a theory. *Has the so-called scientific socialism or Marxism proved successful anywhere in the world in practice?* No. Facts, figures, statistics and ground-level experiences of various countries prove that all brands of leftist politics—Communist, Socialist, Fabian, Nehruvian, and so on—are inherently incapable of delivering anything positive for any nation or for its poor. In fact, they have actually been at the root of poverty, want and stagnation.

Dismal fate of all nations that went socialist proves the point. Take USSR. It claimed to be following *scientific* socialism or Marxism. But, what were its practical results? It drew an iron-curtain so that no one got to see the disaster: the wide-spread poverty and famine and suppression of human rights. Had things been really good, why would USSR be so secretive about it, and not let those interested—journalists, writers, academicians, researchers, politicians, sociologists, and general public—have unrestricted access and see the state of affairs for themselves, especially when they wanted other nations to emulate them, and go communist! Why only guided tours, under strict supervision? Whom were they fooling? Perhaps people like Nehru. One guided tour in 1920s, and Nehru returned fully sold out, like school-boys taken on guided tours! Subsequent guided-tours of both Nehru and his daughter post-independence to the USSR, and both were re-sold!! Ultimately the USSR fell apart, and all its parts are still struggling to throw away the bad old days of communism. Nehru wrote in 'Discovery of India':

"...I had no doubt that the Soviet Revolution had advanced human society by a great leap and had lit a bright flame which could not be smothered, and that it had laid the foundations for that new civilization towards which the world could advance."{JN}

Contrast this with what Bertrand Russel had to say after his visit to Russia:

"...the time I spent in Russia was one of continually increasing nightmare. I have said in print what, on reflection, appeared to me to be the truth, but I have not expressed the sense of utter horror which overwhelmed me while I was there. Cruelty, poverty, suspicion, prosecution formed the very air we breathed. Our conversations were continually spied upon... There was a hypocritical pretence of equality... I felt that everything that I valued in human life was being destroyed in the interest of a glib and narrow philosophy, and that in the process untold misery was being inflicted upon many millions of people..."{BNS/191-2}

There is not a single example of a country which prospered or whose poor were better off under communism or socialism. The democratic countries like the UK which were going downhill with their socialistic policies did course correction under Thatcher and prospered. Extrapolating the time it took Singapore, South Korea and Taiwan to become first-world countries by adopting competitive capitalism, and the time it took West Germany and Japan to rise from the ashes of the Second World War by adopting capitalist economy, it seems reasonable that India would have been a prosperous, first-rate, first-world country by 1980 had it too adopted competitive capitalism and befriended the West.

Unfortunately for the crores of starving Indians and millions of others who had great hopes for themselves, their families and the nation after independence, Nehru guided India into a poverty-and-misery-perpetuating socialistic-bureaucratic black-hole. His descendants, Indira and Rajiv Gandhi, by doing much more of the same, made the situation worse. UPA-I and II, by part reverting to the Nehru-Indira disastrous ways, reversed the Narsimha Rao–Vajpayee upward trend.

Sardar Patel, Rajagopalachari and Rajendra Prasad were opposed to socialism. If only they had led India after Independence, rather than Nehru, India would have been a prosperous first-world country long ago, and it would hopefully have been saved from the debilitating feudal dynacracy (dynastic democracy) founded by Nehru, that is at the root of all miseries.

Nehru just went by what was popular and fashionable among the upper classes in Britain, without any deep study of economics (despite many years in jail where he had all the time in the world, and access to books), or even a reasonable understanding of its basics, although economics is a most vital subject for any political leader.

In fact, Nehru's prejudice—which he picked up at Harrow and Cambridge—against capitalism had more to do with his cultivating himself as an upper-class Englishman, who had a bias against trade, than on understanding of economics or economic history; just as his socialism had more to do with upper-class English Fabians (like Bernard Shaw), than with any genuine experience of or revolt against poverty. Nehru's class or caste bias is apparent in his autobiography where he mentions that "*right through history the old Indian ideal...looked down upon money and the professional money-making class*" and that "*today*" it is "*fighting against a new and all-powerful opposition from the bania* [Vaishya] *civilization of the capitalist West*".

What They Said of Nehru & Socialism

If the future is full of hope it is largely because of Soviet Russia.
—*Nehru*

This permit-licence-raj is not a bee in my bonnet but a great boa-constrictor that has coiled itself around the economy.
—*Rajaji in Swarajya of 15.1.1966* {RG3/415}

Poor countries are poor because those who have power make choices that create poverty. Such countries develop "extractive" institutions that "keep poor countries poor".
—*Daron Acemoglu and James A. Robinson,*
'*Why Nations Fail: The Origins of Power, Prosperity and Poverty*'

Socialist institutions tend to be extractive. Nehru was the founder of the extractive institutions that have been at the root of India remaining a third-rate third-world nation.

To cure the British disease with socialism
was like trying to cure leukaemia with leeches.
—*Margaret Thatcher*

Raja Vyapari taya Praja Bhikhari.
—*Indian proverb*

If you put the federal government in charge of the Sahara Desert, in 5 years there'd be a shortage of sand.
—*Milton Friedman*

People who believe in evolution in biology often believe in creationism in government. In other words, they believe that the universe and all the creatures in it could have evolved spontaneously, but that the economy is too complicated to operate without being directed by politicians.
—*Thomas Sowell*

Mr Jawaharlal Nehru returned from Cambridge with notions of how an all-governing interventionist state can force people into happiness and prosperity through socialism...He sticks to this bias in spite of the demonstration of world experience against it... I hate the present folly and arrogance as much as I hated the foreign arrogance of those [British] days."
—*Rajaji*{RG3/378}

A young man who isn't a socialist hasn't got a heart; an old man who is a socialist hasn't got a head.
—*David Lloyd George, the British PM in 1920*

Nehru's inability to rise above his deep-rooted Marxist equation of Western capitalism with imperialism, and his almost paranoid, partly aristocratic, distrust of free enterprise in its most successful form as 'vulgar', cost India dearly in retarding its overall development for the remaining years of his rule, as well as for the even longer reign of his more narrowly doctrinaire daughter.
—*Stanley Wolpert, 'Nehru: A Tryst with Destiny'*{Wolp2/447}

He [Nehru] had no idea of economics. He talked of Socialism, but he did not know how to define it. He talked of social justice, but I told him he could have this only when there was an increase in production. He did not grasp that. So you need a leader who understands economic issues and will invigorate your economy.
—*Chester Bowles, the then US Ambassador to India*

There is no difference between communism and socialism, except in the way of achieving the same ultimate goal: communism proposes to enslave men by force, socialism by voting. It's the same difference between murder and suicide.
—*Ayn Rand*

MISGOVERNANCE

Blunder–71:
Debilitating Babudom & Criminal-Justice System

Babudom—the IAS-IPS-IFS-IRS combine, those from the criminal-justice system, and the bureaucracy lower down—is very intimately related to socialism, poor rate of growth, continued poverty, injustice and misery.

Nehru did nothing to change the babudom and make it people-oriented, service-oriented and development-oriented—they continued with their feudal class consciousness and arrogant ways, ill-suited to public service. The pre-independence babu culture of living like a rajah, misusing power, exploiting people, becoming rich at their cost, and aping the British ways to look cultured, continued, and indeed became worse with Raj giving way to Nehru-Indira's licence-permit-quota raj. Wrote MO Mathai: *"Members of the Indian Civil Service (ICS) were the most arrogant and perhaps the most ignorant compared to other services which they considered as inferior."*{Mac2/L-2927}

As per 15 October 2013 Times of India, Mumbai news-item '2,600 cops serve in homes of IPS officers in state' by Prafulla Marpakwar:{URL46}

"...The question now is whether [the government] will withdraw the 2,600-odd police personnel deployed at the residences of 280 IPS officers across the state [of Maharashtra]... At least seven to 10 constables are deployed at the residence of an Indian Police Service officer, a senior IPS officer said. If this number is reduced, the state will get enough policemen to fill up at least 10 to 15 police stations... [A conscientious] IPS officer said, 'I am shocked that so many constables are deployed. Occasionally I feel we are still in the British Raj...'" The report states that 5 to 9 constables, 3 orderlies, 1 cook, 2-3 telephone runners and 2 drivers are deployed at the residences of SPs/Commissioners; while 2 to 5 constables, 2-3 orderlies, 2 telephone runners and 2 drivers are deployed at the residences of other IPS officials. The report continues: "'Many officers have even more staffers, depending on their influence. In Pune, a high-ranking officer in the prisons department had 15-20 constables at his official residence,' said a senior IPS officer... What was more shocking, the officer said, was that the staff remained the same even if the officer were to be shifted to another city, and even after an officer retired, the police personnel continued to serve him for a period ranging from three months to a year."{URL46}

So, while the citizens may remain insecure and crimes against women may be a growing menace the IPS babus, like their IAS counterparts, must lord it out. Which other democratic country in the world would allow such shamelessness, brazenness, colonial luxuries, feudal lordliness, priority of services to self over services to people, and utter contempt for the general public! And, can an abysmally poor country like India where millions go hungry afford this? Only a feudal, dynastic democracy like India, where those at the helm similarly lord it out in utter contempt and disregard of the people, can permit such gross insult and indifference to the public!!

What has the Babudom done—especially the IAS at the top, who ought to be accountable for it—to transform the state from a callous exploiter to one that serves citizens. One wonders why that word "Service" is attached to IAS, IPS, IFS and IRS, unless it signifies only self-service or service to their masters. Do they serve the public? Or, do they get served? *The babus indeed have very low IQ—low Integrity Quotient.* Perhaps, compared to the politicians, the babus have been greater culprits. The Indian misgovernance mess and filth can largely be attributed to the IAS-IFS-IRS-IPS combine. They sit at the top of the dung-heap, and are in many ways more powerful than the politicians, who come and go every five years, while they continue, irrespective of their performance, on account of their constitutional sinecure. ICS prospered under the British, while the nationalists suffered jails. Post-independence, the top babus—not all, but an overwhelming majority—have been having a good time: making money, misusing power, contributing little, taking the country to dogs, and then blaming the politicians for all the ills, and how they are not allowed to function!

Wrote Durga Das about the British bureaucracy in India: "Financially secure and socially exclusive, the Civil servant and his wife set about behaving as barons and big landlords did at home, a battalion of domestics to carry out their slightest behest, the club to preserve their social prerogatives and the executive authority to buttress their eminence."{DD/51}

The brown-sahibs, who took over after independence, followed in their foot-steps. In the mid-1930s Nehru denounced the ICS—Indian Civil Service—as *"neither Indian nor civil nor a service"*. He further said that it was "essential that the ICS and similar services disappear completely". Unfortunately, after independence, with himself in power, such pledges, like other promises, faded away.

As if their normal service-period is not sufficient to ruin the country, a large number of retired babus manage a government position in some establishment or the other, and never really retire. No wonder Indian Express [IE] in its series of articles in July, 2012 expanded IAS as *"Indians Always in Service"*. The probability of procuring a *"confirmed gravy train ticket"*, as IE called it, is predominantly influenced by the extent of one's servility to the powers that be. In fact, political class and babudom, mainly IAS, have co-opted each other. Politicians can't amass wealth, handout favours and perpetuate their rule and that of their dynasty without the cooperation of the top babus; and the top babus, in turn, can't keep getting plump postings, a cut in the moolah and gain indemnity for their misdeeds without the kind intervention of the politicians. Being a mutually beneficial combination, the top babus seek and the politicians facilitate their continuation even after retirement.

Thanks to the prevailing system of political patronage, powerful, pliant, generalist babus have long since expanded their tentacles to capture not only governorships, but also most of the critical positions requiring specialist expertise, such as position of RBI governor, CAG, head of TRAI, CCI, NDMA, CERC, and so on. It is, however, worth noting that almost all top positions require high-level expertise, and the generalist IAS—even if they have done some course or taken some training or gained some little experience just to corner those posts—are gross misfits, because top-level expertise demands years of focussed work in that particular field, which the IAS can never gain. IAS therefore has nothing worthwhile to contribute in those areas, and become mere file-pushers passing their time. Why shouldn't the head of TRAI be a telecom expert rather than an IAS babu? Why should the CAG be from IAS rather than from the Indian Audit and Accounts Service? Why shouldn't the RBI governor be an accomplished, experienced economist—why should he be an IAS babu? How come the USA manages to have high-level experts from the concerned fields to head the relevant positions; while in sharp contrast, we put in the IAS babus as square pegs in round holes in all top positions.

Why is it so? Actually, politicians require compliant people who would do their bidding; and IAS babus more than meet that requirement. Why take academic, judicial, social, financial, revenue, security, disaster management, law-enforcing, business, trade, management, information technology, telecom or other technical experts from outside to head those positions and run the unnecessary risk of having honest, conscientious and forthright persons? IAS babus are safe bets, more so the retired ones begging for assignments.

With the economic liberalisation post 1991 it was expected that the bureaucratic stranglehold would loosen. But, sensing the vastly enhanced scope of making the moolah with the unprecedented expansion of the economy, the politician-bureaucratic combine ensured that the plethora of new bodies, especially the regulatory ones, that came into being were hijacked by the babus. With a nod from the politicians, serving and retired babus have captured practically all important decision-making bodies. With IAS babus as heads of regulatory bodies, autonomous, independent, honest, competent and sane regulation is a chimera. Babudom, as it has existed, is incapable of delivering, as the experience of over six decades after independence bears out. There have been some babus who have tried to do good, but that's a miniscule percentage and an exception, and even they could not go very far, as they stood checkmated by the establishment, including their own colleagues.

Isn't it strange that while political parties excoriate one another, TV and print media pans the political class, and NGOs and Civil Society groups fulminate against them, hardly anyone highlights the venality, lack of probity, incompetence and corruption of the babus, without whose complicity or negligence no scam is possible. Khemka, a capable and honest IAS officer who has been at the receiving end, had commented, "*If bureaucrats did their duty, there would be no scams.*"

Indeed, Babudom is a strong pillar in the foundations of India's misery. *The Indian babudom is authoritarian, arrogant, callous, unfair, heartless, ill-mannered, indifferent, incompetent, inefficient, ineffective, nepotistic, sloppy, sluggish, self-seeking and shamelessly corrupt. Bureaucracy is now Kleptocracy.* The only thing that partially saves us from the bureaucracy is its inefficiency.

Among the major factor of India's misery are corruption and poor governance, for both of which the Babudom is responsible. Political class, certainly yes; but, so also Babudom, which is hand in gloves with them. No wonder, PERC (Political and Economic Risk Consultancy: www.asiarisk.com) rates it as one of the worst bureaucracies in Asia responsible for, as an article in *The Indian Express*, Mumbai of 16 October 2013 states, "bottlenecking key policies, widespread red tapism in everyday affairs, massive corruption, being uninnovative and insensitive, and harbouring generalist officers who lack expertise." A report "Corruption's Impact on the Business Environment" for 2013 for Asia-Pacific was published by PERC. It grades countries on a scale of 10, 0 being the best and 10 being the worst—most corrupt. Singapore came at the top with a score of 0.74, Japan and Australia tied at number 2 with a score of 2.35, and India came at the bottom with a score of 8.95!

The India bureaucratic system is actually beyond reform. The only remedy is to dismantle it completely and rebuild it from ground up. When a private company fails or does badly you blame its top-executives, who are generally made to resign. The top executives of the government are IAS-IFS-IRS-IPS combine. You have to blame them for failure of India both at the Centre and in the states. Most of the babus have been supporters of socialism or significant state controls and regulations, not because they think it would do any good to India, but because it results in enhancement of their powers and importance and opens avenues for making money. *Of course, not all babus are bad. It is only 99 percent of babus, as someone said, who give the rest a bad name*! In this connection, the book 'Journeys through Babudom and Netaland'{TSR} by TSR Subramaniam, the ex-Cabinet Secretary, is worth reading.

Looking at the babudom, a parody on the *Metamorphosis* of Franz Kafka takes shape in your mind. What if Kafka was born in India and was witness to post-independence India; and what if he wrote Metamorphosis in the current Indian context? Would it still have the undertone of absurdity and alienation, and of a random and chaotic universe with no governing system of order and justice? Would it still have Gregor, a travelling salesman, metamorphose into a gigantic insect? Or, would it rather have the undertone of a crass, callous, corrupt, rusted, unjust system—all man-made; with Gregor, a babu rather than a travelling salesman, metamorphose into a gigantic cockroach?

Blunder–72:
That Strange Indian Animal: VIP & VVIP

The other day a TV commentator stated that a foreigner visiting a Government office with him asked, "Are there three sexes in your country?" Baffled, the commentator looked at him wondering what to make of it. The foreigner helpfully added, "I notice three toilets: Men, Women and VIPs!" In a conversation on TV a senior IAS lady justifying separate, special toilets for "officers" commented: "People don't know how to use toilets, they make them so dirty!" All these vividly illustrate the extent to which the politicians and bureaucrats since the Nehruvian times have managed to keep India and Indians they are expected to serve so pathetic, like the British before them did, that they need segregation from "common" Indians, again like the British, to carry on. Even taking that silly, bloated IAS lady at her face value, what about the many who have clean toilet habits but are not "officers"? And, what about the officers who have dirty toilet habits? We are still afflicted with a colonial mindset; and given an army of officers like that lady IAS, India is unlikely to see better days.

Nehru himself had an elitist mindset and rather than ridding India of the colonial, brown-sahib culture, he allowed it to flourish—he encouraged it through his own example. The Indian government under Nehru represented in many respects a continuation of British attitudes both in form and substance. Indians, even after the British left, were confronted with the same civil servants, and the same policemen who treated them with the same scorn, arrogance and brutality, and the same master-slave attitude, as under the British rule.

Here is an example from Bhilai Steel Plant [BSP]—a public sector. There were many hospitals in Bhilai run by BSP, and also a main hospital with all facilities in the 1950s and 1960s. The hospital timings commenced at 8am. Patients would try to be there as early as possible so that their turn could come early—especially the employees who had to go to office in the general shift by 10am or 11am; and the students who had to attend schools. If you reached there at 8am, there would already be a long queue, and your turn might come at noon or beyond. So, most tried to be there as early as possible. However, employees belonging to higher grades and their spouses, sons and daughters had a preferential treatment: the first half-hour to one hour after 8am when the doctor came was reserved for them. They had a separate queue, which was always small, as they belonged to a smaller, upper echelon. So, even if they arrived at 8.30am they could see the doctor in the next 15 to 30 minutes. The others, even if they came at 7am, would sometimes wait till 1pm to see the doctor, if the queue was long, which was often the case. This patently unfair and unjust system went on for decades, and may still be prevalent! Mind you, such practices started in the fifties during the Nehru period, and continued. What does it tell about the "socialism" of Nehru and the pro-poor propaganda of his dynasty!

VIP area, VIP security, VIP red-beacon lights on vehicles, inconveniencing hundreds and thousands to let VIP car pass, VIP passes and VIP queues even in temples to let VIPs have darshan while thousands patiently wait: what does this all show? It is a gross insult to the public at large. Why should public, whose servants these politicians and bureaucrats are, suffer and get humiliated by these servants-turned-masters? After independence, and after displacing the British and over 500 rajas and maharajas from their princely states, we have become even more colonial and feudal. Wrote Inder Malhotra in his article, "Very Indian Phenomenon" [VIP], in The Indian Express of 21 July 2012:

"...the 'common person' [in USA] doesn't give a damn about VIPs. Here, of course, the situation is hugely different. The VIP status is flaunted in the face of countless millions every day, round the clock and round the calendar. You don't have to spell out the word; everyone knows what it means. In sharp contrast to what prevails in the US, the super-wealthy in India don't need to proclaim themselves VIPs. They get whatever they want without saying a word. The whole system seems geared to their needs and wishes. The odd tycoon who gets caught on the wrong side of the law lives in jail in greater luxury than five-star hotels can provide. It is the political class, the army of bureaucrats... that form the bedrock of the VIP cult and the perks and privileges that go with it. Like much else, the VIP is a legacy of the British Raj. Independent India has not only embraced it with gusto but also expanded it vastly... English class system and India's deathless caste system must have rubbed off on each other to produce the wonder that is the Indian VIP... Indian scene had added to the woes of the helpless non-VIPs in direct proportion to the burgeoning privileges and pampering of those more equal than the rest..."

Blunder–73:
Corruption in the "Good" Old Days

"Corruption is worse than prostitution. The latter might endanger the morals of an individual, the former invariably endangers the morals of the entire country."
—Karl Kraus, 19th century satirist

Nehru himself was personally honest money-wise. He did keep his hands clean in money matters; although he did not mind others dirtying their hands to raise funds for the Congress Party and for other purposes—what mattered was power for himself.

From the very beginning of his Prime Ministership Nehru adopted a queer and casual approach towards corruption. A resolution on the 'standards of public conduct' at the 1948 Congress session that exhorted 'all Congressmen, members of the central and provincial legislatures and more especially members of the Cabinets... to set an example and maintain a high standard of conduct' was accepted by a majority of 107 against 52. Such a sane and desirable resolution was, however, withdrawn the next day after Nehru threatened to resign, saying the resolution amounted to censure of his Government.{RNPS/102} One wonders why the Congress members bent down to an unreasonable demand. Nehru was certainly not indispensable—he should have been allowed to resign.

There were many cases where Nehru condoned corruption. Or, defended those accused of it. This tended to make corruption acceptable. In a way, the foundation of corruption were laid during Nehru's time, although, unlike Manmohan Singh, Nehru had almost unlimited powers to carry through whatever he wanted.

Sardar Patel's correspondence of May 1950 with Nehru brings out instances where the National Herald (NH) was used as a tool for collecting money on a quid pro quo basis—awarding government contracts to undeserving elements. Feroze Gandhi, Nehru's son-in-law, was then the General Manager of NH. Nehru was not personally involved, but rather than putting his foot firmly down on the impropriety, he tended to soft-paddle the matter, and shielded those responsible. It also brings out Sardar Patel's high standards of probity in public life.{URL47}

A number of his colleagues and confidants at the Centre and in the States were not above board, but Nehru ignored their misdemeanours. Krishna Menon (KM) had engaged in a number of shady deals while in London as High Commissioner. Jeep Scandal Case of 1948 was only one of the scandals. KM finalised a Defence deal with a firm in London with capital assets of barely £605 and placed orders in July 1948 for supply of 2000 rugged, all-terrain army jeeps urgently required for Kashmir operations within five months, with deliveries to commence within six weeks. Menon paid a large sum of £1,72,000 to the supplier upfront, before even a single vehicle was delivered. The first batch, which was to arrive in India within 6 weeks, arrived in March 1949, after 8 months, by when ceasefire in J&K had already been declared—on January 1, 1949. The initial batch of 155 jeeps that landed at Madras port were found to be all unserviceable. Defence official, who inspected the jeeps, rejected the entire shipment. PAC (Public Accounts Committee) conducted an enquiry, passing severe strictures, and recommended judicial enquiry to fix responsibility for the scam. But, the Government did nothing. When there was a clamour in the Parliament, the Government simply tabled its note to PAC to reconsider its recommendation, and asked the House to treat the matter as closed! This was in 1954. PAC, however, again revived the issue in its next report to the Parliament in 1955. Thereupon, the Home Minister Pant, at the instance of Nehru, simple announced in the Parliament that the Government had taken a final decision to treat the matter as closed! How could government close a clear case of gross corruption without taking any action, ignoring PAC's recommendations!!

Mundhra case related to the impropriety of investments by the government-owned LIC into the companies of a financier-investor Haridas Mundhra. The then Chief justice MC Chagla constituted the one-man Tribunal to enquire into the case in 1958. The Tribunal conducted its proceedings in a thoroughly professional manner, and in public, and submitted its report in a record time of one month. Nehru, rather than being appreciative of the exemplary working of the Tribunal (that should have been followed by subsequent such tribunals/enquiry commissions—but, were not), and praising and rewarding Chagla for the same, was cross with him. Why? Tribunal's findings were adverse, and reflected badly on the then Finance Minister TTK Krishnamachari. Wrote MC Chagla:

> "...Nehru addressed a meeting at the Indian Merchants' Chamber, where... he went out of his way to pay a high complement to TTK. I cannot help remarking that it was hardly

proper, when a judicial inquiry was being held involving the conduct of a Minister, for the Prime Minister to pay that very Minister [TTK] a compliment in public..."{MCC/210}

"...I know Nehru was very angry with me, and did not hesitate to show his displeasure. When TTK ultimately resigned, the Prime Minister went to the airport in person to bid him farewell, a gesture that was unique in the annals of our parliamentary history... But all this did not worry me. I had done my work conscientiously, and had come to my conclusions irrespective of whether they pleased or displeased the Prime Minister or anyone else..."{MCC/211}

Rajaji was against Nehru's License-Permit-Quota-Raj not only because it grievously hurt the economy, but also because it was a huge source of corruption. But, it went unchecked. Remarked Rajaji: *"Congressmen look so well off. Have they taken up new avocations and earned money? Then how have they earned money?"*{RG3/371} Rajaji had concluded that it was the socialistic pattern, where the state controlled, 'permitted', and farmed out business that was enriching Congressmen, officials, and favoured businessmen, and harassing the rest.

This is from 'The Hindu' of 9 January 2010, which reproduces what it had said over 50 years ago in its issue of 9 January 1960:

"Prime Minister Nehru categorically ruled out any proposal for appointing a high power tribunal to enquire into and investigate charges of corruption against Ministers or persons in high authority, for the main reason that, in India, or for that matter any other country where there was a democratic set-up, he could not see how such a tribunal could function. The appointment of such a tribunal, Mr. Nehru felt, would 'produce an atmosphere of mutual recrimination, suspicion, condemnation, charges and counter-charges and pulling each other down, in a way that it would become impossible for normal administration to function.' More than half the time of the Press conference was devoted by Mr. Nehru to deal with this question of appointing a tribunal to enquire into cases of corruption as recently urged by India's former Finance Minister, Mr C.D.Deshmukh."{URL27}

That indeed must be a very innovative restriction of democracy! It's like saying a tribunal would subvert democracy and adversely affect administrative functioning. And Nehru suggests no alternative to curb corruption! Wrote Durga Das:

> "...This was the pattern from 1947 to 1951 [stand against corruption], but he [Nehru] gradually began to acquire a tolerance for the malpractices of politicians. He thereupon substituted political expediency for principle in dealing with ministerial colleagues. Unhesitatingly, he turned a blind eye to a demand by C.D. Deshmukh for the appointment of a high-power Tribunal to eradicate corruption when one of the cases listed by him related to the son of a close colleague."{DD/382}

AD Gorwala, a civil servant, stated in his report to GoI: "*Quite a few of Nehru's ministers were corrupt and it was common knowledge*". The Santhanam committee, appointed by the Government in 1962 to examine corruption, said: "There is widespread impression that failure of integrity is not uncommon among ministers and that some ministers, who have held office during the last sixteen years, have enriched themselves illegitimately, obtained good jobs for their sons and relations through nepotism and have reaped other advantages inconsistent with any notion of purity in public life."

Nehru had commented thus on the charges against Pratap Singh Kairon:

> "The question thus arises as to whether the chief minister is compelled to resign because of adverse findings on some questions of fact by Supreme Court. The ministers are collectively responsible to the legislature. Therefore, the matter was one which concerned the assembly. As a rule therefore, the question of removing a minister would not arise unless the legislature expressed its wish by a majority vote."

So, even if a minister is corrupt he can't be removed, unless voted out! So you can buy immunity by manipulating or managing votes. When severe allegations were levelled against Kairon by the critics within the Congress itself, Nehru pooh-poohed them and resisted any enquiry—Kairon had to ultimately resign following Das Commission's findings.

In UPA-I and II, PM Manmohan Singh had advanced excuse of Coalition "Dharma" for corruption—as if Congress people were above board—but in the days of Nehru, Congress was super strong, opposition hardly existed, and Nehru was an unchallenged leader. Nehru could have easily nipped the malaise of corruption in the bud, being himself honest and above board. Sadly, he chose to tolerate it.

Wrote Maria Misra:

"By the early 1960s the Nehruvian project was unravelling. The third plan was in crisis, agricultural reform had stalled, and grain output actually declined in 1962-63...inflation was running at 9 per cent...Congress was confronting a crisis of rising expectations at the very moment that its own reputation was at its lowest, dogged by corruption scandals at every level...The culture of corruption...had begun to penetrate society more deeply. In 1961 the great novelist R.K. Narayan published Mr Sampath, a grimly comic depiction of a city milieu. The eponymous anti-hero is shown to be wholly immersed in fraudulent city life, a liar and an opportunist...Bimal Roy's film Parakh (Test, 1960) dealt with similar themes...offering a scathing satirical attack on venal politicians allied with vested interests...Nehru's non-aligned foreign policy was in disarray, his domestic policy in tatters, and Congress in decline..."{MM/306-7}

The then President of India, Dr Rajendra Prasad had written to Nehru that corruption '*will verily prove a nail in the coffin of the Congress.*' For inquiry into charges of corruption, he strongly advocated the proposal for a tribunal or an Ombudsman under the President or under an independent authority, as suggested by C.D. Deshmukh. Rather than replying to the President's note in the matter, Nehru chose to complain to him for his 'unfriendly act' of sending such a note! Dr Rajendra Prasad wrote to Nehru on 18 December 1959:

"...I must say that I am somewhat disappointed. The question of corruption has been too prominently and too long before the public to brook any further delay in making a probe into it. I think Deshmukh has given enough details about cases to be traced and once the Government makes up its mind and gives immunity to informants against vindictive action, proofs will be forthcoming. I would therefore suggest that thought be given to finding out cases. It is not enough that you are satisfied that all is well. A popular Government's duty is to give satisfaction to the people also...I have been worried by your suggestion that I should send for you and speak to you if I have anything to communicate rather than write. I am afraid this will stultify me in performing my constitutional duty..."{AS/15}

Blunder–74: Nepotism in the "Good" Old Days

Apart from the dynastic streak vis-à-vis Indira, Nehru had a nepotistic streak. During the Nehruvian era of 1947–64 there were many Pandits, Saprus, Kauls, Katjus, Dhars, Nehrus, and their kins in various government posts. Wrote Neville Maxwell:

"An official (non-Kashmiri, non-Brahmin) who worked closely with Nehru for a time wrote that enemies of the Prime minister used to say that his search for talent and gift for talent spotting was limited to those around him and particularly to Kashmiris, and amongst them, those who were in one way or another connected with the Nehru family..."{Max/187}

Wrote MKK Nayar, an IAS officer:{MKN}

"India needed a cadre to do diplomatic work after independence. The Federal Public Service Commission was vested with the authority to create it. Kripalani, an ICS officer, headed the Commission and Grubb, a Tamilian and Puranik, a Maharashtrian were Members.

"Youngsters who had the prescribed qualifications were called for an interview. Based thereon, a list of appointees to the new cadre (now known as Indian Foreign Service) was recommended to the Government. Bajpai and others were annoyed by the list. None of their children or in-laws were in it. They therefore sent Nehru a petition that said, 'We are starting a new cadre. There is no Indian diplomatic service now. The British Foreign Office has done the work. When we start a new diplomatic cadre, youth selected for it must be different from those selected for other services. The Commission does not have the experience to select appropriate persons for such a cadre and those recommended by it are not suitable for us.

"A Special Committee may be formed to select appointees to this cadre. The Special Committee should comprise those who themselves have experience and long service in diplomacy. For this reason, we feel that the list prepared by the Commission may be rejected and a new Committee asked to select the candidates.'

"It is not known whether Nehru considered the repercussions of doing as recommended. But he accepted it. When Kripalani heard this, he resigned. Without mentioning any specific reason, he stated personal inconvenience as his reason for resigning. Bajpai recommended and Nehru accepted it.

"Without considering many of those selected earlier by the Commission, a new Committee [*Special Selection Board*] began a new selection. In the Commission's list Ram and I were ranked sixteen and eighteen. We were not considered by the new Committee and we thus lost the opportunity to enter IFS.

"There were indeed many 'able' persons in the list prepared by the new Committee—not in scholarly pursuits but in selecting their brides. The list of those selected was such that almost everyone was related to someone in high circles. Even children of Committee members made it into the list. It is impossible to believe that Nehru was not aware of what was going on."{MKN}

Nehru's Personal Private Secretary M.O. (Mac) Mathai had something similar to say in his book 'My Days with Nehru':

"...The fruits of labour of the *Special Selection Board* [for foreign services] left much to be desired. All the members of the Board had their own favourites and candidates... "Many people with the right connections and some who did not have the minimum educational qualifications entered the foreign service through the back-door. Leilaraani Naidu, the second daughter of Sarojini Naidu, was also taken in. Unlike Ranbir Singh and Mohommad Yunus, she had ample educational qualifications and teaching experience, but was thoroughly temperamental and patently unsuitable for any diplomatic work. She had to be kept in the External Affairs Ministry throughout her term in the Foreign Service as a lame duck..."{Mac2/L-2946-51}

Blunder–75:
Nehru & Casteism

It is all very well to fulminate publicly against casteism and communalism—it shows you up as modern and liberal. But, what really matters is what you really do in practice to eradicate casteism. With India basking in the glow of freedom, and all charged up, it was a golden opportunity after independence to finally nail casteism. But, did Nehru do so? Sadly, caste of candidates for election in a given constituency was a very important, rather crucial, consideration for their selection. Rather than weakening the foundations of casteism, Nehruvian electoral strategy strengthened it. The sad spectacle that we see today is thanks to the seeds sown since the first general elections of 1952.

The lists of proposed candidates prepared for the consideration of the Congress State and Central Election Committees had an important column on caste of each candidate! This was so even when Nehru was ex-officio member of the Central Election Committee.

One finds many Kashmiri Pandits in Nehru's top circle. Why? Caste loyalty? Incidentally, it is odd why Nehru, who considered himself modern, westernised, forward-looking, secular and above caste, allowed himself to be called *Panditji*?

There is an interesting episode of Nehru's time which illustrates how the upper caste Indian leaders paid mere lip service to the amelioration of the lot of dalits, and how insensitive they were to their pathetic condition: In a Scheduled Caste Conference held in Lucknow, presided by the dalit leader Babu Jagjivan Ram, Nehru in his inaugural address said, among other things, that those who do the menial job of carrying excreta were greater than God. At this, Babu Jagjivan Ram got up immediately and snapped back that having done the said job for ages, the Dalits had already become Gods, and the castes to which Nehru and Gandhi belong should now take up the said task and become Gods!

Blunder–76:
Messy Reorganisation of States

In India, distinct geographical areas have their own distinct language; and associated with them a distinct set of culture, customs, dresses, music, dance, arts, literature and so on. Indian freedom fighters, except perhaps the anglicised-set that included Nehru, were deeply aware of the love and attachment of the people to their mother-tongues and the associated culture, and its power in harnessing them to the cause of freedom; because political freedom would also have meant freedom from English and colonial culture, and its replacement by their mother-tongue and their culture.

It was therefore natural for the leaders of the Indian Independence movements to have worked out back in the beginning of the twentieth century itself that upon independence India should be reorganised along the lines of the major languages so that the people of the concerned regions could fulfil their aspirations, and their language and culture flowers. The Congress Party had committed itself to this way back in 1917. In the constitution that was framed by the Congress under the inspiration and guidance of Mahatma Gandhi, India was divided into provinces, with headquarters and languages as follows:

Province (Headquarters): Language
(1) Ajmere-Merwara (Ajmer): Hindustani
(2) Andhra (Madras): Telegu
(3) Assam (Gauhati): Assamese
(4) Bihar (Patna): Hindustani
(5) Bengal (Calcutta): Bengali
(6) Bombay City (Bombay): Marathi-Gujarati
(7) Delhi (Delhi): Hindustani
(8) Gujarat (Ahmedabad): Gujarati
(9) Karnatak (Dharwar): Kannada
(10) Kerala (Calicut): Malayalam
(11) Mahakosal (Jabalpur): Hindustani
(12) Maharashtra (Poona): Marathi
(13) Nagpur (Nagpur): Marathi
(14) NWFP (Peshawar): Pushtu
(15) Punjab (Lahore): Punjabi
(16) Sind (Karachi): Sindhi
(17) Tamil Nadu (Madras): Tamil
(18) United Provinces (Lucknow): Hindustani
(19) Utkal (Cuttack): Oriya
(20) Vidarbha-Berar (Akola): Marathi

Even Provincial Congress Committees (PCCs) were as per the linguistic zones, like Orissa PCC, Karnataka PCC, and so on. All the leaders of the independence movement from different regions and language areas were agreeable on this—there were no two opinions.

No one thought it would be divisive in nature and a threat to the national unity. That there were distinct languages and cultures was a fact on the ground; and if that meant divisive tendencies, then that would have been there whether or not separate states were carved on that basis. On the contrary, by not carving out the states as per the major-language regions, there was a good possibility of dissatisfaction, frustration, anger and mischief leading to bad blood among people and divisive tendencies.

Misgovernance

Those who were close to the ground and genuinely understood India (and did not have to do "Discovery of India') knew that what held India together through thousands of years and through trying times was the overarching culture of broad Hinduism and associated religions that evolved in the Indian soil like Jainism, Buddhism and Sikhism. This unique Indian combination cut across languages and local cultures and stitched together the larger entity, Bharat Varsh.

However, in the wake of partition, the division of India on the Hindu-Muslim religious lines was extrapolated to include possible future divisions on linguistic lines, and a needless fear psychosis developed. What was decided coolly and rationally in the pre-independence times and was taken for granted, and what most people implicitly looked forward to as a logical post-independence step was sought to be given a go by, as a panic, irrational reaction to communal partition on religious grounds.

Rather than forming a competent body to go into all aspects of reorganisation of India and making recommendations, Nehru's government sought to postpone the whole issue indefinitely.

The issue erupted. First, for Andhra. The government tried their best to suppress the agitation. The more they tried the worse it became. Ultimately, they had to give in, and the state of Andhra Pradesh was formed in 1953. Wrote Dr Dhananjay Keer in 'Dr. Ambedkar: Life and Mission':

"...on September 2, 1953, Dr. Ambedkar criticized Government for its vacillating policy on the formation of linguistic states. He strongly repudiated the view that linguistic reorganization would lead to the disintegration of India. Potti Sriramalu, he observed, had to sacrifice his life for the sake of creating Andhra. If, he added, in any other country a person had to die in order to invoke a principle that had already been accepted, it was possible that the Government of that country would have been lynched."[DK/449]

All the violence, destruction to property, and bad blood among people speaking different languages could have been avoided had the issue been rationally and peacefully settled through a body that could have been set up. Ultimately, States Reorganisation Commission (SRC) was formed in 1954.

The matter of Maharashtra, Gujarat and Mumbai was again allowed to hang for too long, leading to agitations and violence. Eventually, Nehru had to give in. The states of Maharashtra and

Gujarat were created on 1 May 1960.

It showed that the Nehru's government lacked the wisdom to do the right thing at the right time, and created avoidable problems for itself and for the country. Only when forced did they do what people demanded and aspired for. If you indeed had some great and valid principles behind what you did, you should have stuck to your stand, even if you became unpopular and were later thrown out in the elections. What was the down side, if any? Nothing. The linguistic states never asked for secession. Indian unity actually became stronger. The language and culture of different linguistic states flourished—compared to what the status was earlier.

Blunder–77:
Poor Leadership & Administration

Confused & Indecisive; Not Action-Oriented

On many vital issues, Nehru avoided taking actions where required, and substituted inaction with rationalisations. Nehru's inability to take proper and timely decisions was, in a way, related to his lack of clarity and grasp on matters and reluctance to act. Compare the decisiveness of Sardar Patel and Netaji, and their ability to take action, with the fumbling ruminations of Nehru. These are the remarks of Rafi Ahmed Kidwai, a close friend and a confidant of Nehru:

> "You know, I never go to Nehru to seek advice or guidance. I take a decision and just present it to him as a fait accompli. Nehru's mind is too complex to wrestle with the intricacies of a problem. Those who go to him for advice rarely get a lead—and that only serves to delay matters...Nehru does not understand economics, and is led by the nose by 'professors' and 'experts' who pander to his whims and fancies...We should have absorbed Kashmir for good and all...I do not know where we are going. The country needs a man like Patel."{DD/379}

Wrote Brig. BN Sharma: "Consistency in thought and hard-headedness in decisions were not Nehru's strong points. Superficiality of thought and confused thinking led him wondering into the realm of philosophy and metaphysics."{BNS/16}

Misgovernance

Bad Judge of People & Situations

All leaders need to be good judge of people and events. Leaders themselves can't tackle everything, they need to have competent colleagues, reliable second-level leaders and officials under them to realise their national objectives. A leader who is prone to sycophancy and is a poor judge of people would normally end up with an incompetent team. Nehru managed to have people like Sheikh Abdullah, Krishna Menon, BM Kaul, BN Mullik and the like around him, each of whom let down India.

Wrote Durga Das: "Radhakrishnan, who laid down office of President in 1967, was closely associated with Nehru for seventeen years or more. His last homage to Nehru was a panegyric. Yet, to those very near him, *Radhakrishnan once confided that Jawaharlal was a 'poor judge of men' and often extended his confidence and protection to unworthy persons.*"{DD/376}

Nehru was a bad judge of events and situations too. Here is what MO Mathai wrote:

"Nehru was not a good judge of situations. After the partition of India was decided upon, he visited Lahore in 1947. I was with him... At a press conference in Lahore, Nehru held forth and asserted that when partition was brought about, things would settle down and both contending parties would want to maintain peace in their respective areas. Most pressmen were sceptical. They asked, 'What makes you think so?' Nehru replied, 'Forty years of public life.' We all know what happened subsequently."{Mac/110}

Loyalty, Sycophancy & Flattery

Nehru preferred sycophants rather than the competent persons who may have their own mind, and might differ. In short, he preferred 'yes men'. Wrote Rustamji:

"The one test which Nehru applied to men whom he took into the inner circle was loyalty to him. It did not matter if a man had no mind of his own. He must, however, have enough intelligence to avoid irritation. He should be able to understand what the PM said, and if he asked questions, he should do so intelligently so that an opening may be provided for JN to amplify his points for another half an hour or so... He must put all his faith in Nehru, believe in Nehru, admire and adore Nehru, and say worshipful things now and again which could be brushed aside with gratified indifference..."{Rust/194}

"Another fault of JN [Jawaharlal Nehru] was that, like Aurangzeb, he encouraged a peculiar form of flattery. In every forum, someone or the other close to him, spoke in a flattering tone. He was never rude to those people who kept praising him and his work, often in ornate language."{Rust/214}

Nehru's cabinet colleague and admirer Rajkumari Amrit Kaur had remarked about Nehru: "*He is not a good judge of character and is therefore easily deceived. He is not averse to flattery and there is conceit in him which makes him at once intolerant of criticism and may even warp his better judgement...*"{ST/206}

No Delegation

Nehru didn't train others, or gave them an opportunity to develop. For example, he retained foreign portfolio too, doing injustice both to that portfolio and to his own job as PM. He invested overmuch time drafting letters and replies and doing such sundry things, better left to people down below. Wrote Rustamji:

"No big decision could be taken in India by anyone, except Nehru. He kept about and below him men who would always turn to him for decisions, or who, if they took decisions would soon be told that they were wrong... How did this work in practice? It meant that on every major problem when there was a doubt about government policy, that doubt would be removed by the PM... There were good, clever men, advisers in the government, who were able to read the PM's mind, or make an accurate forecast of the way he would think. But these men did not exercise their own critical judgement. They merely anticipated a decision which could be easily done. If it could not be easily anticipated, they awaited the Oracle's pronouncement... Modern government is such a complex affair that if a policy is uncertain, those who function at a distance (like ambassadors and delegates to the UN) or lower below (like Under Secretaries) are constantly kept guessing."{Rust/72}

Wrote MO Mathai: "Nehru saddled himself with more than one portfolio—External Affairs and Atomic Energy and Scientific Research—on a permanent basis... Nehru had neither the aptitude, the patience, the inclination nor the temperament for the drudgery of attention to details. In fact he was a man whose policies could be largely defeated at the level of details by scheming men. Nehru's

Misgovernance

choice of junior ministers directly under him left much to be desired. In any event, having been for so long his own secretary during his long career as a political leader, Nehru never learned to delegate. With only one exception, the junior ministers under Nehru were the most neglected and disgruntled ones in the whole government...{Mac2/L-2901-7}

"One day S.K. Patil asked me privately why the Prime Minister was not encouraging any one or a group of colleagues to come up. I replied that he might as well reconcile himself to the fact that nothing would grow under a banyan tree."{Mac2/L-2914}

Poor Administrator

Wrote Durga Das: "Curzon [Viceroy, British-India, 1899–1905] was an adept at cutting the Gordian knots into which ponderous files had tied a problem over the years. There were few administrative problems he would not himself tackle, zealously and with conspicuous success. Nehru, on the other hand, was more concerned with enunciating doctrines; he had little patience with the details of administration. When confronted with the need for a decision, he would skirt round, weighing the pros and cons, tormented, as it were, by the spirit of self-questioning. Nehru's genius lay in romanticising politics, not in the sphere of administration."{DD/48}

On the basis of what MN Kaul, Lok Sabha Secretary and a close observer of Nehru for many years, told him, wrote Durga Das: "Nehru did not pull his Ministers up when they deserved this treatment. In fact, he was very soft on them. Nehru could not master the administrative machinery. He never rebuked any wrong doer... He bowed before challenges like the language issue and his troubles multiplied. He could never pick out an administrator who could put his ideas into effect."{DD/380}

Contrast the above with Sardar Patel about whom Balraj Krishna wrote: "Common talk among the members of the Indian Civil Service post-Independence used to be: *'If the dead body of the Sardar were stuffed and placed on a chair, he could still rule.'*"{BK/xi}

Blunder–78 :
Squandering Once-in-a-lifetime Opportunity

India's Major Advantages at Independence

Strong Base & Assets

At the time of independence, compared to China and all the countries in SE-Asia like Taiwan, South Korea, Singapore, and so on, India was much better placed in terms of infra-structure like roads, railways, and industries; administrative and criminal-justice infrastructure; and had a large, indigenous groups of entrepreneurs, industrialists and businessmen.

Not only that, India had a favourable balance of payments, with the UK owing millions of pounds to us, which it repaid over the years.

Abundance of Talent

India, and therefore Nehru as PM, was exceptionally fortunate to have a large pool of extraordinarily talent at the time of independence. To have had highly capable and upright politicians like Sardar Patel, C Rajagopalachari, Dr BR Ambedkar, Dr Rajendra Prasad, John Mathai, CD Deshmukh, Dr Shyama Prasad Mukherjee, KM Munshi, GB Pant, Rafi Ahmed Kidwai, and so on, was indeed fortunate. Then, there was a large team of experienced and capable bureaucrats like VP Menon, HM Patel, Girija Shankar Bajpai, etc. Many of the Diwans of the Princely States were highly competent and experienced administrators, like CP Ramaswami Iyer of Travancore, M Visvesvaraya of Mysore, and so on. Indian army had WW-II veterans, and people like KM Cariappa, Thimayya. We also had many reputed educationists, technocrats, economists, and finance persons. India would never have such a mix of talent and such people of integrity again.

Patriotic Fervour & Zeal to Succeed

Post-independence, millions were fired with patriotic zeal, ready to sacrifice, and do their utmost to show to the world what this grand, old civilisation was capable of. They all wanted to disprove the British canard that without them India would go to pieces and would become a basket case. India was the richest nation in the world when the Islamic invaders arrived. Despite their loot and plunder, India still remained attractive, though much less rich. Still, India was far, far richer than England when the English first arrived in India. However, thanks to their loot and disastrous economic management, condition of India became pitiable. That was the time, after independence, to show to the world what India would have been, had the British and Muslims hordes not set their feet in India.

Popular Support & No Opposition

Fortunately for Nehru, support was for the asking. There was no opposition worth the name. He enjoyed unbridled supremacy both over the Congress and the government for 17 long years. He could do what he wanted. People were also fired up. It was once in a millennium opportunity, which India would never again get.

Sadly, Nehru Failed to Rise to the Occasion

Sadly, Nehru woefully failed to leverage the above assets. Even as countries much behind us at the time of our independence picked up, grew fast, and became first-world countries within a few decades, India lumbered on as a forever developing, third-world country under Nehru and his dynasty.

What really pains one is that it was after hundreds of years that India breathed free, and the Indian people, oppressed for centuries, hoped the sun of swaraj would shine for them, lifting the dark days of the Islamic and then the British tyranny—sadly, the sun failed to rise for the overwhelming majority. Nehru just frittered away that once in a life time golden opportunity for the nation. He squandered his political capital. Wrote Brig. BN Sharma:

"He [Nehru] could, but did not rise to the call of destiny and led the country not to glory but ignominy." {BNS/404}

"My chief attempt is to present the unrevealed Janus-like face of the man [Nehru], who to a large extent, shaped the destiny of this subcontinent called Bharat. Placed as he was at the steering wheel of history... he had the power and the authority, unparalleled in democratic polity, to chalk out a path for this country that could lead to progress and glory. Instead, he dithered and fumbled and took us where we stand today. To now correct the course, and reach our rightful destiny, it is incumbent on all of us to know what went wrong and why? It is difficult to imagine how a nation as well-endowed as India in human and natural resources, with a head-start on many other countries similar enslaved, crawled to its present... We are so far behind from where we should have been..." {BNS/xi-xii}

Rather than leaving a strong and prosperous India after seventeen long years of rule, Nehru left India with the largest unsettled border in the world; too militarily weak to effectively defend itself against foreign designs; too isolated and too friendless to get help and support in case of foreign aggression; too poor to adequately feed its millions; too socialistic, babu-dominated, and mired in bureaucratic controls to be able to rise and become prosperous; too illiterate and uninformed to derive benefits from the adoption of a democratic system; too weak politically by not allowing the opposition to rise up, and become an effective player in the electoral system and democratic processes; too pliant a press and media to fulfil their duty as the fourth estate; legislative and executive wings too full of sycophants, "yes-men", and hangers-on at the top-level to deliver anything concrete—overall an oppressive legacy of political, bureaucratic, economic and academic culture that continued to pull India down for decades after, and still afflicts it.

EDUCATIONAL & CULTURAL MISMANAGEMENT

Blunder–79:
Neglect of Education

Neglect of education, especially at the primary and the secondary level during the Nehruvian era sealed India's fate as a prosperous emerging nation and a genuine, enlightened democracy. Among the first things that the countries like Japan, South Korea and Singapore did to become prosperous was to focus on education—both mass education and higher education. Nehru knew only one formula for development: socialism and public sector—which took India to dogs.

Considering how backward the home constituencies of the Nehru-Gandhis have been, despite the fact that they have been representing them for decades, it would appear they have had a vested interest in keeping people illiterate and backward—such people can be easily fooled into voting for you through emotional trickery and sops.

The education under Nehru became elitist. There was regrettable compartmentalisation into the HMTs (Hindi-Medium types) and the EMTs (English-Medium types), with EMTs cornering most facilities and opportunities. There were little efforts to make education universal and of high quality. Policy restrictions and the bureaucratic-maze spread by the Nehruvians ensured peripheral role for the private sector in education, thus severely limiting the already limited educational sector further.

Nehruvians flaunt establishment of IITs and IIMs during the time of Nehru. The question is whether just five IITs and a few IIMs were enough for a country of India's size. Shouldn't there have been several IITs and several IIMs in each state?

Universal literacy and an informed public were the two factors Nehru-Dynasty could not have survived; so it seems they let widespread illiteracy, and grossly inadequate educational infrastructure, prevail.

Blunder–80:
Messing Up the Language Issue

After considerable deliberations the Constituent Assembly agreed that the official language of the Union shall be Hindi in the Devanagari script; but for 15 years from the commencement of the Constitution, that is, from 26 January 1950, the English language shall continue to be used for all the official purposes of the Union—that is, till 25 January 1965. The Official Languages Act of 1963 stipulated that English "may" be used along with Hindi in official communications after 1965. That left it ambiguous. Was it optional? Lal Bahadur Shastri as prime minister stood by the decision to make Hindi official with effect from 26 January 1965, and all hell broke loose in the South. Ultimately, Shastri had to back out.

The question is not Hindi or English, the question is why the matter was allowed to drift for 15 years under Nehru? Why a dialogue was not established among all the stake-holders and why what would happen post 26 January 1965 not thrashed out many years in advance allowing for a smooth transition, or for maintenance of the status quo? If indeed all were not agreeable on Hindi, then it should have been announced well in advance that the status quo would continue till as long as all were not agreed.

Nehru's drift and lack of clarity eventually led to massive agitations and violence and bad blood among people, which were quite avoidable. Shastri too should have been careful not to go along with a decision taken long ago that was not acceptable to a large section.

If it was thought that English is a useful global language, then, as a matter of policy, it should have been made compulsory for all from class-I itself. Government should have pumped in money to ensure there were facilities available in all schools to teach English, apart from the regional language and Hindi. Doing so would have ensured a level-playing field for all students. With all children knowing English, the "English Language Aristocracy" would have been dead. However, this was not done. The brown sahibs managed to create an "English Language Aristocracy" after independence. How to corner good positions, jobs and privileges? Make them conditional upon knowledge of English. Restrict English to chosen schools and colleges, and restrict access to those institutions to only the privileged.

This is not to say that the medium of instruction should have been English. It should have been in the mother tongue in the schools, and optionally also in English or Hindi—with no privileges attached to learning in English or Hindi. But, it should have been compulsory for all to learn English—and good English. That way, English would have been just a foreign language everyone knew. If English became a factor in getting jobs, like in IT or BPO or KPO, then with all students knowing it, it would not have given an edge to the less deserving.

A miniscule English-speaking elite, a miniscule set of Hindi diehards and a non-visionary, incompetent leadership messed up the language issue. A vast majority of people in the South knew neither Hindi nor English, so where was the question of their preferring either? Why should Hindi diehards have tried to impose Hindi? It is a democratic nation, and a consensus should have been evolved; and till that was ensured, nothing should have been done to force any language. If a period of 15 years was found insufficient, it should have been extended well in advance of its expiry, lest there be any uncertainty.

Further, why shouldn't an ancient nation like India have its own national language known to all for easy communication, without in anyway ignoring the regional languages or English or affecting the job-prospects? Who cares what language is so chosen? What is important is that there should have been at least one common language. It could have been Hindi or Hindustani, with liberal borrowing of words from other regional languages and English; or it could have been simplified Sanskrit or Tamil or Telugu or Bengali or any other or a new hybrid language, with borrowings from all!

In sharp contrast to India, it is admirable what Israel did. Upon formation of Israel in 1948, many Jews scattered all over the world came over. They spoke different languages. To ensure a unifying language, many linguists, backed by the State, set about reviving Hebrew, Israel's ancient language, which had fallen in decrepitude. Now, all Israelis speak Hebrew. It has given them an identity, and has greatly helped unify Israel. Most also know English, as it is taught from the primary school itself.

Language Commission setup in 1955 examined the progress in Hindi to replace English as the union language by 26 January 1965 as provided in the constitution, reiterated the constitutional obligation, made various recommendations, but left the decision to the government. A Parliamentary Committee, with GB Pant (the then Home Minister) as the Chairman, was appointed in 1957 to scrutinize the commission's recommendations. Its unanimous (but for one dissent) recommendation was that Hindi should be the principal language from 26 January 1965, and English a subsidiary one, with no target date for the switch over. Pant sent the draft-report of the Parliamentary Committee to Nehru. Here are the extracts from Kuldip Nayar's 'Beyond the Lines' on what transpired:

> "The use of the word 'subsidiary' for English infuriated Nehru, who argued that the word, subsidiary, meant English was the language of 'vassals'. [Various substitute words were suggested by Pant]... Nehru disagreed with Pant and worse, he was quite indignant and reportedly made some harsh comments. Finally, the word subsidiary was substituted by 'additional'. Pant told me, 'Mark my words, Hindi will not come to the country'. He was dejected. That very evening, Pant had his first heart attack..."

Actually, Nehru wanted to carry on with the language he was comfortable in, and it is doubtful if he really cared for things Indian or Indian languages or culture. What is noteworthy is that most of the freedom fighters, irrespective of the language-region they came from, favoured Hindi or Hindustani as a common link-language and national language. Yet, the matter was allowed to become controversial under the watch of Nehru after independence.

Lokmanya Tilak fervently advocated Hindi as the national language, holding the same as a vital concomitant of nationalism. Gandhi had praised Tilak for his discourse on Hindi as the national language at the Calcutta Congress. In London, Veer Savarkar had proposed the resolution on Swaraj not in English, but in what he called the "India's lingua franca"—Hindi. At the Ahmedabad Congress Session in December 1921, Gandhi had proposed three things[BK/74]: Hindi as India's lingua franca, tricolour as national flag, and khadi as the official wear for the Congress members.

Back in December 1925, at the Kanpur Session of the Congress presided by Ms Sarojini Naidu, Hindustani was recommended as the language for Congress Sessions.

Wrote Gandhi in Harijan of 9 July 1938:[CWMG/Vol-73/279-80]

> "...The medium of a foreign language through which higher education has been imparted in India has caused incalculable intellectual and moral injury to the nation. We are too near our

Educational & Cultural Mismanagement

own times to judge the enormity of the damage done. And we who have received such education have both to be victims and judges—an almost impossible feat...

...Up to the age of 12 all the knowledge I gained was through Gujarati, my mother tongue. I knew then something of arithmetic, history and geography. Then I entered a high school. For the first three years the mother tongue was still the medium. But the schoolmaster's business was to drive English into the pupil's head. Therefore more than half of our time was given to learning English and mastering its arbitrary spelling and pronunciation. It was a painful discovery to have to learn a language that was not pronounced as it was written. It was a strange experience to have to learn the spelling by heart... The pillory began with the fourth year. Everything had to be learnt through English—geometry, algebra, chemistry, astronomy, history, geography. The tyranny of English was so great that even Sanskrit or Persian had to be learnt through English, not through the mother tongue. If any boy spoke in the class in Gujarati which he understood, he was punished... I know now that what I took four years to learn of arithmetic, geometry, algebra, chemistry and astronomy I should have learnt easily in one year if I had not to learn them through English but Gujarati. My grasp of the subjects would have been easier and clearer..."{CWMG/Vol-73/279-80}

After the December-1926 Gauhati Session of the Congress, *Gandhi* went on yet another tour of the country, and among other things, expressed in his speeches that "*he felt humiliated to speak in English and therefore wanted every Indian to learn Hindustani. He even went further and advocated adoption of the Devnagari script for all the Indian languages. Once again, he found South India most enthusiastic in its response to him, and he addressed about two dozen public meetings in Madras city alone.*"{DD/124}

After the Congress session in October 1934, Gandhi traversed the country and continued his crusade urging everyone to learn simple Hindi:

"We must give up English as an inter-provincial language and introduce into Hindi–Hindustani words from other provincial languages. A common Devanagari script would help as a common script had helped the development of the European languages."{DD/168}

After independence, once when Gandhi was addressing a meeting at Birla House in Delhi in Hindustani, a few in the audience said they were unable to follow, to which Gandhi said: *"Now we are independent, I shall not speak in English. You have to understand rashtrabhasha if you wish to serve the people."*{DD/290}

According to the then Home Secretary BN Jha the efforts to make Hindi the link-language failed thanks mainly to Nehru and his colleagues. Two big opportunities were lost—one when all chief ministers were agreed in 1961 for Devanagari script for all Indian languages, at the recommendation of President Dr Rajendra Prasad; and the second when a proposal based on parliamentary committee's report was put up in the Cabinet meeting by the Home Minister Pant, to which Nehru had violently responded, "What is all this nonsense? It is not possible to have scientific and technological terms in Hindi," even though Pant's proposal did not cover the latter aspect—Nehru was only expressing his dislike for Hindi.{DD/330-31}

Wrote BN Sharma:

"How is it that after almost five decades of freedom we have not been able to shake off the burden of English and adopt our own national language. That Hindi is the only language spoken by the largest number of people in the largest number of states is an indisputable fact. If a Tamilian or a Keralite can learn English with ease why can he not learn Hindi, whose Sanskrit base is a common source of many words in his own language. Nehru, the Western Oriental Gentleman (WOG) never really made any sincere effort nor did he muster enough political will to implement Hindi... He [Nehru] used specious arguments, such as lack of scientific vocabulary [How have France, Germany, Japan, China, Korea, and many other European and Asian countries managed very well in their own mother tongue?], difficulty in international communications and diversity of local Indian languages as an excuse to stonewall the adoption of Hindi."{BNS/248-9}

No nation is worth its spirit and soul which does not have its own vehicle of cultural articulation that its national language provides.

Blunder–81 :
Promoting Urdu & Persian-Arabic Script

Hindi is written in the Devanagari script from left to right, while Urdu is written from right to left, being derived from a Persian modification of the Arabic script. High variants of Hindi depend on Sanskrit for enrichment, while Urdu looks to Persian and Arabic for its higher variants.

Rather than giving Hindi its due, Nehru insisted that Urdu was the language of the people of Delhi, and should accordingly be given official recognition. When the Home Minister GB Pant told him that the statistics showed only 6% of the Delhiwalas had claimed Urdu as their language, Nehru tried to rubbish the statistics, though he didn't press further with his crazy idea.{DD/329-30}

Nehru was also in favour of Persian-Arabic script in which Urdu is written, rather than Devanagari script in which Hindi and Sanskrit are written.

It seems that anything Indian or Hindu or representing Hindu/Indian heritage, and Nehru had some problem with it, and he tried to abort it. Ram Manohar Lohia had rightly said that Nehru was against anything that would give Indians a sense of Indianness!{DD/373}

Also, Nehru promoted what he was personally comfortable with: English and Urdu. Not what was good for the nation.

Hindi clearly had association with nation, India, Hindu, and Sanskrit; while Urdu has been advocated by Muslim leaders. The states that became West Pakistan and East Pakistan (now Bangladesh) had no association whatever with Urdu; their languages were Punjabi, Sindhi, Bengali, etc. But, the Muslim leaders from UP who migrated to Pakistan imposed Urdu on Pakistan.

What business Nehru had in trying to favour Urdu and Persian-Arabic script can only be understood if we account for his pseudo-secular character, eagerness to appease Muslims for votes, and allergy for anything rooted in India or in Indian culture and Hinduism.

Blunder–82:
Neglect of Sanskrit

With the ascendency of English Language Aristocracy and the Brown Sahibs, work in the Indian languages and Sanskrit suffered a setback. See the condition of Sanskrit—unarguably the greatest and the most scientific language. It is becoming extinct. And unless you have mastery in Sanskrit and other older languages you can't do effective research in past Indian history. Said Will Durant, American historian and philosopher:

"India was the motherland of our race, and Sanskrit the mother of Europe's languages: she was the mother of our philosophy; mother, through the Arabs, of much of our mathematics; mother, through the Buddha, of the ideals embodied in Christianity; mother, through the village community, of self-government and democracy. Mother India is in many ways the mother of us all."

One is told that those who have genuine interest in working on the Indian past now go to certain reputed universities in the US, who not only have a rich collection of relevant books, but also have faculty proficient in Sanskrit! So, to research India, go abroad!! This is what India has been reduced to, thanks to the ill-informed policies of the Dynasty. The comments of Gurcharan Das are worth noting:

"...an Indian who seriously wants to study the classics of Sanskrit or ancient regional languages will have to go abroad. 'If Indian education and scholarship continue along their current trajectory,' writes Sheldon Pollock, the brilliant professor of Sanskrit at Columbia University, 'the number of citizens capable of reading and understanding the texts and documents of the classical era will very soon approach a statistical zero. India is about to become the only major world culture whose literary patrimony, and indeed history, are in the hands of scholars outside the country.' This is extraordinary in a country with dozens of Sanskrit departments in all major Indian universities...The ugly truth is that the quality of teaching in these institutions is so poor that not a single graduate is able to think seriously about the past and critically examine ancient texts... Where is India's soft power when there are fewer and fewer Indians capable of interrogating the texts of Kalidasa or the edicts of Ashoka?...To be worthy of being Indian does not mean to stop speaking in English. It means to be able to have an organic connection with our many rich linguistic pasts...What separates man from beast is memory and if we lose historical memory then we surrender it to those who will abuse it."(URL45)

The adverse fallout of the above is that distortionists of the Hindu cultural and religious heritage like Wendy Doniger of the University of Chicago, and Sheldon Pollock of the Columbia University have become respected global authorities on Sanskrit, Sanskrit literature and ancient Indian heritage. What is more, some rich Indian businessmen have financed them liberally to bring out series based on Indian classics, rather than financing competent Indians. Their interpretations are biased and distorted. It is only lately that people like Rajiv Malhotra and other Indians have begun exposing them. Books by Rajiv Malhotra like 'Breaking India', 'Being Different', 'The Battle for Sanskrit' are worth reading (please check Amazon).

Sanskrit, the most scientific language, and the mother of many Indian and European languages, could have been simplified and modernized (like Israel did with Hebrew), and taught in all schools, in addition to English. It would have revitalized India, and helped unify it.

Blunder–83:
Being Creative with History

There has been little genuine work in Indian history after independence. No worthwhile books on Indian history come from the Indian academe. No importance has been accorded to the study of history, languages, arts, archaeology and such subjects—there is no incentive or encouragement for students to take up those subjects. If brilliant students took these subjects and did research the scene could change. Overwhelming majority of the young go in for graduation in engineering, medicine, law, finance, management and commerce.

The major source continues to be foreign books and foreign writers. Actually, the things have been so manipulated over the last two centuries that anything Indian has been shown in bad light, and anything of West as something superior. And it has been so skilfully done that foreigners or English do not have to do it anymore, it is the Indians themselves who have become self-abusive, and appreciators of all things English or Western.

Part of the reason is that the economy did so badly under the Nehru-Gandhis and India became so pathetic that people felt there was something intrinsically deficient about India and the Indians. Rather than blaming Nehru or Indira Gandhi for their disastrous policies, people began to feel anything Indian was bad, and anything foreign was good. Had India done well after independence, the impression would have been diametrically opposite.

If you have to exploit nations and subjugate its people on a long term basis—for decades and centuries—you can't do it by brute force alone. You have to shake the confidence of people in themselves. You have to make them feel they are nothing—and that they were nothing—before the aggressors. To this end you have to rewrite and reinterpret their history, religion and culture to show how worthless it is in comparison to that of the exploiter. This is what the British politicians, bureaucrats, army-men, writers, novelists and historians did.

You say what you read, and are taught and told. Many books were written by the English and the other foreigners, like Max Mueller, a German, parts of which were either incorrect, on account of limited or deficient research, or deliberately biased and false to serve the imperial or the religious, proselytizing interests. In the absence of books depicting correct position, these books came to be read widely, and some of them became text-books too. Indians have been taught and told what the English and the Christians desired and manufactured to serve their interests. Indians came to believe it. So did others—people abroad in other countries also read these books. Down the generations all started believing the lies as truth. Many Indian writers too based much of their contents on these books written by foreigners, rather than on new research. So, the writings of the Indian authors also started suffering from the same deficiencies. Here are perceptive comments from a genuine scholar Dr KM Munshi in his foreword to his book 'The History and Culture of the Indian People':

> "...Our available sources of information [on Indian past]..., in so far as they are foreign, are almost invariably tainted with a bias towards India's conquerors... The treatment of the British period in most of our histories is equally defective. It generally reads like an unofficial report of the British conquest and of the benefits derived by India from it... The history of India, as dealt with in

most of the works of this kind, naturally, therefore, lacks historical perspective. Unfortunately for us, during the last two hundred years we had not only to study such histories but unconsciously to mould our whole outlook on life upon them... Generations after generation, during their school or college career, were told about the successive foreign invasions of the country, but little about how we resisted them and less about our victories. They were taught to descry the Hindu social system..."{BNS/49-51}

If the British came across something remarkable, which showed India far ahead of the West in the past, they "discovered" its link with the West. If there was something very distinguished about the Aryans, well, they came from the West—India was subject to Aryan invasion and so on. There have been many research-findings and writings to the contrary since, and yet that false impression is allowed to continue in India even today. Apart from further archaeological revelations, an inter-continental research in cellular molecular biology has debunked the AIT: Aryan Invasion Theory. Of course, there is no last word on such things, but there are good reasons to believe that both the so-called Aryans and the Dravidians belonged to India only, and did not come from outside: that has now been proved through DNA study also.

When that racist Aryan-Dravidian theory was propagated, there were many takers for it among the educated Indians themselves, for they felt it enhanced their status—they were not the wretched "natives", their ancestors came from the West! Such was the level of inferiority complex, thanks to successful British propaganda! *Even Mahatma Gandhi, during his South African days, pleaded with the British authorities there that the Indians be treated on par with the British, and not like the native South Africans, for Indians too after all belonged to the superior race, the Aryans—from the West!*

See the cunning of the British in propagating the Aryan-Dravidian theory. It helped create divisions—North vs. South—among Indians, vestiges of which are still there. It helped them show that if there was something superior about the Aryans, it was because they came from the West. It also helped them show that India had been ruled by different groups who came from the West. First, the Aryans, then the Muslims, and then the British. If British were foreigners then so too were Muslims and Aryans. So why crib about foreign rule, that is, their rule—especially, when they had come only to "civilise" the natives and do good for the country! One can understand the purpose and the motivation of the British and other foreigners; but for Indians to talk like them!!

One of the tasks after independence should have been honest and faithful re-writing of Indian history that had been thoroughly distorted by the West by taking the following steps: Setting-up of a large, multi-disciplinary, competent team, free from Marxist, "secular" and biased historians to engage in intensive research, and writing of history and social and economic life of India through the ages in as unbiased a manner as possible, pointing out of flaws and gaps and errors in the existing historical works, and supplementing them; and making available the new researched material and the corrected works in various forms: detailed, academic work, for further research; text-books for schools and colleges; books for general reading in an interesting form; and illustrated books for children. All necessary support should have been given to them—academic encouragement, financial help, incentives, ample opportunities, rewarding career for collection and compilation of all available source materials. Historical fiction too should have been encouraged: we need quality books like that from Amitav Ghosh.

Rather than doing the above, the concerned establishments came to be dominated by the self-serving babu-academics, and the Nehruvians, Marxists, and Socialists who bureaucratised the academics and ensured emasculation of the direction to what suited the Marxist world-view, and the convenience of the Establishment. What we have been having are political hangers-on rather than capable scholars.

Thanks to the above, the biased, distorted version of history written by the West has continued. Rather than demolishing it, our "eminent" sarkari historians reinforced the nonsense. While the English distorted Indian history for their colonial ends, the Indian leftists-Marxists have been further distorting history for their ideological ends, and to please their masters. Arun Shouri's book "Eminent Historians: Their Technology, Their Line, Their Fraud"{AS2} is worth reading in this context. Also the works of Rajiv Malhotra.

These self-serving, dishonest Nehruvian, Marxist academics, apart from the anglophiles, have done great disservice to the profession of writing history. They sidelined the genuine ones, sending them to oblivion. Why have they done so? It paid to do so. You came in the good books of Nehru, himself an anglophile, and thereafter in the good books of his dynasty. You got good positions and assignments. Academic mediocrity was no hindrance to promotions and plum positions as long as you toed the Nehruvian-Marxist-Socialist line. Not only that, by being pro-British or being soft on the British, you got invited by the West for academic assignments, lectures, seminars, and so on. Also, your mediocre writings got published abroad, and were well-reviewed. You also got Indian and international awards. In other words, it paid to be dishonest, unprofessional and abusive to the real India.

The Indian-History-Distortionists did not limit themselves to accepting distorted or false interpretations by the Western historians, they themselves generously contributed to further massive distortion by misrepresenting and misinterpreting the Islamic and the Hindu history. Nehru himself, Nehruvians and Marxists, in their anxiety to appease Muslims, chose to reinvent history, sought to downplay the terrible Islamic excesses and periodic holocausts (mass-loot; burning villages and towns wholesale; mass-killings; unimaginable cruelties; rapes; forced conversions; taking men, women and children as slaves; destruction of thousands of temples, and building mosques over them, or using their material; burning of books, scriptures and libraries, and so on) through the centuries, glorified the Mughal period, ignored the glorious history of many Hindu kingdoms, particularly those in the South, including Vijaynagar, and minimising or ignoring the achievements of Shivaji and Marathas. Wrote BN Sharma: "Nehru's love for English and his leftist leanings spawned a generation of leftist historians who rewrote Indian history in English and put the evidence of history on its head."{BNS/246}

The books that have been authored by the "eminent" Indian court historians during the Nehru-Indira Dynasty era are generally insipid, superficial, distorted, wanting in serious research and insight, and driven by Leftist-Marxist ideological bias. There have been gross distortions. There are parts in Nehru's own books like the "Glimpses of World History" and the "Discovery of India" that contain distorted history ('Blunder-84').

People like Nehru had strangely erroneous notions on how history should or should not be written. If writing of what actually happened in the past—even if it was a millennium or more back—could adversely affect (in their wrong opinion) the present, then give it a spin—that was their view. So, be creative with history—bury or bend or ignore facts, if so warranted. *First*, it is a false notion to presume such adverse effects. *Second*, if different writers presume or interpret differently, should each write a distorted history in his or her own way? *Third*, what really happened would anyway be known through other sources, so why play with facts. When original sources and the writings by the contemporaries are available—those who actually witnessed what happened and wrote about them, like Alberuni and others—why would those who care for history be misled by the creative writers of history? *Fourth*, it is an insult to the intelligence of the general public and readers to be presumed to be gullible enough to swallow wholesale what these creative writers dish out. *Fifth*, it is thoroughly unprofessional to take such liberties with writing of history. It is unwise to try and mould history to suit one's ideological bend or bias, or for political or religious or social or cultural purposes. Truth should not be fiddled with. People should not be taken for granted or taken for fools that they would believe the junk written—like Nehru thought, or Nehruvian-leftist-Marxist historians or the fundamentalists think. There has to be professionalism in writing of history. If history is painful or unpalatable, so be it. It is better to know the truth, whether it is good or bad, palatable or obnoxious. People must learn to face the truth, and learn from history. In fact, the sense of what is good and what is bad also changes from time to time: should history then keep getting re-written? It is a misunderstanding of what the history-writing is all about, and silly, immature socialistic-leftist-'holier-and-wiser-than-thou'-Nehruvian notions of "what is good for the people", and an arrogance that "I know better what people should know" that leads to writing of creative history.

What happened centuries ago is no reflection on people now. Notions have changed. You insult people by twisting the facts. Should the plunder that Qasim, Ghazni, Ghori and other Islamic hordes carried out be swept under the carpet lest it should hurt the Muslims. If Hindu kings did something atrocious in the past, does it mean it should be suppressed, lest it should hurt the Hindus. Christians engaged in terrible atrocities during their campaigns of conversion, inquisitions and colonisation, including the Goa Inquisition. Should it be swept under the carpet? Germans teach their children on Nazi atrocities. Truth must be known. Then only can one come to terms with the reality and ensure the mistakes are not repeated in the future.

Blunder–84:
Distortion of History by Nehru

Books written by Nehru are good, but not great. Many praise Nehru's English. But, going by his books and speeches, one does not feel too impressed. Nehru's contemporaries like Nirad Chaudhuri and many others wrote much better English. Nehru's books betray no research, or breaking of any fresh ground, although they are readable. His works cannot be considered as works of scholarship. What he wrote in 'Glimpses of World History' and 'Discovery of India' are re-narration of the published material, mostly by the British, with their British bias. There is nothing new to learn from it, even at the level of new conclusions or ideas. In parts, it is also wrong on facts and conclusions. His treatment of subjects in his books are superficial. You find no critical appraisals of the topics he dealt with in his books—whether on history or on politics or on economics. Many of his interpretations are stale, copycat Marxist. For a glimpse of the distortion of Indian history by Nehru let us take several examples.

Westernised and anglophile Nehru examined and understood the India's heritage and historical past through the Western glasses, and his writings carried the same bias and misinterpretation. Here is a sample of simplistic, almost juvenile, comment of Nehru in his 'The Discovery of India', driven by an arrogant presumptuousness, and a condescending Western attitude:

"And yet I approached her [India] almost as an alien critic, full of dislike for the present as well as for many of the relics of the past that I saw. To some extent I came to her via the West, and looked at her as a friendly westerner might have done. I was eager and anxious to change her outlook and appearance and give her the garb of modernity..."{JN/50}

Wrote Brig. BN Sharma:

"Nehru's original distortion propounded in the 'Discovery of India' in robbing the Indian culture of its soul of Hinduism, and almost making it appear as a composite culture of diverse religious faiths, mainly Islam and Christianity, had far reaching [negative] influence on our modern historians... The pack of leftist and socialist historians [court/establishment historians] nursed on Nehru's half-baked thoughts lost no time in rewriting history..."{BNS/59}

"Nehru's reading of Indian history was thoroughly flawed by the influence of Western writers and his own predilections of looking at it from his Cambridge perch."{BNS/65}

'The Discovery of India' notwithstanding, its seems Nehru had neither properly discovered the real history of India in several vitals aspects nor grasped the contemporary India, as would be clear from the following faulty interpretation of his in his letter to Lord Lothian dated 17 January 1936:

> "India has never known in the whole course of her long history the religious strife that has soaked Europe in blood... Some conflict arose when Islam came, but even that was far more political than religious... I cannot easily envisage religious conflict in India on any substantial scale... The communalism of today is essentially political, economic and middle class... One must never forget that that communalism in India is a latter-day phenomenon which has grown up before our eyes... With the coming of social issues to the forefront it is bound to recede into the background."{JN3/147-48}

Wrote RC Majumdar, the renowned historian:
"Did Nehru forget the torrent of Hindu blood through which Mahmud of Ghazni waded to India with Quran in the one hand and sword in the other? Did he forget Timur's invasion of India to wage 'war with the infidels'... One would like to know in what sense the iconoclastic fury of Feruz Tughluk, Sikandar Lodi, and Aurangzeb—not to speak of host of others—was political rather than religious? Nor does Nehru seem to have any knowledge of Aligarh Movement and its founder... he [Nehru] was... unable or unwilling to face facts."{Mak/139}

For a glimpse of Nehru's distortion of Indian history let us take another example—that of destruction of Somnath temple. Mahmud of Ghazni destroyed the temple in 1024 CE in his sixteenth of the seventeen raids into India over a period of about 30 years, and carried away camel-loads of jewels and gold. It is said that Mahmud personally hammered the temple's gilded idol to pieces and carted it to Ghazni where they were incorporated into the steps of the city's new Jamiah Masjid [Friday mosque]. Thousands of defenders were massacred, including one Ghogha Rana, who had challenged Mahmud at the ripe old age of 90.

Wrote Zakariya al-Qazwini, a 13th-century Arab geographer:
"Somnath: celebrated city of India, situated on the shore of the sea, and washed by its waves. Among the wonders of that place

was the temple in which was placed the idol called Somnath. This idol was in the middle of the temple without anything to support it from below, or to suspend it from above [might have been so, thanks to magnets]. It was held in the highest honour among the Hindus, and whoever beheld it floating in the air was struck with amazement, whether he was a Musulman or an infidel. The Hindus used to go on pilgrimage to it whenever there was an eclipse of the moon, and would then assemble there to the number of more than a hundred thousand...When the Sultan Yaminu-d Daula Mahmud Bin Subuktigin [Mahmud of Ghazni, who was son of Subuktigin] went to wage religious war against India, he made great efforts to capture and destroy Somnath, in the hope that the Hindus would then become Muhammadans. As a result thousands of Hindus were converted to Islam. He arrived there in the middle of Zi-I k'ada, 416 A.H. [December, 1025 CE]... The king looked upon the idol with wonder, and gave orders for the seizing of the spoil, and the appropriation of the treasures. There were many idols of gold and silver and vessels set with jewels..."{URL55}

In his book "The Discovery of India", Nehru writes about "Mahmud of Ghazni and the Afghans" in 'Chapter-6:New Problems'. A sentence in it goes, "He met with...on his way back from Somnath in Kathiawar." That's all. There is nothing more on Somnath!

But, what Nehru totally omits in "The Discovery of India", he does mention a little bit in his other book which he wrote ten years earlier in 1935—"Glimpses of World History". In "Chapter-51: From Harsha to Mahmud in North India", Nehru writes, "But it was in Somnath that he [Mahmud of Ghazni] got the most treasure..." Nehru further writes:

"He [Mahmud of Ghazni] is looked upon as a great leader of Islam who came to spread Islam in India. Most Muslims adore him; most Hindus hate him. *As a matter of fact, he [Mahmud] was hardly a religious man. He was a Mohammedan, of course, but that was by the way. Above everything he was soldier, and a brilliant soldier.* He came to India to conquer and loot, as soldiers unfortunately do, and he would have done so to whatever religion he might have belonged... *We must therefore not fall into the common error of considering Mahmud as anything more than a successful soldier.*"{JN5}

There could not be worse distortion of history. Nehru is labouring to convince the reader that the havoc that Mahmud wrought was not because he was a Muslim, and that a person of another religion would perhaps have also done what Mahmud did. What utter nonsense! Further, Nehru does not dwell on what all destruction Mahmud wrecked.

The great Indian novelist, Sarat Chandra Chatterjee (Chattopadhyay), had commented:

"They (Muslims) were not satisfied merely with looting, they destroyed temples, they demolished idols, they raped women. The insult to other religions and the injury to humanity was unimaginable. Even when they became kings they could not liberate themselves from these loathsome desires…"{Akb2/226}

Real history is what historians of that time— contemporaries of Mahmud—themselves wrote. As per the contemporary history, when Mahmud of Ghazni was carrying away the Shiva idol of gold from the Somnath temple, many rich traders came together and offered him even more wealth if he returned the idol. Mahmud's retort was: "*I am an idol-breaker, not an idol-seller!*"

Nehru further writes: "Mahmud [of Ghazni] was far more a warrior than a man of faith…" Then about Mathura, he writes, "Mahmud was anxious to make his own city of Ghazni rival the great cities of central and western Asia and he carried off from India large number of artisans and master builders. *Building interested him and he was much impressed by the city of Mathura near Delhi.* About this Mahmud wrote: 'There are here a thousand edifices as firm as the faith of the faithful; nor is it likely that this city has attained its present condition but at the expense of many millions of dinars, nor could such another be constructed under a period of 200 years.'"

What is interesting and intriguing is that nowhere there is any mention by Nehru of how this Mahmud, 'the lover of buildings' as he calls him, mercilessly destroyed Mathura and Somnath!

Wrote Al Utbi, an aide and secretary of Mahmud of Ghazni, in Tarikh-e Yamini: "*The Sultan gave orders that all the temples should be burnt with naphtha and fire and levelled with the ground.*" Utbi wrote that Mahmud first wanted to go to Sijistan, but subsequently changed his mind for "a holy war against Hind", and details how Sultan "purified Hind from idolatry and raised mosques". He also states that the "Musulmans paid no regard to the booty till they had satiated themselves with the slaughter of the infidels and worshippers of the sun and fire." In Tabakat-I Nasiri, Minhaju-s Siraj hails Mahmud for "converting as many as a thousand idol-temples into mosques", and calls him "one of the greatest champions of Islam". No wonder Pakistan names their missiles Ghazni and Ghori.

Nehru wrote: "Of the Indians, Alberuni [who came with Mahmud of Ghazni] says that they 'are haughty, foolishly vain, self-contained, and stolid,'... Probably a correct enough description of the temper of the people." Nehru seems comfortable and fine with anything negative about Indians, but has little negative to comment on the massive destruction wrought, and its wrecker, Mahmud of Ghazni!

Nehru further quotes Alberuni writing about the havoc caused by Mahmud, *"The Hindus became like the atoms of dust scattered in all directions and like a tale of old in the mouths of people. Their scattered remains cherish of course the most inveterate aversion towards all Muslims."* Nehru then comments, *"This poetic description gives us an idea..."* So, Nehru found Alberuni's description of terrible misfortune wrought on India and Hindus poetic!

Incidentally, Alberuni had travelled to India with Mahmud of Ghazni during the first half of the eleventh century CE. The book "Alberuni's India"[ES] is Alberuni's written work on India, translated by Dr Edward C Sachau. Here is an extract from what Alberuni, who was a witness to what Mahmud did in India and to India, and who is referred to by Nehru in the quote of Nehru above, had to say:

"This prince [Sabuktagin] chose the holy war as his calling, and therefore called himself Al-ghazi (i.e. warring on the road of Allah)... afterwards his son Yamin-addaula Mahmud marched into India during a period of thirty years or more. God be merciful to both father and son! Mahmud [of Ghazni] utterly ruined the prosperity of the country [India], and performed there wonderful exploits, by which the Hindus became like atoms of dust scattered in all directions, and like a tale of old in the mouth of the people..."[ES/5,6]

Interesting thing is what Nehru chooses to quote from Alberuni, and what he chooses to ignore. Even God cannot alter the past, but "historians" can!

Blunder–85:
Rise of the Parasitic Leftist-'Liberal' Class

While many studies have documented the predominance of the political left in the academic world, the exceptional areas where they do not have such predominance are precisely those areas where you cannot escape from facts and results—the sciences, engineering, mathematics and athletics. By contrast, no area of academia is more dominated by the left than the humanities, where there are no facts to challenge the fantasies that abound. Leftists head for similar fact-free zones outside of academia.
—Thomas Sowell

Leftists like Rousseau, Condorcet, or William Godwin in the 18th century, Karl Marx in the 19th century, or Fabian socialists like George Bernard Shaw in England and American Progressives in the 20th century saw the people in a role much like that of sheep and saw themselves as their shepherds... The vision of the Left is not just a vision of the world. For many, it is also a vision of themselves—a very flattering vision of people trying to save the planet, rescue the exploited, create "social justice," and otherwise be on the side of the angels. This is an exalting vision that few are ready to give up, or to risk on a roll of the dice, which is what submitting it to the test of factual evidence amounts to. Maybe that is why there are so many fact-free arguments on the left...— and why they react so viscerally to those who challenge their vision.
—Thomas Sowell

In India, you just have to get familiar with the "leftist, anti-American, pro-Arab, anti-Israel, 'secularist', Hindu-baiting, Muslim-apologist, Nehruvian, JNU-type" refrain and jargon to qualify as an intellectual and a "liberal". It's that easy. No serious knowledge or expertise or research work or analytical ability or originality or depth or integrity is required.

Besides, it is safe. Others won't heckle you. Because, these typical Indian leftists have an invisible, informal brotherhood. They support, defend and promote one another, ensure their predominance in the academe and government bodies, and stoutly defend their turf. They are also "eminent" invitees on TV and public functions, seriously ventilating their hackneyed, stale ideas. These windbags have not come up with a single original idea in the last six decades. The Leftist–Socialist–Liberal "Intellectual" is actually an oxymoron, and an anachronism.

The typical Nehruvian-Leftist-Socialist-"Secular"-"Liberal" "Intellectual" parasitic cabal that has spawned the academe, the cultural, literary, archaeological and historical bodies, and sarkari establishments, and has infested and dominated the opinion-making arms like the media unfortunately represents the worst in intellectual traditions, and has become a major stumbling block in progress, for it has managed to pervert sensible discourse. It is even "liberal" and fashionable to be anti-national!

It supports a globally discredited socialistic economic worldview that has practically and amply demonstrated its poverty-perpetuating, misery-multiplying, anti-poor, anti-prosperity, anti-anything-good characteristics. Its "Secularism" does not rise above religion; but is restricted to being anti-Hindu and pro-Muslim, and being unmoved and unconcerned by blatantly illegal proselytization. Its "Liberalism" is being pro-Animal rights while being pro-beef and pro-nonveg; being anti-American while yearning for green-card or assignments in the US; being a rationalist by slamming all Hindu customs and beliefs, while keeping mum on regressive practices of Islam or Christianity; being pro-Arab and anti-Israel; being anti-Sanskrit while being pro-German or pro-foreign language; and so on.

They oppose renaming Aurangzeb road, but never raise a voice against naming of hundreds of government schemes and institutions after the Nehru-Gandhis. They talk of common man and justice and rage about inequality, but find nothing uncommon or no injustice or no inequality in the unjust shameless continuance of the Dynasty! They shout against intolerance, but are themselves the prime examples of intolerance for alternate view (despite it being far superior to theirs)!!

It has been said that true "intellectuals tend to have uneasy relationship with the status quo". However, this deracinated Indian "Intellectual" class has become uncomfortable with the change in the status quo. They feel comfortable only when cocooned in their good, old Nehruvian, "secular", socialistic, I-scratch-your-back-you-scratch-mine, mutually beneficial, incestuous, quid pro quo milieu, at home with the Nehru-Gandhi Dynasty.

Blunder–86:
Mental & Cultural Slavery

Nehru : "The last Englishman to rule India"

We managed to break the shackles of economic and political slavery. But mental and cultural slavery—that we have willingly adopted! That Gandhiji had done much to counter that slavishness is well-known. But, what is strange is that little was done in the post-independence period by Gandhiji's chosen protégé—Nehru—to carry forward Gandhiji's legacy. If anything the mental and cultural slavery increased—in no small measure to the examples set by Nehru himself, and the policies that flourished under him.

Gandhi had once told: *"Jawahar wants Englishmen to go but Angreziat to stay. I want Angreziat to go but Englishmen to remain as our friends."*{DD/261} Knowing this, why Gandhi chose Nehru as prime minister is a mystery. Gandhi used to say that even though Nehru used to fight with him on many issues, ultimately he used to agree with him [Gandhi]. Little did Gandhi know that it was not because Nehru agreed with him, but because Nehru knew that to continue to differ from Gandhi might cost him his position—like it happened with Netaji Subhas—and his goal of becoming the prime minister. Gandhi had also said that after he would be no more, Nehru would speak his language. If Gandhi had watched from heaven, he would have known that Nehru had buried Gandhism along with his [Gandhi's] death. Incidentally, this last thing was told by a Nehru loyalist, Rafi Ahmed Kidwai, himself: *"Jawaharlal has performed the last rites not only of Gandhi but of Gandhism as well."*{DD/279}

Nehru was reported to have said about himself: *"Galbraith, I am the last Englishman to rule India!"*{Wolp2/23} Nehru said this privately in his conversation with the American ambassador JK Galbraith. The remark is also mentioned in Fareed Zakaria's book, 'The Post-American World'{Zak}. We had such great swadeshi nationalists! Nehru had also remarked: *"...in my likes and dislikes I was perhaps more an Englishman than Indian. I looked upon the world from an Englishman's standpoint."*{RNPS/100} It was one thing to feel so, but quite another to be self-complementary or arrogant about it, unless you were not a proud, patriotic, rooted Indian.

In fact, when Nehru had returned to Allahabad from London after his studies, *the then British Governor of UP had hoped that George (as*

Jawaharlal was known in the British Indian circles then) would be Lord Macaulay's dream of a Brown Englishman come true.{YGB/ix} Nehru seemed to fit well with what Lord Thomas Babington Macaulay, the 'Pope' of British–English education in India, had conceptualised in his Minute on Education on 2 February 1835:
"We must at present do our best to form a class who may be interpreters between us and the millions whom we govern; a class of persons, Indian in blood and colour, but English in taste, in opinions, in morals, and in intellect."{URL26}

Effectively, what Macaulay advocated was creation of a new caste: an elite class of anglophiles—the 'Brown Sahibs'. And, that's what the Nehrus were. Motilal Nehru had once banned the use of any language other than English in his house, creating thereby difficulties for those in his large household who didn't know English.{Akb/27}

In his book 'Jawaharlal Nehru, a Biography' Sankar Ghose wrote: "Malcolm Muggeridge, after seeing Nehru shortly before his death, characterized him as *'a man of echoes and mimicry, the last viceroy rather than the first leader of a liberated India'*, and regretted that Nehru was much too British in his approach to have been able to bring about significant or radical changes in India."{SG/193}

Remarked Nirad Chaudhuri in his 'Autobiography of an Unknown Indian, Part-II': "*Nehru was completely out of touch with the Indian life even of his time, except with the life of the self-segregating Anglicised set of upper India who lived in the so-called Civil Lines.*"{NC2} Chaudhuri said that Nehru had little understanding of the actual India life or culture or of Hinduism; and *was a snob, contemptuous of those who spoke English with an Indian accent.*

Wrote Brig. BN Sharma: "Nehru's personality acquired a superficial Indianness and a love for English mores without developing a deep insight into the core of either culture or philosophy."{BNS/10}

NB Khare, the president of the All-India Hindu Mahasabha had said in 1950 that Jawaharlal Nehru was: "*English by education, Muslim by culture, and Hindu by an accident [of birth].*"{Akb/27}

Monuments to Slavishness
Colonial Statues, Names
Right in the heart of New Delhi, at India Gate, staring at all the

passersby—including the freedom fighters, the bureaucrats, the politicians, the ministers—stood the statue of King George V for two decades after 1947!

It was only when Bulganin and Khrushchev visited India in late 1955 that India changed the names Kingsway to Rajpath and Queensway to Janpath in New Delhi, lest the guests feel shocked at our slavishness! However, Khrushchev did not fail to notice the statue of King George V opposite India Gate when driving down Rajpath, and wondered why the relic still stood. But, it was only in 1968 that the statue was removed, and that too upon public outcry!{DD/323}

Colonial Clubs

Bengal Club in Kolkata did not allow Indians till a decade after Independence! Breach Candy Club in Mumbai continued with its sign "Dogs and Indians not allowed" well after Independence!! British openly insulted and humiliated Indians by having such signage in various clubs, train bogies, and other places. Yet, you have many shameless, ignorant Indians still behaving dog-like and praising and admiring the British rule. Khushwant Singh wrote that he was turned away from Madras Club because he was wearing sandals. In another context he wrote that their group was invited to Delhi Gymkhana for a cocktail only to check whether they were properly anglicised and fitted-in!

Colonial Ways

Wrote RNP Singh in 'Nehru: A Troubled Legacy': "Even after independence, Nehru's mental make-up continued to remain as that of the British. He showed a surprise attachment to the old standards set by the [colonial] rulers. At informal dinners at the Prime Minister's house, a liveried attendant stood behind each guest. After twelve years of independence, Harold Macmillan, during his brief visit to India had observed, 'All the etiquette and ceremony were preserved according to the old style. The plates and china remained, with their arms and heraldic devices. The pictures of the viceroys were on the walls... All the pomp and circumstances were unchanged. We were also the chief guests at garden party; there also in the old style with the old viceroy's guard in their splendid uniforms, the trumpeters, the Military Secretary and the ADCs (all in full military).' During the same period, the American ambassador, JK Galbraith [1961–63], after a visit to Wellington in South India noted in his diary, 'The Indian Army officers favour all British Army manners from dress, salute, drill and whisky to moustache. The Queen's picture hangs prominently in the officers' mess.'{RNPS/97}

Western Mores

Wrote Durga Das: "...*several ministers who used to squat on the floor and eat off brass plates or plantain leaves in their homes were now trying to ape Western ways. They contended that Nehru considered only Westernised people modern...*"{DD/292}

Khushwant Singh mentions about an Indian High Commissioner in Canada, who was a member of ICS, and uncle of his wife, in his autobiography 'Truth, Love and a Little Malice', "*...for the Maliks culture meant being well-dressed, knowing European table manners and having a familiarity with exotic drinks like Old Fashioned, Manhattan, ...*"{KS/124}

Like the ICS, the brown sahibs and people like the Nehrus, army was yet another bastion afflicted by the disease. Writes Kuldip Nayar reporting on the position on the front during India-China war:

"I met young army officers sitting in another corner of the lounge. They were bitter and openly spoke of how every requirement of senior officers—soldiers had to carry commodes—were met at the last picket post even while the firing was going on. A captain admitted: 'We are no longer fighters. We think of clubs or restaurants even in the trenches. We have gone too soft; we're no good.'"{KN}

Motilal-Jawaharlal-Tribe vs. Rao-Tribe

There was already a tribe of brown sahibs prior to independence—whose stellar representatives were *Motilal-Jawaharlal Nehru*—but with the departure of the whites, this tribe entrenched itself. Slavishly imitating the West, and adopting their mores was "forward-looking" and being "modern" and "advanced".

Without being jingoistic, one must adopt good things, even if foreign. But, there is a big difference between being rational, scientific, liberal, forward-looking, yet self-respecting; and being slavish show-offs and imitators. You can't start rubbishing your history, language, religion, culture, music, eating habits, medicinal practices, and so on to appear modern. To imitate is a cheap way of appearing forward-looking. Where is the rationality, modernity, scientific temperament and wisdom in panning all things Indian, and in admiring all things foreign!

You notice a sharp contrast between the *Motilal-Jawaharlal-tribe* and the *Narsimha Rao-tribe*? Motilal-Jawaharlal-tribe, that is, the Motilal Nehru dynasty, the imitators like Motilal Nehru, his son, the ICS tribe and the like, went to ridiculous extent to be more English than the Englishmen. They regarded knowing English and being anglicised as enough qualities for gaining positions and privileges, and they bent over backwards to please the English and westerners. They were afflicted by what can be termed as the "Coolie-complex" which resulted in their internalising an inferiority-complex, self-loathing, and a contempt for things Indian, particularly Hindu religion, culture and traditions; and made them ape the West.

On the other hand, the *Rao-tribe*, that is, the current young generation of information technologists, finance professionals, management consultants and the like, who have come up thanks to reversal of the Nehru Dynasty's economic policies by Narsimha Rao, are confident professionals meeting all—English, Americans, Europeans, Australians, Canadians, Japanese, Chinese, Singaporeans—on equal terms, never considering it necessary to know Queen's English (SMS English or Working English being sufficient), or to imitate their mores and habits, merely to look "like them". In fact, if this Jeans generation gets to know of the *Motilal-Jawaharlal-tribe* and what they did, they would be aghast.

Blunder–87:
Distorted, Self-Serving Secularism

Nehru's secularism was not dissociation of religion from the state and politics, as it is supposed to be; rather it was leveraging religious minorities for vote-bank politics. Unlike the minorities, Hindus did not vote as a block. They had their own divisions and sub-divisions, and they didn't vote on religious lines. Therefore, doing injustice to the majority religion (Hinduism) didn't affect votes. However, favouring religious minorities did yield vote dividend, as they voted on religious lines.

Nehru was quick to grasp the convenient road to votes and power, and in the garb of secularism, acted in a way as to procure the votes of the religious minorities. Like in the economic field where Nehru laid the foundations of misery through his debilitating socialism; in the political and electoral field, he laid the foundations of harmful, competitive, religious minoritysm. If minoritysm had led to the prosperity of Muslims and other minorities, one wouldn't mind. But, minoritysm was simply emotional exploitation for votes. In fact, with socialism as the economic creed, neither the majority nor the minority could have prospered.

Ram Manohar Lohia believed that Nehru's acceptance of Anglo-Indian cultural values led to his opposing anything that would give the nation a sense of Indianness. Anglophile Motilal Nehru's upbringing of Jawaharlal was such, and, in turn, Jawaharlal's upbringing of his dynasty was such, that they developed a natural aversion for anything Hindu or Indian.

On the occasion of the opening of the Ramakrishna Mission Institute in Calcutta in 1961, together with the inauguration there of a conference on spiritual life, Nehru burst out in his speech:

"I have always avoided using the word spirituality because of the existence of much bogus spirituality. India is a hungry nation. To talk of spirituality to hungry men does not mean anything... It is no good running away from the daily problems of life in the name of spirituality. I am out of place in this gathering—I am supposed to open this building and inaugurate the conference. I do so."(Croc/136)

What arrogance and ignorance! Was the institute or the conference advocating spirituality to cover up for hunger? Can't endeavouring for a better material life (including, of course, removal of hunger) and search for an enlightened spiritual life go together? If not, in Nehru and Nehru-Dynasty India of poverty-perpetuating socialism, where there would always have been poverty and hunger, there could never have been any place for spirituality!

Author of "Discovery of India" failed to discover that despite different physical features, languages, food habits, costumes, and so on, if there was something that bound India together for centuries from Kashmir to Kanyakumari, and from Dwarka to Dibrugarh, it was Hinduism, and its associated religions like Jainism, Buddhism and Sikhism that arose from its soil. Yet, rather than strengthening those bonds of heritage and unity, Nehru proceeded to either ignore them, or debunk or distort them.

Jinnah's call for observance of 'Direct Action Day' on 16 August 1946 had led to the *Calcutta Carnage*, or the *Great Calcutta Killings*. It was the worst communal carnage committed by the Muslim League that left 5,000 to 10,000 dead, 15,000 injured, and about one lakh homeless! HS Suhrawardy, who was heading the Muslim League-dominated government in Bengal (and who then came to be known as the "butcher of Calcutta"), rather than controlling the situation, further instigated the Muslim goondas. Nehru, as the Vice President of the Executive Council (that became the Interim Government on 2 September 1946, with Nehru as the PM) did little to bring relief to the victims on the specious plea of provincial autonomy—that law and order was a state subject, hence the domain of the Bengal Provincial Government. However, when there was a reaction later to the Calcutta killings in Bihar, Nehru himself rushed to Bihar ignoring the fact of provincial autonomy, even threatening the Bihari Hindus with bombings (!): if Muslims kill Hindus—ignore, or make excuses, or hide behind technical grounds; but if Hindus counter-react to Muslim killings—immediately get into action against the Hindus!

Among many other matters where Patel and Nehru had divergent positions was the issue of Ajmer riots soon after independence. In the Ajmer communal riots, notwithstanding the undisputed mischief of the Muslims, Nehru intervened through his private secretary HVR Iyengar to mollycoddle violent Muslims, and instructed that as many Hindus (though they were not the guilty party) as Muslims be arrested—to maintain balance!

Nehru allowed inundation of West Bengal and Assam by Muslims from East Pakistan (Bangladesh) drastically changing its demographics. It didn't dawn upon him that it was the changed demographics that led to the creation of Pakistan; and allowing demographics to freely change in independent India may again lead to divisions.

Wrote the veteran Congress leader DP Mishra: "...And so far as Nehru was concerned, he had apparently expected secularism to be practised only by the Hindus..." However, when it came to grabbing power, and getting votes, for Nehru, his "secularism" was no constraint. Nehru, Nehru dynasty and the Congress freely indulged in Muslims and minority appeasement to get votes. The Congress so manoeuvred that in the 1957-elections the Bishop of Kottayam issued an appeal to the Kerala Christians to vote for the Congress. The Congress entered into an alliance with the Muslim League in Kerala to grab power. Nehru forgot all about the Uniform Civil Code laid down in the Directive Principles of the State Policy, which could have vastly benefited Muslims women, once he realised that thanks to Mullahs, and conservative but influential Muslim groups, it could cost his party Muslim votes.

Nehru turned a blind eye to illegal and rampant proselytization by the Christian missionaries that adversely affected national interests. This was particularly so in the Northeast where Nehru went by the advice of the Christian missionaries. The net effect was the secessionist movements in the North-eastern states.

The Constituent Assembly's pledge of building one nation with one citizenship became a victim of Nehru's minority-majority syndrome. All those who opposed him were disparaged, labelled non-secular and communal, and weeded out. Gradually, a coterie around Nehru vigorously spread his defective pseudo-secular, anti-Hindu, poverty-perpetuating socialistic claptrap, and sidelined all those who refused to toe Nehru's line. Leaders who differed exited, and leaders who remained became parrots, bereft of individuality and fresh ideas. Commented DP Mishra: *"Gandhiji made heroes out of clay, but under Pundit Nehru's leadership they are being turned into corpses."*{DPM2/262}

Blunder–88:
Nehru & Uniform Civil Code (UCC)

Article 44 of the Directive Principles of State Policy (DPSP) in India sets implementation of the Uniform Civil Code (UCC) as a duty of the State. UCC is meant to replace the personal laws based on the scriptures and customs of various religious communities in India with a common law governing every citizen. These laws cover marriage, divorce, inheritance, adoption and maintenance. The concept of DPSP was inspired by and based on the following: the Irish Constitution, the Declaration of the Rights of Man proclaimed by Revolutionary France, the Declaration of Independence by the American Colonies, and the United Nations Universal Declaration of Human Rights.

In the spirit of the DPSP while the Hindu Code Bills were passed during 1950s, nothing was done to amend the Muslim Personal Laws, despite many prominent Muslims advocating it (with Mullahs and some Muslim bodies expectedly opposing it), including Mahommedali Currim Chagla (MC Chagla), an Indian jurist, diplomat, Cabinet Minister, and the Chief Justice of the Bombay High Court from 1948 to 1958, who had made a vehement plea in favour of UCC. Wrote MC Chagla:

"Consider the attitude of the Government to the question of a uniform civil code. Although the Directive Principles of the State enjoins such a code, Government has refused to do anything about it on the plea that the minorities will resent any attempt at imposition. Unless they are agreeable it would not be fair and proper to make the law applicable to them. I wholly and emphatically disagree with this view. The Constitution is binding on everyone, majority and minority; and if the Constitution contains a directive, that directive must be accepted and implemented. Jawaharlal showed great strength and courage in getting the Hindu Reform Bill passed, but he accepted the policy of laissez-faire where the Muslims and other minorities were concerned. I am horrified to find that in my country, while monogamy has been made the law for the Hindus, Muslims can still indulge in the luxury of polygamy. It is an insult to womanhood; and Muslim women, I know, resent this discrimination between Muslim women and Hindu women."{MCC/85}

For Nehru, power was sacrosanct. Power required getting elected. And, that required votes. Why disturb the apple-cart? If introducing UCC may cost Muslim votes, why do it? Rights and freedom of Muslim women could wait—indefinitely. Let them continue to suffer. Nehru didn't mind "good things" as long as it didn't cost him votes.

Islamic and Muslim-majority countries like Malaysia, Indonesia, etc. have since reformed their personal laws, but NOT the "secular" India. Even during the Nehruvian times, President Ayub Khan of Pakistan and President Habib of Tunisia had changed the Muslim Personal Law in their respective countries. Wrote Brig. BN Sharma:

"His [Nehru's] actions, deliberate and inadvertent, encouraged a separate Muslim identity in the Indian polity whose thoughts and actions were not always co-terminus with the national ethos. By instilling a sense of insecurity in the Muslim minds and thereby encouraging a ghetto mentality and posing as their champion, he berated and denounced the so-called Hindu majority as communal, hoping to create a permanent Hindu-Muslim schism and vote-bank for the Congress... His successors perpetuated the game..."{BNS/264}

To cover-up for his vote-bank politics, Nehru tried to take the expedient plea in the garb of being a "liberal" and a "secular" that a Hindu-majority nation like India would not like to touch the personal laws of the minority, unless the minority itself wants it. The question is: Did Mullahs represent the Muslims? Did Nehru ascertain the wishes of the Muslim women? If Nehru was genuinely a liberal and a secular person, he would rather have said: "We would formulate UCC by involving all concerned. We would educate all Indians on the benefits of UCC. We would educate the Muslims on the reforms that have taken place in Islamic countries. We would encourage wide-ranging discussions. After that, we would ascertain the wishes of each gender in each religious community, including Muslims, through a secret ballot."

It is worth noting that in its judgement of 10 May 1995, the Supreme Court of India reasserted the need of a Uniform Civil Code, commenting that the successive governments till date had been remiss in their duty of implementing their Constitutional mandate enshrined in the Directive Principles; and averred that a UCC was imperative both for the protection of the oppressed and the promotion of national unity.

Incidentally the Goa state has UCC regardless of religion, gender, and caste—Hindu, Muslim and Christians in Goa are all bound with the same law related to marriage, divorce and succession. If there can be a UCC in one state in India, why not in others, especially when it would benefit women.

Notably, when the Indian Penal Code (IPC) for criminal offences is uniformly applicable to all communities, that is, in a way, there is a 'Uniform Criminal Code', why not 'Uniform Civil Code'? Is it because for the Muslims the Sharia is far more stringent on the criminal aspect—cutting off both hands for theft, stoning to death for adultery, and so on—compared to the IPC? Choose IPC for crimes, and for civic cases choose Personal Laws, because they favour males over females!

Blunder–89:
'Sickularism' vs. Somnath Temple

(On Junagadh, please read 'Blunder-31'; and on Somnath and Mahmud of Ghazni, please read 'Blunder-84' above.)

Somnath Temple is on the shore of the Arabian sea in the coastal town of Somnath at Prabhaspatan near Veraval in Junagadh district in Kathiawar in the Saurashtra region of Gujarat. It is 6km from

Veraval, and 80km from Junagadh. It is the most sacred of the twelve Aadi Jyotirlings. The temple is said to have been first built sometime before the common era—BCE. It was destroyed and looted six times: by Junayad, the Arab governor of Sind, in 725 CE; by Mahmud of Ghazni in 1024 CE; by Sultan Allauddin Khilji in 1296 CE; by Muzaffar Shah I, the Sultan of Gujarat, in 1375 CE; by Mahmud Begda, the Sultan of Gujarat in 1451 CE; and by Aurangzeb in 1701 CE. But, each time it was rebuilt.

At the time of liberation of Junagadh in November 1947, Sardar Patel also visited the Somnath Temple (located in the Junagadh State), then in a dilapidated condition, and pledged to reconstruct and restore it to its original glory. Gandhi, when advised by Patel of the commitment, suggested the funds for restoration must come from the public—Patel accepted the advice.

The then Education Minister Maulana Azad, under whom the Archaeological Survey of India (ASI) came, opposed the idea of renovation and suggested that the ruins be handed over to the ASI and preserved in as-is condition. Significantly, he never suggested the same for the Muslim shrines and mosques being repaired by the ASI.{Mak/140}

Upon the death of Sardar Patel, the task was taken forward by the cabinet minister KM Munshi. However, Nehru made no bones about his opposition to the project, and made snide remarks, telling Munshi: "*I don't like your trying to restore Somnath. It is Hindu revivalism.*"{Mak/141}

Cultured and learned Munshi, of course, sent an appropriate and telling reply to Nehru, which included the words:

"...It is my faith in the past which has given me the strength to work in the present and to look forward to our future. I cannot value freedom if it deprives us of the Bhagavad Gita or uproots our millions from the faith with which they look upon our temples and thereby destroys the texture of our lives..."{Mak/154}

KM Munshi had invited President Dr Rajendra Prasad to attend the inaugural function of the rebuilt Somnath temple in May 1951. Protesting vehemently, Nehru opposed Dr Prasad's attending the ceremony, and wrote to him:

"...I confess that I do not like the idea of your associating yourself with a spectacular opening of the Somnath Temple. This is not merely visiting a temple, which can certainly be done by you or anyone else but rather participating in a significant function which unfortunately has a number of implications..."{Swa4}

Nehru also wrote to Rajaji on 11 March 1951 in the connection: "I wrote to him [Rajendra Prasad] that while there was obviously no objection to his visiting this temple [Somnath] or any other temple or other places of worship normally, on this particular occasion the inauguration of the temple would have a certain significance and certain implications. Therefore, for my part, I would have preferred if he did not associate himself in this way..."{JNSW/Vol-16-1/603}

Implications? Anything Hindu, and it hurt Nehru's absurd, defective, and self-serving sense of secularism. Of course, anything Muslim, Buddhist, or Christian never mattered for him in a similar way. Dr Rajendra Prasad, of course, attended, and replied: "I would do the same thing [attend inauguration] with a mosque or a church if I were invited... Our State is neither religious nor anti-religious."{Adv2}

Dr Prasad explained that the significance of Somnath lay in being a symbol of national resistance against invaders. He made an excellent inaugural speech, highlighting, inter alia, that it was the creative urge for civilisational renewal, nurtured in the hearts of the people through centuries that had once again led to the praan-pratishta of the Somnath deity. Somnath was the symbol of economic and spiritual prosperity of ancient India, he said. The rebuilding of Somnath will not be complete till India attains the prosperity of the yesteryear... *Such a grand speech! But, at Nehru's instance, Dr Rajendra Prasad's speech was blanked out by the official channels.*{DD/332}

It is significant that Nehru raised no such tantrums when it came to subsequent restoration of Sanchi or Sarnath, although the same were done through government funds (while Somnath restoration was through public, and not government, funds). Why? They were Buddhist places! Nehru had problems with only Hindu places!

Blunder–90:
Would-have-been Communal Reservation

But for the timely intervention of certain senior, enlightened leaders after independence, Nehru would have carried through yet another major blunder of reservations for Muslims, plunging India further into communal politics under the 'secular' facade, as would be amply clear from the following extracts from the autobiography 'Government from Inside' of NV Gadgil:{Mak/323-5}

"...The temperament of Nehru made simple problems complex and gave cause of anxiety, particularly in the matter of defence of the country... Liaquat Ali [Pakistan's PM] came to Delhi in March 1950, had discussions with Nehru and one fine morning at 10 o'clock Nehru placed before the cabinet a draft of his agreement with him [Liaquat Ali]. I am not sure if Vallabhbhai [Sardar Patel] was consulted before the draft was agreed to. The final two paragraphs in the agreement accepted the principle of reservation for Muslims in proportion to their population in all the services and representative bodies in the constituent states of India. Similar provisions were suggested for the Central Government also.

"Each one of us got the copy of the draft, but no one would open his mouth... I said, *'These two paragraphs nullify the whole philosophy of the Congress. The country had to pay the price of division as a result of its acceptance of separate electorates. You are asking it to drink the same poison again. This is betrayal, forgetful of the last forty years of history.'* Nehru was displeased.

"Gopalaswami Aiyangar said, 'There is substance in Gadgil's objections' and volunteered to redraft the two provisions. I said, 'These two paragraphs must go lock, stock and barrel and no South Indian cleverness would do.' Hearing this Nehru replied with anger, 'I have agreed to this with Liaquat Ali Khan.' I said, 'You must have told him that the agreement can be finalised only after the Cabinet's approval. I cannot speak for other cabinet members, but I am opposed to it hundred percent.' On this Vallabhbhai quietly suggested that the discussions should be postponed to the next day and the meeting was adjourned.

"Vallabhbhai called me for discussions on return home. I told him, figuratively speaking, 'The marriage must not take place simply because the father wants it. The bride is not approved. You must speak plainly now, otherwise complications will follow and we may have to repent. *We have decided on a secular government. This agreement destroys that conception.'* The same night I received from him [Sardar Patel] the papers regarding the revisions suggested by Gopalaswami Aiyangar and his [Sardar Patel's] disapproval of them. I noted on them my agreement with him. When the cabinet met the next day, the last two paragraphs were omitted... The other Ministers congratulated me, but it has to be sadly recorded that at the time of discussion on the draft, none of them opposed Nehru..."{Mak/323-5}

Blunder–91:
Not Seeking Reparations from the British

Said Will Durant, the famous American historian and philosopher in his book 'The Case for India':{WD}

"British rule in India is the most sordid and criminal exploitation of one nation by another in all recorded history. I propose to show that England has year by year been bleeding India to the point of death...

"But I saw such things in India as made me feel that study and writing were frivolous things in the presence of a people – one fifth of the human race – suffering poverty and oppression bitterer than any to be found elsewhere on the earth. I was horrified. I had not thought it possible that any government could allow its subjects to sink to such misery...

"The civilization that was destroyed by British guns... has produced saints from Buddha to Gandhi; philosophy from the Vedas to Schopenhauer and Bergson, Thoreau and Keyserling, who take their lead and acknowledge their derivation from India. (India, says Count Keyserling, 'has produced the profoundest metaphysics that we know of"; and he speaks of 'the absolute superiority of India over the West in philosophy')...

"The more I read the more I was filled with astonishment and indignation at the apparently conscious and deliberate bleeding of India by England throughout a hundred and fifty years. I began to feel that I had come upon the greatest crime in all history...

"The British conquest of India was the invasion and destruction of a high civilization by a trading company utterly without scruples or principle, careless of art and greedy of gain, overrunning with fire and sword a country temporarily disordered and helpless, bribing and murdering, annexing and stealing, and beginning that career of illegal and 'legal' plunder which has now gone on ruthlessly for one hundred and seventy-three years, and goes on at this moment while in our secure comfort we write and read.

"Aurangzeb, the Puritanic Moghul emperor who misgoverned India for fifty years when he died the realm fell to pieces. It was a simple matter for a group of English buccaneers, armed with the latest European artillery and mortars to defeat the petty princes. It was the wealth of 18th century India which attracted the commercial pirates of England and France . This wealth was created by the Hindus' vast and varied industries and trade. It was to reach India of fabulous wealth that Columbus sailed the seas. It was this wealth that the East India Company proposed to appropriate..."

Edmund Burke had predicted in 1783 that the annual drain of Indian resources to England without equivalent return would eventually destroy India. In 1901, Rajni Palme Dutt estimated that one-half of the net revenues of India flowed annually out of the country, never to return: "So great an economic drain out of the resources of the land would impoverish the most prosperous countries on earth; it has reduced India to a land of famines more frequent, more widespread, and more fatal, than any known before in the history of India or of the world."

Commented Rajeev Srinivasan:{URL65}
"A strong case has been made by William Digby quoting Brooks Adams that the Industrial Revolution (circa 1760) could not have happened in Britain had it not been for the loot that came in from India. It is indeed a curious coincidence: Plassey (1757); the flying shuttle (1760); the spinning jenny (1764); the power-loom (1765); the steam engine (1768).

"...Digby estimated in 1901 that the total amount of treasure extracted from India by the British was 1,000,000,000 pounds — a billion pounds. Considering the looting from 1901 to 1947 and the effects of inflation, this is probably worth a trillion dollars in today's money. Serious money, indeed. Shouldn't we ask for some reparation?"

In view of the above, like many countries who had demanded apology and reparations from the countries who had tormented them, India too should have assessed, documented and put a financial estimate to the damages done by the British, should have quantified the loot of two centuries, converted them at 1947 prices, and should then have claimed reparation from Britain, along with written and oral apology. Additionally, a detailed list of all the artefacts, archaeological pieces, precious stones such as Kohinoor and other items stolen from India should have been prepared and reclaimed from the British.

It is worth noting that the arts and treasures that the Nazis took away from the Western countries they attacked and annexed were called loot, and termed unjust, and Germany was forced to return the same to its rightful owner countries. Since the arts and treasures were from the Western countries, and NOT the Asian or African countries, they were loot, and were required to be returned! Loot from the Asian or African countries was not loot. What double standards!!

However, when the ex-colonies like India themselves did not demand return, where was the question of Britain obliging? With anglophiles like Nehru in the saddle, nothing was done in the matter. On Kohinoor, Nehru had made a weird comment:

"To exploit our good relations with some country to obtain free gifts from it [the convenient contention being that Kohinoor was GIFTED (a lie) to the British!] of valuable articles does not seem to be desirable. On the other hand, it does seem to be desirable that foreign museums should have Indian objects of art."

Given such indifferent and baffling attitude, little could have been expected from the anglophile Nehru and his Dynasty.

DYNACRACY & DICTATORIAL TENDENCIES

Blunder–92:
Nehru's Dictatorial Tendencies

"Deep inside his heart, Nehru always was a dictator and first rate politician and manipulator. He feared only Gandhi and Patel—Gandhi because of his moral authority and complete grip on the masses, and Patel because of his firmness, unwillingness to be emotionally blackmailed and the writ in the party."
—Historian Makkhan Lal{Mak/251}

Nehru leveraged the democratic process to gain and retain power, but temperamentally, he was more a dictator than a democrat. He filled the top party posts and the cabinet with "yes-men" so that he could exercise unhindered power, and freely interfere in the workings of the party and ministries not under his direct charge.

Calling Nehru, for the first time, "the Congress dictator", C.R.[Rajaji] also said: "The single brain-activity of the people who meet in Congress is to find out what is in Jawaharlal's mind and to anticipate it. The slightest attempt at dissent meets with stern disapproval and is nipped in the bud."
—Rajaji {RG3/373}

Within months of his tenure as India's first PM, he began acting whimsically and dictatorially without consulting the cabinet and the senior colleagues leading to the well-known rift with Sardar Patel. Patriotic and democratic Sardar Patel was forced to question Nehru's methods leading even to Sardar's resignation in December 1947. The exchange of letters among Nehru, Sardar Patel and Gandhi between November-1947 and January-1948 clearly bring forth the issues of Nehru's dictatorial working. Sadly, Gandhi failed to correct Nehru prior to his assassination on 30 January 1948. (Please also check under 'Blunder-30' Patel's response to Gandhi in January 1950 on the PM's duties and powers.)

Even Acharya Kriplani resigned from the presidency of the Congress in November 1947 protesting timidity of India against Pakistan, its mishandling of the Kashmir issue, and demanding revocation of the standstill agreement signed with the Nizam of Hyderabad. Among the many disastrous results of Nehru's dictatorial working was his series of decision (that were really major blunders) on Kashmir, without taking his cabinet into confidence.

Once the stalwarts like Gandhi and Sardar Patel were no more, Nehru had a free, unbridled play! One can indulge the wise, rational, enlightened, and benevolent semi-dictatorship of people like Lee Kuan Yew of Singapore who within two decades took Singapore from a third-world country to a top first-world country; but can one indulge the blunders-after-blunders of a democratically-elected dictator like Nehru that condemned India to the third-world.

This is what Dr Ambedkar had to say in his resignation letter (from the Nehru's cabinet) of 27 September 1951:

"...The Cabinet has become a merely recording and registration office of decisions already arrived at by Committees. As I have said, the Cabinet now works by Committees... All important matters relating to Defence are disposed of by the Defence Committee. The same members of the Cabinet are appointed by them. I am not a member of either of these Committees. They work behind an iron curtain. Others who are not members have only to take joint responsibility without any opportunity of taking part in the shaping of policy..."

Wrote KM Munshi: "Jawaharlal was a dictator by temperament but had an intellectual aversion to dictators like Hitler and Stalin. He swore by the Constitution but was ever ready to defy or ignore it. Entrenched as he was in unlimited powers, he could never realise the harm that he was doing to the country by twisting the Constitution to his liking."{KMM},{Swa7}

John Mathai (1886–1959) was an economist who served as India's first Railway Minister and subsequently as India's Finance Minister between 1949 and 1951. Being pro-Nehru, he was initially prejudiced against Sardar Patel; but, he soon discovered *Nehru's "feet of clay"*, and remarked:

"Under Nehru the Cabinet had never functioned, and all decisions were taken privately by the Prime Minister and the individual Minister concerned. Even when a decision was endorsed in the Cabinet, the Prime Minister went back on it and reversed the decision... The only time when the Indian Cabinet really functioned was when Nehru was away in Washington for a few weeks towards the end of October 1948 and when Sardar

Patel was acting as Prime Minister. For the first time the cabinet functioned with joint responsibility; and the acting Prime Minister conducted meetings as the British Prime Minister would have."{BK/505}

For his honest and forthright views, especially on the Planning Commission, rather than allowing diversity of opinion and resolving issues democratically through discussions in the cabinet and other forums, John Mathai (then Finance Minister) was eased out by Nehru from the cabinet.{URL34}

How 'democratic' Nehru was would be clear from this extract from Neville Maxwell's book "India's China War":

"There was a Cabinet committee for foreign affairs but that, too, he [Nehru] ignored more often than not, and time and again crucial foreign policy decisions were taken and announced— even acted upon—without either the committee or the Cabinet being aware of them. This was true of the handling of the boundary question with China, which was kept not only from the Cabinet and its foreign affairs and defence committees, but also from Parliament until armed clashes made it impossible to suppress."{Max/91}

If you are arrogant and entertain false notions of your own ability, knowledge and understanding, then you either don't listen to others, or are dismissive of the opinions of the others; and tend to be undemocratic. You don't realise your own limitations; you don't realise you need to involve others, pool the expertise and then evolve a sensible joint solution. Observing your behaviour, people stop telling you the truth; instead they tell you only what you want to hear. You thus cut off honest opinions and feedback. Wrote Rustamji:

"...but when you talked to him [GB Pant, No. 2 in the Cabinet of Nehru], you saw the agility and quickness of a mind that was in strong contrast to his ponderous body. His thinking was quick, incisive: he talked cleverly and had few equals in debate. His English was perfect: and his manner of getting to the root of the problem enviable... Yet when Pant was in the presence of the PM, he was so respectful that he even lowered his standard of intelligence in order that the other may shine..."{Rust/194-95}

Blunder–93:
Nehru—Power Trumps Principles

Despite being already in the powerful position of a PM, Nehru manoeuvred to also become the Congress Party President in 1951, and retained that position till 1954 to ensure a vice-like grip for himself both on the government and the party machinery—even though it flew in the face of the Congress Party principle of one-person-one-post. Nehru then released his presidency in 1955 to his lackey and a nobody like UN Dhebar, and allowed him to continue in that post right till 1959, after which he again manoeuvred to get his daughter Indira Gandhi elected as the party president in 1959.

Ironically, while he himself simultaneously held the post of the Party President and the PM, he got a similar setup banned at the state level—he got a party resolution passed in 1953 forbidding the state CMs from simultaneously holding a post in the PCC (Pradesh Congress Committee), on the ground that the CMs have too much office work to be able to devote time for the party work. (Didn't a PM have as much work? Height of hypocrisy!) Why? He didn't want the state CMs to get powerful, and ever challenge him, or his daughter later. Not only that, he gradually sidelined even the future competitors to his daughter Indira through the Kamaraj Plan of 1963, and other means, to ensure continuance of power for his dynasty. If someone should have first exited the government under the 1963 Kamaraj Plan it should have been Nehru himself for his 1962 India-China war debacle ('Blunder-36'), and for his failure in many other spheres.

Nehru was an agnostic, but his god was power. Principles were fine to enhance one's image, but if they came in the way of power for himself, and after him, for his dynasty, Nehru unhesitatingly and unscrupulously chose power. Nehru ranted on secularism and against communalism and casteism, but when it came to selection of candidates for elections, both religion and caste were critical considerations for him, and for the Congress that was subservient to him. Nehru decried capitalists, but if they obliged his party by filling-in its election war-chest for a quid pro quo, Nehru's "principles" never came in the way. Socialism was not merely a fad for Nehru. What appealed to Nehru and his dynasty in socialism was its vote-gathering and power-grabbing potential by its appeal to the poor and the powerless.

Blunder–94:
Restricting Freedom of Expression

Indian constitution took a regrettable turn on 10 May 1951 when Nehru piloted the First Amendment to the Indian Constitution, that became a law, which, among other provisions, restricted freedom of expression (FoE) by amending Article 19(1)(a).

In sharp contrast to Nehru, the First Amendment to the United States Constitution did the reverse—it expanded the 'Freedom of Expression' (FoE): *prohibited the making of any law* respecting an establishment of religion, ensuring that there is no prohibition on the free exercise of religion, abridging the freedom of speech, infringing on the freedom of the press, interfering with the right to peaceably assemble, or prohibiting the petitioning for a governmental redress of grievances. This First Amendment, along with 9 others, was adopted on 15 December 1791, and constituted the Bill of Rights.

Nehru's amendment was perhaps provoked by the Supreme Court judgment of 1950 on the 'Romesh Thappar vs The State of Madras' case, through which the ban on Thappar's Marxist journal 'Crossroads' was lifted. Through the case, the Supreme Court had effectively recognized unfettered freedom of expression as compliant with our original Constitution, like in the US.

Thanks to Nehru's amendment above, poor Majrooh Sultanpuri, the famous and brilliant lyricist and poet, was thrown into Arthur Road jail in Mumbai in the early 1950s for a year for writing a verse critical of Nehru!{URL36} Dharampal, a highly regarded thinker-scholar, who had addressed an open letter to Nehru after the 1962 India-China war debacle, was also jailed by Nehru.

During the Nehruvian era, a number of books, films and film songs that appeared directly or indirectly critical of the government were censored or banned. For example, the famous poet Pradeep's song in the film 'Amar Rahe Ye Pyaar' of 1961 was censored because of these lines: "Hai! Siyaasat kitni gandi; Buri hai kitni firqa bandi; Aaj ye sab ke sab nar-naari; Ho gaye raste ke ye bhikari."{URL44}

Nehru was not really a liberal in the classical sense, nor was he familiar with the intrinsic Hindu ethos of freedom of expression and free flow of ideas. Hinduism allows, and even encourages, people to discover their own truth.

Blunder–95:
Nehru & Democracy

Not seldom are those who tend to be critical of Nehru reminded it is thanks to Nehru India is a democracy, whose fruits all Indians are enjoying—including criticising him. Does the contention hold?

Elections were conducted in India during the British times too. Congress had not only won the 1937-elections and formed ministries in many states; post elections, with power in their hands, they had already become so corrupt that Gandhi had desired disbanding of Congress after independence. The last pre-independence elections were held in 1946. Independent India inherited many democratic institutions, including election machinery—only it needed a boost to handle universal suffrage.

It was, in fact, the Constitution of India framed under Dr Ambedkar, and passed by the Constituent Assembly comprising scores of worthies and headed by Dr Rajendra Prasad, which had provided for universal adult franchise and democratic setup. So, how can the credit be given to Nehru?

Nehru's own election as the President of Congress in 1946, that led to his becoming India's first prime minister upon independence, was undemocratic. For details, please see 'Blunder-6'.

In the long-term interest of the nation, a responsible democrat would have assiduously worked to establish a multi-party, or at least a two-party democratic system. However, too keen for himself and his dynasty to forever remain in power, Nehru saw to it that India's nascent democracy was not nurtured for a robust opposition. He tried all the tricks to defame, belittle and weaken the opposition.

How can a person like Nehru who introduced dynastic politics (next 'blunder') into India be called a democrat? The biggest menace threatening India is not corruption or lack of governance or reforms or Babudom, but dynasty, because that is at the root of all others. Nehru never worked to make India a really mature democracy. His exertions were to actually turn it into a hereditary, Nehru-dynastic democracy. In doing so, as a collateral to dynacracy (dynastic democracy), India also turned into a nepoticracy, feudocracy, and chamchacracy.

ꞌBlunder–96:
Promoting Dynasty & Dynacracy

Motilal Promotes Jawaharlal
Jawaharlal Nehru was unfairly promoted by his father, Motilal Nehru; and in the true dynastic tradition, Nehru promoted Indira, who in turn, even more shamelessly promoted her progeny. When Motilal Nehru retired as the Congress president in 1929, he made sure by lobbying with Gandhi that his son, Jawaharlal, ascended the gaddi, over the heads of people much more senior and capable than him. Please check 'Blunder-1'.

Nehru Promotes His Sister Vijay Lakshmi Pandit
On how Nehru favoured his sister, please check 'Blunder-11'.

Wrote S. Nijalingappa in 'My Life and Politics'[Nij/102]:
"Another such instance I remember was when Dr. S. Radhakrishnan was president of India...I used to call on him whenever I was in Delhi...In his talks with me, as I believe with others too, he was very frank and open. One day, when I went to him he said, 'Nijalingappa, today I put my foot down. Do you know why?' He then continued, *'Pandit Nehru comes to me and wants me to make his sister, Vijay Lakshmi Pandit, vice-president of India.* I had to tell him, "You are the prime minister of India, your daughter is the president of Indian National Congress and you want your sister to be vice-president. What would people say? I cannot have it." I put my foot down and sent him away.' I think Nehru had promised his sister the post and when she could not get it, she was very angry with her brother. She complained to me about it when she came to my house for breakfast, and said that her brother did not keep his promise. I did not tell her what Dr S. Radhakrishnan had told me."[Nij/102]

Nehru Promotes Indira Gandhi
Although Indira Gandhi had done little work for the Congress, she was made a member of the Congress Working Committee in 1955— entry directly from the top, rather than rising from the bottom. In 1957, Indira was made member of the powerful Central Election Committee.

Durga Das writes in his book[DD] that in 1957 in his weekly

column in Hindustan Times he wrote Nehru was building up his daughter for succession. He says he had checked with Maulana Azad before writing the column, and Azad had said he too had independently reached the same conclusion. Even Govind Ballabh Pant had the same opinion. Later, when Nehru remonstrated with Durga Das on the column, to mollify Nehru, Durga Das assured him that what he had written would bring good publicity to Indira and would stand her in good stead—at which Nehru felt happy and smiled.{DD/370}

In 1958, Indira became a member of the Central Parliamentary Board—Nehru made a vacancy for her by himself resigning from the Board: a deft move! She was then made President of the Congress in 1959, to the astonishment of all, after an intense behind the scenes drama, managed through others by Nehru. Nehru had thus commented on her being made the President: "I am proud of Indira Gandhi as my daughter, my comrade and now as my leader. It is superfluous for me to say that I love her. I am proud of her integrity and truthfulness."

Wrote Rajmohan Gandhi: "Suddenly, at this juncture, Indira Gandhi, Jawaharlal's daughter, was named party president. Her talents were yet a secret, and she had no experience of party work. Several of Nehru's colleagues were offended by the choice but said nothing. *C.R. [Rajagopalachari] was outraged.*"{RG3/373}

Kuldip Nayar wrote: "This was where I first heard that Congress President V.N. Dhebar was resigning and Indira Gandhi was taking over. Pant had supported Nehru at Vinoba's ashram but not at the CWC when Indira Gandhi was nominated as the party president. He was careful not to oppose Nehru's daughter directly but argued that her frail health would come in the way of the extensive travels the Congress president was required to undertake. Raising his voice, Nehru told Pant that 'she was healthier than both of us' and could put in longer hours of work. The subsequent discussions, as I noted, were to fix the date on which she would assume charge. *This was the first time that dynastic politics came to the fore, and the Congress since then has been following the practice of invariably having a member of Nehru family at the helm of affairs*...Left to Nehru, he would have liked Indira to succeed him as prime minister, but too many Congress leaders, with a long stint of sacrifice and struggle for the country's freedom, were still on the scene at the time."{KN}

Nehru had also started developing Indira as a public figure. By making her the official host, Nehru gave her exposure to foreign dignitaries and guests. Nehru also sent her on various foreign assignments like India's representative to the UNESCO's Executive Board, and tour of foreign countries on Nehru's behalf.

After the 1962-debacle, and his plunging popularity, Nehru used the Kamaraj Plan of 1963 to clear the way for Indira from the seniors. Morarji Desai, who had not objected then, later told Michael Brecher about the Kamaraj Plan: "It seemed to have been motivated not only to get rid of him [Morarji] but also to pave the way for Mrs Gandhi to the Prime ministership, just as Motilal [Nehru] had passed on the Congress presidency to him (Nehru)."{IM2}

Acharya Kripalani believed that the evils in the country emanated from the top and that Nehru was the pace-setter in abusing patronage and power.{DD/371}

One may say that Nehru did not make Indira Gandhi the PM. But, he was working towards it. However, before he could fulfil his mission he passed away. Though he had done the ground work—given the necessary visibility to her. Lal Bahadur Shastri had himself told that *"in Panditji's mind is his daughter"*. Writes Kuldip Nayar: "I ventured to ask Shastri one day: 'Who do you think Nehru has in mind as his successor?' '*Unke dil main to unki saputri hai* [In his heart is his daughter],' said Shastri...Nijalingappa said he was pretty sure that Nehru had his daughter in mind as his successor. In his diary, he wrote on 15 July 1969 that Nehru '*was always grooming her for the prime-ministership obviously and patently*'."{KN}

Wrote MO Mathai: "A couple of years ago Vijaya Lakshmi asked me, 'Why did Bhai [Nehru] drop me completely during the last phase of his life?' I did not wish to answer that question at the time, and managed to change the subject. I have already given in this chapter part of the reason. The other part is that Nehru did not want to build up a rival to his daughter who was much younger. More about this in the chapter on Indira!"{Mac/142}

Nehru Laid the Foundations of Dynacracy: Dynastic Democracy

Democracy grafted on a nation with a strong feudal mindset is likely to degenerate into dynacracy, unless the leaders who matter consciously devote themselves to ensuring it does not happen, both by setting an example themselves and by putting in place appropriate systems. Nehrus did the reverse. The dynastic politics that Nehru started and thus sanctified, and what was even more shamelessly promoted by his daughter, has now vitiated and poisoned our whole democratic system. Following in the footsteps of Motilal, Jawaharlal and Indira, now most leaders promote their own dynasty in politics. We are now already in the era of blooming dynacracy! It has become all pervasive and has vitiated and poisoned our democratic system. The whole democratic process would soon get reduced to jockeying for power among select dynasties!

It's not just Nehru's heirs—we now have heirs in nearly every state. Abdullah & Sons and Mufti & Daughter in J&K; Mulayam Singh Yadav, Son & Family in UP; Badal & Sons in Punjab; Chautala & Sons, Hooda & Sons in Haryana; Lalu-Rabri & Sons in Bihar; Sharad Pawar & Daughter & Nephew, Thackery & Sons & Nephew in Maharashtra; YSR's Family in Andhra; Karunanidhi & Sons in Tamil Nadu; and, of course, spouses and sons and daughters and relatives of many other politicians. Many legislative and parliamentary constituencies are now private estates.

As per a study detailed in Patrick French's book 'India: A Portrait'{PF2}, about 28.6% of the MPs in the Indian parliament are HMPs—Hereditary MPs. Even more revealing are the figures that while over two-thirds of the 66 MPs aged 40 years or less are HMPs, all the MPs below 30 are HMPs! Going by this trend, we would soon be back to where we were in the "good" old pre-independence period: ruled by hereditary rajas and maharajas and princes. Strangely, this trend was started by the one who vexed most eloquent against rajas, maharajas and the feudal setup in the pre-independence days—Jawaharlal Nehru.

Defending the Indefensible: Dynacracy

Among the biggest crimes of the Nehru Dynasty is that they have taken the guilt and the shame out of dynastic politics, and have encouraged others to follow suit, through their example. However, India is a country whose culture and thinking has been so vitiated by the dynasts and their hangers-on and direct and indirect beneficiaries that even the indefensible—dynastic democracy—is defended. Dynacracy-tolerant "intellectuals" often question: Are the dynasts trying to get in undemocratically? No. Then, what is the problem. If one fights an election, gets elected, and becomes a political leader, what illegality or wrong is committed—everything is democratic and above board.

Although obviously absurd, one is not surprised to hear such pleas. What is happening dynasty-wise, be it Nehru-Gandhi or DMK or Lalu or any of the scores of other dynasties, is so obviously wrong that it should neither attract any defence, nor any arguments to demolish that defence. However, the original Dynasty has been able to do such publicity over the decades through the compliant MSM, intellectuals and netas that the reverse has happened: questioning the dynastic succession has become questionable!

A prominent argument advanced goes like this. Dhirubhai Ambani's sons are also businessmen. That is, businessmen's wards generally become businessmen. Progeny of artists—singers, musicians, writers, and others—also become artists. Sons and daughters of Bollywood actors also become actors. Doctor's wards also become doctors. Farmer's son is often a farmer. Dynasty is everywhere. So why pick on only political dynasties? This superficial argument can fool only the gullible. Progeny of doctors, artists, actors, businessmen becoming also doctors, artists, actors, businessmen affect them only, not others. However, progeny of a neta/politician becoming a neta affects people at large. It is the requirement of a democracy to be representative and hence non-dynastic. Business houses or art houses or professional establishments are not required to be representative.

In politics too, you once had hereditary rajas and maharajas and kings and queens. But the days of those retrograde systems are gone—now replaced by a democratic system. In a way, therefore, hereditary or dynastic succession is unconstitutional. Then, why bring it in from the backdoor. It is against the spirit of the Constitution. Dynastic succession is feudal, inappropriate, unjust, and harmful for the nation, whether it happens in the communist North Korea or the Islamic Saudi Arabia or in the democratic or dynacratic India.

To the pro-dynasty "Don't they fight elections and win" argument, the question is: How do they win? A far more competent competitor would not even get the party-ticket. But for the dynasty scion, it is for the asking. They get on a platter the constituency nursed for years by their parents. And they have money to splurge to get elected. After getting elected, a high position within the party-organisation or the government is assured to them—something denied to the many much more competent but less-connected contenders. The whole thing is unjust, unfair and undemocratic.

The sophists question: "Are you saying that children of a politician should be denied a political career? Would that be democratic?" It is not that the progeny or relatives of a politician should be denied a political career. Only thing is that they should not be allowed to derive an unfair advantage. That is possible when things are enforced to be genuinely democratic, nepotism is rooted-out, and talent and ability take the front-seat. Is there any inner-party democracy in the political parties? What if the person from the so-called dynasty also has merit? Well, does he or she have more merit compared to the many with merit? If yes, fine. But, let there be a fair comparison, competition and debates.

Why is Dynacracy Disastrous?

Dynacracy (Dynastic Democracy) is bad not just because we resent some having unfair advantage, it is bad because it results in mediocrity, and it discounts merit. The quality of leadership emerging out of a dynastic process can never be really good. For proof, check for yourself the unutterable underachievements of the underwhelming leadership of the dynasts, at the state or at the Centre, and how it has become worse and worse down the generation: for example, the reverse geometric progression of woefully falling standards from Nehru down to Rahul Gandhi.

Don't those who defend dynasties on the specious plea that "after all they get elected" realise that it is thanks to their running, or rather, running down the country for decades that India could do no better than rank among the poorest and the most corrupt countries in the world and remains in "dark" ages as a third-world country.

The principal hazards of dynasty politics are the following: (a)It discounts merit and prevents competent from rising. (b)It thwarts internal democracy in political parties. (c)Dynastic politics, nepotism, institutionalised corruption and non-accountability go together. (d)Dynastic politics is always at the expense of the nation. (e)It is the biggest menace. It's the foundation of India's misery.

Blunder–97:
Not Limiting the Term of the PM

If Nehru was a true democrat, he should have taken a page out of the US Constitution, and limited the term of a prime minister to just two terms—like the President of the US. Not only that, on completion of two terms passing on the baton to one's kin should also have been prohibited, to ensure dynasties did not take over politics. Dynasties have a vested interest in continuance at the expense of the nation. They also have a vested interest in covering up all the wrong doings of the dynasty.

Following Nehru's footsteps, you find a strange spectacle of people—whether young or old, and whether in a political position or a bureaucratic position or a position in a sports body—not wanting to ever quit. Where extension is not possible, bureaucrats would seek some position or the other post retirement.

Contrast the above with George Washington, co-founder of the USA. He was proclaimed the "Father of the Country" and was elected the first president of USA in 1789 with virtually no opposition. Washington retired in 1797, firmly declining to serve for more than eight years—two terms—despite requests to continue. His tremendous role in creating and running America notwithstanding, he didn't harbour or propagate self-serving notions of indispensability. The 22nd amendment to the US constitution setting a maximum of only two terms for the president came only in 1947. Prior to that it was only an observed good practice for over a century.

Thomas Jefferson, the third President and one of the founding fathers of the US, famous for his many achievements and for having originally drafted the Declaration of Independence of the US in 1776, was also requested, pressurised and persuaded to consider continuing as President after completion of two terms in 1808, on account of his excellent performance on multiple counts—during his tenure the geographical area of the USA almost doubled, upon purchase of Louisiana from the French, which in turn ended the dispute about the navigation of the Mississippi. However, stressing the democratic and republican ideals, Jefferson refused, even though there was no legal bar then, and people would have loved him to continue.

EVALUATING NEHRU

Can a country attain greatness even if its leaders are Lilliputs; and vice versa, can the country's leaders be considered great even if the country goes to dogs—or remains wretchedly poor and achieves only a fraction of what it could have?

You can't do justice to evaluating a person by just talking in general terms like: "He was a great patriot...he sacrificed so much... he ensured unity of India (as if under someone else, India would have got divided) ...he made India a democratic country... he was founder of India's foreign policy... and so on."

Often, when we talk of "greatness" of a political leader in India, it is "greatness by definition", not "greatness evaluated by factual, material achievements"! For a fair evaluation, you have to adopt a right approach, a proper set of rules, the "dos" and the "don'ts":

Rules for Evaluation

DOs

Rule-1 (Dos)

When evaluating a national leader, evaluate his or her contribution to the nation on a set of vital parameters, for example, GDP, Per-Capita Income, Relationship with Neighbours, Internal Security Position, External Security Position, Literacy Level, Spread and Availability of Quality Education at all levels, and so on. Determine those set of parameters at the start of the tenure of that leader, and also at the end of his or her tenure. Check the difference.

Rule-2 (Dos)

The above, by itself, is not sufficient. Some progress would anyway be made with the passage of time. The point is whether the progress was as much as it could or should have been. For example, say 5 IITs were opened in 17 years. Could or should they have been 50? Were only 5 out of the possible 50 opened? That has to be evaluated. For this, also determine a set of developing, but fast-growing countries against whom you would like to benchmark your performance. Evaluate the progress of those countries for the same period. Compare.

DON'Ts

Rule-3 (Don'ts)

Do not mix the personal with the professional or the political. There is little point offsetting poor political performance against good personal traits, and vice versa. If you are evaluating a politician, evaluate political contribution. Other aspects may be evaluated, but separately, so as not to mix up issues. For example, Gandhi as a person must be evaluated separately from Gandhi as a politician.

Rule-4 (Don'ts)

Greatness has nothing to do with popularity—media can be managed, popularity can be purchased, general public can be manipulated and led up the garden path. Nor has greatness anything to do with winning elections and ruling for a long time. Hosni Mubarak ruled for 41 years—does that make him great? Gaddafi had been ruling for decades—did that make him great? The point is, after winning an election, what you did for the people and the country. If you did little, you actually wasted the precious time of the people and the country.

Rule-5 (Don'ts)

Don't go by generalised descriptions or attributes that don't measure the real comparative position on the ground. For example, statements like, "He was a great democrat, thoroughly secular, highly honest, scientific-minded person, who loved children, and gave his all to the nation," or, "He was my hero, he inspired generations, and people loved him," don't help the purpose of evaluation.

Rule-6 (Don'ts)

Don't go by what the person wrote or spoke or claimed. A person may talk big on lofty ideals and make grand claims, but the real test is what concrete difference he made to the nation and to the lives of the people—that measurement alone is relevant. Did the person walk the talk? Did he really help achieve the goals he talked about?

I may make big claims on being democratic. But, is my actual conduct democratic? Do I respect the opinion of others? Or, do I act dictatorial? Am I above nepotism? Or, do I promote my own? I may talk big against social injustice. But, has it substantially come down during my tenure? Mere talking is not enough.

Unless a leader scores high as per rules 1 and 2, he or she cannot be adjudged as great. This is quite logical. You do not evaluate Sachin

Tendulkar's cricket on his personal goodness, you evaluate it on his performance on the field, on the runs scored—not in isolation or as an absolute, but in comparison with others.

On these criteria, one can say that LKY—Lee Kuan Yew—of Singapore was indeed a great leader.

You evaluate Ratan Tata for his business performance by evaluating not Ratan Tata, the person, but the Tata Group—its actual business and financial performance. What was the business and the financial status of the Tata Group when Ratan Tata took over, and what was it when he relinquished control; and how did it compare with the progress made by other business houses. If the performance of the Tata Group is evaluated to be bad, then it is the performance of Ratan Tata which would also be evaluated as bad. You would not try to lessen Ratan Tata's bad performance by either blaming his subordinates or colleagues; or offset the same against his stellar personal qualities.

This is the right approach. You evaluate Ratan Tata or Mukesh Ambani or Narayan Murthy by evaluating the performance of the companies they are heading. If the companies are doing well, you give credit to them. But, rare is a case where a company does badly or goes into bankruptcy, and you still evaluate the person heading it as good and competent. *Strangely, this common sense approach goes for a toss when you try to evaluate a political leader—a country might have gone to dogs, but the leader was great!!*

Nehru Evaluated As Per the Rules Above

Keeping the above rules in mind, and checking the major blunders of the Nehruvian era that we highlighted above, Nehru's 17 year period stretching from August 1947 to May 1964 appears to be an unmitigated disaster! Nehru fails to measure up both as per Rule-1 and Rule-2 of evaluation explained above. Nehru's balance-sheet is therefore in deep red on all the major counts.

Unfortunately for the millions of Indians, particularly its poor, Jawaharlal Nehru, despite his best intentions, ended up as an all-round comprehensive failure, unwittingly laying the foundations of India's misery. Sadly, Nehru's dynasty, rather than retrieving India from the mess, reinforced those blighted foundations.

"Greatness" by Definition

Often, when we talk of "greatness" of a political leader in India, it is "greatness by definition", not "greatness evaluated by factual, material achievements"! Very often you find Nehru evaluated as per rules 3 to 6 given earlier, the "don'ts". People—even intellectuals, social commentators, politicians, senior journalists and writers—make generalised statements to eulogise him, even as they show indulgence to his gross failures.

Unfortunately, this led to giving him a stature he didn't deserve. Falsehood is always harmful to the nation. He was so drunk on his own false image that he arrogantly went about with his own "wisdom", ignoring or belittling others, and committed blunders after blunders, with no one to stop him. Ultimately, it harmed the nation. It didn't stop at that. He was given such a projection, that his descendants found it easy to claim the top-most position without working for it or deserving it. So, those who unjustly praise or eulogise a national leader do a disservice to the nation. One wonders where Nehru would have been had he not been Motilal's son, and had Gandhi not anointed and sold him.

Alternate Posers to Help Evaluate

If we were to evaluate on the basis of a set of posers keeping the above Rule-1 and Rule-2 in mind, the questions would most likely be as under.

Were the Indian borders more secure and peaceful by the end of Nehru's tenure compared to what they were when he became the prime minister? That is, were we better off with our external security?

The answer is a big NO: Please check 'Blunder-33–47'.

Did India have all friends as its neighbours by the end of Nehru's tenure, thanks to his reputed foreign policy?

No. Friends like Tibet disappeared. China, a friend, became an enemy. Sri Lanka gave you no "bhav"—weightage. Pakistan remained an enemy. Please check 'Blunder-48–58'.

Was India a more respected nation by 1964, thanks both to our foreign policy and our achievements?

Unfortunately, no. It became an object of contempt, a country others ignored, and an international beggar.

Was India's internal security better by the end of Nehru's tenure compared to that at the beginning?

Again, NO. Please check 'Blunder-59-63'.

Did poverty decrease significantly in the 17 long years of Nehru's rule?
No. Poverty and misery multiplied: Pl. check 'Blunder-64-70'.

Did India become self-sufficient in food during Nehru's tenure?
No. Rather, it became a land of hungry millions, and an international beggar. Please check 'Blunder-65'.

Did India become a highly industrialised nation during Nehru's tenure?
No. India's industrial growth was actually throttled by Nehru thanks to his socialist fad and putting severe restrictions on the private sector. Only the grossly inefficient public sector expanded, financed among other sources, by the British debt-repayment. Public sector became a huge money-sink and a white elephant. : Please check 'Blunder-64'.

Compared to the nations in SE Asia, did India do better economically?
No. It was left far, far behind by them, even though India started off with a huge advantage. : Please check 'Blunder-67, 68'.

Did India emerge as a prosperous nation, 17 years after independence?
Certainly not. Please check 'Blunder-64-70'.

Did literacy rate dramatically improve?
No. Please check 'Blunder-79'.

Was the curse of untouchability eradicated? Was the lot of Dalits better?
No. Please check 'Blunder-63, 75'.

Did minorities, including Muslims, feel more secure?
No. Please check 'Blunder-63'.

Did criminal-justice system improve to provide justice and security to aam-admi?
No. We carried on with the callous colonial system, and actually made it even worse. Please check 'Blunder-71, 72'.

Did elitist babudom become service-oriented and empathetic to the poor?
No. Among the worst things that happened under Nehru,

accentuated later under Indira, Sanjay and Rajiv, was India's Babudom: the IAS-IPS-IFS-IRS combine, those from the criminal-justice system, and the bureaucracy lower down. Babudom is very intimately related to socialism, poor rate of growth, continued poverty, injustice and misery. It became more corrupt, self-seeking, indifferent and vicious. Pl. check 'Blunder-71–74'.

Did corruption and dishonesty come down in the political and the bureaucratic setup?
No. It got worse. Please check 'Blunder-73, 74'.
Unfortunately, it's a series of "Nos"!

The above posers are not exhaustive, they are only illustrative in nature. There are many more vital posers whose answers too are in the negative.

Defending the Indefensible

Dreamer & an Idealist (or a *Nabob of Cluelessness*)

Unable to rebut Nehru's faulty handling of many issues like Kashmir, India-China war, economy and so on, his admirers have invented an *innovative alibi*: Nehru was a dreamer and an idealist! "Dreamer" implying he had great vision, and "idealist" implying that he was a man of high principles, lofty moral standards, and impeccably cultured and hence, thanks to the machinations of his unprincipled adversaries, he lost out on certain counts.

Rather than a dreamer or an idealist, Nehru was indeed, as someone has said, a *'Nabob of Cluelessness'*.

One would have highly appreciated Nehru as a dreamer if he had helped millions realise their dreams that they had upon independence. Sadly, the fond dreams of millions turned into nightmares! Was dreaming of a political leader at the top-most responsible position an elitist luxury and an indulgence afforded by the exclusive environs of Lutyens' Delhi!

Talking of "idealism" and "high principles", may one ask what were those high principles that prevented Nehru from finding a negotiated settlement of Indo-China borders? What was that lofty ideal that allowed Nehru to mutely accept erasure of our peaceful neighbour Tibet as a nation? What were those principled compulsions that drove Nehru to refuse Tibet's repeated pleading to raise its issue in the UN? What were those high moral standards that forbade Nehru to ensure Sri Lanka treated its Tamil citizens fairly?

What was that idealism that allowed nepotistic promotion by him of his daughter? Where was the great morality in protecting the corrupt—which he tried for some of his colleagues? Was it conscionable for him to continue as a prime minister after the debacle in the India-China war? Why the cultural "finesse" of many of his acts upon the death of Bose, Patel and Rajendra Prasad (highlighted earlier in the Unabridged Edition: 'Blunder-106–121') questionable?

Further, being a dreamer and an idealist may be excellent personal qualities, but when evaluating a person politically and as a leader, the relevant points to evaluate would be if the dreamer-idealist managed to convert those dreams into reality for the masses and whether the nation moved towards some great ideal.

Innovative Counterfactuals!

Unable to eulogise Nehru on facts, many admirers, on the self-serving assumption that a person other than Nehru would not have been able to do what Nehru did, resort to innovative counterfactuals like: "Had it not been for Nehru India would not have remained united and secular. But for Nehru, there would have been no democracy, and the citizens would not have enjoyed freedom..." (Pl. check 'Blunder-89, 90, 92 to 102') *If facts don't help you, go by presumptions and probabilities!*

What if one advanced an alternate counterfactual and argued that an alternate person (like say Sardar Patel or C Rajagopalachari or Dr BR Ambedkar) as prime minister would have made India more united, more secure, more secular and free from communalism, more democratic and much more prosperous, and India would have been well on its way to becoming a first-world nation by 1964!

Conclusion

Nehru's leadership is unique not only in terms of the paucity of achievements, or the large gap between the potential and the actuals, or a very poor show compared to other comparable nations; but in the blunders that he made. Other leaders too make mistakes, but Nehru can beat them all hands down. The number, the extent, and the comprehensiveness of the Nehruvian blunders can't be matched. Comprehensive? Other leaders blunder in one or two or three areas. Not Nehru. His was a 360 degree coverage. He blundered in practically all areas (and sub-areas, and in very many ways): external security, internal security, foreign policy, economy, education, culture,... it's a long list. An examination of his record leaves you gasping. Here is a very cryptic label to capture the essential Nehru: "*Nabob of Cluelessness*".

Nehru bequeathed a toxic political (dynastic and undemocratic), economic (socialistic), industrial (inefficient and burdensome public and state sector), agricultural (neglected and starved), geographic (most borders insecure), administrative (incompetent and corrupt babudom), historical (Marxist and Leftist distortion), educational (elitist, and no universal literacy), and cultural (no pride in Indian heritage) legacy.

Of course, quite irrespective of the fact that the balance-sheet of the Nehru-period was deep in red, it cannot be denied that Nehru meant well: it is another matter that his erroneous understanding of economics, foreign affairs, external security and many more things led to policies that proved disastrous for the country. Also, *he was well-intentioned. But, then, road to hell is often paved with good intentions!*

* * * * *

BIBLIOGRAPHY

A Note on Citations
Citations are given as super-scripts in the text, such as {Azad/128}.

Citation Syntax & Examples
{Source-Abbreviation/Page-Number}
e.g. {Azad/128} = Azad, Page 128

{Source-Abbreviation/Volume-Number/Page-Number}
e.g. {CWMG/V-58/221} = CWMG, Volume-58, Page 221

{Source-Abbreviation} ... for URLs (articles on the web), and for digital books (including Kindle-Books), that are searchable, where location or page-number may not be given.
e.g. {VPM2}, {URL15}

{Source-Abbreviation/Location-Number}... for Kindle Books
e.g. {VPM2}, {VPM2/L-2901}

{VPM2/438/L-2901} = Page 438 for Printed/Digital Book; and L-2901 for Location 2901 for a Kindle Book. Applicable, where citations from both type of books given.

Bibliography

Column	Contains
A	Abbreviations used in citations.
B	B=Book, D=Digital Book/eBook on the Website other than Kindle, K=Kindle eBook, U=URL of Document/Article on Web, W=Website, Y=YouTube
C	Book/Document/Web URL Particulars

A	B	C
AA	B	Alice Albinia—*Empires of the Indus*. John Murray. London. 2009.
AD	B	Anuj Dhar—*India's Biggest Cover-up*. Vitasta, New Delhi, 2012.
AD1	U	Author Anuj Dhar writings and tweets. https://twitter.com/anujdhar/status/1013302357092790273 https://twitter.com/anujdhar/status/1013299350976397314
AD2	B	Anuj Dhar—*Back from Dead: Inside the Subhas Bose Mystery*. Manas, New Delhi, 2011.
Adv2	U	Lal Krishna Advani Blog—*Dr. Munshi's historic letter to Pandit Nehru: VP Menon calls it a masterpiece*. Times of India, 11-Oct-2013. https://blogs.timesofindia.indiatimes.com/lkadvanis-blog/dr-munshi-s-historic-letter-to-pandit-nehru-vp-menon-calls-it-a-masterpiece/

A	B	C
Akb	B	M.J. Akbar—*Nehru : The Making of India*. Roli Books. New Delhi. (1988) 2002.
Akb2	B	M.J. Akbar—*The Shade of Swords*. Roli Books. New Delhi. 2002.
Akb3	B	M.J. Akbar—*Kashmir: Behind the Vale*. Roli Books. New Delhi. 2002.
AL	B, D	Alastair Lamb—*The China-India Border*. Oxford University Press. London. 1964.
AL2	D	Alastair Lamb—*Treaties, Maps and the Western Sector of the Sino-Indian Boundary Dispute*. http://www.austlii.edu.au/au/journals/AUYrBkIntLaw/1965/4.pdf
AL3	B, D	Alastair Lamb—*The Sino-Indian Border in Ladakh*. https://openresearch-repository.anu.edu.au/bitstream/1885/114831/2/b10941575.pdf
Amb	Y	B.R. Ambedkar in 1956. YouTube. https://www.youtube.com/watch?v=CO3wtmkuZT0
Amb2	U	Dr BR Ambedkar—*What Congress and Gandhi have done to the Untouchables*. https://drambedkarbooks.com/dr-b-r-ambedkar-books/ http://guruprasad.net/wp-content/uploads/2014/06/What-Congress-and-Gandhi-have-done-to-the-Untouchables.pdf
Amb3	D	Dr BR Ambedkar—*Pakistan or the Partition of india*. 1945. https://drambedkarbooks.com/dr-b-r-ambedkar-books/
Amb5	U	Dr BR Ambedkar—*Dr. Ambedkar's Resignation Speech of 27-9-1951*. https://ambedkarism.wordpress.com/ 2011/03/10/dr-ambedkars-resignation-speech/
Amb6	U	Dr BR Ambedkar—*Selected Works of Dr BR. Ambedkar*. https://drambedkarbooks.files.wordpress.com/2009/03/selected-work-of-dr-b-r-ambedkar.pdf
Arpi	B, D	Claude Arpi—*1962 and the McMahon Line Saga*. Lancer. New Delhi. 2013. https://books.google.co.in/books?id=F-Lmt7J-vYgC
Arpi2	D	Claude Arpi—*Born in Sin: The Panchsheel Agreement–The Sacrifice of Tibet*. Mittal Publ. New Delhi. 2004. https://books.google.co.in/books?id=38RAiJ3ApeIC
Arpi3	U	Article by Claude Arpi—*The Blunder of the Pandit*. Rediff.com. 16-Jun-2004. http://www.rediff.com/news/2004/jun/16spec3.htm
Arpi5	U	Claude Arpi : www.claudearpi.net http://www.claudearpi.net/wp-content/uploads/ 2016 /12/1947-12-23-Nehru-to-Patel.pdf
Art	A	Article "*Nehru ditched Bose!*" in Mumbai Mirror of 28 August 2005 (based on a biography of Dr VJ Dhanan, an INA recruiting officer).
Aru	D	Arunima Kumari—*Encyclopedia Of Bihar*. Prabhat Prakashan. New Delhi. 2013. https://books.google.co.in/books?id=18MwBQAAQBAJ
AS	B	Arun Shourie—*Are we deceiving ourselves again?* ASA Publ. Rupa & Co. New Delhi. 2008.
AS2	B	Arun Shourie—*Eminent Historians: Their Technology, Their Line, Their Fraud*. ASA, New Delhi. 1998.
ASJ	B, D	Arthur M. Schlesinger Jr—*A Thousand Days: John F. Kennedy in the White House*. Houghton Mifflin, New York, 1965.

Bibliography

A	B	C
		https://books.google.co.in/books?id=uFhNxX5lrNEC
AW	B	Andrew Whitehead—*A Mission in Kashmir*. Penguin-Viking. New Delhi. 2007.
Azad	B	Maulana Abul Kalam Azad—*India Wins Freedom*. Orient Longman. New Delhi. 2004
Bali	D	Amar Nath Bali—*Now It Can Be Told*. Akashvani Prakashan. Jullundur. https://archive.org/details/NowItCanBeTold
BK	B, D	Balraj Krishna—*Sardar Vallabhbhai Patel : India's Iron Man*. Rupa & Co. New Delhi. 2005 https://books.google.co.in/books?id=sLr7z6gNcV0C
BK2	B, D	Balraj Krishna—*India's Bismarck : Sardar Vallabhbhai Patel*. Indus Source Books. Mumbai. 2007 https://books.google.co.in/books?id=sLr7z6gNcV0C
BNM	B	BN Mullik—*My Years with Nehru: The Chinese Betrayal, Volume-1*. Allied Publishers. New Delhi. 1971
BNM2	B, D	BN Mullik—*My Years with Nehru: Kashmir, Volume-2*. Allied Publishers. New Delhi. 1971 https://archive.org/stream/in.ernet.dli.2015.131607/2015.131607.My-Years-With-Nehru-Kashmir_djvu.txt
BNS	B	Brig. (Retd) B.N. Sharma—*India Betrayed : The Role of Nehru*. Manas Publications, New Delhi. 1997.
Bose	B	Subhas Chandra Bose—*The Indian Struggle 1920–42*. Oxford University Press. New Delhi. 2009.
Chee	D	Brigadier Amar Cheema—*The Crimson Chinar. The Kashmir Conflict: A Politico Military Perspective*. Lancer. New Delhi. 2014. https://books.google.co.in/books?id=Qc25BwAAQBAJ
Chur1	U	WikiQuote: Winston Churchill https://en.wikiquote.org/wiki/Winston_Churchill
Croc	B	Walter Crocker—*Nehru: A Contemporary's Estimate*. Random House India. Noida. 2008.
CT	B, D	Chris Tudda—*Cold War Summits: A History, From Potsdam to Malta*. Blooomsbury. London. 2015. https://books.google.co.in/books?id=sM62CgAAQBAJ
CWMG	D, W	*Collected Works of Mahatma Gandhi*. Volumes 1 to 98. http://gandhiserve.org/e/cwmg/cwmg.htm
Das	D	S.C. Das—*The Biography of Bharat Kesri Dr. Syama Prasad Mookerjee with Modern Implications*. Abhinav Publications. New Delhi. 2000. https://books.google.co.in/books?id=MczOO0f1DYEC
DD	B	Durga Das—*India: From Curzon to Nehru & After*. Rupa & Co. New Delhi. 2009
DFI	U	*Defence Forum India* (DFI). http://defenceforumindia.com/forum/threads/1962-india-china-war.10061/page-2
DG	B	C. Dasgupta—*War and Diplomacy in Kashmir 1947-48*. Sage Publications. New Delhi. (2002) 2009.
DGL	B, D	(Editors) Amit R. Das Gupta & Lorenz M. Lüthi—*The Sino-Indian War of 1962: New perspectives*. Routledge. London. 2017. https://books.google.co.in/books?id=hFRuDQAAQBAJ

A	B	C
Dix	B	JN Dixit—*Makers of India's Foreign Policy*. HarperCollins Publishers India. New Delhi. 2004.
DK	B, D	Dhananjay Keer—*Dr Ambedkar: Life and Mission*. Popular Prakashan. Mumbai. 1995. https://books.google.co.in/books?id=B-2d6jzRmBQC
DKP	B, D	Maj. Gen. DK Palit—*War in High Himalaya: The Indian Army in Crisis, 1962*. C Hurst & Co. London. 1991. https://books.google.co.in/books?id=ukw1PuEt8IcC
DL	B	Dalai Lama—*Freedom in Exile: The Autobiography of His Holiness the Dalai Lama of Tibet*. Abacus. London. (1990) 2002.
DPM	B, D	Dwarka Prasad Mishra—*Living An Era: India's March to Freedom, Volume 2*. Vikas. New Delhi. 1978.
DPM2	B, D	Dwarka Prasad Mishra—*The Nehru Epoch: From Democracy to Monocracy*. Har-Anand. New Delhi. 2001.
DW	B	Dorothy Woodman—*Himalayan Frontiers: A Political Review of British, Chinese, Indian and Russian Rivalries*. Barrie & Jenkins. London, 1969.
ES	B	Dr Edward C Sachau—*Alberuni's India*. Rupa & Co, New Delhi, (1888) 2009.
FaM	B	Dominique Lapierre & Larry Collins—*Freedom at Midnight*. Vikas Publishing House. New Delhi. Tenth Imprint 2010.
FG1	U	Francois Gautier Blog Post: *Haunted by Macaulay's Ghost*. 16.Apr.2008. https://francoisgautier.me/2008/04/16/haunted-by-macaulay%E2%80%99s-ghost/
FM	B	Frank Moraes—*Witness to an era: India 1920 to the present day*. Vikas. New Delhi. 1973.
FY	B, D	Francis Younghusband—*India and Tibet*. John Murray 1910. LPP 2002. https://www.gutenberg.org/files/48996/48996-h/48996-h.htm
GD	B	Gurcharan Das—*India Unbound*. Viking/Penguin, New Delhi, 2000.
GD2	B	Gurcharan Das—*The Elephant Paradigm: India Wrestles with Change*. Penguin, New Delhi, 2002.
Gill	B	Gill S.S.—*Gandhi: A Sublime Failure*. Rupa & Co. New Delhi. 2003
Gla	B	Glancey, Jonathan—*Nagaland: A Journey to India's Forgotten Frontier*. Faber & Faber. London. 2011
GSB	B, D	GS Bhargava—*The Battle of NEFA*. Allied Publ, New Delhi, 1964.
Hin1	U	Article by Kallol Bhattacharjee—'With Nehru writing to its PM, Israel gave arms to India in 1962'. TheHindu.com. 27-May-2017. http://www.thehindu.com/news/national/with-nehru-writing-to-its-pm-israel-gave-arms-to-india-in-1962/article18591835.ece
Hing	B, D	Aman M. Hingorani—*Unravelling the Kashmir Knot*. Sage Publications India. 2016. https://books.google.co.in/books?id=Aco2DAAAQBAJ
HJS	U	Article '*India pays for Nehru*' by A Surya Prakash. https://www.hindujagruti.org/news/3927.html
HK	K	Henry Kissinger—*On China*. Allen Lane, an imprint of Penguin Books. London. 2011.
IFJ	U	India Foundation Journal, Jan-2014.

Bibliography

A	B	C
		http://www.indiafoundation.in/wp-content/uploads/2016/08/January-Journal.pdf
IM1	U	Article "*How to make foes and alienate people*" in 'The Indian Express' of 6 February 2012 by Inder Malhotra. http://indianexpress.com/article/opinion/columns/how-to-make-foes-and-alienate-people/
IM2	U	Article "*A purge with no losers*" in 'The Indian Express' of 19-Mar-2012 by Inder Malhotra. http://indianexpress.com/article/opinion/columns/a-purge-with-no-losers/
IT1	U	India Today: Who freed India? Gandhi or Bose? 26.Jan.2016. http://indiatoday.intoday.in/story/who-freed-india-gandhi-or-bose/1/579840.html
ITV	U	India TV Article '*Why Gandhi opted for Nehru and not Sardar Patel for PM?*' by Raj Singh, 31-10-2015. http://www.indiatvnews.com/politics/national/why-gandhi-opted-for-nehru-and-not-sardar-patel-for-pm-6689.html
Jag	B, D	Jagmohan—*My Frozen Turbulence in Kashmir*. Allied Publishers. New Delhi. 2006. https://books.google.co.in/books?id=CWjLtfi-ssIC
JC	B, K	Jung Chang, Jon Halliday—*Mao: The Unknown Story*. Jonathan Cape, 2005/ Random House, 2007.
JD	B	Diwan Jarmani Dass—*Maharaja*. Hind Pocket Books. New Delhi. 2007.
JD2	B	Diwan Jarmani Dass—*Maharani*. Hind Pocket Books. New Delhi. 2008.
Jha1	U	Prem Shankar Jha—*Kashmir 1947, Rival Versions of History*. Oxford University Press. New Delhi. 1996. http://www.rediff.com/freedom/0710jha.htm
JN	B, D	Jawaharlal Nehru—*The Discovery of India*. Oxford University Press. New Delhi. (1946) 1985. http://www.rediff.com/freedom/0710jha.htm
JN2	B, D	Jawaharlal Nehru—*An Autobiography*. Oxford University Press. New Delhi. (1936) 1982. https://archive.org/stream/in.ernet.dli.2015.98834/2015.98834.Jawaharlal-Nehru-An-Autobiography
JN3	B, D	Jawaharlal Nehru—*An Bunch of Old Letters*. Asia Publishing House. New Delhi. (1958) 1960. http://krishikosh.egranth.ac.in/bitstream/1/2027646/1/HS826.pdf
JN4	U	Jawaharlal Nehru's Note on '*Policy regarding China and Tibet*' dated 18-Nov-1950. http://docplayer.net/24127812-Policy-regarding-china-and-tibet-1-jawaharlal-nehru-november-18-1950.html
JN5	B, D	Jawaharlal Nehru—*Glimpses of World History*. Oxford University Press. New Delhi. (1934-35) 1989 Seventh Impression. https://archive.org/details/in.ernet.dli.2015.108462
JNSW	D	*Selected Works of Jawaharlal Nehru*. Edited by S.Gopal. Second Series Volumes 1 to 61. http://nehruportal.nic.in/writings
JPD	B, D	Brig JP Dalvi—*Himalayan Blunder : The Curtain-raiser to the Sini-Indian War of 1962*. Natraj Publishers. Dehra Dun. (1969) 2010. http://krishikosh.egranth.ac.in/bitstream/1/2027646/1/HS826.pdf

A	B	C
JS	B	Jaswant Singh—*Jinnah : India–Partition–Independence.* Rupa, New Delhi, 2013.
JS2	B	Jaswant Singh—*India at Risk: Misconceptions and Misadventures of Security Policy.* Rupa & Co, New Delhi, 2009.
Kaul	B	Brij Mohan Kaul—*The Untold Story.* Allied Publ. New Delhi. 1967.
KC1	U	Kumar Chellappan—*Revealed: Nehru wanted to scuttle Sardar's Hyderabad plan.* The Pioneer of 30 October 2012. http://bharatkalyan97.blogspot.in/2012/10/revealed-nehru-wanted-to-scuttle.html
KMM	B	KM Munshi—*Pilgrimage to Freedom.* Vol-1&2. Bhartiya Vidya Bhavan, Bombay, 1967.
KN	K	Kuldip Nayar—*Beyond the Lines.* Roli Books. New Delhi. 2012. Kindle Edition.
KN2	B	Kuldip Nayar—*Between the Lines.* Konark Publ. New Delhi. 2014.
KNR	B	K. N. Raghavan—*Dividing Lines: Contours of India-China Conflict.* Leadstart Publishing. Mumbai. 2012.
Krip	D	J.B. Kripalani—*Gandhi, His Life and Thought.* Publications Division, Ministry of Information & Broadcasting. 1970. http://www.mkgandhi.org/ebks/gandhihislifeandthought.pdf
KS	B	Khushwant Singh—*Truth, Love and a Little Malice: an Autobiography.* Penguin, New Delhi, (2002) 2003.
KS2	U	Article by Khushwant Singh—*Iqbal's Hindu Relations.* 'The Telegraph', 30 June 2007. https://www.telegraphindia.com/1070630/asp/opinion/story_7992715.asp
Lala	B	R.M. Lala—*The Joy of Achievement: A Conversation with J.R.D.Tata.* Penguin. New Delhi. 2003
LMS	B, D	Dr LM Singhvi—*Parliamentary Democracy in India.* Ocean Books Pvt. Ltd. New Delhi. 2012. https://books.google.co.in/books?id=0wN0BQAAQBAJ
MA	B	Lt Manwati Arya & Ram Kishor Bajapai—*Judgment: No Aircrash No Death.* Lotus, New Delhi, 2010.
Mac	B	M.O. (Mac) Mathai—*Reminiscences of the Nehru Age.* Vikas Publishing House. New Delhi. 1978. *Mathai was Personal Private Secretary/ Special Assistant to Nehru during 1946-59.*
Mac2	B, D	M.O. (Mac) Mathai—*My Days with Nehru.* Vikas Publishing House. New Delhi. 1979. https://archive.org/details/in.ernet.dli.2015.147284
Mak	B	Makkhan Lal—*Secular Politics, Communal Agenda : A History of Politics in India from 1860 to 1953.* Pragun Publication, DK Publ., New Delhi, 2008.
Mal	B, K	Manohar Malgonkar—*The Men Who Killed Gandhi.* Roli Books, New Delhi, (1977) 2008.
Mani	B	*Inside Story of Sardar Patel: Diary of Maniben Patel: 1936-50.* Chief Editor: PN Chopra. Vision Books. New Delhi. 2001.
Max	B	Neville Maxwell—*India's China War.* Natraj Publishers. Dehradun. (1970) 1997.
Max2	U	Article by Neville Maxwell—*Remembering a War: The 1962 India-China Conflict.* Rediff.com. 18-Oct-2002.

Bibliography

A	B	C
		http://m.rediff.com/news/2002/oct/08max1.htm
MB	B, D	Michael Brecher—*Nehru: A Political Biography*. Oxford University Press. London. 1959.
MB2	B, D	(Edited by) Michael Brecher—*Studies in Crisis Behaviour*. Transaction Books, New Jersey, 1978. https://books.google.co.in/books?id=IIfqktFeW2IC
MCC	B	Mahommedali Currim (MC) Chagla—*Roses in December*. Bhartiya Vidya Bhavan, Mumbai, (1973) 2000.
ME	B, D	Michael Edwardes—*The Last Days of British India*. Cassel London; Allied Publishers Pvt. Ltd.London. 1963 https://archive.org/details/LastYearsOfBritishIndia
ME2	B, D	Michael Edwardes—*Nehru: A Political Biography*. Allen Lane. London. 1962. Vikas Publ. New Delhi.
MG	B	Madhav Godbole—*The Holocaust of Indian Partition: An Inquest*. Rupa & Co, New Delhi, 2006.
MiM	B	Minno Masani—*Against the Tide*. Vikas, New Delhi, 1982.
MKN	K	MKK Nayar—*The Story of an Era Told Without Ill-will*. DC Books. Kottayam, Kerala. (1987) 2013.
MLS	B, D	ML Sali—*India-China Border Dispute*. APH Publishing Corp. New Delhi. 1998. https://books.google.co.in/ books?id=Z6y2E9gw5oIC&pg
MM	B, D	Maria Misra—*Vishnu's Crowded Temple: India since the Great Rebellion*. Penguin. London. (2007) 2008. https://books.google.co.in/books?id=GTTRzJzJ_W4C
MND	B	Manmath Nath Das—*Partition and Independence of India: Inside Story of the Mountbatten Days*. Vision Books. New Delhi. 1982.
Moon	D	Penderel Moon—*Divide and Quit*. University of California Press. California. 1961. https://books.google.co.in/books?id=WpViCTc-YAgC
Moon	D	Penderel Moon—*The British Conquest and Dominion of India*. India Research Press, New Delhi, 1999. https://books.google.co.in/books?id=20TAWsOaq4cC
Mos	B	Leonard Mosley—*The Last Days of the British Raj*. Jaico. Mumbai. (1960) 1971.
Muld	B, D	Andrew Muldoon—*Empire, Politics and the Creation of the 1935 India Act: Last Act of the Raj*. Ashgate. Surrey, UK. 2009. https://books.google.co.in/books?id=2ovcJWTsgVAC
Na1	U	V.S. Naipaul. The New York Review of Books. *India: Renaissance or Continuity?* 20.Jan.1977 http://www.nybooks.com/articles/1977/01/20/india-renaissance-or-continuity/
Nag	B, D	Kingshuk Nag—*Netaji: Lving Dangerously*. Rupa, New Delhi, 2016. https://books.google.co.in/books?id=duHwCgAAQBAJ
Nat1	U	K Natwar Singh's article '*Jawaharlal Nehru and the Mountbattens*' in *The Hindu* of 14-Nov-2008. http://www.thehindu.com/todays-paper/tp-opinion/Jawaharlal-Nehru-and-the-Mountbattens/article15341646.ece
NC	B	Nirad C. Chaudhuri—*Autobiography of an Unknown Indian, Part-II*. Jaico Publishing House. Mumbai. 2011.

A	B	C
NC2	K	Nirad C. Chaudhuri—*Autobiography of an Unknown Indian, Part-II*. Jaico, Mumbai, 2011. Kindle Edition
Nij	B	S Nijalingappa—*My Life and Politics: An Autobiography*. Vision Books. New Delhi. 2000.
Noor	B	A.G. Noorani—*India-China Boundary Problem 1846-1947: History and Diplomacy*. Oxford University Press. New Delhi. 2011.
NP	B	Major General Niranjan Prasad—*The Fall of Towang, 1962*. Palit & Palit. New Delhi. 1981.
Pani	B, D	Panigrahi D.N.—*Jammu and Kashmir, The Cold War and the West*. Routledge. New Delhi. 2009. https://books.google.co.in/books?id=WcXHRVYzV4MC
Pani2	B, D	Panigrahi D.N.—*India's Partition : The Story of Imperialism in Retreat*. Routledge, Taylor & Francis Group. London and New York. 2004.
PB	B	Prasenjit K Basu—*Asia Reborn: A Continent rises from the ravages of colonialism and war to a New Dynamism*. Aleph, New Delhi, 2017.
PC	B	Peter Clarke—*The Last Thousand Days of the British Empire*. Allen Lane (Penguin). London. 2007.
PF	B, K	Patrick French—*Liberty or Death: India's Journey to Independence and Division*. Penguin. London. 2011.
PF2	B, K	Patrick French—*India: A Portrait*. Penguin. London. 2011.
PP	B	Pankaj K Phadnis—*Freedom Struggle: The Unfinished Story*. Abhinav Baharat, Mumbai, 2002.
Rao	B	Gondker Narayana Rao—*The India-China Border: A Reappraisal*. Motilal Banarsidas. Delhi. (1968) 2009.
RCM	B, D	RC Majumdar—*History of the Freedom Movement in India, Vol-I*. Firma KL Mukhopadhya, Calcutta, (1962) 1971. https://archive.org/details/history1_201708
RCM3	B, D	RC Majumdar—*History of the Freedom Movement in India, Vol-III*. Firma KL Mukhopadhya, Calcutta, (1962) 1971. https://archive.org/details/in.ernet.dli.2015.125612
R&R	B, D	Amiya Rao & BG Rao—*Six Thousand Days: Jawaharlal Nehru, Prime Minister*. Sterling Publ. New Delhi. 1974. https://archive.org/details/in.ernet.dli.2015.118430
Red1	U	Colonel Anil Athale, 'The Untold Story: How Kennedy came to India's Aid in 1962'. rediff.com. 4-Dec-2012. http://www.rediff.com/news/special/the-untold-story-how-the-us-came-to-indias-aid-in-1962/20121204.htm
RG	B, K	Rajmohan Gandhi—*Patel–A Life*. Navjivan Publishing House. Ahmedabad. 2008 Reprint.
RG2	K	Rajmohan Gandhi—*Patel–A Life*. Navjivan Publishing House. Ahmedabad. 2008 Reprint. Kindle.
RG3	B	Rajmohan Gandhi—*Rajaji–A Life*. Penguin Books. New Delhi. 1997.
RG4	B	Rajmohan Gandhi—*Understanding the Muslim Mind*. Penguin Books. New Delhi. (1986) 2000.
RG5	B, D	Rajmohan Gandhi—*Mohandas: A True Story of a Man, His People, and an Empire*. Penguin Books India. New Delhi. 2006. https://books.google.co.in/books?id=TEyXCoc76AEC
RNPS	B	RNP Singh—*Nehru: A Troubled Legacy*. Wisdom Tree. New Delhi. 2015.

Bibliography

A	B	C
Roy	D	M.N. Roy—*Men I Met*. Lalvani Publishing House. Bombay. 1968. http://lohiatoday.com/CollectedWorks/MNRoy/MMNR-09-MenIMet.pdf
Roy2	B, U	M.N. Roy—*Legal Murder in India*. International Press Correspondence, vol. 3, no. 9 (24 January 1923). Reprinted in G. Adhikari (ed.), Documents of the History of the Communist Party of India: Volume 2, 1923–1925. New Delhi: People's Publishing House, 1974. https://en.wikipedia.org/wiki/Chauri_Chaura_incident
RP	B, D	Dr Rajendra Prasad—*India Divided*. Hind Kitabs Ltd. Bombay. 1946. (Also, Penguin India, New Delhi, 1946) https://books.google.co.in/books?id=D9FzePpOA60C
RP2	U	Article "*Legacies of former Presidents & their controversial events*" by Prashant Hamine dated 7-Jul-2017 in 'The Afternoon Despatch & Courier' http://www.afternoondc.in/city-news/legacies-of-former-presidents-their-controversial-events/article_199025
RPD	B	Rajni Palme Dutt—*India Today*. Manisha. Calcutta. (1940) 1970.
Rust	B	PV Rajgopal (Editor)—*I was Nehru's Shadow: From the Diaries of KF Rustamji*. Wisdom Tree. New Delhi. 2006. *Rustamji was Nehru's Chief Security Officer between 1952 and 1958.*
RZ	B	Rafiq Zakaria—*The Man Who Divided India*. Popular Prakashan, Mumbai, (2001) 2004.
Sar	B	Narendra Singh Sarila—*The Shadow of the Great Game: The Untold Story of India's Partition*. HarperCollins. 2005
Sch	B	Howard B. Schaffer—*The Limits of Influence—America's Role in Kashmir*. Penguin/Viking. 2009.
SB	B	Sumantra Bose—*Contested Lands*. HarperCollins. New Delhi. 2007.
SB2	U	Sumantra Bose—*How the Pandit Lost the Valley*. Open Mag. 14-Nov-2014. http://www.openthemagazine.com/article/voices/how-the-pandit-lost-the-valley
SD	B, D	Sandip Das (Edited By)—*Jayaprakash Narayan: A Centenary Volume*. Mittal Publ, New Delhi, 2005. https://books.google.co.in/books?id=U9U0LiT3dtMC
SG	B, D	Sankar Ghose—*Jawaharlal Nehru, a Biography*. Allied Publishers Ltd. New Delhi. 2006. https://books.google.co.in/books/about/Jawaharlal_Nehru_a_Biography.html?id=MUeyUhVGIDMC
SH	B, D	Sanjoy Hazarika—*Writing on the Wall: Reflections on the North-East*. Penguin, New Delhi, 2008. https://books.google.co.in/books?id=rXx2oczz9sYC
Shak	B, D	Abida Shakoor—*Congress-Muslim League Tussle: 1937-40*. Aakar Books. New Delhi. 2003 https://books.google.co.in/books?id=XTn77Ix5-uwC
Shan	D	V. Shankar (Sardar Patel's Secretary)—*My Reminiscences of Sardar Patel Vol-I & II*. S.G. Wasani for The Macmillan Company of India. Delhi. 1974. URLs: Pl. see below.
Shan1	D	V. Shankar (Sardar Patel's Secretary)—*My Reminiscences of Sardar Patel Vol-I*. S.G. Wasani for The Macmillan Company of India. Delhi. 1974. https://books.google.co.in/books?id=ya1AAAAAMAAJ
Shan2	D	V. Shankar (Sardar Patel's Secretary)—*My Reminiscences of Sardar Patel Vol-II*. S.G. Wasani for The Macmillan Company of India. Delhi. 1974.

A	B	C
		https://www.scribd.com/document/180707518/My-Reminiscences-of-Sardar-Patel-by-V-Shankar-Vol-2
SJ	B	Shakunthala Jagannathan (CP Ramaswami Iyer's granddaughter)—*Sir CP Remembered*. Vakils. Feffer & Simons Ltd. Mumbai. 1999. https://srajahiyer.wordpress.com/2016/01/23/how-nehru-sold-kashmir/
SKV	K	Shiv Kunal Verma—*1962: The War That Wasn't*. Aleph, New Delhi, 2016. Kindle Edition.
SNS	B, D	Shashikant Nishant Sharma (ed.)—*New Perspectives in Sociology and Allied Fields*. EduPedia Publications (P) Ltd. New Delhi. 2016. https://books.google.co.in/books?id=YjGpDAAAQBAJ
SRG	B, D	Sita Ram Goel—*How I Became Hindu*. Voice of India, New Delhi, 1982. http://www.voiceofdharma.org/books/hibh/
SS	B, D	Sanjeev Sabhlok—*Breaking Free of Nehru: Lets Unleash India!* Anthem Press, New Delhi, 2008. https://books.google.co.in/books?id=zU9utu7wZpQC
ST	B	Shashi Tharoor—*Nehru: The Invention of India*. Penguin Books. (2003) 2007.
Stat1	U	The Statesman: *The War & the Freedom*. Article by Suman Saket. 13.Aug.2015 http://www.thestatesman.com/features/the-war-amp-the-freedom-82191.html
Swa1	U	Article *'The Butcher Of Bengal' And His Role In Direct Action Day* by Jaideep Mazumdar. SwarajyaMag.com. 16 Aug 2017. https://swarajyamag.com/politics/its-a-crying-shame-that-the-butcher-of-bengal-has-a-road-named-after-him-in-kolkata
Swa2	U	Article *'Balraj Madhok (1920-2016) Gave Us Definition Of Indianisation'*. SwarajyaMag.com. 5-May-2016. https://swarajyamag.com/columns/balraj-madhok-1920-2016-gave-us-definition-of-indianisation
Swa3	U	S. Kalyanaraman—*Was The Non-Aligned Movement Ever Relevant For India?* SwarajyaMag.com . 29-9-2016. https://swarajyamag.com/world/was-the-non-aligned-movement-ever-relevant-for-india
Swa4	U	"*When Nehru Opposed Restoration Of Somnath Temple*". https://swarajyamag.com/politics/the-somnath-saga-a-precursor-to-debates-around-secularism-in-india
Swa5	U	"*When Nehru Shunned Einstein's Request To Support The Jewish Cause*" by Manish Maheswari in Swarajya of 13-Jan-2017. https://swarajyamag.com/politics/when-nehru-shunned-einsteins-request-to-support-the-jewish-cause
Swa6	U	Article "*Indus Waters Treaty: Nehru's Original Himalayan Blunder*" by Rakesh Krishnan Simha in 'Swarajya' of 2-Oct-2016. https://swarajyamag.com/world/indus-waters-treaty-nehrus-original-himalayan-blunder
Swa7	U	"*Indian Nationalism: Nehruvian And Marxist Conception Of India – Part II*" by Manish Maheswari in Swarajya of 10-Nov-2017. https://swarajyamag.com/ideas/indian-nationalism-nehruvian-and-marxist-conception-of-india-part-ii

Bibliography

A	B	C
Tho	B	S.P.P. Thorat—*Reveille to Retreat*. Allied Publishers. New Delhi. (1986) 2013.
Tim	D	Tim Leadbeater—*Access to History: Britain and India 1845-1947*. Hachette UK. London. 2008.
TR	B	Tathagat Roy—*My People, Uprooted: The Exodus of Hindus from East Pakistan and Bangladesh*. Ratna Prakashan, Kolkata, 2002.
TS	B	Tsering Shakya—*The Dragon in the Land of Snows: A History of Modern Tibet since 1947*. Penguin. London 1999.
TSR	B	TSR Subramanian—*Journeys through Babudon and Netaland: Governance in India*. Rupa, New Delhi, 2004.
TSR2	B	TSR Subramanian—*GovernMint in India: An Inside View*. Rupa, New Delhi, 2009.
Tunz	B	Alex Von Tunzelmann—*Indian Summer : The Secret History of the End of an Empire*. Simon & Schuster. 2007.
URL7	U	Article *'Why Partition?'* by Perry Anderson. London Review of Books, Vol-34, No-14, 19 July 2012 https://www.lrb.co.uk/v34/n14/perry-anderson/why-partition
URL8	U	Article *'After Nehru'* by Perry Anderson, Professor of History and Sociology at UCLA. London Review of Books, Vol-34, No-15, 2 August 2012. https://www.lrb.co.uk/v34/n15/perry-anderson/after-nehru
URL10	U	*Indian Partition and Neo-Colonialism*. http://coat.ncf.ca/our_magazine/links/issue47/articles/a04.htm
URL11	U	*'Operations in Jammu and Kashmir 1947-48'* by Rohit Singh. 2012. http://www.claws.in/images/ journals_doc/SW%20i-10.10.2012.150-178.pdf
URL12	U	*Letter from the Maharaja Hari Singh to Sardar Patel* of 31-Jan-1948. www.claudearpi.net/ wp-content/ uploads/2016/12/1948-01-31-Maharaja-to-Patel.pdf
URL13	U	"*For a century and beyond, the 'Kashmir Conflict' remains a euphemism for 'Islamic Jihad'*" by Shwetank Bhushan. MyIndMakers. 12-Sep-2016. https://www.myind.net/Home/viewArticle/century-and-beyond-kashmir-conflict-remains-euphemism-islamic-jihad
URL14	U	Article *'UN reforms—a fading mirage?'*. The Hindu Business Line. 16-Sep-2009. http://www.thehindubusinessline.com/todays-paper/tp-opinion/article1062010.ece
URL15	U	Article *'Nehru vs Patel: Ideological Rift, Hardly a Trivial One'*. Rakesh Sinha, Sunday Express. 10-Nov-2013. www.pressreader.com/india/sunday-express8291/20131110/282033324959792
URL16	U	*Rao Bahadur IGP PK Monnappa*. wikivisually.com/wiki/Rao_Bahadur_IGP_P.K.Monnappa
URL18	U	*Jinnah's presidential address to the Constituent Assembly of Pakistan* on 11 August 1947. http://www.pakistani.org/pakistan/legislation/constituent_address_11aug1947.html
URL19	U	Article *'The War We Lost'* by BG Vershese in Tehelka.com dated 13 Oct 2012. http://www.tehelka.com/2012/10/the-war-we-lost/

A	B	C
URL20	U	Letter from PM of China to PM of India, 23-Jan-1959. digitalarchive.wilsoncenter.org/document/175951
URL21	U	Chou En-Lai's Letter to Nehru of 7 Nov-1959. https://www.marxists.org/subject/india/sino-india-boundary-question/ch04.htm
URL22	U	Article "1962 war: When Nehru decided to strike against China despite Army chief's advice" by Mohan Guruswamy dated 15-Oct-2107 in www.dailyo.in. https://www.dailyo.in/politics/india-china-1962-war-nehru-cuban-missile-crisis/story/1/20089.html
URL23	U	The Sino-India Border Dispute. http://shodhganga.inflibnet.ac.in/bitstream/10603/21118/4/chapter%202.pdf
URL24	U	Article "J.N. to JFK Eyes Only" by Inder Malhotra in 'The Indian Express' of 15-Nov-2010. http://indianexpress.com/article/opinion/columns/j-n-to-jfk-eyes-only/
URL25	U	"China's Decision for War with India in 1962" by John W. Garver. http://indianstrategicknowledgeonline.com/web/china%20decision%20for%201962%20war%202003.pdf
URL26	U	Minute by the Hon'ble T. B. Macaulay, 2-Feb-1835. http://www.columbia.edu/itc/mealac/pritchett/00generallinks/macaulay/txt_minute_education_1835.html
URL27	U	The Hindu, 9-Jan-1960: "Enquiry into charges" http://www.thehindu.com/todays-paper/tp-miscellaneous/dated-January-9-1960-Enquiry-into-charges/article15958471.ece
URL28	U	Jawaharlal Nehru's Presidential Address at the Lucknow Congress in 1936. https://www.marxists.org/history/international/comintern/sections/britain/periodicals/labour_monthly/1936/05/x01.htm
URL29	U	Article "Manmohan did not correct map error to protect Nehru name" in 'The Sundat Guardian' of 23-Aug-2014 by Madhav Nalapat. http://www.sunday-guardian.com/news/manmohan-did-not-correct-map-error-to-protect-nehru-name
URL32	U	Article 'Nehru wanted Army scrapped' in Hindustan Times of 26-Aug-2006. https://www.hindustantimes.com/india/nehru-wanted-army-scrapped/story-4pCTLAT4tXlKRnBUtJqz9O.html
URL33	U	Blog: 'Some Independence, please, for armed forces' by Col (Dr) Sudhir Sakhuja in NDTV.com dated 9-Aug-2013. https://www.ndtv.com/india-news/blog-some-independence-please-for-armed-forces-531096
URL34	U	"The complete truth about how Jawaharlal Nehru forced John Mathai to resign". http://indiafacts.org/complete-truth-jawaharlal-nehru-forced-john-mathai-resign/
URL35	U	Atanu Dey's Blog-post 'Nehru and the Indian Economy (...Why is India Poor?)' https://deeshaa.org/2005/01/21/nehru-and-the-indian-economy-why-is-india-poor/
URL36	U	"Of Commonwealth & Majrooh" https://www.dawn.com/news/1073415

Bibliography

A	B	C
URL37	U	"Not at the Cost of China: India and the United Nations Security Council, 1950" https://www.wilsoncenter.org/publication/not-the-cost-china-india-and-the-united-nations-security-council-1950 https://www.wilsoncenter.org/sites/default/files/cwihp_working_paper_76_not_at_the_cost_of_china.pdf
URL38	U	"Mistakes Of Jawaharlal Nehru And Vijaya Lakshmi Pandit" https://www.linkedin.com/pulse/mistakes-jawaharlal-nehru-vijaya-lakshmi-pandit-atul-juyal/
URL39	U	Saswati Sarkar, Shanmukh and Dikgaj—*Did Nehru betray Chandrasekhar Azad to the British? Dailyo.in* 27-Feb-2016. https://www.dailyo.in/politics/chandrasekhar-azad-jawaharlal-nehru-mahatma-gandhi-hinduism-freedom-struggle-sardar-patel-subhas-chandra-bose/story/1/9233.html
URL40	U	"How Bangladeshi Muslims wiped the Assamese out in their own land" http://www.assam.org/news/how-bangladeshi-muslims-wiped-assamese-out-their-own-land
URL41	U	'Nehru: Planning For Poverty' by J Nair. http://varnam.org/2013/05/nehru-planning-for-poverty/
URL42	U	Nehru's legacy – The Somnath Temple treachery. http://www.opindia.com/2017/11/nehrus-legacy-the-somnath-temple-treachery/
URL43	U	'Nehru and the China-Tibet blunder'. http://indiafacts.org/nehru-and-the-china-tibet-blunder/#.WYiqK5XO2QM.twitter
URL44	U	Anand Ranganathan. https://twitter.com/ARanganathan72/status/922422036655366146
URL45	U	Blog-post 'The loss of inheritance' by Gurucharan Das in ToI of 9-Sep-2012. https://blogs.timesofindia.indiatimes.com/men-and-ideas/the-loss-of-inheritance/
URL46	U	'2,600 cops serve in homes of IPS officers in state' by Prafulla Marpakwar in ToI of 15-Oct-2013. https://timesofindia.indiatimes.com/india/2600-cops-serve-in-homes-of-IPS-officers-in-Maharashtra/articleshow/24168369.cms
URL47	U	"Blast from the past—Patel-Nehru letters expose the frauds in fund collection for NH". By Team PGurus - December 9, 2016 https://www.pgurus.com/blast-from-the-past-patel-nehru-letters-exposes-the-frauds-in-fund-collection-for-nh/
URL48	U	Article "Water diplomacy: Skating on thin ice" by Brahma Chellany in The Economic Times of 10-May-2012. https://economictimes.indiatimes.com/water-treaties-diplomacy-india-faces-difficult-choices-on-water/articleshow/13073011.cms
URL49	U	The Hindu on 13-Jun-2016: "Had Nehru accepted U.S. offer, India will not have to try for NSG membership: Rasgotra". http://www.thehindu.com/news/national/Had-Nehru-accepted-U.S.-offer-India-will-not-have-to-try-for-NSG-membership-Rasgotra/article14420389.ece
URL50	U	Article "Why I blame Nehru for India's failure at NSG" in DailyO.in of 27-Jun-2016 by Abhishek Shrivastava.

A	B	C
		https://www.dailyo.in/politics/jawaharlal-nehru-nuclear-suppliers-group-xi-jinping-india-china-ties-unsc-narendra-modi/story/1/11424.html
URL51	U	Article *"Nehru's Pacifism and the Failed Recapture of Kashmir"* by Sandeep Bamzai in ORF dated 13-Aug-2016. https://www.orfonline.org/research/nehrus-pacifism-and-the-failed-recapture-of-kashmir/
URL52	U	Article *"Nehru As Seen By A Hindu Nationalist"* by NS Rajaram in IndiaFacts.org dated 24-Nov-2015. http://indiafacts.org/nehru-as-seen-by-a-hindu-nationalist/
URL53	U	DFI https://defenceforumindia.com/forum/threads/1962-india-china-war.10061/page-2
URL54	U	Article *"India pays for Nehru"*. https://www.hindujagruti.org/news/3927.html
URL55	U	Blog '*Somnath*' by Pravin Agrawal. https://www.speakingtree.in/blog/somnath
URL56	U	Article "*Nehru Termed Bose 'Your War Criminal'*" in The Pioneer of 24-Jan-2016. http://www.dailypioneer.com/todays-newspaper/nehru-termed-bose-your-war-criminal.html
URL57	U	"*No crash at Taipei that killed Netaji: Taiwan govt*", Outlook, 3-Feb-2005. https://www.outlookindia.com/newswire/story/no-crash-at-taipei-that-killed-netaji-taiwan-govt/277465
URL58	U	Article "*Remembering Netaji: How Nehru denied India her true freedom hero*" by DIPIN DAMODHARAN in DailyO dated 22-Jan-2016. https://www.dailyo.in/politics/netaji-subhas-chandra-bose-birth-anniversary-death-nehru-congress/story/1/8596.html
URL59	U	Article '*A Case For Bhim Rajya*' by S Anand in the Outlook magazine of 20 August 2012. https://www.outlookindia.com/magazine/story/a-case-for-bhim-rajya/281924
URL60	U	Article '*Was Mahatma Gandhi a hypocrite?*' in DailyO by Saswati Sarkar, Shanmukh, Dikgaj and Divya Kumar Soti dated 3-Jul-2015. https://www.dailyo.in/politics/mahatma-gandhi-subhas-bose-ahimsa-non-violence-british-raj-independence/story/1/4756.html
URL61	U	Article '*Nehru and the China-Tibet blunder!*'. http://www.socaltibet.org/the-great-indian-prime-minister-nehru-and-the-china-tibet-blunder/
URL62	U	Article '*Nehru's Arrogant Ambition*'. https://deeshaa.org/2008/04/06/nehrus-arrogant-ambition/
URL63	U	Hindustan Times report titled '*Incorrect maps given to China led to 1962 war*' of 22 October 2012. http://mahitiadhikar.blogspot.in/2012/10/incorrect-maps-given-to-china-led-to.html
URL64	U	SA Aiyar in Swaminomics—*Lessons for India from Singapore*. ToI Blog, 29-Mar-2015 https://blogs.timesofindia.indiatimes.com/Swaminomics/lessons-for-india-from-singapore/

Bibliography

A	B	C
URL65	U	"*The uncouth reality of the present is not the only possibility for India: in our many pasts lie the seeds of our future*" by Rajeev Srinivasan in Rediff. http://www.rediff.com/news/aug/04rajee1.htm
URL66	U	"*A Measure of the Man*" in Outlook. https://www.outlookindia.com/magazine/story/a-measure-of-the-man/281949
URL67	U	Jaya Jaitley—"*#NehruSnooped: Truth behind Netaji files*", 25-May-2015. https://www.dailyo.in/politics/netaji-nehru-renkoji-temple-saigon-kk-chettur-national-archives-netaji-gold-sa-iyer/story/1/3954.html
URL68	U	"*Jansangh founder SP Mukherjee was killed: Atal*", ZeeNews, 7-Jul-2004. http://zeenews.india.com/news/nation/jansangh-founder-sp-mukherjee-was-killed-atal_166864.html
URL69	U	"*Jawaharlal Nehru failed to appreciate foresight of General Thimayya, Field Marshal Cariappa*" by Anirban Ganguly, FirstPost, 4-May-2018. https://www.firstpost.com/india/narendra-modi-is-right-jawaharlal-nehru-failed-to-appreciate-foresight-of-general-thimayya-field-marshal-cariappa-4456431.html
URL70	U	"*Here are the 5 most popular lies that leftists peddle against Veer Savarkar*" by Ashish Shukla in www.opindia.com on 28-May-2018. http://www.opindia.com/2018/05/here-are-the-5-most-popular-lies-that-leftists-peddle-against-veer-savarkar/
URL71	U	Bhagat Singh. https://en.wikipedia.org/wiki/Bhagat_Singh
Vee	U	Blogpost: '*Biography—Lt. Gen S.P.P. Thorat, KC, DSO*'. http://veekay-militaryhistory.blogspot.in/ 2012/10/biography-lt-gen-spp-thorat-kc-dso.html
VK1	B	Autobiography of Dr Verghese Kurien of Amul Dairy fame, as told to Gouri Salvi—*I Too Had a Dream*. Roli Books, New Delhi. 2005.
VM	B	Ved Marwah—*India in Turmoil*. Rupa, New Delhi, 2009.
VPM1	B, D	V.P. Menon—*The Story of the Integration of the Indian States*. Longman, Green & Co. London. 1955. URL: http://lib.bjplibrary.org/jspui/bitstream/123456789/132/1/V.P.Menon%20-%20Integration%20of%20Princely%20States.pdf
VPM2	K, D	V.P. Menon—*The Transfer of Power in India*. Orient Longman. Chennai. (1957) 1997. Kindle Edition 2011. https://books.google.co.in/books?id=FY5gI7SGU20C
VR	B	Valerian Rodrigues—*The Essential Writings of B.R. Ambedkar*. Oxford University Press, New Delhi, (2002) 2003.
Wav	B, D, K	*Wavell: The Viceroy's Journal*. Edited by Penderel Moon. Oxford University Press. London. 1973. https://archive.org/details/99999990080835WavellTheViceroysJournal
WD	B	Will Durant—*The Case for India*. Strand Book Stall, Mumbai, 2007.
Wire1	U	Article '*How India Paid to Create the London of Today*' by Kannan Srinivasan. The Wire. 20-Apr-2017. https://thewire.in/125810/how-india-paid-to-create-the-london-of-today/
Wolp	B	Stanley Wolpert—*Jinnah of Pakistan*. Oxford University Press. London. (1984) 2008.

A	B	C
Wolp2	B	Stanley Wolpert—*Nehru: A Tryst with Destiny*. Oxford University Press. London. 1996. https://books.google.co.in/books?id=Cg9uAAAAMAAJ
Wolp3	B	Stanley Wolpert—*Shameful Flight: The Last Years of the British Empire in India*. Oxford University Press. London. 2006.
YGB	B, D	YG Bhave—*The First Prime Minister of India*. Northern Books Centre. New Delhi. 1995. https://books.google.co.in/books?id=Ye3VUMLhaz8C
Zak	B	Fareed Zakaria—*The Post-American World*. Viking. Penguin India. New Delhi. 2008.